I0746931

Also by Jack J. Wyatt:

Lions in the Water

Blood Stone Mountain

Jack J. Wyatt

ISBN: 978-1-7341083-3-0 (hardcover)
ISBN: 978-1-7341083-4-7 (paperback)
Library of Congress Control Number: 2022905832

JackWyattBooks.com

For Dad, who taught me nothing cool comes without struggle.

You may choose to look the other way,
but you can never say again that you did not know.

— William Wilberforce

PROLOGUE

Weary Lorenzo stirred in the mud. Isabella, please be safe.

Rain stung his half-naked body. Sleep, when it came, lasted two hours at best. Most nights, he lay awake in the filth, shaking and staring into the darkness.

Where was this place? The Southern Cross peeked below the clouds. South America, somewhere. Deep in the jungle. Quarry pits, rimmed in a prison of towering trees. Land they were forced to mine for minerals.

Captives—all of them. They'd been reduced to creatures, weak and sickly. Fed rancid fish and murky water. No comforts, no shelter. They defecated in waist-deep holes, slept on sodden ground, clutching anything for warmth.

Lorenzo wiped the moisture from his eyes.

Half a year, maybe longer, since they'd taken him. His shirt was gone, jeans threadbare. No shoes, his feet raw and lacerated. In these dreadful pits, the bitter haze of kerosene stung the air. It kept the mosquitoes away and kept them working.

The downpour thickened. Black clouds hung low.

Living a slow death, he had to escape.

A guard in a poncho pushed a wheelbarrow through the slop, a rifle slung over his shoulder.

Lorenzo rose, careful not to wake the others curled around him.

The guard and his wheelbarrow slipped into the trees.

Lorenzo scurried to the undergrowth, feet squelching in sludge. He secretly trailed the man along the muddy path.

Water hammered the canopy. A narrow path winding beneath through the untamed rainforest.

Tire ruts and muddy boot prints marked the trail. Lorenzo crept over the soft soil, slipping past the palms. The path sloped into a dark, misty canyon.

Ahead, the guard's boots sloshed through the mud, and wheels squeaked. Lightning flashed. The trail snaked down a hillside. The poncho-clad man vanished into a canopy of trees.

Lorenzo slunk low and quiet through the foliage. Branches clawed his torso, and pebbles hobbled his steps. Far from the quarry now, his heart raced—capture meant death, but he would die regardless.

The guard came to a ridge, stopped his cart, and set aside his rifle. With a heave, he tipped the wheelbarrow forward. Two lifeless bodies slid down the hillside.

Lorenzo gasped.

The guard gathered his weapon and headed back.

Lorenzo crouched behind a veil of undergrowth. He tapped his forehead, chest, and shoulders, whispering, "Amén."

The guard and his cart sloshed by.

If he had the strength, Lorenzo would have attacked—disarmed him, snapped his neck—but his muscles were frail, too weak.

The rolling cart moved up the trail, vanishing into the bush, back toward the quarry.

Veiled by the storm, Lorenzo made his way to the bluff. A deep ravine stretched below, thick with vines and saplings. He peered over the muddy ridge.

Below, the ravine was shrouded in darkness. A gagging stench of sulfur and rot clawed at his lungs. He carefully made his way down the slippery slope.

A jolt of lightning lit the scene.

Lorenzo recoiled in horror.

A human body lay sideways at his feet, limbs askew. Tattered pants and bare-chested like himself. Throat slashed, eyes cloudy and open.

He knew the man—Hector. Another prisoner, like them all, taken by the men who ran these pits. Far from this awful place, Hector had a family—a son, Emilio. Emilio was Lorenzo's age. Hector and Emilio loved fishing together. They cherished their long chats. He'd told Lorenzo about his patient wife, who always boiled potatoes in case they caught nothing.

Out here, they'd toiled until Hector fell and broke his hip. Unable to walk or work, he was no longer worthy of their filthy food and water. Now he lay here, discarded.

Lorenzo's jaw clenched. He should've died by now too. Maybe that was the plan—let them all rot until the rain washed them away. But he wouldn't give them that victory.

Trembling, he swept a palm over Hector's face to close the eyelids. In the heavy brush lay another body, its throat sliced. Three more appeared sprawled in the bushes. Men he'd known, faces from the pits. Their lives snuffed out, dumped like refuse.

A coldness pressed his chest, twisting his gut.

He wanted to weep, but his starved body refused. He knelt by Hector, clutching his cold hand, and bowing in silent prayer.

Mist beaded on Lorenzo's sunken cheeks.

No one here gets out alive.

The fortunate died early. The rest suffered until their final breath, then tossed into this leafy grave.

CHAPTER

1

Rain fell like judgment in the suffocating jungle. Near Colombia's border, an abandoned town decayed in silence, its streets choked by creeping foliage and shadow. Howler monkeys shrieked above the hum of insects, their cries muffled by the dense downpour.

Outside a crumbling church, a black Mercedes SUV idled, its engine a low growl—a sleek intruder in this forsaken place. Nearby, a sludge-covered 4Runner sat idling, its driver's door missing.

Inside the decrepit church, a voice sliced through the thick, stagnant air.

"Appreciate men bringing you here." Yuri swept a hand toward the crumbling altar, his smile sharp, unsettling. "Excuse surroundings, but it is important we meet."

Diego wiped his palm on his trousers.

The men shook.

Diego's shoulders tensed, his hand damp against Yuri's.

Two locals stood in the shadows, their muddy boots sinking into the moss-coated floor. Rifles in hand, their barrels gleamed faintly in the dim light seeping through the broken stained-glass. One fixed his gaze on Yuri, unblinking, while the other scanned the church, his eyes tracing the water that streamed through a jagged hole in the ceiling, splattering into a murky puddle below.

The sanctuary lay in ruin—lianas draped from the rafters like nooses, and ferns sprouted from the pulpit. The air was heavy with mold and the relentless buzz of the jungle outside. It was a place forgotten by time, swallowed whole by the wilderness.

"Is good to see you, señor," Diego said. His voice carried a nervous edge.

Yuri towered over him—his ash-black hair hung wet to his neck. He straightened a crease in his slacks.

"How is family?"

Diego forced a smile. "Bien, señor, bien."

"English, please." Yuri's thick accent was firm but polite. "It is not native tongue either, but halfway we meet."

Diego nodded.

"You are having more issue on routes?"

Diego cleared his throat. "Sí. Trouble hit four trucks. Bandits everywhere."

Yuri's eyes narrowed. "And this requires more money?"

Diego swallowed. "Jungle is brutal—bandits hit hard."

"I already pay to handle danger." Yuri rubbed his chin. "And this is not first time of problem."

"No," Diego admitted.

Yuri's smile faded. "What is it my last monies bought?"

"Señor?"

"First ambush. You lost two trucks. I paid more to fix it. What did money buy?"

"More men, more vehicles," Diego stammered, head dropping.

"Yet ambushes keep coming." Yuri said, twisting the rings on his fingers. "Your trucks stay under canopy—satellites cannot see us. So how did they find you?"

Diego shrank under his gaze, shoulders hunching.

"Explain how your useless team still lost six trucks in a month?" Yuri barked. "Every lost trailer is payment! Delays weapons, delays progress! And makes Americans blame me!"

"Señor, we—"

Yuri's studded fist smashed Diego's cheekbone. Blood sprayed and he crumpled.

"I would not trust you to escort grandmother across fucking street!" He shouted. "Your team should be fighting to death to protect vehicles. It is what I pay for! Which means either you are worthless, or you are stealing!"

The gunmen raised their rifles, aiming at Diego.

Kneeling, Diego threw his hands up. "Please, no, señor!"

"Who then has taken?" Yuri roared. "And do not tell me it is Colombians—I trust counterpart like brother. They never cross border into that shithole country. Those people know better."

"Not us!" Diego cried, shaking his head frantically. "¡No traicionar!"

Yuri seized Diego's throat, his grip iron-tight, raising him to his feet. "Once as comrades, but that has passed."

The gunmen grabbed yellow nylon rope and bound Diego's wrists and ankles, as he squirmed and screamed.

Yuri stuffed a rag into Diego's mouth, wrapping silver tape around his neck, and jaw to secure the gag.

"My men have seen the ambush sites." Yuri patted the tape on Diego's cheek. "Marks point to the Soles cartel."

Diego fell to his knees, eyes wide with terror.

Yuri circled him, his oxblood boots pounding the rotting floor. "How is it military cannot find jungle pathways, not even from air, yet disorganized lowlife in jungle can find, follow, and steal from me?"

Diego struggled against the rope, but it held firm.

"Which leads back to you." Yuri's brows rose. "Valuables crossing routes in this hideous country. You and your men get greedy, work deal with Soles cartel, choose to steal because you are disloyal."

Diego shook his head. Tears welling in his eyes.

"And this means you are working against me." He snatched Diego by the hair. "For you, this is profit. For me, it is to achieve end. But now cargo is missing from my roads—roads crawling with uncivil vermin. And I will ask question now, on which life of your daughter Sofia and wife Maria depend."

Muffled cries escaped the gag as tears streamed down Diego's face.

"Where has cargo gone if not to seaport? Who are you working with?"

He tore off the tape, removing the gag.

Diego gulped air. "Men are loyal! We would never—"

Yuri shoved the cloth back in, slapped the tape over it, and pushed Diego to the ground.

A powerful kick struck Diego's ribcage.

Bone cracked.

Yuri inspected his boot for scuff marks.

The gunmen stood by, rifles ready.

"Alright, I am done with this." Yuri straightened his shirt. "And this fucking country melts me."

Blood soaked through Diego's gag.

"Alright. Finish it," Yuri commanded.

The gunmen hoisted Diego up, but the larger one froze, his eyes on the crooked cross.

"Problem?" Yuri snapped, jaw tight.

The gunman motioned toward the altar.

"Fine. Then take far from here," Yuri said coldly. "Jesus is for you to fear. But if authorities find him, I find you."

The two bowed their heads.

Yuri turned to Diego. "Your betrayal to protect has single punishment. Penalty I should have enforced after first incident."

Diego's eyes pleaded, wet with tears.

"I have cargo to move." Yuri turned. "You are done."

CHAPTER
2

Maria clutched the fresh bandage on her shoulder and scurried away barefoot.

Hannah sighed. The children never thanked her, and the elders didn't trust her. Seventeen patients today. Bruises, bumps, rashes, cuts, and a broken ankle—which the poor farmer had hobbled on for a week before their arrival. His crooked smile after she'd administered the local anesthetic was worth every ache of the day.

Hannah drew in a half yawn. She'd resolved months ago that this work mattered more than comfort. Readjusting the elastic tie in her long, unwashed, brown ponytail, she stretched, feeling the jungle's weight settle into her bones.

Each patient received a basic physical and treatment for urgent disorders. Next came vaccinations—tetanus and varicella—with vitamin injections for the elderly and frail. They managed minor surgeries, scheduling tougher cases for transport. Levels four and five meant quick fingers on the satellite phone, a clear landing zone, and many prayers. Her three-person team, thankfully, had faced none of those.

On the tent's other side, Alisha held six-year-old Nyla by the elbow, cleaning her arm with an alcohol wipe. Nearby, Dan yanked a syringe from Tio's tiny shoulder, his laugh echoing faintly through the canvas.

Hannah retrieved a plastic 5-gallon canister from an open supply crate and a water filtration hose.

"All better? Todo mejor?" Dan tossed a used syringe into the sharps container.

Tio nodded.

Dan pointed toward Hannah. "Ayuda a rio?"

The young boy rubbed his arm and bobbed his head, then shuffled over and seized the empty canister from the lady doctor.

"Thank you, Tio." Hannah grinned. "Such a gentleman."

Dan smiled at the twosome. "When you return, we've got some celebrating to do!" He nodded to a half-empty bottle of Zinfandel resting on their folding supply table.

A rosy blaze scattered across the wax palms and Andean oak trees as the sun retreated behind the lush mountainside. Jungle—once a cartoon of leafy creatures in her mind. Ten months ago, it was a distant fantasy. Now, after humping through Colombia's humid mountains and valleys to villages like this, she knew better. "Appreciation" wasn't right—it was grudging respect for this uncomfortable, unpredictable, sweaty pain in the ass. Slithering dangers, winged threats, clawed beasts, toothy predators, and every bloodsucking insect imaginable. Plus, they'd run out of coffee 47 days ago. Mornings dragged without mercy.

"De esta manera." Tio pulled her hand.

Hannah knew the way, but his company warmed her.

The river ran east beyond a knoll, 200 meters from the medical tent. Tio whistled and marched along the dirt trail. Like most children here, he was healthy beyond a lack of iron. That wouldn't last long— they'd leave a crate of chewable multivitamins, candy-like treats to tide them over for months. Another team would resupply next year.

She hadn't decided on reenlisting. This was the most important work she'd ever done. But the question lingered. It'd taken a month to unplug from the world and embrace this low-resource existence—code for looking and smelling like hell. Ditching traffic, work pressures, and deadlines was simple. She didn't miss her computer or the incessant beeps of that sentient cell phone. But air conditioning, warm baths, and M&Ms? Those stung. Two months back, a refrigerated vending machine in a random town had yielded two ice-cold Fantas—grape and orange. She'd have fought off a crocodile to keep them.

Even with split ends and no makeup, focusing on others had shifted something in her. Alleviating a child's tears, a parent's worry, or warding off disease with a Band-Aid or a booster felt raw and real—gratification no lab could match. Alisha and Dan had become good friends, and even their Scottish guide, Phinn, with his odd phrases she now understood, fit the team. But another year? Alisha's condition meant she and Dan would leave soon.

Hannah peered out toward the distant river. Could she handle two new teammates and this sweltering wilderness for fourteen more months? The question gnawed at her.

Unusually, the air was still. No chirping insects, no breeze—just a faint hush.

She and Tio entered the warm flowing water at the river's edge. Twenty feet wide, two or three feet deep, the channel ran from the mountains, the lifeblood of this remote place. Alongside vitamins and first-aid kits, they'd leave reusable water containers like Tio's to guard against drought.

Hannah slid the supply hose underfoot to steady it. Tio set the canister beside her, and she began pumping. Liquid filled the inlet, clean water draining into the plastic.

Tio skipped a stone across the rushing water and giggled. He searched for another, tried again—a second laugh.

Socializing was never her strength. As an undergrad, she'd buried herself in pre-med courses and hospital shifts, too shy to lift her eyes from books or screens. Sorority invites never came—mingling felt messy. After failed blind dates, she'd resolved that college was for studies, not parties. Med school was better, surrounded by others as awkward as she, outside labs and study groups. Professional medicine demanded everything, leaving little room for social pressure—or dating. That could wait. Much later.

At thirty-one, single, in a jungle with a nine-year-old, her shyness had faded—burned away by a decade of education and residencies in medicine and virology. If only Tio were twenty years older…

The container filled slowly as Tio perfected his stone skipping. A distant hum grew louder, a mechanical growl piercing the jungle's drone. Still kneeling, Hannah gazed across the river.

Her job back in the States had hollowed her. She fetched coffee, scrubbed samples, and watched older men win grants with jokes and handshakes. This jungle "sabbatical" was her escape, a year to figure things out.

Teaching was an option—her credentials were solid—but academia teemed with self-important lecturers chasing open bars. Atlanta's research hub called to her. She craved hands-on risks, leading experiments in cellular replication and genetics. Challenge drove her, and this dreadful jungle delivered it.

The rumble closed in. A low vibration tickled her skin—something deeper than thunder.

Tio stopped mid-toss, the stone falling from his hand.

An off-road vehicle sped across the opposing riverbank, tearing through young banana trees and bouncing over dirt trenches. A 4Runner, missing a door.

She slowed her pumping.

The vehicle halted.

Two men exited and wrestled with the rear hatch. They struggled with something inside.

Her breath caught.

A third man emerged, blood staining his clothes, a dirty cloth over his mouth, yellow nylon rope binding his hands and torso.

Hannah's pulse raced.

Tio grabbed her arm. "Miss—" he said.

"Silencio!" she whispered, throat tight.

They huddled beneath a draping logwood at the river's edge.

One man raised his rifle, shouting over the water's rush—words lost to the current. His partner stepped forward and struck the bound man's face. The body dropped.

This was bad. They had to sneak up the embankment before being spotted. Hand on Tio, she edged back, watching the men across the waterway.

One leaned down, tugging the prisoner up by his nostrils. A muffled squeal.

The short one aimed his rifle. More words exchanged.

The bleeding man cried.

The taller, thickset gunman nodded.

Sharp cracks tore at her ears, a sizzling numbness locking her limbs. Muzzle flashes lit the dusk, and the bound man crumpled to the dirt.

"Miss, miss!" Tio's voice rose, tugging her shirt as the ringing faded, snapping her back.

The short man glared across the river, raised his rifle, and shouted their way.

Her stomach twisted. She squeezed Tio's hand.

"Run, Tio!"

They spun to flee, but the hose snagged her foot. She tumbled over the container into the shallow river, a rock striking her nose. Pain flared, vision blurring.

Bullets whizzed by.

"¡Rápido!" Tio yanked her elbow.

She tore the hose free. They sprinted up the ridge, Tio's little legs matching her pace, leaves rustling overhead.

Splashing echoed behind them.

Blood gushed from her nose, spilling down her face and neck.

They raced over barbed grass, through dense flora, onto the trail, branches darkening their path.

Fifty meters from the river, the dirt lane forked.

Tio darted north toward his village.

Hannah turned east, glancing back—no gunmen yet, still climbing from the river. Her denser, shadowed path hid her slender frame as she zigzagged through branches, bounding over rocks and sticks.

A turn led to a thick tree line. Something clawed her neck, but she kept her pace, dodging what she could, pain blooming where she couldn't. Through weeds and bushes, she burst into the clearing where her team's tent stood.

She stopped, breath ragged, hands trembling. She thought of the man's scream—how it had ended so quickly. There was no honor in what she'd seen. Just cruelty, efficient and cold. And it had seen her back.

She had to warn the others.

CHAPTER

3

Dan uncorked the zinfandel. He poured two plastic cups, then filled a third with orange juice before handing it to Alisha.

The mesh flaps broke open.

"Ah, right on time!"

Dan and Alisha raised their drinks.

Breathless, Hannah shook her head.

"Good lord, love, what happened?" Dan rushed over.

A swollen lump between her eyebrows dripped with blood.

Hannah waved him off. "River… something… bad."

"Dear!" Alisha rose. "Your nose is bleeding."

"Dangerous people. Must… quiet."

"I'll get the antiseptic." Alisha moved toward the crate.

"Please, keep your voices down." Catching her breath, Hannah did her tired best to explain what she and Tio saw.

Dan fetched gauze and disinfectant, grabbing a first-aid field kit from a crate as Alisha examined Hannah's injuries.

"That man by the river may need our help," Dan said.

Alisha tried to tend to Hannah's facial wounds.

"They executed him."

"Jesus mighty!" Alisha gasped.

Hannah hushed her.

Dan leaned closer. "But you lost them at the fork?"

"Can't be sure," Hannah whispered. "Didn't see them behind me."

Dan paced across the tent's vinyl floor, sagging with heat.

"I'm sorry, ladies, I must be certain that man they shot isn't lying in pain."

"Dan, you're not listening. These guys are killers."

"Killers?"

"Probably cartel," Hannah said. "If you go outside, they're going to shoot first."

"Daniel Paul Bannister." Alisha seized his wrist. "You're not going out there. I won't raise this child alone!"

"Lower, please!" Hannah pleaded.

Dan turned. "My God—the village!"

Hannah shared the fear—would little Tio make it back safe and warn his parents of the dangerous men by the river? The tribe's 150 inhabitants knew how to deal with goons in this area. Many were armed, and confrontation wasn't uncommon here. Still, she had to put trust in two things: the villagers' knack for keeping peace with murderous thugs and their silence about the doctors camping over the ridge, opposite their farmlands.

"Where's Phinn? We have to warn him," Alisha whispered.

A muffled crack sounded outside.

"What was that?"

Hannah snatched a reflex hammer from their portable exam table.

Dan pivoted, hands ready.

The tent's LED lights powered to a high glow.

Leaping for the generator's switch, Dan stumbled over an electrical cable but righted himself, smashing the kill button. The generator died. The tent plunged into darkness.

Alisha exhaled. "That scared the hell out of me."

"Where's the satellite phone?" Hannah fumbled through objects on a nearby table.

A scuffle erupted outside, drawing closer.

The three inside turned toward the tent's entry.

"Dentro!" a deep voice commanded from outside.

The tent's mesh flaps parted, canvas rustling in the humid air. A twitching hand emerged—followed by the stocky man staggering forward, a wet wheeze escaping as he clutched an oozing red patch on his stomach.

It was Phinn.

Alisha screamed.

Phinn collapsed face down on the dirt.

Dan sprang toward him, but Hannah grabbed his forearm.

A nasal cackle cut through the night outside. Something scraped across the canvas, pushing through the flap. A black gun barrel poked inside, rotating to each of their faces.

The satellite phone sat next to gloves and a portable x-ray machine on a folding table at the tent's far side—Hannah raced across and lunged for it.

"Alto!" came a shout.

A short, lean, brown-skinned man wearing a red bandana on his head waltzed into the tent. He pushed her aside, seized the wireless handset, hurling it to the ground. The large phone bounced but didn't break.

Grinning, he inverted his rifle and smashed the device into the dirt. It split open, exposing its fragile electronics. He pounded the circuitry over and over, cackling in amusement.

A larger man carrying his own rifle stepped inside the tent, yelling something. The smaller man ceased his smashing.

Alisha and Dan huddled in a far corner.

The fat one aimed his rifle. The skinny one joined him.

Dan stepped between Alisha and the gunmen, shouting and pointing at their weapons.

Hannah's eyes darted between them and the scattered phone pieces at her feet. She dropped to a knee, snatching as many broken components as she could, jamming the parts into her khakis.

The large man's barrel swung her way.

"Arriba ahora!"

Slowly she rose, hands in the air, and stepped to her friends in the corner.

She stared down at Phinn, his face hidden. Had blood stopped seeping from his stomach? A bad sign—clotted or still? Was he breathing? Her vision struggled to focus.

Grimly, Hannah realized how little she knew of Phinn—his laugh silenced now.

"Ahora!" one shouted.

The tubby man with the rifle pulled out his cell and left the tent. His partner corralled them into a corner, aiming his rifle at Alisha's belly.

Dan's fingers curled inward, and his nostrils flared.

But the rifle held steady on its target.

CHAPTER
4

"Sí, doctors. One man, two women."

The fat man sounded excited.

Under the evening sky, Foster blinked away his double vision. He took a deep breath, switching hands with the cell phone.

On the bustling pier, workers hurried here and there, loading cargo into the docked freighter. Toiling under a faraway hook, a workman extended his arm and raised a thumb. The soaring crane grappled the leashed containers, rotated them seaward, and coupled them with other metal boxes jutting above the ship's highest deck. The twist locks clicked into place, and the boom released its hold on the stack. Across port, others with forklifts jostled intermodals into position for the next hoist.

Venezuela was a detestable shithole filled with the ignorant, helpless, and hopeless. A dead economy, rotting infrastructure, and a collapsing power grid. Two-thirds of its people had no running water, and those who did had to boil out the poisons. Death and chaos riddled its cities—vandalism, rape, murder spilling into the streets. A week ago, an innocent man wrestled a carjacker and suffered a gutting in broad daylight. Territory disputes over drugs and sex work often ended in savage butchery. No longer third-world—Venezuela had rotted into something darker.

Foster frowned as a crane's groan echoed.

Yuri had killed Diego without consulting him. One of his best men, someone he counted on to move loads from the mines to the ports, was gone. He was expected to suck up the loss without comment or complaint. Then he was told Yuri's men would oversee the semi-trucks.

This deal was getting worse.

When Foster had agreed to the conditions, the Russian had assured him he could manage things as he saw fit. But now the dishonest Slav was encroaching on his territory.

And why? Because a truck or two went missing? It's a fucking jungle—losses are to be expected. But Yuri dictated the money and equipment out here, something Foster wished he'd have negotiated for when they made their deal.

His face twitched.

The Russian controlled this pier. He managed the exports, spoke with the buyers. He made deals worth millions, while Foster was stuck deep in the country managing those mines. Yuri's men had taken the routes, expecting Foster to take a cut on his end for the extra security. That greedy motherfucker.

A warm wind carried the stench of rotting fish across the pier.

Above, the humongous crane powered down. Pairs of men waltzed shoreside near the freighter's hull, unhitching the chunky mooring lines from their sizable anvil dock cleats. The bow thruster bubbled toward the wharf, and the freighter's ass-end churned the sea.

He would figure out what to do about Yuri later. For now, there was still the main job to attend to. Resources to manage, control, squeeze more work from like he'd done with the Bantu. And he could use more help.

Foster flexed the fingers of his hand as the cellphone's signal wavered in and out.

"Do not kill them." He tweaked the rim of his straw hat. "Bring those doctors to me."

CHAPTER

5

Sweat clung to Hannah as their kidnappers cursed and pounded the 4Runner, one under the hood and the other working the ignition. Crammed in the rear seats, Alisha and Dan huddled beside her, the trio locked in the vehicle the entire frightening night.

The revival efforts failed—the 4Runner's motor was dead—a victim of the gruesomeness a day before.

Morning exposed the murdered man—gagged, roped, dime-sized holes staining his bloody shirt—sprawled before the vehicle, killed while Hannah and Tio fetched water. No excess bleeding—fortunate. A bullet had pierced his heart, ending his suffering quick.

But the 4Runner had succumbed to the same fate. In the hasty execution, one of these goons had also shredded the vehicle's engine with their bullets on accident.

The large one yanked the door, pulling Dan outside.

"Transportation?" The rifle raised to Dan's face.

"We were dropped off," Dan lied. "We had the satellite phone for pickup. We don't have a vehicle."

Hannah fingered the sharp pieces in her pocket. Dan was wise not to give up the fact that their truck and trailer were a mile away, off a trail where Phinn had driven them weeks prior.

Thinking of him—a sadness hit her. Phinn's grumbling strength— the way he'd fuss if she carried her own gear. "Missy, you need to save your energy for doctoring," he'd say. Phinn was sweet, old-fashioned that way. She could not believe he was murdered.

Working to find new transportation, the larger of the two thugs pulled out his mobile and dialed. His name, it turned out, was Marko. Pacing and cursing, he told of his partner's stupidity for shooting the 4Runner's engine. They needed a new vehicle, pronto. Whomever he called was not near. There would be a meeting point, several kilometers away, but which direction Hannah could not make out from the call before Marko clicked off.

They pulled her and Alisha from the vehicle and hiked into the jungle. Their only nourishment was a jug filled from the river, pausing only when allowed for quick gulps.

Hot, hilly, and her legs throbbed. A growl rumbled nearby, swallowed by the foliage. There'd been no food—but she didn't feel hungry. The anxiety of having a gun pointed at her killed her appetite.

Their dreaded march continued under the high afternoon sun. Sweat dribbled from her pores, and the bug spray had completely worn off. Tiny, winged critters dive-bombed her face and neck.

She swatted bugs, tearing a stud from her ear—her father's gift from graduation, back when she'd stomached that son-of-a-bitch. She pressed a thumb and finger to her ripped ear to check if the blood had dried. It had not.

Marko led them onward, sun-beaten and unwashed like his partner—the stench was unforgiving. The short one had wiry brown hair corralled in a red bandana, but there was something not medically right with the man. His hands shook, and he'd stumble occasionally, even on flat terrain, before catching his balance and laughing. The high, grating laugh made Hannah believe he may be a few cards short of a full deck.

Marko was taller and wider than his companion—about six feet, she guessed—with beefy hands and greasy brown hair. He didn't shake like his partner, but the lower part of his ample belly did jiggle whenever he moved.

Bandana and Marko forced them down a trail of thicker and thicker foliage toward whatever rendezvous Marko had agreed to with the caller. But Bandana staggered every few yards. After a stumble, he'd right his balance, check his weapon, and giggle. Was the idiot high on drugs?

Marko stomped ahead through the jungle. He'd push branches aside, give Hannah a creepy look, then release the shrubbery for her to catch—when she was lucky. When she wasn't lucky, he'd let go of a loaded branch and it would strike her like a whip. Asshole.

Each had a long gun, though she didn't know the type. Rifles with crescent-shaped attachments at the bottom. If she tried to escape, she'd get mere steps before bullets hit—and her corpse became dinner for the growling and howling creatures out here.

On occasion, Marko shouted, "Silencio!" They'd pause—Marko panting, checking his device, barking at Bandana in the rear—then trudge on. She could tell, though, by the sopping wetness of Marko's dirty t-shirt that the excruciating hike was getting to him.

But Alisha had to be feeling the worst of it. Nearly seven months pregnant, the humid sun wasn't helping. Dan held her hand, protecting his wife from whipping branches. Dan also shouldered a canvas medical bag of supplies they'd been allowed to take from the camp.

An hour later, gasping, Marko moved several branches, and his mood changed. A clearing. Relief from the jungle. Maybe now they'd stop for more water?

They entered a small clearing, a muddy road cutting north. Bandana pointed excitedly, then the two men conferred in the clearing, leaving Hannah, Alisha, and Dan a few yards behind.

She couldn't hear what either was saying, but Bandana's laugh erupted now and again.

"Why did they take us?" Alisha sobbed.

Dan caressed her, and her head fell onto his shoulder. His cropped dusky hair was sweaty, and beads streaked down his forehead and temples. His shirt collar was torn from an earlier scuffle with Marko back at the tent.

Dan whispered something into Alisha's ear, then locked eyes with Hannah. "Ransom?" he mouthed, ensuring his wife wouldn't hear.

Hannah glanced at the two gunmen in the distance, nodding once.

They scanned the maze of hills and jungle—no civilization, just birds and beasts. The dirt trail was their only road, and no help was in sight. They'd also traveled far from the river, and this area's absence of streams and running water was concerning. If they tried to escape on foot in this sweltering heat, they'd need hydration and fast.

But it was Marko that worried her most—dragging them through the jungle at gunpoint. Their destination? No place good.

Dan made a clicking noise with his mouth, which got her attention. His eyes tried to signal something to her, which Hannah had difficulty interpreting. He tapped his right pant leg, then pointed to Alisha.

Thankfully, weeping Alisha had been wearing her knee-length maternity dress when they'd taken them from the tent. In happier times, she'd boasted that it was the least itchy outfit she had with her. But as Hannah's eyes followed its length past Alisha's waistline and rounding belly, she found the reason for Dan's concern.

A dark red streak of blood trickled down her inner thigh.

Oh my God! Hannah gasped, and her neck tightened.

Dan glared at her and shook his head.

Their kidnapping was becoming more terrifying—there were four lives at stake. Dan was right. They shouldn't tell her now. The burden of pregnancy, the physiological toll of that alone in this dangerous environment, never mind the two pricks forcing them to only God knew where in this jungle, was already toiling with her body and emotions.

Luckily, Alisha couldn't see the blood herself, not while standing. But they needed to get someplace fast where they could adequately examine her.

Marko and Bandana marched back in their direction. Marko motioned with his rifle. He glanced at the dark lines trickling down Alisha's legs.

"Ella caga?" Marko grunted.

Dan tightened his jaw.

Bandana pointed, grabbing Alisha's arm.

Dan shoved him, and Bandana fell.

"No, me!" Dan insisted.

Marko squinted, walking up to Dan. The two men stared each other down.

Marko took a step back, turned, pretending to retreat before hoisting the rifle's butt end, striking Dan's forehead with a sickening thump.

Dan fell backward, crumpling to the ground, out cold.

Alisha screamed.

Bandana squealed with laughter.

Hannah tried to approach, but Marko pointed his rifle at her. His evil stare held like it had moments before. She took a frightened step back.

Bandana pulled Alisha from her husband's body, and she screamed hysterically. He shoved her toward Hannah, and it took all Hannah had to keep her pregnant friend from falling. She held Alisha as the woman screamed and struggled.

Marko yanked back the slide on his weapon and clicked the bolt into place. He lifted the rifle eye level, his finger floating on the trigger, and aimed its barrel at Dan, who was now stirring in pain on the ground.

"No!" Hannah shouted.

Marko's aiming eye looked her way.

Alisha cried and wailed as Hannah held her in a bear hug.

The psychotic man's eyebrows raised.

"Es el doctor?" he asked.

"What? Yes! We're all doctors!"

Bawling, Alisha struggled, but Hannah held her steady and faced away from the scene with Marko and his gun.

Marko's gaze returned to the gun sight and held its target.

"Don't you do it, you motherfucker–"

The rifle swung up and away from Dan. Marko turned and walked off with Bandana.

Hannah was stunned and relieved. She let go of Alisha and rushed over to Dan. The dripping cut on the side of his head went from his frontal bone to his right ear. A quick probe of the injury showed the laceration had reached the periosteum layer, the final membrane before the bone. She grabbed peroxide and gauze, patching the gash as best she could. She prayed the blow hadn't cracked his skull.

Bandana and Marko ordered the three to stay put while they scouted the grounds and the nearby trail.

Dan stirred, coming to his feet, and the gunmen shoved them back onto the trail.

Shooting pain from Hannah's ankles hobbled her footing. Blisters inside her wet and muddy shoes had broken open, and now those sores rubbed raw against the inside of her socks as they restarted their hellish hike. But there was no use in complaining.

A broken branch caught her foot, and Hannah fell to the ground.

Marko leered back at her.

Bandana jabbed his rifle into her shoulder blade.

Painfully, she rose to her feet.

CHAPTER

6

Kendrick leaned against the oak railing at the far end of the bar. Across the low-lit saloon, a sandy blonde woman with a velvety voice strummed her acoustic guitar. Overhead, a squad of ceiling fans swished the air while chatter rose and fell around him.

A few stools away sat a brunette with large trundling curls, adorned in a light lavender summer dress, sipping a chardonnay. Her soft young face gazed outward like someone he'd once known. Even the way she held her wine glass was hauntingly familiar. A sudden squeeze hit his chest, and he stared at the suds in his pint glass, inhaling deeply.

An unforeseen political makeover had retired him at fifty. The current intelligence administration wanted fewer human assets, more technology, wireless surveillance, drones, and whatnot. Their revised definition of "surgical military strike" in this soulless circus of automation now included higher percentages of civilian casualties. It was a cold calculation designed by university-bred bureaucrats and accountants who'd never served, never seen the tragic costs of conflicts launched with their biros.

Two years adrift now, unused and aging. Shown the exit despite a bevy of knowledge and skills. The first sprouts of gray, and they'd made him a pensioner. A document "honoring" his thirty years of service spit out from a thoughtless computer, dispatched without an autograph, and sent Royal 2nd Class to his flat in Cardiff.

At first, he saw it as an opportunity—a new place, a chance to be alone. Why not? A change in scenery, fresh surroundings, a location where he might be alone to reflect. He wasn't tied to anything in his home country and found the weather in many southern American coastal states agreeable, akin to being on holiday, every day.

He'd settled in this quiet Florida town, bought a flat, tried jogging and books—but his mind became restless. Weeks of reflection turned out to be more uncomfortable than enriching. Time at the pub ate up more of his day. His life had slowed down too much. It was far too soon for all this "relaxation."

Kendrick cupped his Guinness and drew a swig, his eyes flicking to the doorway.

There was nobody he was close to here. Some acquaintances, sure, but none in which he'd genuinely confide. On occasion, he'd regale an amusing story to a pub chum. He'd certainly gained an array of exceptional knowledge throughout his career. But he never spoke of his own life. Revealing the intimate was ill-regarded in his prior profession. He'd spent decades as an instrument, thrust into complex, dangerous, and often violent conditions all around the globe, and had come to see himself mainly through the eyes of those unsettling deeds. An untidy life filled with risky missions, unfit for pub conversation, let alone courting tales with which to woo the fairer sex.

Yet, he was qualified for nothing else. And, on this barrier island, there wasn't a high demand for furtive intelligence work among residents more concerned with sunrises and sea turtles.

Kendrick glanced at the clock on his cell.

Though, strangely, concern had arisen in this island's modest shipping port—a matter with unverified connections to a questionable ground transportation business that caught the international police agency's attention.

He hoisted his pint and swallowed.

Interpol needed help. A reach-out from a former colleague connected him with the bureau. Though not a hefty assignment—possible light reconnaissance—the inquiry for his aid had rekindled a sense of usefulness. Sought for his unique abilities, skills he feared would remain dormant, even rot, as his days flew by on this coastal shoreline without challenge. In twenty minutes, they'd brief him on its next steps.

He'd cleaned himself up for the occasion—in case he'd need to meet his handler face-to-face at some point. Gone was the stubble. His salt and pepper hair cut high and tight by a bubbly stylist who doted on her two children. She'd even trimmed his eyebrows. The remarkable transformation made him look, and feel, a decade younger.

He was about to order a second stout when a familiar face hobbled through the doors, wincing in pain.

Jed ordered a whiskey, which was highly irregular since Kendrick had only seen him consume pints. The wide compress around the shrimper's leg also caught his attention. He'd figured there to be a harrowing story behind it and wandered over to his friend.

They'd spoken on a handful of occasions, and Kendrick found conversations with the fisherman far more interesting than chit-chats with the neck-tied and pop-collared.

Jed was a long-haired, strapping man north of thirty who'd spent his working life in the sea, "railing for catch"—a term Kendrick quite liked. Jed shared stories of Florida's rough waters and those in the Gulf, which he and his mates traversed according to season. It was a fascinating lifestyle. Most interestingly, recent chinwag with the shipman had included conversation surrounding this Island's remarkable history, something Kendrick had also keenly studied before his relocation here.

A stool opened next to Jed, and Kendrick took it. Jed, though, didn't seem to recognize him for a moment. Probably his new haircut.

"Hey Tommy," Jed finally said. The two engaged in another discussion about old ships, privateers, and historical mischief… until a cellphone rattled.

"So sorry, one moment."

Kendrick held the mobile tight to his ear and tapped the rim of his glass.

"Subjects ETA ten minutes. Confirm ISO, report back," the agent said, clipped Italian accent cutting through. "No engagement—keep it clean, capisce?"

"Yes, dear," Kendrick said. He glanced at Jed, curious how the young fisherman had damaged his leg. But there would not be time for that now.

He needed to leave the saloon right away without arousing suspicion. That shouldn't be difficult, as he'd already laid the groundwork with Jed for an exit.

"Debrief in ninety minutes." The Interpol agent cleared his throat. "And remember U.S. has not recognized red notice. Activities, these persone, we are without jurisdiction. Be cautious, we cannot offer assistance."

"But of course, dear."

Kendrick made kissing noises into his mobile—he'd told Jed he was expecting a call from his wife. He dropped the device into a shirt pocket, downed the rest of his Guinness, and turned to the shrimper.

"I apologize." He rose from his stool. "But I must be running along, so good seeing you again. How I do enjoy our historical chats."

Jed rubbed the dressing around his leg, gazed up with a soused smile, and the two shook hands.

Kendrick didn't enjoy lying to him. The truth was he hadn't a wife, or any close family left.

Here, he'd vanished into ordinary life, unnoticed. His current façade, as a retired professor of history, borne of an ironic background because most of his sanctioned charges had been to change its direction.

A strange excitement filled him. It was time to return to the field.

Outside, darkness hung over the streets.

Kendrick headed north for a few blocks, passing the last of shops, restaurants, and marina outbuildings. The asphalt ended, and so did the streetlighting. He left the road and cut across a field of ruddy buttonbush and cattails toward a long fence line which boxed in the area's seaport. The sound of small waves crashing ashore replaced the calls of frogs and cicadas.

He paced the enclosure's perimeter in the darkness, then halted.

A suspicious box truck ambled over an unlit dirt path from the east at a curious break in the fence line.

The headlights of the vehicle were not turned on.

CHAPTER

7

Mangrove trees and cordgrass swirled in the night breeze, providing Kendrick with excellent cover.

On the other side of the fence, three sizable men exited the box truck, fitted with hard hats and matching rain pants. They huddled in the darkness behind a row of powered thermal stacks. A 40-foot-long, corrugated metal shipping container sat on a heavy-lift bombcart, a low-speed trailer used to move cargo within the freight yard.

The tall one stepped aside, switched on his flashlight, and worked the lock on the nine-foot metal door using a tension rod and rake pick, while the other two maintained a lookout.

Kendrick held still behind the wired barricade. Under the yard's orange floodlights, he noted the container's 11-digit alphanumeric and memorized it.

After that, he should have left and reported his findings to the agent. But the night had more secrets to spill. He gripped the chain-link fence, hunching low in the darkness. Despite the whiskey, Kendrick moved like a man half his age.

Alexandra Island's port was a sprawling hub—1,200 feet of pier, three cranes, and steel tracks snaking through the freight yard. The seaport was a massive mechanical sorting center.

Diesel smoke drifted in the air. Regrettably, this evening's armed detail had assigned itself to the other side of the port, far from the activities Kendrick was observing. A massive cargo ship had arrived at its dock, a football pitch away in the northern zone. Half a dozen tan-shirted guards stood in a semi-circle, gazing skyward as the crane's gantry swung a triple-stack from ship to shore, its hoist motor rumbling to lower the containers onto the asphalt with thrumming precision.

The guards congratulated one another on its success as a radio crackled faintly, issuing routine updates about the unloading process.

Unloading a ship wasn't normally a spectator event. However, tonight's colossal cargo vessel stretched three-quarters of the pier's length, and its sheer size broke the monotony of smaller freighters that typically berthed here on Alexandra.

The crane's throaty motor also provided noise cover for the three Kendrick was watching. If any security persons spotted these three men, they'd appear as regular dockworkers from a distance. If one or more tan shirts began to stroll their direction, the three had plenty of time to collect themselves and make a getaway.

"Rudy!" one said in a low shout.

Rudy rounded the front of the container and jogged over. Kendrick saw no lanyard ID around his neck, and knew he wasn't a real longshoreman.

Kendrick couldn't hear the discussion, but Rudy lowered the cart's swing tail once they split up, allowing the container door to open fully. Rudy entered while the other two observed the guards.

Kendrick shifted position to get a closer look.

Rudy emerged carrying an elongated wooden crate.

"Nine crates?" the tall one hissed from the ledge.

"Yeah, nine," Rudy snapped. "One's busted—can't haul it."

"Cargo intact?"

Rudy gave a sharp nod.

"Duffel's here." The man grabbed a black canvas sack from the truck, tossing it into the container. "Pack it. All of it. Alexi will skin us if we're short."

The man pulled out his cell, but the phone's glow was not enough for Kendrick to get a good look at his face.

Minutes later, Rudy appeared. Whatever items he crammed inside the bag were each around three feet long. *We're they weapons?*

He offloaded the final crates and jumped to the asphalt, swinging the container's large steel door to a clanking close.

"Quiet!" Rudy hissed, wrestling the door.

"You'll get us nabbed!" his partner shot back.

"This damn door's a bitch!" Rudy growled.

The taller one reappeared. "I don't want to be cellmates with either of you two ass monkeys. Now get these on the truck before they spot us."

Once loaded, the trio returned to the box truck, and sped off without headlights.

Kendrick returned his attention to the shipping container.

Rudy had forgotten to padlock it.

Kendrick reached under his shirt flap and slid the chambered SIG Sauer 9mm from his waistband. Carefully, he laid the pistol at the base of the fence and concealed it with wet leaves.

Scaling the fence at a U.S. Customs port—a heavily regulated zone—could land him in serious trouble. Trespassing, Border Protection laws, and steep fines. But if they caught him with the SIG, Homeland Security would lock him away on a federal weapons charge, so he'd better not risk it.

With the guards' attention elsewhere, Kendrick climbed the fence and slid behind a double stack of steel container pods. This section was a maze of dry cargo, awaiting turn as boxcar transport on the dock's parallel rail tracks to the north.

While the crane's trolley loudly crawled over the ship for another fetching, he sprinted through the yard's southside to the refrigerated row, hustling in the faint light across the wide tarmac. Wearing black shirt and trousers, not a single security crew member glanced his way.

Kendrick removed the open padlock, pulled the door's lever, and the rod raised from its keeper. A soft crack sounded, and the shipping container's tall entry broke from its seal.

Diesel motors rumbled in the distance, and the crane plucked more freight from the massive ship.

From a pocket, Kendrick fished out a penlight. He grabbed the steel door's rod, hoisted himself onto the bombcart, and entered the pitch-dark 40-foot container, smudging the door with his prints.

The beam scanned its interior. Dozens of crates lined the rectangular box's metal floor, some stacks four and five high, with a squeezable path up its center. A noticeable gap in crates at the container's rear caught his eye, along with two open boxes.

A logo. A globe, two clasped hands. He knew it. Everyone knew it. One of the largest nongovernmental organizations on the planet. But why would NGO branded goods be in the imports section at an American harbor?

He opened one of the boxes, finding a stuffing of shredded crinkle paper with cellophane-wrapped smartphones—those pay-by-the-minute deals. It appeared the trio in the truck had helped themselves to at least half a dozen of these burners.

But the second crate was filled with sand and clay. Nearby, a crowbar rested against the wall. He pried open another chest, then another, and several feet away yet another. All crates had the same markings on their exterior. In fact, each wooden box did except for the open cellphone carton. These crates also appeared much larger than the five the men had taken. And each one he opened was filled with the same soggy earth.

Digging into the soil, he found several hard lumps and pulled them from the box. Rocks. He fished out more and examined them. Some were reddish-yellow, others smooth and dark—more murky cobalt than black, with faint, etched lines that didn't look natural. Not clumpy like coal. Instead, the edges were soft with rust-colored lines and pits. Like river rocks.

At his feet sat the remains of a crate—the one Rudy identified—crushed by over stacking. A rifle magazine lay in the remnants, along with a discarded, half-sheet of paper. He snatched the piece.

A torn manifest. Weights, times, and some descriptions. Ancillary cargo, no count. Hydro packs, 1,200 units. Fem, 28. Binder Resin – 20L, 10 units.

The sheet was incomplete, but a name appeared, Garner Wodehouse. Kendrick winced. Senator Wodehouse? A name like that didn't belong here. Why would it be on this manifest?

He seized the gun magazine, its casing scratched. Slight curve, a distinctive locking lug. Military, 5.56 millimeter.

Why ship stones halfway across the world? He flipped the magazine over. Rocks and ammo—using the cover of an NGO for transport. What the hell were they hiding?

He examined the stones again, slipping a few into his pocket for later research.

Outside, a voiced barked.

"Contact—over there!"

Kendrick darted for the container's exit, heart pounding.

Footsteps came near to the trailer.

He eased the steel door shut and wrenched the door lever. The rods slid into their keepers, and he clicked the padlock closed.

"What was that?!"

The footsteps quickened, and then another pair joined, equipped with jingling keys.

They were too close. Leaving the SIG behind limited his options and there was no time to reach the fence line. The guards would spot him. They might even shoot him.

Kendrick grappled the container's locking rods and swiftly clambered up its backside. He pulled himself onto the container's rooftop and went silent.

"Check the other side, I know I heard a noise."

Kendrick slowly lifted his head. The container's owner code, PELG, caught his eye—it didn't match the alphanumeric code he'd memorized on the door earlier.

Below, a third guard approached from the north.

With three sides surrounded, Kendrick hoped one of them wouldn't fetch a ladder and scale the container. What would he do if they spotted him up here? Run? Where? And once they got his fingerprints, it would trigger a whole mess of complications. No, he'd take measured breaths and make no sudden movements. They'll probably get bored in a few minutes and leave.

A dull wiggling sounded.

"Locked tight," one below said. "No breach."

"Caffeine's got you twitchy, Frank," another grunted.

"Screw you, there was a—" Frank cut off.

Buzz. Buzz. Buzz. A vibration echoed from the container's metal roof.

"That's real!" Frank snapped. "Check it!"

Flashlights, feet, and clattering keys jostled below.

Belly-down, Kendrick frantically worked at his shirt pocket, cursing himself. Why hadn't he left the bloody phone at the fence line with the SIG? One mistake, and he'd be done.

"Denny, climb the trailer—hoist me up," Frank ordered. "Something's moving."

Kendrick's breath caught a flashlight grazing the container's edge, inches from his shadow. With no weapon and no escape, he had one desperate play. He rose to a knee, pulled the stones from his pocket, and lobbed them at a far container stack, aiming for a hollow spot. It had to work, or he was finished.

A perfect strike—a clatter rang out.

Drawn by the noise, Frank and Denny abandoned their two-man totem pole.

"Over here!"

Flashlights split, two racing toward the distraction, but Frank stayed, his beam probing the container's rooftop.

"Something's up there," he muttered.

Kendrick dropped flat, still.

Frank's light swept closer, then paused as his radio crackled.

"All hands, debris on the tracks from unloading—move now!" a voice barked.

Frank held, inspecting smudges on the container's door, inching closer to Kendrick's rooftop perch.

Another crackle. "Frank, get over here now!"

He muttered a curse, gave the rooftop a last glance, then turned away, his footsteps fading.

CHAPTER

8

Noodle readjusted his rear and washed a paw.

Twenty-seven-year-old Ernie Nelson rinsed off the trowel, pointer, and mixer. The burgundy bricks he'd laid on the bungalow's exterior surpassed his expectations. The work had been grueling—but this was his first house, and he was determined to take honest care of it.

He stowed the tools in the small wooden shed, Noodle trailing behind. Evening had fallen, and a tepid rain drummed the roof. He wiped his wet hands on his soiled jeans as Noodle waited inside.

"We're done, pal," Ernie said. "Let's get some grub."

Noodle had shown up during the landscaping phase. The bold black-and-white feline had watched Ernie for hours before sauntering from the brush, claiming a patch of fresh sod, and sprawling out. Scrawny but twice the length of a normal cat, with a whip-like tail and quick legs, he didn't belong to anyone—same as Ernie. They'd traded glances that afternoon: Ernie grading the property, Noodle lounging. Later, when Ernie heated canned spaghetti, the cat slinked to the screen door. Their bond—and Noodle's name—solidified when Ernie shared some pasta with the whiskered one.

They crossed the yard from the shed when Ernie's pocket buzzed. He answered the call as they entered the bungalow.

"Hello?"

Silence.

"Hello?"

A gruff voice came through.

"Good evening, Petty Officer Nelson."

Ernie didn't know the voice.

"Sailor, where does my call find you?"

"Home, but—"

"Good. Warm there?"

"Raining. Who the hell is this?"

"Listen," the voice said. "I've got a deal for you."

A deal? Ernie hadn't spoken to anyone from the military in over a year, and he'd rather keep it that way.

"Dorsey, if this is you, it ain't funny. Kiss my ass!" A finger hovered over the end-call icon.

The caller cleared his throat. "Son, I'd rather not."

Ernie eyed the unknown number.

"This is Commander Campbell, Special Operations. Can we speak freely?"

Spec Ops? Why were these bastards calling now, after all this time, at this hour?

"What do you want?" he snapped.

"Good. This is confidential. As a former serviceman, you're bound to secrecy."

"You discharged me for conduct unbecoming, sir."

A sigh. "Yes, son, I know. I've reviewed your case. With my help, we might get you reinstated."

"Reinstated? The Navy painted me as the villain. I'm lucky my squad didn't frag me. It was bullshit!"

Another sigh. "Agreed. It was bullshit. You were in a tough spot. I get it. I'm sorry."

After eighteen months, hearing that felt good, even from a stranger.

"Thank you, sir," Ernie muttered, grudgingly.

Campbell cleared his throat. "We need your help."

"What's the situation?" Ernie asked, surprising himself. Though one apology didn't erase what they'd done—tossing him out, leaving him to scrape by with a dive business on Alexandra Island. No wetsuit, a shaky breather, borrowed fins—he'd worked the docks, cleaning hulls, scrubbing bird shit, anything for cash. At least the Navy hadn't stripped his dive cert, or he'd have been fighting alongside the seagulls for scraps.

It took everything he had to rebuild his life. A customer once traded him work for a beat-up dinghy. Two months later, he'd bought a Chevy 4x4 with a hitch, towing his skiff along the coast. For a year, he'd risen at 5:30 AM, taken every job—underwater or otherwise—seven days a week. He'd saved enough for this rundown bungalow by the inlet, a place he'd fixed with his own hands. Why should he give a damn about the service after they'd screwed him? Still, he'd listen—if only to hang up later.

"We've got a situation I'm not fully briefed on, and this line isn't secure."

Ernie scoffed. This already smelled like bullshit.

Rain pounded the roof as he pulled out smoked salmon for dinner. Noodle dashed across the kitchen, leapt onto the counter, and made biscuits on a dish rag.

"What's this got to do with me? I've been out over a year. The Navy ditched me. I've moved on." He sliced the fish, plated it. Noodle licked his chops.

"Hold on. This operation's top secret. The targets are high-value."

"High-value? The Navy's got jets. Are airstrikes off the table?"

"Son," Campbell grunted, "I don't blame your anger. But let's keep this civil. I'm trying to help."

Ernie set a plate by Noodle, who tore into it, while he chewed a piece himself. He'd listen, but he'd stay sharp. They wouldn't burn him again.

"Set your anger aside for a minute. Remember what it took to be in this country's service. Time is critical."

"Yeah, whatever," Ernie said, eyeing his plate.

"Good. I misspoke—assets, not targets. We need them retrieved."

Ernie froze. "Human assets?"

"Yes."

"Civilians?"

"Yes."

"Are they resisting, or—"

"No, Nelson. They're missing."

Despite the grime, the salmon in his hand, and the thousand miles between them, six-foot-two Ernie straightened and paced the tile floor.

"Last known, sir?"

"We have it. Time's tight. I can't debrief here. Are you willing to give me a chance, like I'm offering you?"

"Sir?"

"Plainly put, I'll fight to restore your rank. I can pay you a retainer—a year's former salary—if you meet me in Norfolk for a briefing. That's it."

A year's pay? That'd nearly cover what he'd lost when they'd booted him.

"Confirm—a year's pay?"

"Yes. More upon mission completion. Can you fly tonight, zero hundred?"

"Midnight?"

"Affirmative. If not, I've got other names. But your location, your skills—we've made preparation for your retrieval."

Noodle leapt over the sink, helping himself to Ernie's plate.

Two hours to shower, pack, and reach Jacksonville.

"How long, sir?"

"If you accept? A week, maybe two."

He'd need a sitter for Noodle. A photographer lived down the road—a young woman he'd waved at a few times while retrieving his mail. He'd likely be back in a day, but the cash was tempting. Eight years of his life, flushed by those bastards. Taking their money felt like payback, but it meant trusting them again—something he'd sworn never to do.

"How many civilians?"

"Not on the phone, son."

If it stank of bullshit, he'd take the cash and walk. He glanced at Noodle.

"Alright, I'll meet."

Campbell exhaled. "Good. Get to Jekyll. There's an airstrip."

"Jekyll Island? Why not Jacksonville?"

"We can't do that."

"What? Why, exactly?"

"In the brief. Get there by midnight, pack lightly. If you agree to the assignment, it'll be warmer than your current location. We'll gear you up."

"But sir—"

"That's all for now."

"Why me? You've got all of Spec Ops."

A pause. "Because I'm not authorized to use active forces."

Not authorized? What the hell was he hiding?

"More in Norfolk," the commander grunted.

"Sir?"

"Jekyll by balls, petty officer."

The call ended.

Odd as hell, but Campbell had called him by rank twice—no scorn, no accusations. It'd been over a year since anybody had done that. Tugging Noodle's tail, a corner of Ernie's mouth twitched upward.

CHAPTER

9

Heavy rains led to a steamy afternoon as the five of them trudged through the muddy jungle. The blisters on Hannah's ankles stung more than they throbbed.

Darkness was setting in. Their two captors decided to make camp in a small clearing near the dirt road, in a remote wooded nowhere.

Marko instructed them to collect timber, watching as they stacked branches. He'd foolishly given Bandana the lighter. The idiot lit the kindling, then waved a burning branch like a sword, swatting embers, cackling as he danced. Minutes later, Marko barked at Bandana. Bandana stared at him, deflated, dropped the stick to the bonfire, and fell silent. This clown was high on their jungle brew—whatever that was.

Marko paced the perimeter, struggling to get a signal. Frustration mounted with each step. He jabbed the screen, muttered, and moved, repeating the process.

Alisha, Dan, and Hannah sat on a busted log near the fire. Dan was awake, but his head ached from the blow. The gash had stopped bleeding, and she'd checked his pupils. He appeared stable, but she couldn't know the true extent of the damage without an x-ray. Their only medical resource was the bag they'd brought.

Along with antiseptics, bandages, painkillers, and gauze, it held Alisha's prenatal vitamins. She'd thought to pocket the vitamins, but the hidden satellite parts might draw notice.

Despite his injury, Dan laid his shirt on the log for his pregnant wife. He and Alisha held each other. College sweethearts, they'd been inseparable since Alisha found "Alisha and Dan, together forever" in his textbook weeks into dating. Both trained as GPs, eager to give back before starting their practice. The pregnancy had been a happy surprise. When she told Dan, the reserved man eagerly suggested baby names.

Hannah watched the fire, her tummy rumbling. Amid the danger, she envied Alisha and Dan, as she had for months. Though their age, they had a closeness she lacked. Watching them now deepened her sense of emptiness.

In Atlanta, there'd been Roland, a junior chemist. He was nice and quirky, but lacked spark. On their last date, he'd lit candles, played his band's demo—"The Coworkers," all hospital staff—and served undercooked pasta. She appreciated his efforts, though they had little in common beyond the lab. Was it her fault?

She stared into the fire.

When the Colombia assignment arose, she called Roland repeatedly over two days. Maybe time together might ignite things? What would he say? Would he consider going with her? Were they even that close? After her messages, Roland finally texted: "Thanks for the laughs," with a smiley. That ended any delusions she had about breaking his heart.

Alisha and Dan were married and expecting. She dated guitar-playing boy-men who couldn't cook pasta. Now, marching through the jungle under threat from these two guerillas—drug soldiers, whatever they were—her loneliness turned to hollow pain. Only her friends would worry. Nobody else would fear she'd been taken or care if she died out here.

Bandana sang and danced by the fire, lost in a drugged haze. Marko had wandered from sight, still chasing a signal in the dense rainforest.

The two gunmen had supplied them water, and now she had to pee. "Baño," she said in Bandana's direction.

The erratic man nodded, or perhaps it was a twitch. Whichever way, she took it as permission.

She found a spot behind trees at the clearing's edge and crouched to relieve herself. While there, she noticed a sharp stone jutting from the ground. She checked for Bandana and Marko, then dug around the stone.

If small enough, she could conceal it. Perhaps stun Bandana if she got near? Yes. Next march, she'd trail Bandana and strike his skull.

Her fingers raked at the earth.

Could she grab Bandana's gun and shoot Marko? Did she even know how the rifle worked? Maybe she could threaten Marko instead? Would that be enough to get him to surrender his weapon? Then, could she find help and return Alisha, Dan, and herself to safety?

It was possible, but she needed the stone first.

Her eyes darted between Alisha and Dan through the trees and the dancing buffoon near the flames.

Three fingers worked the rock.

Her heart pounded. She'd never fought anyone. Yet, her pupils widened, and her thoughts raced.

If Phinn were alive, he'd have taken down a gunman by now. But they'd murdered him at the tent. A strong man with a Scottish lilt, he'd dug trenches and hauled gear around the villages for months, outworking men half his age. These bastards had cut him down cold.

If Dan were healthy, this would be easier. She'd strike Bandana, and they could overpower him for his gun. But Dan hadn't fully recovered, and with Alisha pregnant, she didn't want to risk the expectant father.

She zipped her pants and knelt for leverage.

The more she edged the dirt, the more stone she exposed. She moved carefully, as firelight may betray her. Bandana might start yelling or barking. Marko, wherever he was, might halt his hunt for a cell signal and come running—or take aim and shoot her.

A hard twist left, then right. The rock came loose.

Its sharp, arrow-like tip, perfect for cutting, had caught her eye. Its wide base fit her hand.

Hannah raised the rock—perfectly shaped for a weapon.

A boot smashed her free hand.

Marko towered, eyes reflecting the fire.

She dropped the stone, clawing his leg.

But he didn't move.

His boot ground her skin raw.

The pain was unbearable.

Her screams brought no help.

CHAPTER
10

A year's salary just to board a flight didn't convince Ernie Nelson. Commander Campbell's offer came too fast, too smooth, and suspicion twisted in his gut. If he sniffed out a lie on this Virginia trip, he'd pocket their cash and tell them where to shove their mission.

The Chevy's headlights pierced the night, lighting up a small runway hidden behind crooked trees. Ernie drove through the entry gate, tires bouncing over rough stone and stirring dust.

The airfield's parking lot was a mix of empty spaces. Ernie parked near the end and cut the engine. Idle Cessnas and Beechcraft sat nearby, but a sleek private jet stood out on the tarmac ahead. It was a monster of luxury, the kind he'd only seen online—rides for rich athletes, musicians, and influencers full of ego and silicone.

He grabbed his rucksack from the passenger seat, its weight loaded with clothes, his Desert Eagle, stolen Bellevilles, and a half-eaten carton of trail mix. If Campbell delayed his return, he'd at least have comfortable boots and snacks to tide him over while he figured out how to spend their money. He slung the bag over his shoulder, stepped out into the humid night air, and locked the Chevy with a beep that echoed faintly across the deserted lot.

The jet loomed, its white fuselage glowing under the runway lights. Ernie eyed the plane and its silver stripes that ran from nose to tail.

A man stood at the base of the aircraft, early forties, broad-shouldered, with ruffled brown hair and a five o'clock shadow that looked more neglect than intent. Loose cargo pants, Converse sneakers, and an unbuttoned short-sleeve flapping over a ratty t-shirt. Ground crew, Ernie figured.

Approaching, Converse man snapped a sharp, palm-down salute to his hairline.

"NCO Nelson?" he asked, offering a hand.

"Ernie Nelson, yes."

They shook, his grip firm and calloused.

"Colonel Michael James Bennett, United States Air Force. Good to meet you, Nelson."

"Colonel?" Ernie froze. A senior officer dressed in civvies, sent to fetch him personally? This mission was either desperate or a complete shitshow.

"Semi-retired." Bennett grinned. "On retainer now. I fly the brass around—hush-hush stuff, mostly. Meetings, spy missions, the occasional assassination or two."

"What?"

Bennett clapped Ernie's shoulder. "Kidding, chief. Relax. Come on, let's get you aboard."

Ernie shook his head.

Bennett gestured to the jet. "Kept her paint civilian. No military markings. Just a registration number on the turbines. Certain service members love their secrecy. Con-prop."

"Con-prop?" Ernie said.

Bennett nodded. "Confiscated property. Seized from some unsavory types. Your partner's already inside."

"Partner?" Campbell hadn't mentioned a partner.

"Yeah, the other guy. Arrived a while ago. Interesting fella—you'll see." Bennett smirked.

They climbed the airstair. The jet's interior was like nothing Ernie had ever seen. Six beige leather armchairs, high-backed and plush, lined the cabin, each empty and screaming luxury. A long couch stretched across the rear, flanked by a galley bar with a sink, two refrigerators, a microwave, and a trio of silver dishes. Two large monitors hung on the walls—one on the forward bulkhead, the other opposite a small table—both displaying an inflight map. The setup was nicer than Ernie's bungalow. What the hell kind of mission was this?

"Hell of a plane," he said, dropping his rucksack onto a seat.

"A $65 million airliner," Bennett said from the doorway. "A gift from a smuggler. The ATF confiscated it a year ago. It hauled automatic weapons until some idiot overloaded it, landed hard, and bent this door's frame." He shoved the entry panel with his shoulder, producing a groan but no seal. "Torqued the rails. Takes a few hits to close properly."

Ernie settled into a chair.

At the aircraft's rear, a mahogany door swung open.

A man stepped out—mid-forties, athletic, with low-trimmed, speckled gray hair. He gave Ernie a curt nod but made a beeline for the galley bar. Eight glasses sat beside several decanters, and his fingers danced over them.

"Let's not bore the liver," he announced. His accent was thick, not quite English—but regional.

He grabbed a tumbler, held it eye level, then struck it against the mahogany bar. The glass thudded dully.

"Remarkable," he said, his speech slow and deliberate.

Ernie squinted. That voice, that face. He'd seen this man before—somewhere, sometime—but the memory wouldn't surface.

"Summoned by posh aircraft," the man said. "Fine seating, fitted buffet, flat screens, unbreakable dishes—everything the flying elite could want or need." He raised his voice toward Bennett. "But the door to this winged palace doesn't close properly?"

"Not standard Air Force stock," Bennett shouted back. "They don't keep G650 parts on the bases I fly into. This is a luxury vessel, and the officers I haul don't give a sloppy shit about a busted door."

"Interesting idiom." The stranger dropped ice into his tumbler and poured a generous splash of liquor from a decanter.

Bennett, still wrestling the door, shot him an annoyed glance. "Listen up, British Intelligence. I'm not sure what you've heard about our military, but we don't drink Martinis or drive Aston Martins."

The man swept an arm outward, laughing. "Evidence suggests otherwise."

Bennett frowned. "If I complain about this door seal, they'll stick me into a stripped-down C-20, where you two will be lucky if your seatbelts work."

The man sipped his drink.

"No whiskey bars, either."

The tumbler sank from the stranger's lips. "How barbaric."

Bennett shoulder-rammed the panel, clicking the door into place. "Strap in, wheels up in ninety-seconds."

The stranger cupped his drink and approached Ernie.

"On the ship, as it were," he said. "Instead of a salute, I offer the Assyrian greeting."

He stuck out a hand, firmly snatching Ernie by the palm.

"Thomas Ryan Kendrick. Born in Rumney, Cardiff. Proud Welshman, former British operative. Now trapped on this aircraft with you, Petty Officer Nelson."

Kendrick took a seat across from Ernie.

Bennett stomped down the aisle, a small notebook in hand, muttering to himself, stopping near the two men.

"Strap in for takeoff—tightly, both of you."

"Planning aerobatics, are we?" Kendrick fumbled with his harness, but kept his tumbler level.

"Runway's a bit short," Bennett said.

"Short?" Ernie's pulse quickened. He'd flown plenty with the Navy, but always on big transports with long, forgiving runways.

Bennett knelt, pressed a button on the underside of Ernie's chair, locking it into position. Then, he did the same for Kendrick's seat.

"This could be rough—stay belted in. If you need to hurl, put your head between your knees." He eyed them both. "I don't want you choking on your own vomit."

Ernie's face went pale. "Exactly how short is this runway?"

Bennett tugged at each man's harness, ensuring they were secure. "We call it "shit your pants short.""

"Vivid," Kendrick said. "But I'd feel better with a standard measurement."

Bennett tilted his head. "About 3,700 feet. After that, it's a fat bay of saltwater, and this ain't no boat. With our weight, fuel, and no wind, we need nearly a mile. The plane's base weight is 54,000 pounds. Add fuel, reserves, cargo, and us, we hit 72,300 pounds—3,000 over the limit." He smirked at Kendrick. "Feel better?"

"I'll need more whiskey," Kendrick announced.

Ernie's eyes darted to the exits, counting the steps to the nearest one.

Bennett turned to him, placing a hand on his shoulder. "Listen, kid. I've flown everything from crop-dusters to F-117s, including classified rigs I can't tell my great-great-grandkids about. I've got a million hours in the air, and I know this craft. No headwind today, front moving in, but I'll get us up."

"Just the shortness is concerning," Kendrick said.

"Gentlemen, we're on a tight timeline." Bennett stood. "And it's time to kick the tires and light the fires. Sorry to be abrupt, but we've got no choice."

Kendrick raised his glass. "Trousers prepared."

Ernie wondered if his seat cushion could be used as a floatation device.

Bennett headed to the cockpit. "I need to spool to max before releasing the brake. We'll need 125 knots for pullup. You'll feel increased G-force—might get uncomfortable. If you get queasy, stay buckled, and remember what I said. She'll be hauling ass when I yank up her nose. You'll feel like you're glued to your seats."

Ernie's mouth fell open. This wasn't a transport—it was a $65 million deathtrap. He should've demanded two years' salary, a life vest, and a fucking helmet.

Across the row, Kendrick leaned back in his seat, swirling the amber liquid in his glass. His gaze fixed on Ernie.

"You ever hear about the Darien Expedition, Nelson?"

The only thing on Ernie's mind was how far to shore he'd need to swim when this thing hit the water. "No?"

"Late 1600s," Kendrick said, voice low. "Thousands of Scots aimed to settle a Panama jungle patch they called New Caledonia."

Ernie leaned in, hoping talk would calm him. "New Caledonia?"

"They wanted a trading post to link the Atlantic and Pacific—make a fortune off world trade."

"Like the Panama Canal?"

"Not quite," Kendrick said. "Same spot, but they planned a land route for carts and horses, not a canal. But the aim was the same—no sailing around South America needed."

"Really?"

Kendrick took a slow sip. "These men were full of piss and vinegar. They loaded up their ships and supplies and sailed south."

The cabin lights dimmed.

Kendrick raised his chin. "But these poor souls had no idea what they were walking into, you see."

Ernie shifted uncomfortably. "What happened?"

A grim edge crept into Kendrick's tone. "After they landed in Darien, everything went to hell. Thick forest all around—miles of it, choking the coast. No roads, no trails, just green swallowing everything. Determined, they built a fort, hacked out a settlement, but the jungle fought back. Mosquitoes brought fever—malaria, dysentery—killing many. Supplies rotted in the humidity."

"Shit…"

"Yes." Kendrick raised an eyebrow. "But that was only the crust of the matter. The natives weren't thrilled about uninvited guests, either, you see. Hit-and-run raids, arrows from the trees."

Ernie swallowed.

"And the Spanish, who'd claimed the whole damn region a century earlier, caught wind of this Scottish plan to build a land-route."

"They didn't know?"

"No." Kendrick shook his head. "They sent ships and soldiers to finish the job. By the end, most Scots were dead or begging to leave. Survivors limped back north, half-mad, speaking of shadows moving in the woods, voices whispering in the dark. Almost two thousand souls lost to that mess."

"You're kidding?"

"Serious as a gravestone. And all because some big shots in Edinburgh didn't tell them the whole truth—didn't warn them what they were really up against."

The hum of the plane's engines broke into a roar.

Kendrick stared over Ernie's shoulder, out the oval window into the black void beyond. "History buries stories like that. But here's the rub—those Scots weren't the only ones who disappeared down there."

"No?"

"Spanish explorers, English pirates, even some American surveyors in the 1800s—all went into that jungle looking for something. Gold, land, shortcuts. Most didn't come back. And the ones who did? They talked about the same damn thing—feeling watched, losing their way in the trees, like the forest itself didn't want them there." Kendrick gulped the rest of his drink. "Makes you think, doesn't it?"

Ernie's mouth went dry. "Think what?"

"About all this." His eyes flicked toward the cockpit. "What they're not telling us about this mission. What they're hiding."

The aircraft howled to life, spitting cobalt flames into the night. The turbines gyred to maximum, a deafening roar. The Gulfstream thundered down the runway, shaking hard. Ernie's teeth knocked together as gravity pressed him into the leather. Runway lights flashed by in white and red streaks, tears pooling in his eyes as the speed climbed.

Bennett's voice crackled over the intercom.

"Few more knots, and we'll have it!"

Clutching his chair's armrests, Kendrick turned to Ernie. "Grand. Shit-the-pants-short with play-by-play."

Ernie closed his eyes, but visions of splashing into the ocean flooded his mind—metal crumpling, water rushing in, the jet sinking into the dark Atlantic.

"Here we go!" Bennett shouted.

The aircraft's nose torqued upward.

Ernie felt three times his weight.

But the rear of the aircraft was still rolling on the asphalt.

Would the tail strike the runway? Could they fly without it? If they hit a freighter in the bay, would they missile through its hull, or pinwheel into the sea like a fiery piñata? Sweat soaked his neckline.

A growl boomed through the fuselage.

The rear gear lifted, and the jet caught flight speed—yards from the runway's end.

"Climbing to eight thousand," Bennett announced.

The jet careened skyward at a steep angle, mashing Ernie into his chair. Pressure built in his ears.

Finally, the plane's nose eased its angle.

The lump in Ernie's throat receded.

"I hope Virginia's runway is longer than that one," he said, voice shaky.

Kendrick unbuckled. "Virginia, you say?"

Ernie nodded. "Norfolk. About an hour's flight."

Kendrick glanced at the inflight map. "We're headed North? To Virginia?"

Ernie nodded again.

Kendrick's brow furrowed. "Does the pilot know?"

JACK J. WYATT

CHAPTER
11

Marko's stomp dislocated the middle and ring fingers of her left hand. When he was satisfied he'd inflicted enough damage, he allowed Hannah to get up and leave.

Pain seared up her arm, white-hot and relentless, her vision blurring. When Marko stepped back, his shadow loomed over her, satisfaction glowing in his shadowed eyes.

She staggered to her feet, clutching her mangled hand to her chest, salt stinging her cheeks as tears carved trails through the grime.

She stumbled toward the fire's glow, its heat pulsing against her skin. Alisha's sharp voice cut through the haze, clashing with Dan's low growl as they faced Bandana. His rifle gleamed in the flickering light, barrel swaying lazily between them.

Hannah dropped beside the flames, the smoky tang of burning wood filling her lungs as Alisha and Dan turned to her. They moved quickly—wooden tongue depressors set against her swollen fingers, the rough scrape of medical tape binding them tight. Realigning the joints was a fresh hell, a jagged bolt of agony that ripped a gasp from her throat, her stomach churning as the bones grated into place.

She reached for the medical bag, fingers trembling toward the painkillers, but Marko's meaty hand darted in first.

He snatched the bottle, grinning as he upended it over the fire. The pills scattered into the blaze, popping and hissing as they melted into oblivion.

Bandana's laughter erupted, a wild, hyena-like cackle that grated against her raw nerves.

Later, they slumped onto the massive log by the fire, its bark digging into her thighs. Alisha's arm slid around Hannah's shoulders, a warm anchor against the chaos, but it did little to dull the throbbing in her hand. Her fingers ballooned, skin stretched tight and glistening in the firelight, each pulse a fresh stab. She lifted her arm, holding it high above her heart, and the ache eased—just barely—into a sharp, persistent sting.

Across the flames, Bandana sprawled, his chest rising and falling in jagged snores. His rifle rested against his knee, a coiled threat even in sleep. How the manic bastard had finally crashed, she couldn't fathom—maybe the jungle itself had worn him down.

Beside her, Alisha nestled into Dan, his arm curling protectively around her. Their breaths soon synced, softening into the steady rhythm of sleep.

Hannah's eyelids drooped, heavy with envy, but the pain kept her tethered to wakefulness.

The fire wasn't for comfort—sweat already beaded on her brow, the humid night pressing down at a sticky 80 degrees. No, the flames were a flimsy shield against the jungle's unseen hunters. Moths swarmed the light, their wings a frantic blur, drawn into a hypnotic dance. One veered too close, and the fire claimed it—a sizzle, a flash, then a spiraling plunge into the glowing maw below. Hannah flinched at the sight, the scent of charred wings lingering in the air.

For a fleeting moment, adrenaline had whispered rebellion—grab a rock, smash it into Bandana's skull, run. But the fantasy dissolved as fast as it came. Her crippled hand mocked her, and the weight of

Marko's pistol, tucked into his waistband, anchored her to reality. She'd been lucky to escape with broken fingers instead of a bullet.

The fire dwindled to embers, casting long shadows that danced across the clearing. Marko stirred, his boots scuffing the dirt as he tossed more branches into the pit. Sparks flared, the crackle snapping through the stillness.

Hannah ducked her head, letting her hair curtain her face, her breath shallow as she mimed sleep.

Marko's grunt rumbled low, followed by the sharp prod of a stick into the coals, coaxing the flames back to life.

They were being moved—dragged somewhere, she didn't know where. A town, maybe? A place with a rusted truck she could hotwire, or a phone to plead for help? Her mind raced, grasping at possibilities—could she slip away, vanish into the trees? But coordinating a breakout for all three of them felt like chasing smoke. She exhaled, the damp air clinging to her lungs.

Plans were a luxury she couldn't afford, not here, not now. This wasn't some city escape—this was a third-world hellhole, a tangle of wilderness and gunmen. Food, water, survival—all dangled at the whim of these filthy captors. Running meant death, alone or together, in a day or two tops.

Marko's phone buzzed, its screen casting a harsh glow across his scarred face. He swiped at it, voice low and guttural, words half-lost to the jungle's hum.

Hannah could hear both sides of the call, not clear, but some. She made out, "Morning… coming for us…" The rest blurred into static—trucks, schedules, nonsense that didn't fit their stranded nightmare.

Marko chuckled, a rough sound that scraped her nerves, then glanced over, eyes skimming the hostages. Satisfied, he lumbered off, still muttering into the device.

Somehow, Hannah's eyes closed, and she nodded off.

CHAPTER
12

"Where's this plane going?" Nelson demanded.

Bennett sat in the pilot's seat, scanning the dash's flat-screen panels—radar, direction, airspeed. Switches and knobs cluttered above, while a console between the seats bristled with thruster controls, fuel levers, and a radio.

"Hell of a liftoff. Hope it didn't get too hairy back there," Bennett said.

"Where are we going?" Nelson repeated from the doorway.

Bennett fidgeted with buttons on the center console.

"Insurance hates solo pilots on a bird like this. Safety thing." He tapped the copilot seat. "Jump in here—we've got a tight window to hit the coast."

Nelson hesitated.

"Chief." Bennett turned, grinning. "Step over the console and slide into the coolest shotgun position you'll ever experience."

Nelson ambled over the center console, settling into the vacant copilot seat. He acclimated to the forward position with a light belch.

"Buckle in, put your cans on."

Nelson strapped in tight, then slipped the headset over his ears. Bennett's voice came through its small speakers.

"Good," Bennett said. "Want to take the stick for a bit?"

"Told us you had a million hours in the air?" He ignored Bennett's question. "You look good for your age."

"Just trying to relax you." He smiled. "You guys seemed a bit, uh, tightly wound?"

Another quiet belch left Nelson's belly.

"Didn't expect we'd hit Mach five."

"I apologize, orders and all. Time's a factor."

Dark clouds zipped through the atmosphere below. On the western end, large flashes of lightning came and went from huge gatherings of vapor.

"Cyclone's coming." Bennett nodded at the windscreen. "Saw those wispy cirrus spikes earlier."

"The puffy ones out there?"

"Cumulus. But that big bastard—" He pointed to a towering, flat-topped cloud flashing with lightning. "That's a cumulonimbus. Mean as hell, cloud to cloud bursts."

Outside the windscreen, a horizontal bolt swam across the clouds, branching through the hovering vapors.

"What happens if lightning hits the plane?"

Bennett chuckled. "Nothing good."

Nelson stiffened.

"Relax, chief. The jet's got a metal body. We'd feel a huge bang followed by a hard jolt." His head tilted. "Might scare the piss out of us, but the jet's fine." He motioned to the outside again. "But over there, in that big-ass vertical, black thunder cloud is dangerous mean shit. Hailstones, heavy rain, and downdrafts that'll plummet this aircraft thousands of feet in seconds."

Nelson stared, unblinking.

"Best to stay away," Bennett concluded.

Nelson had seen massive thunderheads like that from a boat, and knew it could create deadly waves in the ocean. But he never considered what it might do to an airplane if one flew through it. His shoulders eased the farther the jet angled away from its path.

"See the stick to your right?"

"Yeah?" Nelson's eyes shifted.

"Place your hand on it, gently."

Nelson gripped the sidestick.

Bennett unbuckled.

"Hold her steady for a minute." He leaped over the center console. "I need to take a leak."

"Wait!" Nelson shouted. "I don't have–"

But the pilot disappeared without another word.

What the hell was wrong with this guy? Oh sure, the jet was on autopilot. Of course. Nice joke, Colonel Shithead.

Nelson released the stick.

A moment later, the plane dipped downward. He blinked—Christ, this wasn't a joke.

He seized the control. The jet swayed right and upward. Sweat pooled at his neckline. What an absolute asshole! That jerk had really left him flying this thing. His grip tightened, pulse hammering—then steadied. The jet responded, smooth and alive under his hands.

Minutes passed, and Bennett was still MIA.

What if an engine caught fire? Or a lightning strike decided to shoot out from the heavens and fry off a wing? What was he supposed to do? He scanned the dash.

The cockpit door swung open.

"Passed your first test!" Bennett smirked. "Knew you could do it."

"Damn you, what test?" Nelson shouted.

"Haven't crashed yet, so that's good."

"You do realize I want to rip your head off, right? It's dangerous to leave someone in control of something they've no training on."

Bennett returned with two Styrofoam cups. He placed them into the beverage holders, seated himself, and strapped in.

"I can't believe you would—"

"You, sir, are flying the next generation of pilot controls here. Side-mounted, it looks like a video game controller and even feels like one. Remember to keep your movements small and slow. These devices are sensitive and reactive."

Nelson blinked in his direction.

"Now, push the stick forward."

Nelson shoved the light apparatus ahead, and the Gulfstream dropped at a hard angle.

"Slowly! That's the Atlantic down there, and I don't have my swim trunks on. Small and slow, remember?"

Nelson eased the controller back and the plane's nose rose.

"More."

The dark skies scrolled upward.

"Getting the feel?"

He was. The sidestick was firm but pliable, like a handshake. A tilt of his wrist was all it took to move the craft one way or another. It surprised him how much power was in his palm.

"Alright. A few things, thrusters on your left." Bennett touched the hefty split nickel handles. "Most times we push and pull in tandem unless maneuvering on the runway or the engines go out of balance. Forward is power-up, and backward takes us to idle."

Nelson glanced at the center console. The engines currently ran at near full power.

"That's right," Bennett said. "We're moving at 560 knots, about 650 mph. That's a full 100 mph faster than commercial aircraft."

Six-hundred fifty miles an hour. Shit, this was cool.

"And you're doing it. You're flying us." Bennett raised his soda.

A wide grin overtook Nelson's face.

Bennett scanned the sky. "See any other planes out there, check the wingtips—red light on the left, green on the right. Tells you which way they're headed."

"Same as ships and boats," Nelson said, nodding.

"Something I didn't know," Bennett said.

He rose, pulling a thick manual from behind Nelson's seat pocket. "Alright, this is a quick guide to emergency and weather procedures. ATC calls to help you gain an ear for tower chatter and an index of general aircraft terms. If you get bored, have a glance."

He set the paper guide on Nelson's lap.

"We're squawked at 1443. That's our current transponder ID." Bennett pointed to a small screen and its tiny keyboard. "That ID lets ground control know what type of craft we are, so they don't mistake us for another plane."

"Okay." He was getting a crash course in flying, and it was exciting.

"There's other stuff. Take-offs and landings and such. Trivial details, really. Other than that, you're ready for your pilot's license." Bennett chuckled.

Nelson hoped Bennett wouldn't take back control right away because this was frickin awesome. He figured the best way to stay flying was to keep the man talking.

"How'd you become a pilot?"

"First oath was boots and bullets, standard stuff." He leaned back. "But when it came time to re-up, I decided to enter flight training. Humping's too hard on the body, and I'd always wanted to fly." He took a sip from his cup. "But I didn't know what I was in for."

"How do you mean?"

"Well, I made solo and squad attached at the end of 2000. I was itching to fly in combat, but I was young and stupid. Had a case of antsy-antsy training pants. Started praying for action."

"Oh." Nelson knew where this was going.

"Never forget that morning. All-deck call, command losing it, screams in the tower." Bennett sipped his drink. "Air traffic said that second plane nearly clipped two others—feet away—before I scrambled my F15 out of Langley."

Nelson's head shook.

Bennett stared ahead, voice low. "Then the order came. Thrust to the front line of a war I didn't even know existed until earlier that day. Combatants are one thing, but firing on commercial airliners?"

The tips of Nelson's fingers nudged the sidestick.

"Things that change us." Bennett's gaze drifted out the window.

Minutes of silence passed until Bennett spoke again. He pointed to the flat panels on the dash, talked a little more about altitude control and related adjustments, explained the basics of screen readout, which alarms to watch for, switches never to touch or he'd kill them both, and things like that.

He quizzed Nelson, corrected him once, leaned back, and closed his eyes. "Keep the night sky above. Wake me in an hour, and we'll switch off."

Nelson kept the jet steady at 41,000 feet, hand firm on the stick. Stars gleamed in the gathering dark. He didn't know their destination— and right now, it didn't matter.

CHAPTER
13

The villagers were a smiling lot and generous with what little they had. Aldous Phinn tried to make himself useful while the three doctors tended to health needs.

He'd dug a septic line in one community and set the drainage tank far away from the river, their main water supply. In another, he aided in the raising and resetting of their huts using four long bamboo fulcrums he'd fashioned. He'd helped these villagers grade their foundations and mix concrete to set proper footings and steady the structures against rampant seasonal flooding.

They marveled at his tools. His sight level was a huge hit. The children had never seen the beam of a laser, and he had fun flashing it on their foreheads and making them chase the red spot around the grounds like a herd of kittens.

He spent the rest of his time patching roofs alongside the owners and performed other odd jobs when he saw the need. The entire experience here and elsewhere in the other modest towns they'd traveled provided him that feeling of being needed. No judgment, no apprehension.

In appreciation, they stuffed him with rice and fish, sometimes potatoes and ham. Whatever they served, he ate. It was wonderful. He was a part of something. Although their time together would be short before he and the others moved onto their next community, he relished the accomplishments and nurturing thankfulness.

But that evening, something happened. His usual stroll between the village and the campsite, some unknown loon snuck upon him in the dark, bashing the side of his skull. Momentarily blinded, he stumbled, but he didn't go down. He turned to see a small man holding a rifle, butt-end first. His assailant gave an eerie smile, releasing a queer laugh.

The second strike landed fast—an unusual punch to his gut. He had no time to defend or strike back before the assailant scurried into the dark underbrush and vanished. Then came the warmth, the burn. He pressed a palm to his abdomen, feeling moisture.

That was not a punch. The sleekit bastard had slipped a knife into him. He rushed toward the medical tent, his pulse pounding in his ears.

Breathing became difficult, and a sharp pain throbbed in his stomach. He swatted through branches, forging ahead to the only safe place out here and the people who could fix him.

Numbness hit his legs, and the run slowed to an unsteady jog. Fifty yards ahead, he saw a lit tent, then the light was rapidly extinguished.

He pushed forward as fast as he could, but the bends, bushes, and rocks became harder to navigate. The trail went hazy. Almost there, he stumbled.

Coldness chilled his spine, his balance affected.

Behind came footsteps. And that strange laugh.

Paralysis seized his legs as his bloodied hand reached for the tent. A scream erupted, and he fell forward into blackness.

When the morning sun met his face, no one was more surprised than he. Anna, Pablo, Gevia, and others drifted in and out of his field of vision, floating above him like angels. At first, he wasn't sure if his imagination had assembled them as protection against his inevitable entrance into the afterlife, making the passage from earth to the unknown a bearable journey to the mind.

But they were not imaginary.

The faces were real.

They patched his injuries, fed him water and rice. But then he'd drift out again. When he woke, so came the food and liquids.

On the second day, he was able to sit up by himself.

Anna brought him a bowl of soup.

"What… what happened?" he rasped.

She raised her head, eyes heavy with sorrow. "The doctors—they took them."

CHAPTER

14

Airport Ricardo Domini, San Felipe, Magdalena, Colombia. Three freighters loomed at the northern port, cargo Nelson clocked from mid-air as the Gulfstream hit the tarmac.

"Need to secure a place in the hangar," Bennett barked. "Dress in. Transportation's minutes out." He motioned to a cabinet near the plane's bar. "They provided us a box of greens and blacks, all sizes. But blend the clothing with your streetwear." He nodded to a window. "Lots of eyes in Colombia. We shouldn't dress alike."

He had already switched to jeans and swapped his Converse for a pair of well-worn Timberlands. Kendrick donned a pair of black trousers, boots, and a camel-colored overshirt.

Nelson opened his rucksack. He hadn't worn footwear most of the past year and a half. But now, as he prepared his boots, it brought back a memory he'd been avoiding.

Massive debt for stale classrooms and useless coursework, all to rot in an office fifty years, had him itching for a noose. He'd joined the military for an experience no college provided. It offered him a hands-on quest to learn skills and trades, instead of from some boring textbook. And he'd managed a successful career for near eight years.

But then came the bullshit incident that wrecked his life.

After the trial, Nelson had to ditch everything Uncle Sam had issued over eight years—blues, whites, fatigues, his M16, M9, dive gear, even the sheath. And he returned everything, except for his black Bellevilles—the first piece of equipment he was ever issued. He'd earned them. They could take away his service and most of his equipment, but nobody was getting his fucking boots.

He laced up tight and stood, pulling his phone from his pocket— Eden's text glowed onscreen, her lips pressed to Noodle's head. A smirk tugged at him. The auburn-haired stranger next door had his buddy handled.

Cabin lights cast a soft sheen across the floor, turbines churning humid air around him, until a sharp noise beyond the hull drew him down the Gulfstream's ramp.

Scarlet flushed the horizon east of him, across the dark taxiway. On the runway's far side, a medium-sized craft rested with its strobe lights pulsing.

Nelson hit the asphalt, boots scuffing as he scanned for Bennett and Kendrick—nothing but empty tarmac staring back. The air was hot and heavy, like a sauna at dawn. A boxy truck rolled out of the shadows, its loud beep piercing the quiet. A green light flashed briefly, then the jet's hum drowned it out again.

He didn't yet know what kind of mission they were in for, but when Bennett ultimately disclosed their destination while the two were chatting in the cockpit, Kendrick's strange story about the jungle now made sense. Colombia was strange, and far different than any country he'd seen before. Outside the cities, the place was overrun with jungle, and bordered five peculiar countries it didn't always get along with. The people spoke a language he barely understood. Bennett also said many regions outside Bogotá were lawless and infested with cartel. He told them they needed to remain cautious, alert, and ready.

For now, as he scanned the dark tarmac and adjacent buildings, it was probably better if he waited inside the aircraft until Bennett and Kendrick returned.

"Que tal!"

The voice jolted him, adrenaline surging.

Nelson spun in the darkness, glimpsed a figure, and seized a fistful of fabric, yanking to drop them. But the stranger countered—hard.

A deft arm snaked under his, fingers locking his wrist and twisting it inward. He broke free, lunging for their throat, only to snag a fistful of long hair.

A woman.

She darted behind him, her grip clamping his wrist again. An arm hooked under his shoulder, her other hand pressing the back of his neck, pinning him.

Nelson's single option was to push himself backward and fall, hoping to startle the enemy and break the holds.

He readied his legs.

Laughing erupted.

It was Bennett.

The person behind him released their hold.

"NCO Nelson, I'd like you to meet Specialist Catalina Rosales," Bennett said.

Nelson turned, red faced. "I'm sorry, I—"

"No apologies, sir. Nice spar." She grinned, extending a hand.

Nelson shook it, wrist pulsing, masking the sting. Five-eight, ponytail taut, brown eyes—Rosales stood sharp.

"Superior hand-to-hand." Bennett chuckled. "Top-tier linguist, too—aced phase four."

"Special Forces?" Nelson's brow lifted.

"Guard to Green Beret," she said. "Q-Course scheduled next month, once we're done out here."

"Green Beret?" Kendrick appeared. "That's extraordinary."

Kendrick was correct—Nelson worked hard, earning his trident through intense training. Green Berets shared that intensity, training both mind and body, skilled in combat and survival in any environment.

He suddenly didn't feel so bad about being bested in the scuffle moments ago.

"Where you from, soldier?" Bennett asked.

"Born in Bayamón, outside San Juan, sir."

"Puerto Rico. Beautiful place."

"Family moved stateside in my teens. Virginia."

"Got us a genuine brat here," Bennett grinned.

"Proud parents?" Kendrick asked.

"Father was KIA in Afghanistan, sir. Mom's retired with her husband in Florida. But yes, she's proud, sir."

"I'm sorry about your father," Bennett said. "Tough war."

"He was the best of us, sir." Rosales gave a tight nod.

"You've been briefed?" Kendrick asked.

"Yes, sir. Four subjects in country. Present location and condition unknown. Possible missing or kidnap scenario."

Nelson jumped in. "Do you know this region?"

"Read-in some, but the orders came fast, sir. I know the terrain, probable list of hostiles. But the geopolitical I'm less familiar with. There wasn't enough time before deployment."

"That's alright." Bennett motioned toward Kendrick. "British Intelligence here knows everything about every place on the planet. Isn't that right Major?"

Kendrick ignored the cynical accolade.

"Where's the rest of your unit? Don't Special Ops teams come in pairs?"

"Unsure, sir. The orders came fast, top-down, and not through my CO."

"Three in to fetch four?" Nelson muttered.

"Don't like the odds either," Kendrick said. "I think we're still short."

The man now had a different tone than he'd had on the plane, a serious one. Perhaps this was the sober Kendrick, the soldier?

"Forgot to mention I'm detail, too," Bennett shrugged. "Time to dust off those field skills."

Nelson and Kendrick turned to the pilot.

"What? I'm not as handsome as Nelson here, but I can bird dog with the best of them."

Nelson fought a grin.

"Got the gear in the hold," Bennett said. "Suggest we break it out and see what gifts the military provided us?"

They paced to the aircraft's rear, and Bennett opened its luggage hold. He dragged out a large metal rolling case.

Rosales eagerly stepped forward.

"First choice to you, soldier," Bennett said.

Her eyes lit up. She snatched a black and white camouflage rifle from the gunnery.

"You know this weapon?"

"Hell yes, sir. M14 Mod Z." She seized the rifle. "Pistol grip, 22-inch barrel, laser-sighted—light and lethal." She flicked out the bipod, then snapped it back. "Solid pick, sir."

"Guess we know your specialty, yes?"

"No, sir." Rosales shook her head. "My concentration is in electronic warfare. But as our weaponry take on more gadgetry, I've found it helpful to familiarize myself with every modern type and model."

"Gadgetry?"

"Yes, sir. We have smart sights with smart rounds now. Next-generation computer-guided missilery that can navigate barriers, plunge underwater, resurface, and hit targets miles away. I've seen it. I've fired it."

"Submarine bullets? Now I've heard everything." Bennett lifted another rifle from the chest. "I prefer the simple, old M4 myself." He held the firearm close, inspecting its chamber and attached suppressor. "Because it all comes down to pulling the trigger, doesn't it?"

"Yes, sir." Rosales winked. "Point and click."

Nelson selected an M4A2.

Kendrick eyed the remaining three rifles and five handguns. He picked up a nylon shoulder harness with two Beretta pistols and extra ammunition clips.

"Uhm, pal," Bennett said. "You do realize we're going in-country here? Hostiles and shit? Are you sure you don't want more firepower than that?"

Kendrick pulled the harness over his head and fed his arms through the slots. "We're headed into treacherous jungle—most of which is controlled by dangerous militants, to retrieve four civilians and return them here for transport." He buckled the harness tight to his ribcage. "I can assure you we'll be outgunned and outmanned, no matter what we bring."

The others held, eyes on Kendrick.

"Incursion won't be the problem." He stuffed extra ammunition into his pockets, scanning the faces of Rosales, Nelson, and Bennett. "But once we reach our objective and find those four assets… I suggest you each prepare to run."

CHAPTER
15

Dawn broke. Marko woke Hannah with a rifle poke to her chest. She gasped, blinking at the muddy trail ahead. Her fingers still throbbed. Marko stomped past her to the trail with his phone.

Shards of gravel jabbed at Hannah's back, and sand fleas gnawed at her exposed skin. In these highlands, the frigid morning wind sent shivers rattling through her.

Alisha and Dan sat to her right in the dirt, the wounded but dutiful husband covering his wife's midsection and shoulders with his cotton shirt.

Hannah's dirty khakis still hid the remnants of the broken satellite phone. If she could piece the components together and connect the battery, maybe she could call for help. But as they traveled deeper into the jungle, she realized how badly disoriented she was. No landmarks. No trails she could describe to a dispatcher. Even if the phone worked, she couldn't tell anyone where to find them. But she had to protect it.

Bandana had killed something—too small for a pig, too slimy for anything she wanted to name—his machete glinting in the dawn light, still wet with gore.

He turned the thing over a fresh fire, meat hissing and popping. When it browned enough, he tore it into pieces and tossed a chunk to each of them.

She forced down what she could, not knowing when they'd eat again. They passed around a filthy plastic jug, and the brown liquid helped wash down the awful meal.

Bandana wandered off behind the trees, leaving a pacing Marko in the distance.

Hannah eyed the half-full water jug. Would she get far if she ran? Could she take a burning log from the fire, sneak up on Bandana while he relieved himself, and bash his skull in? Her gaze drifted to Alisha and Dan—and cold truth snapped her back.

She'd already lost the function of two fingers. If she tried and failed, Marko would shoot her dead. Maybe Bandana would toss her corpse on the fire, cook her like game meat, and force-feed the remains to her friends.

Marko finished his call, muttering, "El jefe no espera," and headed back toward them.

Hannah kept her dead stare locked on the flames, trying to savor the fire's warmth.

Marko crept closer.

"Fría?" he said.

Cold? Yes. The winds in these overgrown mountains were bitter. Yes, she wanted a real breakfast. Yes, she wanted to get the hell out of here. But she said nothing.

Marko reached down, fondling her hair.

A low, pleased grunt rumbled from his throat.

Her fist clenched—the other stiff with two throbbing fingers.

He pawed her ear, slithering down her cheek, a sweaty thumb angling for her lips.

Her father had walked out when she was young, leaving her with a hard-earned lesson: depend on no one. She and her mother had scraped by—secondhand clothes, spaghetti dinners, library books. Every step afterward—retaking exams, faking loan forms, earning her MD and PhD—was a fight she won alone. She hadn't come this far to fold now.

Marko's eager thumb pressed against her mouth.

Hannah slapped his arm.

Marko stepped back, hoisted his rifle, and aimed it between her eyes. "La perra!"

She glared up at him, her fingers twitching. Clutching a mound of soil beneath her, she readied herself. Dirt wouldn't save her, but if it came to it, she'd blind him, shove his flabby ass into the fire. Yes, he'd cut her down with bullets. But he'd live the rest of his wretched life marked by the flames she fed him to.

He pressed the muzzle harder into her skull.

She stared him down, unblinking.

Running feet pounded across the dirt.

"El camión! El camión!" Bandana sprinted into view, pointing as an engine growled closer.

A bullet-pocked Datsun pickup rattled up the mucky track like a coffin on wheels, windshield webbed with holes. Its scrawny, brown-skinned driver and his passenger seemed to know Marko very well.

Inside the filthy cab, she spotted two military-type rifles leaning against the seats.

"En tus pies!" Marko barked, yanking the rifle back and motioning at them.

She, Alisha, and Dan got to their feet and trudged toward the truck.

Marko stepped closer as they passed, the rifle loose in his hand, a grin curling his cracked lips as he grabbed himself.

Hannah met his stare, her sore fingers twitching as she walked past, head high, the phone's hidden weight the only thing anchoring her. She eyed Marko.

Not on your best day, you filthy sack of shit.

16

Kendrick texted the Interpol agent a quick synopsis of Alexandra's port activity, including the conflicting ISO numbers he'd memorized. But he also relayed that he was now out of the country, on a new assignment. The grateful agent thanked Kendrick but implored him to message right away once his mission was complete.

Kendrick found the request interesting.

Sunlight scorched the tarmac. Bennett secured the Gulfstream inside a large hangar. Outside, a Range Rover with a spider crack in its windshield sped toward the building. The vehicle parked, and an unfamiliar Latino man with a cleft lip got out. He handed the keys to Bennett without a word, gazed at the jet, then, as quickly as he appeared, scampered away.

Bennett shrugged.

"Ground transport, I guess."

A mid-90s model, dirty blue or black, he couldn't tell which under the dried mud, with several rust patches dotting the truck's underbelly.

Bennett surveyed the dents and warped roof and laughed. "I think this thing's been rolled."

Rumpled and inconspicuous, the old four-door vehicle looked as if it belonged in this part of the world, barreling through the hills in this godforsaken jungle.

Rosales and Nelson circled toward its rear.

"At least we know she can take a beating, sir."

Rosales placed her weapon into the Rover's cargo area, then returned to the open gunnery case and sorted through its contents. She outfitted herself in a sleeveless black jacket and slid ammo clips into pockets on its front. Finally, she retrieved all remaining weapons and their respective shells, and packed them in the Range Rover.

She and Kendrick shared a glance.

"Prepping for the run, sir."

Kendrick nodded, impressed. Smart soldier.

She handed him a rifle. "For the ride, sir. Keep it up front with you."

Kendrick took the weapon without arguing.

"Had breakfast yet?" Bennett tossed Kendrick a small package, then unwrapped his own and took a bite. "Tastes like shit, but you can live on them."

"Don't forget," Nelson called out. "Four pints of water, minimum, per day." He held up a canteen. "These self-filter, but we should change out the sieve every couple of days."

Kendrick and Bennett nodded.

Rosales rounded the vehicle with something in her hands, passing a set to each man.

"Sirs, our eyewear. High-density polyethylene and clear aluminum. They look and feel like a normal set of eyeglasses."

"No thanks, got my own spectacles, soldier." Bennett tapped a bulge in his shirt pocket.

"No, not like these you don't. In addition to the EVS, these are secure, encrypted com devices. The newest self-contained headgear with built-in solid-state battery." Rosales held up her pair. "Once fitted, tiny tubes slip over your ear's antitragus." She pointed to the side of her head. "This directs sound into your auditory canal, which, unlike a normal magnetic speaker, cannot be overheard unless that person's ear is literally pressed against yours."

A bizarre image came to Kendrick's mind, two people ear to ear.

"The EVS augments at distance."

"What?" Bennett interrupted.

"Sir?"

"That "augments at distance" bit—it sounded like gibberish and hurt my brain." He squinted.

Rosales grinned. "Sorry. EVS—enhanced vision system—boosts what we see, sir. It's augmented reality. Picks up heat signatures, sharpens anything from infrared to ultraviolet, and enhances targets up to 3500 feet away."

Bennett scratched his chin.

"Think of it like night vision on steroids, but in broad daylight too. Clear targets over a thousand yards, even in pitch-dark," Rosales said.

"Ah, yes, I see," Bennett said.

"Plus, they have normal vision enhancements, store full mapping, and they're true all-way communication. We don't need to worry about stepping on each other when we speak."

"But I like saying "over,"" Bennett said. "It's so official."

She nodded. "And they're voice-controlled."

"That's all fine, Rosales," Bennett said. "But will the glasses make me look cool?"

"Put them on, sir." She smiled.

The three men did.

A small screen appeared in the upper left of Kendrick's eye line. Inside, miniature green boxes appeared, and small captions identified Rosales, Nelson, and Bennett by name. A tiny six-digit clock floated above the left side of his vision. He rotated his sight across the taxiway and amazingly found the eyewear supplied a pristine view of every object around him.

A creature rustled from a distant bush. A yellow box framed it in the smart glasses, tagging it "Capybara" as the dog-sized rodent ambled off. Fascinating.

Kendrick's eyewear fixed its sensors on the Range Rover. Service and repair warnings floated into his field of vision, Low tire pressure, service engine, check brake fluid. Colombian rental—sounded about right.

"Well, son of a bitch," Bennett exclaimed.

Kendrick heard him perfectly through the eyewear's earpieces.

"The more your eyes use them, the sharper the images become, sirs. They take readings from your retina and self-adjust the optics like a dynamic prescription."

It sounded like Rosales was inside his head.

"Absolutely incredible." Nelson paced around in his new visual world.

"These glasses are prototypes, sirs. Ground signals stay secure between us using radio frequency. For anything beyond," she pointed skyward, "they scramble through satellite relays—military-grade, no interruptions, even in storms."

"I like these." Bennett turned to her, and the two grinned at one another.

"And they self-tint," Rosales added.

"Submarine bullets and self-tinting, augmented reality glasses?" Bennett smirked. "The world's a video game."

"That it is, sir," Rosales replied.

"I bet these glasses come with a fancy name?"

"They're 524-73s, sir."

"Sounds like half a phone number," Bennett snickered.

"Some in field ops call them Rickrollers, sir."

"Rickrollers?"

"Never want to give them up, sir."

Kendrick laughed aloud.

"And they'll never let you down?" Nelson chuckled.

Bennett frowned, clearly lost. "What's that supposed to mean?"

A tone pulsed in Kendrick's ear.

"A beeping noise inside here?" He pointed to his eyewear.

"It's a private call, sir. Say "Kendrick, answer com.""

He did as she instructed. Commander Joyner's voice popped into his ear.

"All set there, major?"

Kendrick walked away.

"This is it? This is everyone?"

"Small team, I'm afraid, best we could manage. There are things at play which, well, I can't say much more because I don't know much more."

"What's the backstory with Rosales?"

"Pistol, isn't she? Second-generation military, both parents served. Father died in Afghanistan, mother worked in intelligence, like yourself, until she retired not long ago. Rosales is also very inquisitive. If I didn't know any better, I'd say she was a younger Kendrick and will wind up in intelligence one day. Now, she might be young, but she has combat training, though hasn't seen much. A technical specialist, self-solver, excels in everything, and on-course to graduate special forces." Joyner hesitated before continuing. "But she may have a lot to prove, so watch out for her."

"But we need at least two more, even with the equipment. This is questionable country."

"Nelson's a SEAL, an incursion and recovery specialist. He was the point man for operation Jupiter."

Kendrick looked over at Nelson. A handsome, tall kid, six-two at least, without an ounce of fat on his muscular, lean body. He was in better shape than Kendrick had ever been in his entire life.

"Jupiter? The Nord-Lawrence rescue? Those contractors in Niger?"

"Yes, extraordinary success, despite the odds. But his military later released him in a sordid doing, I'm afraid. He doesn't have any issues, per se, but Nelson's dismissal left him furious from what I understand. He'd done near a solid eight years but was abruptly discharged without pension. So, I can't blame him. However, subsequent video of Nelson's incident shows another story altogether." Joyner paused. "I can't elaborate, but Nelson's commander would really like him to return full time. Though, politics are mucking things up. But do your best to get him back into the mix. Make sure he's still got that edge. Nelson needs challenge to regain that confidence, much like yourself."

"My confidence is fine," Kendrick said. "But we're well short here."

"Don't overlook Bennett. No offense, the man may appear seasoned, but he knows his stuff. Came up through their Marines, with serious ground time in Afghanistan. Part of a hit-and-run squad. Bennett may be a pilot, but he was hammered tactical, just as you."

Kendrick looked the wide-shouldered, unkempt jet pilot over, who was standing by the hangar and speaking through his eyewear to someone else.

"Second Lieutenant Adler and I will remain your com points through duration. And one last thing." Joyner continued. "And I say this with restraint as your friend and former commander. We've paired you with smart soldiers. Treat them as such. I know you're used to working alone but talk with them, you're good at that. Use their abilities. You're not in your thirties anymore, Kendrick. The days of shouldering all the burden and going maverick are behind you."

Soon after, the communication ended.

Kendrick turned to the Range Rover.

Bennett swung the glasses up on his forehead, his smirk fading as Kendrick approached.

"Marines?" Kendrick said. "Hit and runs?"

"Picking off the bad guys. What about you, British Intelligence? My command had shit for background. What are you? MI6? Five?"

"Something like that."

"That's crap," Bennett snapped. He tossed the eyewear onto the Rover's hood. "You know my history, but all I've got on you is you drink like a fish and spin crap that won't stop bullets."

An uneasy silence swept between them.

"Fine, then. Keep your damn secrets. But since you're in charge of this thing, I need to know you've got my back." He jabbed a finger at Kendrick. "Each of our backs."

"I do," Kendrick said.

"Actions will tell. But so help me, if I get stuck saving your ass…" Bennett shook his head.

"You won't." Kendrick lifted his chin. "We're both professionals. Let's keep focus. This mission isn't about you or me."

Bennett's jaw firmed, but he nodded.

"Any other detail?"

"Nelson," Bennett said. "Been working with him already, trying to get his mind right. Then there's Rosales. She's everything that you think she is. Green as hell, but that's not what bothers me."

Kendrick looked over his shoulder at the pair.

"I was told this mission wasn't authorized to use actives, but she appears to be," he said.

Interesting. Kendrick had also been informed no active-duty personnel would be used. This was a secret, off-the-books operation. The flying Marine was right. Rosales was the odd one out. His gut tightened.

"Curious," he said.

CHAPTER
17

Marko and the other man crammed into the pickup's cab as she, Alisha, Dan, and gun-toting Bandana rode in the Datsun's bed. Trash rattled with sand and rocks in the truck's bed as it jolted over potholes and swerved around corners. Tree branches lashed out, forcing them to duck, as if the driver aimed for the woods to torment his helpless passengers.

No other vehicles dared the route. After three grueling hours dodging branches and fording a swollen river, the Datsun lurched up a hillside and stopped.

Marko stepped out, clutching a small package, and ordered them from the truck's bed.

The driver waved. The Datsun's mismatched tires turned the dirt, vanishing up the muddy corkscrew trail.

Marko brushed past, his stench trailing, the narrow path barely wider than his bulk. He grunted, shoving through the foliage. The four captives followed at a distance with Bandana, his rifle, and his laugh bringing up the rear.

Around the bend stretched a swampy valley, downed trees strewn everywhere. Crude shelters of scavenged wood, draped in tattered cloth and plastic, dotted the wetland. Unkempt men lined up before a smoking firepit.

All appeared male. More than a hundred, but it was impossible to count because they were everywhere, waiting for whatever the person working the fire, who was soiled with dirt themselves, would put onto their tin plate.

Across the way sat three open tractor-trailers spattered with muck and filth. Dirty buckets and shovels, saws, pickaxes.

Were they living out here? The tools—were they excavating something?

Marko and a companion approached. The white man beside Marko wore dark jeans, a far cleaner shirt than any in the camp, and a straw hat. Marko handed him the package he'd received from the Datsun's driver but gave a curious sneer when he turned and stepped away.

The slender man in the straw hat moved in front of Alisha, Dan, and herself.

"Good morning."

The man's English shocked her.

"My name is Foster."

He stood just shy of six feet, lean, with gray-blonde hair and alabaster skin that seemed primed to blister in the sun. Light stubble shadowed his angular jaw. His voice carried a vibrant confidence, tinged with a smarmy accent she couldn't pin down.

"Please address me as Foster or Mister Foster." He circled the group. "I run this area."

Hannah scanned the murky field again. It looked like an outdoor factory for crafting mud pies. What could these people possibly be doing this far in the middle of who-the-hell-knows-where, with all these farming tools? It wasn't drugs, or drug manufacture. Unless their customers preferred sludge in their cocaine. Maybe bridge or canal construction? But wouldn't that take earth moving equipment? Bulldozers, dump trucks, excavators?

"You are all doctors? Am I correct?"

The three stood in silence.

"Please answer. Each of you," Foster demanded.

Alisha nodded, cradling an arm beneath her belly. Dan also replied in the affirmative.

Foster leered at Hannah.

"Yes," she said, as stone-faced as possible.

"I'll get to know your names over time." Foster's clean fingertips stroked the brim of his straw hat. "For now, I need you to understand a few things. Some are critical to your personal survival, so please listen close before contemplating journey elsewhere."

Scanning the grounds, a shiver struck Hannah.

Foster squinted, then pointed to Marko and the two men standing next to him. "While your escorts brought you here involuntarily, you will only see a few guns in this camp. Mostly we use them to defend against the wildlife." He pointed to the tree lines around the area. "You're in the greater Amazon rainforest. Things in this jungle are extremely aggressive."

Bandana laughed.

"First, there's no one else around for several kilometers in any direction. Not a soul. Second, and most important, these lands are home to the largest creatures in the world."

He put a hand on the back of his neck and closed his eyes. Yet, an instant later, his clasped hands returned behind his back, and he resumed pacing the perimeter.

"Anacondas stretch six meters, swamp-dwellers. Their bite's not the danger—it's nonvenomous. But if one coils around your body, it'll crush the life out of you. No metaphor does it justice."

Bandana cackled and Marko grinned.

"In dry areas, the pit viper slithers about. Its toxic bite paralyzes its victim, leaving one vulnerable to the half-meter Amazon Centipede to sting and feast." He flashed a grin. "You must also stay far away from riverbanks and sizeable pools of water. The Black Caiman, similar to an alligator but much bigger and swifter, is the most dangerous creature in this area. Stand in the waters, which are bustling with piranha, and a Caiman may grab a leg and have you for dinner. I can assure you that being eaten alive is a painful death." He rubbed at his forehead. "But you may get lucky and only find yourself face to face with a jaguar if you try to escape into these mountains."

He smirked, examining their faces.

"Beyond that, various lethal insects and colorful amphibians crawl about. The Amazon has many killers. Therefore, please stay close to camp. We cannot protect you otherwise."

The blood drained from Alisha's face somewhere between "anaconda" and "lethal insects." Dan froze beside her, eyes wide with terror.

Foster paused, letting the jungle's dangers sink in, his lip twitching upward as he motioned to the pits.

"There is a job for each. Those you see behind me are the precious workers. Our assets. Your task is to tend to their health needs, much the same way you were doing when my men found you." He raised a finger. "Think of this as a relocation of your needed skills. A strong worker is a productive worker. And production is what we do here."

Production of what? This entire place was nothing but slimy swamp and dead trees.

"The accommodations are lacking, but you'll make do."

The native beside him grinned and nodded.

"You'll find supplies and such in your medical shack. If you are needing anything, please inform myself or Marko. We will see what we can do."

Marko? Was this scumbag really Foster's second in command? Yes, I do need some things. How about a handgun to kill you assholes, a helicopter to leave this dreadful place, and a few sandwiches for the ride?

Foster scanned the group again. "Beyond the wildlife, there is one major rule here. If any of my workers become incapacitated, and by that, I mean stop breathing and expire, please notify one of us immediately. Dead bodies attract unwanted animals. We must relocate the corpse right away for everyone's safety."

Panic shook Hannah. What the fuck were they doing to these people? What was this awful place?

"I'd take questions, but I realize each of you must be anxious to see your new quarters and get to work."

Marko and Bandana stepped aside, clearing a path for Foster and his straw hat.

"This way," Foster said.

Hannah, Alisha, and Dan sloshed up a small hill behind Foster to a dilapidated, doorless shack. The structure was built of discarded logs and mud, and sheets of tin served as a roof. At best, the shed would protect them from rain, but little else.

Climbing the embankment to the wretched hut, she gagged on the inescapable stench of death.

CHAPTER

18

After two fuel stops, the Range Rover trekked southeast. They traded driving duties in four-hour shifts. As Route 46 ended, they veered onto an easterly non-surface road in the direction of the physician's last campsite.

The four agreed to hit that campsite area first to see what they could learn from their missing asset's last known location.

Soaring Brazil Nut and Vogel palm trees bordered the Rover's path. The undergrowth thickened, the trail twisting through sharp bends and jolting over ruts.

They were well outside the mapped towns and far from any paved roadways when Rosales alerted them.

"We might have a tail." Rosales peered back.

Bennett was at the wheel and eased off the accelerator.

"Hostile?" He glanced through the rearview.

"Not sure." Rosales slipped on her eyewear.

Kendrick turned. "Do you see a firearm?"

An older model, grubby, chocolate-brown jeep was gaining on the Rover. The vehicle's rider emerged from its open roof and pointed a long gun in their direction.

"Affirmative," Rosales shouted. "Passenger is hot."

"Weapons up!" Nelson called.

Three rounds chambered in as many rifles, and Bennett lowered the windows.

"Don't shoot unless–"

Something struck the vehicle's outer shell.

Rosales and Nelson aimed their rifles, returning fire. An incoming round shattered the Rover's rear window and zipped past Bennett's head through the windshield.

"Fuck this!" he cried.

The Rover hit an incline. Bennett maneuvered up its face. Accelerating, he torqued the steering wheel left, and the 4x4 ripped through heavy underbrush. Branches and loose rocks scraped the Rover's undercarriage as it weaved and bumped through the jungle.

For two kilometers, the others held their attention rear, waiting for the pursuing jeep to reappear.

"I don't think they followed," Rosales shouted forward.

"Anyone hit?" Nelson hollered.

None of them were.

The Rover stopped in a clearing, engine ticking as it cooled, the air thick with humidity and the buzz of unseen insects.

Nelson wiped sweat from his brow. "Who the hell do you think they were?"

"Colombian welcome wagon." Bennett scowled.

"Exactly." Kendrick cleared his chamber. "Probably local growers sending a warning."

Nelson raised a palm. "I don't think we should go back that way."

Rosales nodded. "I agree."

Cutting across the jungle, they found a secondary dirt road, and Bennett steered onto it. Within an hour, the Range Rover crested another peak.

Rosales stiffened. Her gaze locked on something down the hillside.

"Convoy below us—two, no, three vehicles on a path," she reported, scanning the hillside.

Bennett slowed to a stop.

"What type?" Nelson asked.

"Trucks. I think it's another road, but the eyewear's chart doesn't bring it up." She pointed. "Two o'clock."

Nelson and Kendrick followed her direction.

"I see them, three klicks down the hillside."

"Military?" Kendrick asked.

"Negative. Semi-trucks with container trailers."

Bennett rubbed his chin. "Bet whatever they're hauling is interesting."

"We need to leave this mess anyway. Let's go down for a closer look."

Bennett plowed the Range Rover through the foliage and pulled close to a heavily wooded gorge at the hill's bottom.

"Just in case these aren't friendlies."

"Say that's likely," Nelson nodded.

The team hid the Rover in a grove of trees and bushes and set out on foot.

"How far are we away from the doctor's camp?"

"About nine klicks, sir."

"What are you thinking?" Nelson asked.

"Not sure," Kendrick replied.

As they emerged from the tall ceiba and mahogany tree line they came upon a strange passageway. The dirt road tunneled under the jungle canopy, stretching several hundred meters north. The "road" the convoy had traveled on was worn only where the vehicle's tires had rolled the ground. Grass and other high greenery on the path appeared undisturbed.

Rosales pointed. "Abandoned vehicle south."

"We're hell and gone from civilization. Why would anybody be out here?"

Kendrick scanned the area. "Wondering that myself."

The abandoned truck alongside the dirt trail had broken windows, and bullet holes pocked its outside. Specks of blood dotted the shards of glass littering the front seat. The ground had been disturbed, indicating someone had removed the truck's trailer.

"This is fresh." Bennett eyed the blood streaks inside the vehicle.

Kendrick scooped up the pebbles, thumb tracing their rust-colored veins—too damn familiar, and too far from Alexandra to be chance. A small red-yellow nugget gleamed among them.

"Wonder what they were hauling?"

Kendrick raised his head. "Nine kilometers to the camp?"

Rosales nodded, glancing at a bullet hole in the door.

"No idea where this goes," Bennett said. "But they've been using it for a while. Check out the south end." He pointed. "Cuts right through those trees, like a tunnel. That's some heavy regular use. Does the same thing north and disappears into the trees."

Bennett was right. The tall saplings at both ends had grown around the trail and burrowed a canopied path large enough for semi-trucks to pass through.

"Tried a few ways, but my eyewear still doesn't show anything. This road shouldn't exist. I checked out satellite imagery, but once the trail hits the tree line, there's no place I can find that it re-emerges. Most of those trees are a hundred feet tall or better. The dirt path snakes below them in both directions, hidden from the skyline."

Very odd. They were in the middle of nowhere, and if Bennett hadn't taken the Rover off-road through the uncharted jungle thicket into these mountains, they never would have found this road. From the splattered blood and the bullets in this abandoned truck, it appeared whoever used the road had enemies. Plus, whoever disabled that semi and stole its trailer knew its cargo was valuable. Valuable enough to kill the driver over. And all of this meant their missing assets were undoubtedly in grave danger.

A kilometer away, a flock of birds took swift flight.

Nearby, puffs of gray smoke ascended in the sky, and a rumbling came in the distance.

"Bogeys approaching." Nelson pointed. "Let's move."

Rosales scooped up a collection of shells, and the four sprinted from the broken-down truck into the thicket of woods towards their hidden Range Rover. Each remained behind the trees and bushes, staying low and out of sight.

Two large tractor-trailers rumbled by. On top of each, men with semiautomatic rifles scanned the route.

"More semi-trucks, sirs," Rosales whispered, peering through the forest.

"How many do you see?" Nelson asked.

"Two, no three. But sirs, there's men on top the trailers with rifles."

"Hijackers?" Bennett said.

"No, sir, looks like they're detail."

Bennett nodded. "Now I'm very curious to know what's inside those rigs."

Kendrick was, too. These had to be loaded semi-trucks. Otherwise, why would they need protection? And the cargo was headed northwest on this hidden jungle path, but where had it come from?

"I don't think we're supposed to be here." Bennett gripped his rifle.

Rosales and Nelson readied their weapons.

"I wonder if our doctors wandered into the middle of this?" Kendrick said.

"That'd be bad." Nelson grunted.

Rosales checked her mag. "Bad's too tame—those rifles mean war."

"Yeah," Kendrick squinted. "We've stumbled onto someone's Silk Road—hidden, deadly."

The trucks rumbled toward the trees and vanished. The heavy scent of diesel hung in the air.

Nelson shot Kendrick a look. "Silk Road? Like that online drug site?"

"Right, the hitmen-for-hire thing," Bennett said. "Dark web crap."

"There was an online black market with the same name, yes." Kendrick muttered. "But it took the term from a bygone route."

"You mean the Silk Road was an actual road?"

"It was." Kendrick nodded. "And it changed the world far more than you understand."

Bennett smirked. "Alright, British Intelligence, I'll bite. How?"

Kendrick slung the rifle Rosales had given him to his side. "Before GPS and AKs, people still needed to move valuables across dangerous places." He gestured at the canopy overhead. "Think caravans. Camels. Guards with spears instead of rifles. Goods. Mail. People. Plagues. Anything that required transport. The network stretched nine thousand kilometers long. From Asia to Europe, to Africa. If it moved, it moved on that road."

Rosales wiped sweat from her brow. "Thought it was just silk?"

Kendrick shook his head. "Silk was just the start. Spices, metals, livestock—everything moved on that ancient road, including dark commerce."

"Dark commerce?" Rosales asked.

"Gunpowder, human trafficking. Even in the Middle Ages, slaves were frowned upon by many—but safe in-route, so long as they stayed on the trail. Protection at all costs, even for the illicit cargo."

Nelson shot Kendrick a look. "Some things don't change. Just the weapons get louder."

Bennett chuckled. "And the trucks get bigger."

"Exactly," Kendrick said, motioning to the dirt trail. "Whatever's moving up that jungle road—someone's guarding it like gold. Which means it's worth blood."

Rosales tapped a shell casing against her boot. "Got the blood part right."

"Question is—what the hell's the cargo?" Bennett said.

Kendrick signaled to Rosales. "Best guess, Sergeant?"

Rosales fished the spent shell casings from her pocket. "Something worthy of 39mm, 12 gauge, and .44 caliber shells, sir."

"So, not silk?" Bennett chuckled.

Kendrick ignored the joke. "Any 5.56 caliber?"

Rosales shook her head. "No, sir."

"NATO rounds?" Nelson said.

But Kendrick didn't elaborate. Instead, he scanned the canopy. "We're knee-deep in someone else's supply chain—and they'll kill to keep it moving."

Rosales frowned, turning a casing between her fingers. "Sir... I don't think they're just local cartel guys."

Kendrick sharpened his gaze. "Explain."

"Different calibers. Mixed weapons. Not cartel clean," she said, rattling the spent shells in her palm. "These look rebel. Maybe Fuerzas Armadas Revolucionarias de Colombia. Terrorist left-wingers."

"FARC?" Nelson's gaze met hers. "But that guerrilla group disbanded years ago."

"Maybe on paper. But those rebels always had a hodgepodge of firearms and a bunch of them began working with the cartels after the ceasefire, training Mexican syndicates."

Nelson blew out a breath. "That's a party I don't want to crash."

"From rebel to protection for drug smugglers," Kendrick said. "An instant army, going where the money is."

The others nodded.

They broke from cover, slipping through the trees. Within minutes they reached the Rover, still cloaked beneath branches and brush.

"Been thinking," Rosales said as they settled in. "Insurgents with nothing else to do but work to rebuild their militia—and that'd be my guess who these guys are." She hesitated. "Except one thing doesn't fit."

Kendrick caught her in the rearview. "What's off?"

"The truck drivers," she said. "They were locals. But the shooters on the trailers were all white guys. Not Colombians."

"They were?" Kendrick said.

"Yeah, plus this is rainforest, wilderness—extremely remote. And FARC is pretty tight. They don't like outsiders."

Bennett muttered from the driver's seat, "Yeah, this is bigger than drugs."

Kendrick locked eyes with Rosales. In this deep green hell, their missing assets were in serious trouble—and trouble out here didn't leave survivors.

CHAPTER
19

Dead organics—rotting microbes and algae from long-gone creatures—smothered acres of stagnant ponds. Workers with hand tools clawed into the sunbaked wetlands, stabbing through an oxygen-starved crust of decay. Out hissed hydrogen sulfide, carbon dioxide, and methane, the swamp's foul breath rising to choke the air.

Hannah's eyes burned—a gag hovering in her throat. This festering lowland was death's own furnace.

Foster strode up the hillside, unbothered by the toxic haze, while she, Alisha, and Dan stumbled after him.

He led them into a shabby, doorless shack perched above the basin. Mud and logs propped its walls, and inside, four plywood planks sprawled across the dirt. Grubby blankets tangled over them, flanked by stained, caseless pillows.

"Welcome to your new home office." Foster chuckled, rasping his throat. "We do not have laundering facilities. Please keep what you wear as clean and functional as possible. Consider the days ahead your probationary period. Do well, and I'll see what I can do regarding a change of outfit for each of you."

Hannah froze, horrified. This dump made the medical tent's lumpy cot and itchy blanket feel like a palace. This place was a fucking nightmare. No shower. No toilet. Just filth.

Foster flexed his fist, a twitchy habit, then motioned. "Supplies are on the back wall."

Stacked plastic crates brimmed with ripped cardboard boxes—cold packs, adhesive tape, burn dressings, wipes, a few sterilization scraps, metal splints, and a pair of mismatched crutches propped in the corner.

Hannah edged closer. Everything for a broken leg, tourniquets, and large compression bandages for major lacerations and traumatic injuries. But no analgesics or sedatives. What were they using for painkillers?

"We're only treating the most critical injuries here, a MASH unit for the workers. Cuts and scrapes heal on their own, whereas bones and large gashes will require your aid." His leer pinned her—cold, indifferent.

Dan held Alisha's trembling hand, eyes unblinking.

Foster steered them to a second room where plastic sheeting coated the dirt floor. More crates hugged the log walls, stuffed with half-clean rags and battered boxes. A plywood slab balanced on sawhorses loomed in the room's center—like a workbench at a construction site.

"Your examination table," Foster declared. "For probing and patching."

Hannah's jaw unhinged. Nothing gleamed, nothing sanitized—staph and sepsis lurked, poised to strike. This was no clinic. It was a butcher's stall.

Foster smirked faintly. "Best we can do out here. I trust you each to make do."

A lanky figure stumbled into the mud shack—tangled gray hair, trembling hands, neck jerking like a broken puppet. Breath wheezed through his nose.

"Ahh, your colleague, Doctor Malum," Foster said.

Grimy scrubs sagged off Malum's bony frame, a stained shirt clinging beneath. He chuckled to himself, eyes glued to the dirt, lost in some private haze. What was wrong with him? How long had he been out here?

Shouts and howls erupted outside.

Foster bolted from the shack, Hannah on his heels.

Down the hill, near the firepit, a dozen shirtless men slung plates and fists in a muddy scrum. A scrawny boy, barely a teen, dove into the mess, clawing at a brawler. One thug snatched a thick stick, smashing it over another's skull. The victim crumpled to the slop.

Foster's sharp whistle cut the air.

Marko and another rifleman waded in, shouting orders, but the madness raged on.

Three quick whistles followed.

Marko glanced up, caught Foster's nod, and fired.

A crack split the valley.

Stick-man collapsed, clutching his arm.

The mob scattered.

"What the fuck?" Dan muttered behind Hannah.

The wounded man thrashed in the muck, shrieking.

Foster's chin turned. "Expect your first two patients here in moments."

Hannah flinched as he ushered her and the others back inside.

"Doctor Malum?"

The old man's head steadied, hands still quaking. "Yes, yes," he croaked.

"Please help with any questions our new arrivals may have," Foster said. "Familiarize them to our procedures."

Malum responded without looking up. "Yes, yes."

Foster addressed the group, his voice steeled. "In this enterprise, it becomes necessary from time to time to settle worker conflict. My philosophy is to cripple, not kill—unless necessary. For the human resource is a critical asset."

Human resource? Critical asset? What the fuck was this place?

"For you each, the goal is not to lose patients. Good workers are difficult to come by. Any patient deaths will be examined by me, and I will ensure you're providing the utmost care. If I find any malfeasance, punishment will occur. These include lashes and a liquid-only diet. For the most severe infractions, you will live and work among the others below for a duration of my choosing." He eyed Alisha. "Pregnant or not."

Dan balled a fist, glaring.

Hannah's gut twisted. Foster was a monster.

"I shall leave you to it." He dipped his head, vanishing.

Alisha gasped, clutching Dan's arm.

They stood silent, Hannah's mind spinning. This place was a hellscape. What would happen if they were trapped here for months, years? And Alisha—what would happen to her baby? Raised in this swamp or taken away?

She faced Alisha and Dan, a heavy truth slicing deep.

They might never escape.

CHAPTER

20

The Range Rover tore through the Colombian mountainside, tires spitting gravel as it climbed the rugged incline.

Rosales' voice cut through the engine's growl. "Sir, there's a vehicle."

Ahead, a four-door GMC Yukon loomed in the haze, its attached trailer sagging like an afterthought. Grime smeared the SUV so thickly its original color was a mystery—mud and dust had claimed it entirely.

The Range Rover rolled to a stop beside it, and the four piled out, boots crunching on the rocky earth.

Kendrick circled to the Yukon's rear, crouching to scrape a crust of gunk from the license plate with his knife. The numbers emerged reluctantly, streaked but legible.

"How do I contact my base?" he asked, straightening.

"Say your name, sir, and then 'start com.'" Rosales tapped her own eyewear. "It'll prompt you for the number."

Kendrick nodded, then followed her instructions. "Kendrick. Start com." A faint beep hummed in his ear, followed by a robotic chime requesting digits. He rattled them off.

"Sir, Second Lieutenant Adler here," a voice crackled, tunneling through the device into his skull.

Kendrick read the plate aloud, and Adler's response came swift.

"Registered to Feliz Expedición a la Montaña—translates to "Happy Mountain Expedition." Sole proprietorship, owned by a 50-year-old, Aldus Patrick Phinn."

"Phinn?"

"Hold on, sir—there's more."

"More?" Kendrick's brow furrowed.

Hesitation crept into Adler's tone. "Phinn's a Scottish expatriate. Got a criminal record."

Kendrick stepped away from the others, lowering his voice as the wind tugged at his jacket. "Violent crime?"

Adler's keyboard clattered. "Original charge was murder. Reduced during trial. Public record shows a five-year sentence for culpable homicide."

"He killed someone?"

"I can dig deeper, run it through our system for details."

"Later. We're two kilometers from the campsite. Status update at 17:00."

"Seventeen hundred. Yes, sir."

The connection severed with a soft click. Kendrick stared at the Yukon, its filth-crusted shell hiding more than just its paint.

Culpable homicide, downgraded from murder? He hadn't studied Scots law, but he knew it paralleled manslaughter in Welsh courts— intentional or not, someone had died by Phinn's hand. Adler's intel might reveal what this Scottish guide was truly capable of.

The remote village of Guajira lay north of Cesar, tucked within the Department of La Guajira—a two- or three-kilometer slog through unforgiving hills. They'd have to go on foot from here.

"It's got to be 200 fucking degrees," Bennett huffed. He mopped his brow with a sleeve. "Sun's barely up, and I'm sweating like a politician at an ethics convention."

Rosales and Nelson chuckled.

They trudged west by northwest, the trail winding through scrub and stone as morning bled into afternoon. Dust clung to their boots, and the heat pressed down like a living thing. A wall of jungle rose ahead, dense and unyielding, halting them cold.

Bennett yanked a machete from his pack, hacking at the underbrush with grunts of effort. Vines parted, but the tangle was like an impossible maze.

After several minutes, Rosales spoke. "I'll check the perimeter, sirs." She pivoted, slipping back down the path, vanishing into the haze before anyone could protest.

Bennett thrust the blade at Nelson. "Your turn, SEAL."

Nelson gripped the machete, slashing at the foliage, sweat beading on his temples. He carved a jagged scar through the green, but it was slow going.

Bennett stepped back, rolling a stiff shoulder with a grimace. "Thick shit out here," he muttered.

Kendrick squinted at the impenetrable snarl of vines. "I doubt the group took this route off the main road."

Nelson eked out three or four paces before pausing, his chest heaving. He rubbed his shoulder, dropping the machete to the dirt.

The jungle seemed to thicken ahead, mocking their efforts.

"Hold up, chief. Take a swig." Bennett lobbed a water bottle over.

Nelson caught it, ripped the cap off, and chugged. Water dribbled down his chin.

"Not sure we're on the right path." Kendrick wiped sweat from his eyes.

"No shit," Bennett shot back. He cracked a second bottle, gulping it down like a man dying of thirst.

"Sirs?" Rosales rang out from behind.

Kendrick turned. She emerged from the trail, unscathed by the heat—no flush, no sweat, just steady calm. Fucking youth.

The three men straightened, trying to mask their exhaustion, but their flushed faces and soaked shirts betrayed them.

"Found another way, sirs," she said. "Fifty paces back, the path snakes east a bit, then opens to a wider trail. Spotted a clear hundred meters—might lead into a shaded treebank." She gestured with a confident sweep of her arm, then paused, eyeing their wilted forms. "Suggest we check it out, sirs."

They nodded in unison, relief in Bennett's eyes.

Kendrick grunted. Anything beat this hellhole, baking under a merciless sun, slashing at the relentless Colombian wilds.

CHAPTER
21

Bennett spotted a 4Runner several yards south, parked crookedly near the river. The team edged closer, and he broke into a hustle to secure it, his boots clomping the dry earth.

"Thing's flashing a warning in my screen," he said, voice crackling through the eyewear. "Says vital service required."

"Analysis program, sir," Rosales relayed. "It's picking up a critical failure. One or more systems are failing—engine, maybe brakes. The vehicle probably won't run."

Bennett huffed a laugh. "Reminds me of the rust-bucket I had in high school."

Rosales and Kendrick broke off, fanning out along the perimeter, scanning for signs of life—or trouble. Nelson headed toward Bennett and the 4Runner, rifle at the ready.

The waterway's sandy banks stretched wide, fringed with gnarled trees and dense, vibrant shrubs. The river churned fast, its surface glinting under the sun.

"Sir?" Rosales nodded across the stream.

Kendrick turned. Half-submerged in the shallows on the far bank lay a green canister—its metal dulled by water and silt.

"I'll check it out, sir." She splashed through the current, rifle hoisted overhead, water swirling around her thighs.

Kendrick stood fast. Rosales was a force—conscientious, bold, a natural leader who didn't hesitate. He'd never seen her falter, not once, and her drive outmatched anyone he'd served with.

"Water vessel," she called. Wading deeper, she drew a long tube from the murk. "Looks like a filter. Someone might have been filling the canister when they got interrupted."

In the distance, Bennett and Nelson examined the 4Runner.

Kendrick swept his gaze over the immediate area, then farther out, searching for structures or movement. Eastward, white smoke rose in thin, curling tendrils—hazy, controlled, like a village fire.

Determined to work the eyewear himself, he fumbled through commands. "Map. Show me a map." His voice tight, impatient. "Please—show me a damn map!"

But the eyewear's lenses were blank.

"Sir," Rosales cut through his earpiece. "Say your last name first, then the command."

"Kendrick. Show me a map."

The display flared to life. After a few clumsy verbal adjustments, he scaled the digital chart, its grid pivoting as he turned his head. The smoke aligned with a village marker—three, maybe four hundred meters off. The missing physicians had been on a mercy run, bringing aid to remote corners of this underdeveloped stretch. This river had to be the lifeline for that community.

Rosales climbed the far bank, ascending a mound beneath a sprawling tree, her silhouette sharp against the sky.

"Christ," Bennett's voice crackled. "This truck's riddled with holes." He exhaled hard. "Engine's shot to hell—bullet damage, no question."

Kendrick swung his gaze back to the 4Runner, unease coiling in his gut. "Check the plate if it's got one." Gunfire, shit. Maybe he should ping Adler for that full dossier on Phinn?

"Sirs," Rosales reported in from across the river, her tone steady but edged. "I see tracks up this hill. Four sets, maybe five. Two are scuffers."

"Scuffers?" Kendrick pivoted her direction.

"Front-heavy prints, no heel. They were sprinting, sir. Fleeing or chasing, I can't be sure."

Rosales entered the water, wading back across.

Damn it. They were three days late to whatever went down here. That village by the smoke was their next move. Kendrick prayed the doctors hadn't been caught in something ugly, but the clues—the truck, the tracks—pointed to bloodshed.

"Ah, shit," Nelson's voice dropped low.

Kendrick clenched his jaw, dread filling his chest. He gazed downriver toward the scouting pair and the 4Runner.

"This isn't good. We've got a body over here."

CHAPTER
22

Shirtless workers, slick with filth, hauled two injured men into the shack. One pointed to the man with the bleeding arm, whispering to Hannah, "Lorenzo."

The bullet from Marco's rifle had torn through Lorenzo's forearm. It wasn't gushing—radius and ulnar arteries spared, Hannah guessed— but without x-rays in this festering wetland, who could tell? All they could do was patch and pray.

Someone had knotted a bloody rag around the wound, tied tight. Hannah watched Dan slice it open with unsterilized scissors, his fingers probing the raw flesh.

Malum hovered behind her, muttering—words too soft to catch, like a prayer gone sour.

Foster loomed over them, hands clasped behind his back, leaning in like some grim overseer. The second patient they'd dragged in lay unconscious in the other room, head cracked from a thick stick in the fight. Hannah wanted his name, but Foster shooed the grimy workers out before she could ask.

She couldn't believe Lorenzo. Early in her career, on ER rotation, she'd seen gunshot wounds before—excruciating, red-hot, searing through muscle and tendon until the pain shocked men into unconsciousness. But not Lorenzo. His glassy eyes stared up at her, calm as a man getting a shave. No anesthesia, not a sound. He just lay there, letting them dig into his torn flesh.

When Alisha doused the hole with alcohol, Hannah braced for a kick that never came—not even a flinch.

"Excellent." Foster nodded, eye twitching, a tear streaking his cheek. His breath caught, a faint tremor rippling through his neck. He stared at Alisha's hands, jaw clenched.

"Do we have a suture kit?" she asked.

"This isn't a—" His voice cracked, strained, then steadied. "Hospital. No fancy sutures."

Alisha recoiled.

Foster blinked hard, calm settling unevenly, his fingers twitching once, then again, before stilling—like a storm passing too fast

"Doctor Malum," Foster said, low and sharp. "Glue and tape, please?"

The muttering man shuffled to the plastic crates, head jerking, whispers trailing him like smoke. He returned with the supplies, dropped them beside Alisha, then backed off, head down and silent.

Lorenzo had gone still—passed out or asleep, Hannah couldn't tell.

A shout turned Foster's head toward the small slit of a window.

"I see your first challenge is well on the mend," he said, voice steadying. "I'm needed elsewhere. Please direct any questions to Doctor Malum."

He left the medical shack, a faint twitch tugging his cheek.

Dan edged toward Doctor Malum. "Doctor, what the hell is that pit for?"

It was a mineral pit, sure—but for what? Lorenzo was out, the other patient still senseless.

"Doctor Malum?" Hannah tried to make eye contact. "What is this place mining?"

Malum twitched, mouth opening then closing, but no words came.

Dan frowned. "Let's hope we don't have too many questions for the good doctor." He cracked the glue cap, running a bead along Lorenzo's wound. "Do we have any locking forceps?"

Hannah rummaged through the plastic crates—tweezers, pliers, no surgical gear. "Nothing," she muttered.

"Forget it. We'll tape it." He sealed the gash with glue and Alisha wrapped it tight with adhesive.

"What about antibiotics?" Alisha asked.

Hannah sifted through rows of crates—aspirin bottles, promising but weak. She knelt to the lowest stack.

A trembling hand, cold and clammy, grazed her shoulder.

She froze, a chill racing through her.

Malum leaned in, foggy eyes wide, pointing left. There, Hannah found antibiotics and ibuprofen. Not strong—but they would do.

"Thank you," she said.

Malum loomed, fingers curling, uncurling.

She stared, throat tightening. "Doctor, what's wrong with this place?"

Malum rasped, his breath hitching. His eyelids clamped shut, then snapped open. "Danger, poisons!"

CHAPTER
23

"I'm not getting a damn thing," Nelson growled. He smacked the comms unit over his ear, sweat trickling from his hand as he shook his head in frustration.

"Same here, sir. Everything else is operational, but command's gone silent." Rosales slipped off her eyewear, inspecting the lenses under the jungle's shady canopy, and frowned. Then she slid the glasses back over her ears. "Satellite might be down—or someone's jamming it."

Kendrick's link worked, tethering him to Adler. His American counterparts—Rosales, Bennett, and Nelson—however, were cut off from the U.S. base, their signals swallowed by some unseen glitch. For now, they'd have to lean on his command, a lifeline threading back to the Crown's network. He cocked his head, listening to Adler's words.

"Name's surfacing now, major." Adler's tone cut sharp through a hiss of static. "That 4Runner belongs to a Diego Riverian."

"That was fast," Kendrick said with a spark of surprise.

Adler chuckled dryly. "The Crown knows how to burn through the people's coin." Rapid keystrokes punctuated his words. "Apprehended years back in Colombia, 2002. Labeled a political prisoner, but the file's thin on specifics."

"Safe to assume he had connections?" Kendrick's mind was already spinning with possibilities.

"Affirmative, sir. Deep ones, I'd bet. But I'll need my commander's access key to go any deeper. He's offsite—slipped out yesterday with other senior brass. I'm not in the loop on his whereabouts."

"Any word on his return?"

"No telling, sir. He's been cagey since that delegation rolled in. I'll ping you if he resurfaces."

"Thanks, Adler. We'll keep moving. Wait—one more thing." Kendrick dug into his pocket, fingers snagging the jagged edges of a stone he'd pried from the riverbank. He held it up, its dull sheen flickering under the eyewear's scan.

"Major." Adler's tone spiked with surprise. "Where the hell did you find that?"

"Eyewear wouldn't tag it," Kendrick said. He turned the rock slowly. "What's your system saying?"

"I don't need a database to clock that," Adler replied.

Kendrick's brow twitched. "Lay it on me."

"That's coltan, major. Col-tan," Adler emphasized. "An ore packed with tantalum—those grayish veins running through it. It's a rare earth mineral. Handles heat up to 4000 degrees Celsius." His tone fixed. "Tantalum is the most corrosion-resistant metal in the world, and most acids won't even break it down."

"That answers my next question," Kendrick said flatly.

"Who'd kill for it?"

"Exactly."

"Every cell phone maker, circuit board manufacturer, space agency, government, and military."

Kendrick whistled low. The implications stacking fast. He pocketed the stone, and fished out another. A reddish-yellow chunk, heavier than it looked, which he held up for Adler's view.

"And this one?"

"Bloody hell," Adler spat. "Sorry, sir, but that's a raw nugget of gold."

"Gold?" Kendrick squinted, tilting it in the light. "Are you sure?"

"Dead sure. That reddish tint is surface grime—clean it up, and it'll gleam like the sun. Where'd you find it?"

Kendrick's voice tightened. "Same place as the coltan."

"Sir, those are conflict minerals." Adler's words carried a heavy warning. "Both of them."

Conflict minerals. The term coiled in Kendrick's gut. This was bigger than he'd thought, and the doctor's lives were in grave danger.

Was there a mine nearby? That would explain the armed trucks—hulking, dust-caked rigs bristling with overly protective escorts. If coltan was anything near gold's price, anyone hauling it would kill to keep it. But where were these minerals going? And where had they dug it up? The vehicles they'd seen hauling were not government issue. This was an underground operation.

Rosales had pegged the men as ex-FARC, and that tracked. Guerrilla fighters turned profiteers, already armed to the teeth. This corner of the world was a tangled mess—lush with resources, rotten with corruption. If FARC were clawing their way back, they'd need cash to rearm, retrain, rebuild. Mining, though? That didn't fit. These were rebels, not rock-breakers. Someone else was pulling strings here, and he needed more information to pin it down.

He'd share Adler's intel with the team but keep his theories close until they had more evidence. No sense stirring the pot with half-baked guesses.

Kendrick turned to the others. "Adler ID'd the stones. Coltan and gold—conflict minerals, high value."

Rosales nodded, her jaw tight. "Had my suspicions, sir. That's what's in those trucks?"

"Looks like it," Kendrick said. "I'd bet they're mining it nearby."

Bennett grunted. "Explains the firepower."

The Marine seemed to be warming up to him, which was good. But his animosity from time to time was still puzzling to Kendrick. A grudge? Rivalry? He'd figure it out later.

The killing they'd witnessed—the bound man at the river—might tie into this mining op. Blood spilled over rocks like these wasn't rare. But the bigger questions loomed. Where were these trucks going? Who was selling, who was buying? And why had one of those containers made its way up to Alexandra, of all places?

Kendrick signaled the group forward, boots sinking into the damp earth as they pressed through the woods toward the village, unanswered questions settling deeper with every step.

CHAPTER
24

The unconscious man in the first room had stirred while they tended to Lorenzo's arm.

Despite the dried blood crusting the second worker's scalp, he sprang up, wild-eyed, chest heaving—then bolted out of the shack, feet slapping the dirt.

Hannah and Dan raced after him. But the skinny, shirtless man slipped through the crooked doorway, melting into a swarm of figures laboring in the mud below, swallowed by the chaos.

They skidded to a stop outside. From their hillside perch, the basin sprawled like a festering sore.

"What a god-forsaken place," Dan grumbled.

Laborers clawed the grime with blackened hands. A crew member loomed over a barrel every few men, eyes lifeless. One slapped a fistful of sludge into the drum. The barrel tender rocked it in slow, deliberate circles, and a metallic sheen—liquid silver, sharp and unnatural—spilled over the rusted rim, glinting briefly before sinking into the muck.

The satellite phone parts jabbed Hannah's thigh. She had to fix it—cracked casing, frayed wires, their only shot at escape.

"I need to see what this place is, head down there," Dan said.

"No, Dan. It's too dangerous—we don't know how they'll react."

"Which is exactly why we have to, Hannah. We'll learn nothing from these broken men up here." He scanned the edges of the valley, squinting. "Spot that Foster chap anywhere?"

The sun blazed overhead, white-hot, marking noon. Armed figures prowled the muddy expanse below, their shouts cutting through the air as they barked at the sluggish and prodded the idle with rifle butts. Dust clung to their boots, their faces shadowed under wide-brimmed hats.

The pit gouged the earth, three football fields of ruin. Craters gaped beside mounds of slop where teams of five or six dredged the soil, their movements mechanical, relentless. Men waded neck-deep in stagnant ponds, diving under. Some surfaced with clumps for the barrels. Others surfaced with nothing but gasps, their chests heaving, eyes vacant.

The stench was thick, rotting, unbearable.

"I don't see him. But those guards are everywhere," Hannah said.

"We'll have to explore it eventually. How else will we—" Dan stopped midsentence.

Staring down at the pits, she felt it too—a crushing despair radiating, a silent scream etched into every bent back and trembling hand down in that muddy valley.

Men toiled under a vast, cruel weight, their lives reduced to this endless grind. Danger pulsed in the air, sharp as a blade against the skin. Yet Dan turned and strode down the slope with purpose, his silhouette shrinking against the vastness below—leaving Hannah torn between fear and helplessness.

At the valley's far end, a long aluminum trailer hummed atop a hill, its surface dulled by dust. That echo? Was it a generator? Did that trailer have power?

A gaunt man wheeled a barrow through the filth. Workers dumped small, mud-caked lumps from their barrels into his cart, the grim pile growing with each stop.

She couldn't make out the objects from this distance, just dark specks against the rust-streaked metal.

On the hilltop, the trailer door opened. Marko stepped out with another man, both gripping rifles, their knuckles white around the stocks.

Where was Dan? The mass of bare backs and heads shifted below.

A scuffle flared west—fists flying, a sharp cry tearing the air. Dan's voice? It had to be.

Marko and his companion trudged into the valley, their scowls fixed on the commotion. Had they spotted Dan?

Dread seized her, cold and heavy. "Dan, where are you?" she rasped.

Alisha lingered inside, unaware. What would she say if she saw her husband down there? Her scream would shatter them all—she'd loved him too long.

Marko gestured sharply into the distance. Hannah's gaze followed, darting across the swarm of muddy figures.

Dan was nowhere—only endless rows of bent spines and hollowed-out men. She edged closer to the drop-off, mud slick under her feet.

"Hannah?" Alisha called from inside, insistent.

Hannah didn't answer. She scanned the pits, pulse drumming in her throat.

Foster stepped from the trailer, his icy stare aimed her way, slicing through the distance like a blade.

CHAPTER
25

Down in the marshy valley, the air was thick with chemical rot and decay. Gray pools of sludge stretched out, their surfaces slick and shimmering, like spilled oil. It wasn't just a smell. It was a putrid organism, clawing at his throat, coating his tongue with every shallow breath.

Life didn't belong here. Yet a few crooked trees stood defiant, their bark peeling away—like burned skin—revealing raw, blistered wood beneath.

Workers moved in the sludge, hunched and hacking with dull blades, against the gray sky. Dan stopped at the edge, his boots sinking into the unstable ground. The men around him drifted through the haze, their faces blurred by exhaustion and grime.

On the perimeter, Foster's men prowled. Their rifles slung across their chests, watchful and ready.

He had to move fast, blend in, become one of them, even just for a moment. He peeled off his shirt, stuffing it into the back of his jeans. The scorch of the sun radiated on his bare skin. Sweat beaded on his neck, trickling down his spine.

The air grew dense with the tang of rust and sweat.

He slipped into the mass, terror tightening his chest—but three lives depended on him, he had to know more and find a way out. Mud sucked at his trainers with a wet, grasping gurgle. Each step coated his shoes in a thick brown muck, slowing him, pulling him down.

He trudged to a squatting man chopping at the earth with a small pick, the tool's clink swallowed by the valley's drone.

He whispered low. "Yo estoy Dan."

The man didn't look up, didn't flinch, and kept swinging.

"I'm Dan, do you speak English?" he tried again.

A backhand brushed him away like a fly.

Dan lowered and moved on. He wiped a hand across his brow, the grime smearing, and trudged deeper into the marsh. The valley buzzed around him, clanks of metal, the soft scoop of shovels, the occasional splash of liquid hitting the ground. Voices were scarce, stolen by a terror he could feel in his bones. He didn't know what they were digging for, but their silence filled him with dread.

Farther in, he came upon a crew working with pickaxes. A bare-chested man stood over a pile of dirt, scooping handfuls and tossing them into a rusted drum with a hollow clang.

Nearby, another tended the barrel, a frail man, his thin frame dotted with bruises and scratches. The drum sloshed as he rolled it, shimmering liquid spilling over the rim, staining the mud with a glossy sheen.

Dan stepped closer, his shadow falling across the man's work. "Hola," he whispered.

Sunken eyes glanced up—and slid away.

"Yo estoy Dan," he said, leaning in.

The barrel creaked under the man's trembling grip. Dan caught a faint metallic whiff from the shimmering liquid inside, its surface unnaturally still and thick.

"¿Qué estás haciendo ahí?" Dan nodded at the barrel.

The frail man glanced at him, lips sealed.

A hefty guard drew near, boots sloshing, rifle low but ready. As he passed, fear rippled through the workers, hands tightening on tools, gazes dropping to the ground.

Strange movement in the haze. Dan stepped back from the barrel, unease crawling up his spine. A shout split the air. A worker had flung a shovelful of mud into another's hole, splattering a man clutching a pickaxe. A glare, knuckles whitening around his tool.

A fight erupted, bizarre and brutal, shovel versus pickaxe. The shovel swung first, missed, but now two enemies closed in. One flipped his tool, whipping the wooden handle like a sword. Timber cracked against timber, sharp and jarring, vibrating through Dan's chest. The valley seemed to swallow the noise, its mud muffling the clash. A sour wind struck his lungs. The ground pulsed, as if fed on their violence.

Wet feet jostled in the muck. A spade smashed a shoulder, bone splintering with a sickening crunch. The victim shrieked, his weapon tumbling into the filth. A second blow landed, ribs cracking, doubling him over.

Dan clenched his fists, adrenaline spiking. He had to stay hidden, but part of him braced to fight.

A shrill whistle sliced through the noise.

Guards closed in, voices barking orders through the haze.

Each fighter instantly changed from warrior to worker, without so much as a parting shot—as if nothing had happened.

Dan crouched beside the 55-gallon drum, breath shallow, praying the guards would pass. He needed answers. What was this hellhole? What were they mining? Who was in control? Anything to aid an escape—but the rifles were coming too close.

The dirty man lifted his sunken gaze from the barrel, locking eyes with Dan. "You and your friends must leave this place," he rasped. "Or you will die."

CHAPTER
26

Hannah edged closer to the hill's crumbling lip, pulse racing like a trapped animal. Dan disappeared, swallowed by the sea of mud-soaked bodies churning below, their faces blurred into a filthy smear.

Alisha called again from the shack, her voice sharp with worry. Hannah pretended not to hear, but her heart went heavy. Soon, her pregnant friend would stagger out and face the brutal truth. Her husband had gone down into the worker's treacherous gorge.

Shouts rolled across the valley, mixed with the clang of tools swung like weapons. Hannah tensed. More shattered men would land on the shack's splintered plywood, half-dead, reeking of rot and despair.

Foster's shrill whistle cut through the noise.

A familiar face flashed in the chaos below, maybe Dan, before it vanished into the muck.

Alisha's scream jolted her.

"He's having a seizure!"

Hannah tore inside, breath ragged. Lorenzo, their gunshot victim, lay still on the table, dried blood caked around his arm.

Alisha was crouched over Doctor Malum, grappling his jerking arms while his legs flailed. She grabbed his jaw, prying open his mouth.

"Airway's clear," she said. "Count 38, 39, 40…"

"What happened?" Hannah cried.

"Keep his legs still, 45, 46…" Alisha pinned his thrashing knees until he went limp. His breathing slowed and his eyes opened to a vacant stare.

For a moment, the only sound was rain against the roof. Hannah's fingers hovered over his ribs, unsure if he'd start seizing again. She watched the rise and fall of his chest like it might convulse at any moment.

"Doctor Malum, can you hear me?" Alisha peered into his glassy eyes. "You've had a seizure, out for almost a minute."

He didn't blink, just stared past them.

"I'll check his pulse." Hannah grabbed for his wrist, feeling a weak thud. "How did it happen?"

"He was pacing, muttering, then collapsed." Alisha pressed one hand to his chest, the other to his sweaty forehead. "Do we have a stethoscope?"

Hannah shook her head. "Not in the crates."

"We need to roll him."

They lifted his slack body onto his side. Hannah bent his knee to steady him. His blank gaze held.

"He might be catatonic," Alisha muttered.

"If it's a tumor or aneurysm, we're helpless here." Hannah sighed.

"This place has nothing for real care." Alisha's tone was bitter.

She was right, of course. No electricity, a mud hut, a hodgepodge of supplies that didn't make any sense. And who knew what sickness was festering in those pits?

Alisha gazed up from Malum. "Where's Dan?"

Hannah's stomach sank. Dan was still down there, maybe caught, shot like Lorenzo, or forced into that demonic pit. What could she say? That she'd failed to stop him?

Malum's arm twitched. Hannah caught it and held it down.

A harsh wheeze sounded at the door.

Dan stumbled in, coughing, his eyes wild.

"Dan!" Hannah called. A wave of relief hit her chest.

"Dan, where were you?" Alisha kept position over Malum.

Dan hacked, wincing with exhaustion.

Hannah rose, helping him inside. "What happened?"

Panting and doubled-over, Dan gasped. "They're using the barrels... sifting something..." He heaved a breath, trying to stand upright. "They're searching… something down there."

He slapped a rough, amber-red lump into Hannah's palm. The lump was slick, sticky against her skin. She didn't know what it was yet, but it felt like some strange truth—rough, ugly, undeniable.

"What is this?"

"They're digging for—"

"Daniel!" Alisha screamed.

Two men stormed into the shack, boots pounding, weapons aimed.

CHAPTER
27

"Put them down, slowly."

Kendrick counted twelve rifles aimed at their skulls, the barrels glinting under the jungle's canopy—and those were just the firearms he could see. Another four, maybe six, lurked in the rustling bushes and trees at the edge of his vision, their presence betrayed by the snap of twigs underfoot.

The natives wore a patchwork of handmade tunics and faded store-bought shirts, threads fraying at the seams. Some barefoot on the damp earth while others wore thin sandals, toes exposed.

"Hands off those triggers, quarter speed." Nelson's tone was steady and taut. "Cool as summer rain."

Sweat rolled down Kendrick's neckline. He lowered his sidearm, sliding it gently into its holster.

"Hello there," Bennett crooned. He let the M4 fall on the weight of its strap, flashing a cautious grin. "Fine day to be alive, eh?"

Nelson's whisper was terse. "Rosales? Put it down."

"I don't like it, sir." Her finger twitched above the rifle's trigger.

"Best warm up to it," Bennett growled under his breath. "Before they start putting holes in us."

Kendrick's gaze bounced between faces. This wasn't a tangle they could win. His chest tightened at the thought of bloodshed.

The air thickened with the scent of wet leaves and smoke, and a whirr of insects buzzed.

"Buenos días, ¿cómo están?" Rosales lowered her rifle, forcing a smile.

None of the tribespersons answered, their faces stone-still.

"Keep hands at your midsection where they can all see them. Right. Right," Nelson spoke through his teeth. He waved a slow hand at the cadre of natives.

A few appeared more hostile at the gesture.

Kendrick caught their body language, cagy and suspicious.

"What the hell's going on?" Bennett droned low.

"That action is confusing them," Kendrick said calmly.

"What?" Nelson turned, brow cocked. "I'm trying to say hello."

Kendrick stood, arms at his sides—his stare fixed on those in front of him. "They don't look like they understand. In fact, these natives are probably unfamiliar with the greeting. And if you keep it up, they may think you're either deaf or trying to cast a spell on them."

Nelson shrugged. "Should I try to shake their hand?"

"That would be employing a gesture traditionally used to show you intend no malice and harbor no weapon, while strapped around your neck is a gas-operated machine gun that could cut down their entire tribe with one pull of its trigger."

Bennett sneered. "If you know all about this, then what the hell do we do, British Intelligence?"

"Try presenting them a gift." Kendrick took a slow, measured step forward.

Nelson seized a water bottle from his pouch.

"No," Kendrick said. "They have water, and if you show them that plastic bottle, they may believe you're down to that last container and have come to rob them of their supply."

"Shit." Nelson returned the bottle to his pouch.

"Let's try to offer them something they don't have."

"Like what?"

Kendrick's mind raced, until a young boy strolled up to Bennett, pointing at the jet pilot's shirt collar.

Bennett instinctively covered his dangling aviator sunglasses with a hand.

"Gafas de sol!" the boy cried, jumping up and down.

Rosales smirked. "He likes your sunglasses, sir."

"Yes. I like my sunglasses, too," Bennett grumbled. "I like them very much."

Kendrick shot him a glance. "More than your life?"

Bennett grunted.

"Best warm up to it, sir."

"Ah, fuck," Bennett scoffed. He unhitched the aviators from his neckline. "Here you go."

The young boy snatched the pair.

"You little thief," Bennett said under his breath.

"Right, yes," Kendrick said, smile tight. "Put them on. You'll look smashing."

"I'd like to smash–" Bennett began.

"Holes, sir," Rosales warned. "Remember the holes."

"Three hundred dollars those cost me."

"Small price out here." Kendrick stared straight ahead at a tall native holding a rifle pointed at his chest. He took another, cautious step beyond his three teammates.

The young boy fit the oversized sunglasses over his tiny ears.

"Dammit," Bennett scoffed.

"Let it go, sir."

"We are looking for doctors," Kendrick said loudly. "Bannister. Mitchum. Their guide, Phinn." He nodded to Rosales.

"Buscamos médicos que pasaron por aquí. Bannister. Mitchum. Su guía, Phinn." She gazed at a shorter man aiming a long Remington in her direction.

An older woman with long gray hair moved past the fire line toward the four.

"Phinn! Phinn!"

"Here we go." Nelson gritted his teeth. "Stand guarded."

"Phinn está herido. Descansando." The woman pointed to a parting in the trees and a path behind them.

Rosales locked eyes with Kendrick. "Says he's injured, sir."

Kendrick grimaced. But if the man was still alive, he might be able to help them. "Can you ask about the others?"

Rosales and the woman conversed. Seeing the exchange, most villagers lowered their weapons. The young boy who'd sped off with Bennett's sunglasses had disappeared.

"The gist, sir, is they believe the doctors were taken. They say two men approached with guns wet from a river in the vicinity. The village chased them off. They found Phinn bleeding on the trail leading to their tent."

"Where is this tent?"

"Already asked, sir. I know the way. Phinn's there right now, and they say he's able to talk."

"We need to be careful." Kendrick studied the path, its shadows twisting like a trap waiting to spring. "Phinn's an ex-convict. Manslaughter."

Rosales and Nelson both nodded.

"I'll follow you guys in a minute. Need to find out where my "gafas de sol" ran off to. That little shit's around here someplace."

Rosales smirked. "Let it go, sir."

CHAPTER
28

They took him.

Rain pummeled the tin roof. Alone in the corner, Alisha sat in wet dirt, her shaky hands guarding her unborn child, the air thick with the damp stench of mildew.

Hannah had tried to console her, but there were no words. Alisha's screams as the filthy thugs ripped her from Dan. The terror in her eyes watching them drag him away, and then the silence of his absence.

With Dan taken and Alisha in emotional ruin, any chance at rescue—a signal to anyone out there—was up to Hannah.

As the downpour continued, the tin roof creaked under the rain's weight, groaning with the damp.

In the doorway, a man with a rifle stood puffing reefer, before a distant whistle sounded, and he vanished without a word.

Hannah crept to the shack's doorway, watching as he descended the hill into darkness. She felt for the fragments in her pocket and retuned inside.

She found a clean spot near the plastic crates to use as a workspace. She removed the phone fragments from her pockets and counted them. Thirteen. The green board with the circuitry was primarily intact, minus the torn red and black wires. Power wires—that much she'd figured out. The battery, which she'd carefully kept in its own pocket, was unbroken as far as she could tell. But that was it as far as good news went.

The phone's LCD display suffered a sizable crack down its middle. The keypad's guide was gone, and only minuscule dots remained where user-friendly digits had once been. The remaining pieces were a mixed collection of busted black plastic.

She arranged them by type and put the plastic in one corner of the crate, the electronics in another. Figuring the entire effort might be for nothing unless she could get a signal out, she worked at the antenna first. Hooking the battery to a half-put-together device might be dangerous and could destroy it, and she'd save that task for last.

Nine wires. Four gathered into as many slots on the cream receptacle, but a majority left dangling. The receptacle was more like a clip. It mated with something on the circuitry board. But where?

In her hand, two cable housings. One green and one yellow. For these two lines, inside the clip, she found damaged ends of the same wires. She pulled and cleaned the broken wire from the clip, stripped the lines, and jammed them into their respective slots as far as possible.

But the clip's interior gave her no help configuring the other three. Blue, white, and black. Where did they fit?

"Please, please, please." Alisha's head was down, her hands tented in prayer, her voice a ragged sob. "He's gone," she choked out, eyes lost in the dirt.

Hannah stopped her work.

"Honey, it's going to be okay. We've got to be strong."

But the words were bullshit. She didn't know it was going to be okay. She didn't know what strong meant, not when failing Alisha would break her too. She put an arm around her friend and hugged her tight.

They had one another, at least for now.

Hannah steeled herself, Dan's laugh flashing in her mind—faint, fleeting, a memory she couldn't lose. She would do her best to make sure they got out of this alive. She rose to fetch Alisha some water, but a rustling from the exam table startled both of them.

CHAPTER
29

"Fuckers nabbed them." The Scot sat up and coughed. "I's lying on the ground, leaking from the wound and losing to the pass-outs." He rubbed his forehead. "Couldn't do nothing." He huffed. "I's supposed to be taking care of them." Phinn's eyes reddened, wet with failure he couldn't choke back.

Kendrick's suspicions were momentarily quelled. The story that Aldous Phinn told did sound plausible, and his expressions matched his words… so far.

The three physicians, Phinn said, had been taken by cartel members, or guerrillas that roamed these areas looking for white faces like tigers hunting for prey. These fanatical groups were small, armed, trained, and motivated. They could've gone in any direction. The assets were doctors, and this gave him hope. They were much too valuable to kill. He'd check with Adler to see if any demands had come for a ransom.

Rosales pulled apart the wrapping on Phinn's midsection and examined the injury. She probed the crude stitching done by the villagers.

"Seen worse, a lot worse." She angled her head. "No black or discharge. I have antibiotics in my pack. He should take a cycle of those to fight any potential infection. The scar might be nasty, but I think he's good."

"Conversation wound," Bennett flexed his jaw. "Got a few of those in this group."

"Yeah, but the bastard who shanked me, oh I's want a piece of him," Phinn growled.

"Anything else distinctive about the men?"

"Not a spec. It was dark as anything. Never saw them types before that night. Came in from nowhere and caught me off guard on that trail. Got into a scrum with one of them. Didn't know I'd taken a hit in the gut for a bit."

"Any idea which way they went?"

"Bastards were gone for a solid day until I woke from this." Phinn scratched his chin. "Could quiz the villagers. It's where the two bastards went first."

"They did?"

"Aye. Got a fork in the river trail. The most beaten path rounds to the village. That knifer got me on a soft path to this tent. Harder to see. Plus, they came from behind, so the two fuckers must've gone the village's direction first."

"Is anyone in the village wounded? How did they–"

"Wouldn't worry about that lot. They's deal with cartel crews all the time. Heard they gave you the same greeting?"

"Yes." Bennett crinkled his forehead. "And one of those little muggers has my sunglasses."

"Aye," Phinn said. "Surrendered me wristwatch when we arrived. But they nice folks and got a stockpile of weapons. Collected from past skirmishes and whatnot. Most inaccessible communities are equipped like this one. Seen plenty. Keeps the tribe safe, good deterrent for fending off the odd character now and again. Gave me a tiger-claw necklace—protection, they said, against the cartel's black luck." He rubbed at the wound on his chest.

"Itching's good, sir, but don't scratch. Ointment will help." Rosales sat next to Phinn on the cot, fished a tube from her pack, and smeared it on.

"We got no direction." Bennett shook his head.

He was right. Without a clue to their course, there was no way to tell who might have them. Kendrick, again, hoped someone would call in a ransom. After all, kidnapping was South America's third oldest profession.

This place was as remote as any he'd ever seen. Thick jungle and hostiles everywhere. They could, and would, scout the perimeter for strange footprints and other clues. The rain hammered the tent, a relentless drum over the jungle's wet hum. Then a shout—harsh, guttural—pierced the drops, monkeys scurrying in the trees.

"I'm coming too," Phinn declared. He spun his legs off the folding bed, put his feet to the floor, and reached for a shirt.

"Sir, that's not a good idea. There still isn't much scabbing on the wound yet, and those stitches may not hold under any kind of strain."

"Appreciation for the concern, missy. But that bastard and me have us a dance to finish." Phinn grunted. "I'll snap the fucker's neck. He's got it coming."

"We need to scout the area and check for movements," Nelson said.

"I'll hold here, help Phinn pack his gear," Kendrick said.

"If we find something, we'll come get you," Nelson said. Then he turned to Phinn. "Do you need anything in the meantime? Water, food?"

"I need to put a long spear up the man's arse who done this!"

"I'm beginning to like this guy," Bennett grinned.

Kendrick, though, wasn't so sure. He'd need to learn more. The Scot's checkered past begged a lot of questions. Would they be in danger if they brought him along? Even simply to guide the man out of this jungle to a hospital? And, if they met any problems on the way back, which was likely, could he put a weapon in this man's hands?

Rosales, Bennett, and Nelson stepped from the tent, leaving him with Phinn.

Kendrick dragged a canvas chair beside Phinn's bed, sat, and drummed his fingers against the seat's edge. Could they trust this man?

CHAPTER
30

They didn't want him dead, not yet—not while he was still valuable to them.

Lorenzo lay motionless on a dirty plywood table, humid rot thick in his lungs. The bullet that ripped through his arm had caused his legs to buckle and dropped him to the ground. Voices from the pits, scurrying feet. Then came a sharp stabbing pain in his thigh.

The contents of the syringe propelled him into a horrible cloud of nothingness, an impossible place where logic vanished, and the concept of time melted away. He struggled to fight the sensation again, but the opioids were too embracing, too pure, too potent. They sped through his body in seconds, confusing every sense, until he drifted powerlessly, suspended in the zero space of sheer euphoria.

They'd moved him from the muddy grounds below and placed him here. But the poppy's last alkaloids were detaching from his brain cells and cycling through his kidneys. The drug's absence was replaced by a painful throb in his left arm. Someone had patched his bicep.

He welcomed the hurt. Pain was real, awakening.

His skin prickled everywhere.

Two women nearby sat on the dirt floor. The pregnant one was weeping, as the other embraced her.

Lorenzo shut his eyes, fighting for consciousness.

Isabella had warned him not to go. "Nobody pays that well, Lorenzo—nobody." But he was too excited, too eager. Youth, agility, and confidence were on his side. The economy was getting worse every day, but a hardworking man like himself would stand out, he assured her. He'd earn for them, as his own father had done.

Isabella's unusual eyes made her self-conscious. One blue iris and one green. There was a name for the condition, but he could never remember it. In town, she wore her chestnut hair over a brow, draping one of her eyes so the others wouldn't stare. But she never hid them when they were alone. He loved all of her, and she loved him.

He put a hand on Isabella's cheek and made her a promise. If the job in the city felt dishonest or turned out no good, he'd return home swiftly and search for another. Don't worry, mi amor, he'd said. They agreed he should at least travel into Mérida and check it out. He hugged her tight, kissed her goodbye, and listened as she locked the door behind him.

A long line of jobless men showed, hungry for work. A man in a short-sleeved white shirt and skinny tie sized them up. He directed each man to one of three buildings in the rundown complex. A pulp factory that had produced its last materials in the '90s, went out of business, caught fire, and partially burned down.

At first, everything seemed normal. The questionnaire asked for the usual contact information. Lorenzo anxiously filled it out and waited.

Two hours later, they called his name.

Behind a heavy door was a windowless, humid, smoke-filled room. Two men in collared shirts and loose neckties greeted him. Another man, overweight and sweaty, sat behind a thick walnut desk smoking a cigar. The space had two doors, the one Lorenzo had entered, which automatically closed behind him, and a second door to the desk's rear.

Lorenzo sat in the only vacant chair.

"Last job?" The man behind the desk looked Lorenzo over, puffed his cigar, and coughed.

"Factory," Lorenzo said, voice catching. "F-fabrication and welding, sir." He'd fudged his duties a bit. Okay, a lot. Bending tinplate into cans and repairing a friend's fence with an oxy-acetylene rig hardly made him an expert metallurgist. But Isabella had told him to build himself up.

"Position has long hours," the fat man hacked again. "Can't have you late or getting sick out there."

"No, sir." Lorenzo straightened his posture, swallowing hard.

One of the men behind him snorted. "This one'll snap before the week's out."

Lorenzo shook his head. He'd work anywhere, do almost anything.

On occasion, the two well-built men standing inside the office chimed in on whatever point the deskman conveyed. But mostly, each paced around the small space behind Lorenzo.

"Family?" the deskman asked.

"Just married," Lorenzo replied.

The two behind him laughed, and the fat man hacked.

Then, the deskman parked his cigar in an ashtray, looked up at his two partners, and uttered those words Lorenzo had longed to hear since losing his job at the paint factory.

"Let's give you a try," he grumbled.

Lorenzo's shoulders relaxed. He and Isabella would be okay. In a couple of weeks, he'd have enough money to properly fill their cupboards. He'd surprise her with an oversized bag of those American barbeque potato chips she loved so much.

They'd supply him with new boots and safety gear. There was even a rideshare program to the site.

"Write your address here," the sweaty man coughed and pushed a blank sheet of paper forward on the desk.

Lorenzo rose from the chair. They already had his address on the application, but he wrote it again. When he finished, the deskman snatched the sheet, and the room's mood changed.

The reek of body odor floated behind him.

The second door flung open.

Lorenzo's smile faded.

A pair of arms squeezed his torso.

Lorenzo struggled, but it was no use.

Fingers and a rag crammed into his mouth.

Terror and panic surged through him.

And a black canvas cloaked his face.

No paycheck. No free boots. He was theirs now.

They tossed him into the bed of a pickup truck with several others. Blindfolded, hands tied, feet bound. Each bounce on the unpaved road knocked his skull against the base of the vehicle. Four, maybe five others were trapped with him, moaning through their cloth muzzles. The wagon drove for hours and hours over steep inclines, down ridges, and crossed water at least four times.

When they stopped, the driver uncovered their faces. Jungle in every direction as far as he could see. No car horns, no powerlines, no signs of civilization. They were forced to hike through the wilds several kilometers at gunpoint until they reached this horrible location.

Six months now, maybe longer, captive in this mud-riddled underworld, a stagnant zone hidden deep within the rainforest. A chasm devoid of trees, flowers, or weeds. While tropical showers fed the lush hills above, Amazonian leftovers washed down their high slopes flooding the valley's murky trenches. Fallen trees and dead creatures from the upper forest plummeted into the basin, creating a sickening grotto of rotten slurry.

Sunup to sunset, Lorenzo was forced to mine these muddy holes, held prisoner by the remote location and the men with weapons. There were many others here, too, slaving away beside him. Some believed they'd be set free once the grounds were picked of all their value. Others whispered rumors of pay and release after a year.

But Lorenzo knew the deadly truth.

Each day, since returning from the awful bluff and those discarded bodies, he hunted and hoarded for any nourishment he could find. He needed protein to be strong.

At night he pictured a faraway world, happy and safe. Someplace without danger and death. Someplace warm with food. Someplace with his Isabella. His fist clenched—I won't die here, he swore silently.

The rain was letting up. The marijuana-smoking men and their rifles retreated to their quarters. One woman rose from the dirt and brushed herself off, while the sad pregnant lady held on the ground.

The bullet they fired into his arm burned. Inside a torn pantleg he hid the broken hammer's claw—its cold heft a secret against his thigh— he wrestled it away from a worker before they shot him. Another tool for his plan.

Seeing Hector's dead body in that gully enraged him. But when he snuck back to the mine that night, he thought he saw a light in the distance, far away from this hellish place.

He rose from the plywood and rubbed his bandaged bicep.

Tomorrow, he'd eat as much as he could, even if the food was killing him.

He'd nurse the injury to his arm, keep it clean.

He'd leave this place.

He'd reach that light—if it was real.

He'd return home to Isabella.

CHAPTER
31

Lorenzo stared at them, his gaze no longer glassy but soft and curious. Long, grubby, dark hair tied with string fell to one side, cresting a shoulder. A tatty beard covered his cheeks.

Alisha stopped crying.

The two women stared at Lorenzo.

He looked around, examined the injury on his arm, then massaged the gauze dressing with his fingertips, wincing. Little by little, he raised himself up, swung his legs off the plywood table, and placed his bare feet on the floor.

Hannah spoke low, deliberate. "Despacio, ten cuidado. Me llamo Hannah."

Lorenzo nodded.

He was possibly still in shock, and he might get an infection. She wanted an excuse to convince Foster that the wounded Lorenzo needed rest, anything to save him from that pit of death below for a little longer.

"Hannah, the pills," Alisha sniffled.

"Right, yes." She kept her gaze on Lorenzo, raising a hand. "Wait, alto."

She stood, slow. Even if he was determined to leave like their earlier patient, she didn't want to scare him off too early. From the scratches and cuts on his bare chest and back, it seemed he'd survived the horror of this place for a long time.

Lorenzo eased off the table, his breath hitching.

Hannah fetched a bottle of antibiotics she'd found earlier in the crates. She couldn't find an expiration date—regardless, they were better than nothing.

She held up the bottle and two fingers. "Twice a day," she said, voice unsteady. "Dos veces al día. Okay?"

Lorenzo couldn't be more than 20 years old. She'd noticed the white spots on his fingernails during their repair of his arm. He was low on zinc. Each side of his nose was scaled and red, which showed a lack of B2. At the peak of each shoulder was a patch of rough, bumpy skin. In the center of his chest, the beginnings of a dip. Appalling signs of malnourishment. She wanted to take him stateside, hook him up to an IV, blend a cocktail of multivitamins for him, and jam a large pizza down his throat.

Yet somehow, he was surviving out here. Working as a slave in the middle of these jungled muddy wilds. His loose pants meant rampant hunger had already put his muscle tissue in decline, and one day it would become too much. The digging, the scavenging, the unclean air he breathed circling through his bloodstream. His body was in decay. How much longer could he last out here? Months, maybe weeks? Before his undernourished heart would take no more and beat for the final time?

Lorenzo blinked. He snatched the pills from her hand, scanning the bottle. One side of his mouth hitched upward.

Despite the sunsetting, a remarkable gleam radiated from his eyes. A hope, a determination. She was lost inside his stare for a quiet moment.

Lorenzo drew her hand, and his head lowered.

"Gracias damas," he said. "Que dios las mantenga a salvo."

May God keep you both safe? Hannah's heart sank, his words tearing at her. Down that dark hill, this young man labored in dangerous toxins under threat of disease and death at the behest of a madman who viewed him as nothing more than a minion.

Lorenzo was withering to nothing, and he'd taken a bullet, likely not for the first time, which could have killed him. And for what? Most in his situation would be fighting to find a reason to keep going, to live. But Lorenzo was different. He had a noble, unselfish spirit. How incredible, after all the burdens on him and the hopelessness he must feel in those pits, to still think of her and Alisha's safety.

Hannah didn't want him to leave.

But the quiet, kind man with the injured arm slipped from the shack and melted into the pouring night rain.

She stood frozen in the doorway, rain prickling her face, as the downpour swallowed him whole. Something inside her twisted—the urge to call him back, to tell him he mattered. But she said nothing. In this place, kindness was a currency too costly to spend.

CHAPTER
32

"Second time I caught a stab," Phinn said, and looked down at his patched wound. He wrapped his midsection front to back several times with the tape Rosales had supplied, careful not to cinch his lungs into suffocation. After at least ten revolutions, he bit a notch in the vinyl tape, ripped it off, and dropped it to the cot.

The others were scouting the village and its surroundings for traces the gunmen might've left when they took their hostages. That gave Kendrick time to assess this man and decide if he posed any threat.

"Tell me of the first time," Kendrick said. He leaned forward in the folding chair.

"Aye. Knowing the past, are you?" Phinn replied. Gingerly, he pulled a trouser leg over a foot.

Kendrick stared him in the eyes.

"Years ago, back home in me flat, damp chill seeping through the walls, watching the Celts on the screen, second half." He leaned back on the cot, shimmying his trousers to his waist. "Got the wifey dressed in her goonie sitting together with my son and me on the couch." He paused. "Apology. Goonie is a sleeper, a nighty. When I get the excites, my native creeps out."

Kendrick understood. When he was in the throes of drink, the same occurred. His accent thickened, and his vocabulary blossomed. Though without the suds, he adopted the American's lingo and toned down his natural ictus for the most part. But right now, he needed Phinn to be forthright and unfiltered with him.

"Welshman. I get the lingo," he said.

"Ah," Phinn's stare held on Kendrick. "Caught a tinge of shore in your speak, din't I?"

Kendrick's stare remained fixed on the man.

"Quiet night, really. Having a bite. Downing a pint of suds, but not overdoing it, you know. Comes this banging on the door, horrid racket. Tattie slices slitter down the shirt. Thinking a pished loon outside has got the wrong place, or a ween needs help. Cleaned me self and sprang to sort it out."

Phinn drew a deep breath and exhaled.

"Next thing happens, this dobber busts the door in, breaks into my place, swinging a blade. Dunno what he wants, so I's asking him. I mean I got the kid and the wife. Feared he'd take a jab at one or the other. Now my purpose is, well, best give the madman what he needs and send him on his way, right?"

He rarely broke eye contact with Kendrick.

"Idiot's spouting on about money and valuables. 'Where's the jewels?'" Phinn's voice raised. "Jewels? I ain't got no jewels! Where's this walloper think he is? Fucking Edinburgh Castle? Do you see any heraldry on these walls, you twat?"

Kendrick huffed a chuckle.

"He rambles on and on. "Where's the cash?" and all that. I's try tell him we don't got much in the flat, but I'll give him whatever I can rustle."

He rose from the cot and coughed.

"And then what happened?" Kendrick said.

"Fucker dabs at me." He mimed the action. "I snatch his arm, toss him fler bound. I's shitting scared. His blade is thrusting and poking."

Another pause. Phinn patted sections of the tape around his chest.

"Now, cause I tossed this bampot further into me hoose, he's between my fam and me. His eyes go darty and I know he's fixing to take a turn at one of them with that claw in his clutch. So I grab what I could from a stand in the scullery, and I lunge fury at the fucker."

Kendrick watched for the usual signals. Change in voice, fidgeting, avoiding eye contact. He observed none of this in Phinn.

"We's tussling, got one arm pushing me kin away from the madman. Blade pokes me side, stings like a fucker." He pointed to a surface near his stomach. "Not deep, but now the minge has got hell coming. I take me blade and thrust. Hitting flesh. Dig and twist. Dig and twist. His legs get shoogly, till finally the fucker falls to the boards."

So far, this sounded like self-defense. An armed intruder enters a house, threatens a man and his family, and meets his end when the owner stabs him to death. But there had to be more to the tale.

"Authorities show. Check the place, tell the tale. My lady clinging, son's holding me hand. Into the early morn, take the photos, remove the dead fucker, answer questions, do the signings." Phinn cleared a cough. "Then they tell us it's over. We can tidy the blood and mess ourselves or hire some trained types. Handed us cards and copies, and they're off."

Unless he skipped the part where he killed the officer during the card exchange, this didn't sound like murder to Kendrick.

"Fortnight trickles by, and different authorities show up. Seems they done a proper death-look and are leveling me with murder."

Something was missing. This wasn't right. Why would the authorities arrest a man for defending his home? His kid? His wife?

"Caged me for the crime," Phinn's head dropped, and he let out a long breath before continuing. "I stabbed the man seventeen times. Too many, they said. Deemed it excessive." He cleared a tickle in his throat. "Lost me job, sliced the pension. Said "Went beyond what was necessary." But all's I did was stabbed the menace from the fucker! And any man worth the feet he's standing on would've done the same!" He tightened a fist and pounded it into an open palm. "Utter shite!"

If the story was true, then Phinn was the victim here. Not outside the realm of possibility, but what kind of damn fools would see it this way?

"But them judges don't know me spot. Not too many mawkit bampots in Bearsden. Are there, you turds? How many stabs is your family worth, Lordship? Mine's worth seventeen! Seventeen fucking stabs! And I'd do it again, you pricks!"

Phinn blew a raspberry with his lips.

"High court sorted it to culpable homicide. Passed a sentence of five years. SPS early released in three. But I got the tick on my record. Scotland jobs are scarce when everyone thinks you dangerous."

Kendrick admitted he'd been guilty of this too. He'd pre-judged the man himself before even meeting him. Now, though, after hearing the story and watching his expressions, he realized that'd been unfair.

Phinn closed his eyes and said nothing for the next several seconds.

"Didn't mind the cage. Didn't care of the tawdry food. The years in prison was slow, but I dealt them."

He looked up and exhaled.

"But she never visited, never wrote, never rang. Sheriff's Court served me the papers in the cage second year. She and the wee moved on, don't know where. Ain't seen or heard from them since." He fished a folded photo from his pocket, then wiped a tear. "All I got left of the gap-tooth fella now."

He handed the photo to Kendrick. Faded, creased, it showed a grinning boy holding a football.

"Seventeen times, self-defense. Protecting my lady and son. Now neither want nothing to do with the likes of me." His voice cracked. "Missing the wee's growing up years, can't ever get those back."

Kendrick clutched the photo. They'd taken away Phinn's freedom, employment, and family. But he was in his own home? Defending his loved ones? All because the courts didn't agree with the number of times he'd stabbed an armed intruder?

The two finished their conversation. Phinn, anxious to leave with the team, wanted to pack a few things. Kendrick shook the Scottish man's hand and left him to it.

Kendrick didn't bother to call Adler because he didn't need verification. He'd witnessed the raw emotion in Aldus Patrick Phinn's face, the rage in his voice. If he harbored a secret, it was likely a plot to blow up The Scottish High Court, something Kendrick was now tempted to help him plan.

CHAPTER

33

Hannah coaxed Alisha to the exam table and had her lie down. She grabbed a grubby blanket, shook off as much dirt as she could, and wrapped it around a brown-stained pillow from the adjacent room. Then she dusted a second blanket and draped it over her. Alisha wept until she finally drifted off.

With her friend resting, Hannah's thoughts turned to Lorenzo. That expression on his face. That smile. His positive, peculiar attitude infected her with energy, and she couldn't sleep. She said a silent prayer for Dan, hoping that wherever they'd taken him, he was still alive. Now, it was up to her to get them all out of this.

Foster's guards wouldn't visit until daybreak, but she only had a few hours. At the plastic crate stacks, she found the collection of phone parts. Again, she picked up the broken antenna. But the wires didn't make any sense to her. She worked for near an hour, the candle wax dripping down on the crates. But she was no closer to solving the mystery.

A stirring from the corner. Malum sat up on his plywood bed. He coughed and hacked phlegm for at least a minute until his airway settled, and his usual heavy breathing returned.

He was harmless. Weak, feeble, and lost in the head—except that strange warning he'd barked earlier. Poisons. She wondered if he'd ever become sane enough to explain what he'd meant. But that cough—his cough—what if that poison was in the air? Could they all be in danger? Eyeing Alisha, it was too horrible to even think about right now.

Her attention returned to the scattered phone parts.

Malum rose, glanced outside at the night sky—eyes sharpening for a split second—then shuffled over to her workspace.

She held the antenna in her palm, twisting wires around, trying to determine the different possibilities. If her guess was wrong, the device would never work—and they'd all rot in this underworld.

A shadowed hand appeared.

Hannah recoiled.

Candlelight struck Malum's face, lighting wrinkles and smudges of dirt. His gaze fixed to hers.

"Please?" he uttered. His fingers trembled, but slightly less than they had earlier. Sleep had calmed whatever was going on inside of his body.

Her eyebrows descended. The phone piece was a lifeline—there was no way she'd hand it off to someone who didn't seem all there in the head. For all she knew, he might eat it. Then what? She'd be fucked, that's what.

"Doctor Malum. I'm working here," Hannah scolded.

"Please?" he said once more. His expression shifted to a smile, and his eyes glowed with the flickering candle.

For reasons she didn't understand herself, except that his gaze reminded her of Lorenzo's, she offered him the piece.

Malum snatched it.

Her heart skipped.

But he took the candle and the device over to the plywood bed. He set the candle down and placed the antenna next to it, then situated himself on the floor and grouped the ends of the five wires she'd been working with between his fingers.

"Soft," he said. He straightened the cords that dangled, but he didn't pull on them. No, he lightly brushed at the wires as if he were petting the device. "Soft," he repeated.

Malum's fingertips pressed the wires against the flat plywood, all the way down to their broken endings.

"Memory," he muttered. "Memory."

Holy shit. The friction his light fingers created caused the wires to slowly jostle themselves back into their natural positions. A configuration she'd not considered before.

Malum was a genius. A very mad, heavy breathing, babbling genius.

He pointed to the wires, pressed them between his fingers, then handed the contraption back to her with both hands.

"Thank you," she said.

When she returned to the table, so did Malum. But this time, she didn't mind his breath on her shoulder.

Over the next hour, they worked together repairing the satellite phone piece by piece.

Doctor Malum patched and secured the phone's plastic casing using medical tape. They both worked to replace the circuit board and keypad, whose ribbon required another female receptacle which she found on the green circuit board.

This was working. Soon, all the pieces would be in place. And when they put the battery in and powered it up, she could call…

Wait.

Call who?

How many chances would she have at this?

Malum coupled the green circuitry board to the phone's body, then snapped the keypad panel into place.

The phone's cracked LCD screen glowed deep orange, and words emerged.

Hannah's hand trembled.

Irimus…

Registered…

Call Ready.

She gasped. The phone was working!

It was impossible to determine the battery icon's remaining charge through the shattered display by the dim candlelight.

Carefully, she aimed a fingernail onto the teeny black dot and pressed.

The number "1" appeared on the screen. She sighed, and Malum giggled. They were getting the fuck out of here!

She pressed a second digit before Malum's hand grazed hers.

"No," he wheezed. "Seven."

"Seven?"

"Seven." His eyes moved from her to the phone.

Could he be right? Could she be that far off? No, she'd try her number first, which was one-two-one.

She pressed the last digit, and Doctor Malum swiftly shook his head.

She pressed the place where the send button would have been, and then put her head as close as she could to the earpiece without moving the phone from the ledge.

It rang, but then came a queer tone.

"This call cannot be completed as dialed. Please check the number and dial again," the stale voice repeated.

Shit. Hannah had no idea which button would end the call. Her fingernail hit more spots, and other numbers appeared on the LCD screen. Working this unmarked grid of keyboard dots blindly was going nowhere. It might be best to shut it down and power it up.

"We may need to disconnect the battery," she told Malum.

He didn't understand. Or maybe he did. He reached for the phone.

"Wait," she said.

He pointed to a button on the side.

She pressed it, and the phone's LCD screen cleared itself.

Irimus…

Registered…

Call Ready.

The madman had surprised her again. She was convinced there was a lot more to Doctor Malum still inside somewhere. He understood what they were trying to do. He'd been helping her all night. She needed to trust him.

Gently, she pressed the tiny black dot for number one. After that, as Malum had instructed her, she pushed the dot for a seven. Both gray digits glowed against the phone's amber screen.

Her finger floated over the small field of black dots. Which one was next?

She turned. Doctor Malum held up one finger.

"One? The number for rescue is one-seven-one?"

Malum smiled and gave a slow nod.

Strange. Hannah didn't recall that during the briefing when they entered the country ten months ago. Had she forgotten? Or was she overly tired?

"Alright," she said. Her fingernail poked at the black dot for the number one again.

"Uno siete uno. Emergencia, ¿en qué puedo ayudarle?"

The stranger's voice startled her. It had come from the world outside. Hannah squeezed the phone.

"Hola, necesito ayuda… I'm some place," Hannah stammered. "Lo sentimos, estamos–"

"Miss, I can speak English if you prefer?"

"Oh, yes, please! I'm not sure where I am. I can't, we were, I think we're somewhere in the eastern Colombian mountains, and–"

"Miss, you need to call the Colombian emergency service number. Hold, please."

The line clicked twice, and static resonated through the phone before the line reconnected.

"That number is one-two-three, thank you."

"Wait, wait, I'm—"

"Miss, please dial one-two-three for the services in your location."

"But—"

"You have dialed the emergency services of the wrong country. Goodbye."

No static. The signal simply went dead.

Malum had given her the wrong number, and they'd wasted a call. Well, if it wasn't for him, she'd still be messing with wires. Besides, something was going on with the man, and this hadn't been his fault. Thanks to Malum's mistake, the operator had provided the correct number to dial. Maybe the error wasn't so bad after all?

She pressed a fingernail to the correct digits. Once they showed on the screen, she hit the send button.

Malum grunted.

She leaned into the earpiece. Having this moment to think also gave her an idea. Although this was a satellite phone, not a cellular, it still had GPS capabilities. She could ask them to trace or triangulate, or whatever the term was to identify their location. And, according to several movies she'd sat through and trashy novels she'd read, they only needed to keep the line open for a few seconds until the proper authorities pinpointed their location.

The call went through.

An emergency operator answered.

But before she could reply, the amber glow flickered out against her cheek, and a sharp hiss swallowed the operator's voice.

CHAPTER

34

At dawn, steady rain fell on the village. The four had spent the night in a hut offered by the townspeople. The space included a soft bed and blanket for each.

When they rose, Rosales and Nelson spoke with several villagers. Kendrick and Bennett scouted trails around the medical tent, but there weren't many conversations between the pair.

After an hour, they met in the center of town, in an open-air pavilion. The structure was thatched with twine and held in place by bamboo poles. Most days, the locals used it to trade wares and crafts. Today, the outdoor dome sat empty as a steady downpour prattled the roof.

The villagers offered food and drinks. The team declined the meal but welcomed the tea, delivered minutes later. Little eyes stirred from every village corner after Rosales fished a candy bar from her knapsack for the child who'd brought them the hot drinks. It started a flurry of incomers, and more smiling faces surrounded her, wet by the rain. Each delivered a "please" and departed with a "thank you" until she ran out of chocolate supplies. Soon after, the townspeople gathered their clans and left the four alone under the gazebo.

"As I said, sir, we spoke with the villagers. They all give the same description. Two male hostiles, both armed with AKs, came from the river. A child was also down at the waterway escorting one of our missing three assets, Doctor Mitchum, but he says they split up on the run back. The kid warned the others in his village, and when the two hostiles arrived, they were met by the residents who'd fortified themselves with firearms. The hostiles changed course and ran down another path. Seems that's how they came upon Phinn and the doctors, sir."

Nelson nodded.

"Any direction?" Kendrick asked.

"No, sir. They said it was near dark, and the residents have a policy. Anytime they turn outsiders away, the villagers always remain near the village to protect it. They say trying to chase down an outsider, guerrillas or cartels has turned bloody in the past. These folks only seek to defend their property and their people anytime they meet with aggressors."

"Seems wise," Nelson said. "Wouldn't be smart to agitate unknown militias any further after making a stand like that. No advantage to being drawn farther out into the jungle, possibly into some ambush a hostile might be baiting them toward."

Kendrick agreed. Don't go running after danger once you've chased it away.

"Sir, I continued scouting this morning but didn't find anything on the trails," Rosales said. "There were boot prints west of here, but the tracks were pretty washed out."

She didn't say it, but Kendrick caught her expression—time was slipping, and the rain wasn't their only enemy.

"I followed a set for twenty meters," she said. "But they stopped in a patch with at least three other paths in various directions. We could try searching them one by one, but when I spoke to a local, they said each trail went on for kilometers and through thick jungle. It may take a while if we attempt it, sir."

Kendrick watched the rain fall outside their enclosure.

Phinn arrived holding a backpack. He greeted the four with slang only another Scotsman could understand. Next, an announcement was made that Phinn would be joining them, by Phinn, who punctuated his intentions with arm movements and lingo that sounded like a hammer hitting glass. He was pleased when Rosales, Bennett, and Nelson didn't object to his tagging along.

"Where to now, British Intelligence?"

Kendrick eyed the sarcastic Marine.

That, though, was the question. The team now understood how, when, and partially by whom the doctors had been taken—but they still had no idea where they might be. It was a big, big jungle out there. If they continued on foot they were exposed, and might stumble onto a poppy field, marijuana farm, or cocaine plantation if they went exploring. Even places like this village might deliver each a bullet if they didn't like their looks.

"I think we better head back to the vehicles," Kendrick said.

"Waste a time! Them twats got our mates!"

"Yeah, them twats got our mates!" Bennett chuckled.

Kendrick looked at Rosales and Nelson. He wanted everyone to have their say.

Nelson stepped forward. "Green Berets are the best strategists in the forces," he said. "I defer my vote to Rosales."

The men waited as the rain fell.

"Watch this," Nelson whispered to Kendrick.

Rosales bobbed her head. "Sirs, I think we should head back."

"No, lass!" cried Phinn.

"We'd lose a good four hours," Bennett frowned.

"Please, everyone gets to speak," Kendrick said.

Rosales continued. "I believe our best option is to return to the vehicles. We don't have any confirmed intel as to the doctor's direction. We're four days behind their capture and movement. If they went on foot, they're at least a day in one direction or another, and probably more. We could continue our hunt around these trails, but the rain and dangerous territory are against us. My guess is the assailants commandeered another vehicle after their transport was disabled by the river. And, if they did, it means they could be kilometers away in any direction." She motioned to the forest. "The five of us marching through these hills would never catch up to them, even if we did know their course. Returning to the vehicles also gives us transport, which equates to speed and directional opportunities we do not have on foot. We could return with both vehicles and scout a wider perimeter in far less time, including more of that route the semi-trucks were on, negating the hours we'd spend hiking back."

There was a silence. Even the rain trickled out.

"Fucking Spec Ops," Bennett smiled. "Best strategy, she's right."

"Plus, sirs," Rosales smirked. "It'll be lunch soon, and my map shows a cantina approximately ninety minutes north from our vehicle's location that serves barbeque."

"Oy!" Phinn's hand shot up. "I change me vote."

"Me too!" Bennett laughed.

Nelson nudged Kendrick, and both men grinned.

Rosales was one of the best assets Kendrick ever had the fortune of working with. Her field reasoning was rational, strategic, and impeccable. He secretly wished his country could steal her away from the American Forces. He'd once lost a mission to inflexibility—and Rosales would've seen the angles he'd missed.

On the other hand, Nelson had a keen understanding of team dynamics. Rosales had diplomacy training. But the trust Nelson placed in Rosales to persuade the others was unexpected. For Kendrick, self-reliance was so deeply entrenched that he would have never considered such a move. Hardened by a career that taught him to avoid things he couldn't predict or control. And it appeared he'd just received a remarkable lesson from the SEAL.

Joyner was right, these were good soldiers. Bennett, though, was still a mystery.

The four grabbed their gear.

Bennett stood for a moment, his grin faded, eyes tracing the jungle's edge.

CHAPTER
35

Clouds unleashed a relentless downpour as the unfortunate workers in the muddy pits began laboring once more.

Hannah stood alone, outside the adobe shack, struggling to locate Lorenzo. Below, more than a hundred dug, squatted, and sifted through the sludge—prisoners of Foster's endless quarry, mining for something she still didn't understand. Rain and shadow blurred one poor soul into the next.

She and Doctor Malum were not able to get the phone working. They'd lit a second candle, checked everything, but that amber glow never returned. Malum wandered outside before dusk, mumbling to himself, perhaps sensing the tears of disappointment she was holding back.

Alisha slept restlessly on the plywood exam table.

Hannah's heart ached for her friend. She returned to the shack's crates and carefully pulled out the dead phone.

She'd been stunned to hear that voice from the outside world—crackling through the speaker—until the connection went dead. The medical tape they'd used to mend its cracked shell had held, briefly. But now the device was worthless.

"Good morning," Foster said.

Startled, she fumbled with the phone. What would he do if he found her with it? Would they take her away like Dan, leaving Alisha all alone here?

She lobbed the device into a random crate, then stood to face her captor.

"I said, "good morning!"" Foster shouted.

Was the son of a bitch really expecting a greeting?

"Just looking for something for a headache," she lied, nervously placing both hands on her hips.

"Oh, allow me," he said.

He brushed past her to the collection of crates.

Her palms went sweaty. He'd find it for sure. She scanned the room for a weapon and spotted a box of metal stints above Foster's head. But would any of them be sharp enough to puncture skin?

Foster's rummaging stopped.

Hannah held her breath.

"Here you are."

He presented a bottle of aspirin.

She almost threw up.

"Breakfast is over. Did Malum not inform you?" He sniffed the air. "When the campfire rages, it's time for chow," he crooned oddly. "Anyway, I understand. First night settling and all. I brought these for you."

He handed her a square package of aluminum foil.

"Cast-iron cornbread. I make it myself now and again. A special treat for your first full day. Keeps the energy up!" Foster's left eye twitched slightly, almost imperceptibly, as he spoke. He blinked hard, as if clearing dirt from his eye.

She was starving. But this was so strange. This man holding them hostage in the middle of hell was bringing them… cornbread? She took the offering with caution.

Foster glanced toward the examination table. Alisha was now sitting, head down, wiping tears. His gaze returned to Hannah, but he spoke loud enough for Alisha to hear.

"Oh, and your friend is fine." Foster grinned, his cheek twitching. "He understands how he mustn't wander below. Not without proper escort. A night in the elements will do that. I'll send for his return later, so be sure to save him a piece." He pointed to the wrapped foil in her hand.

She nodded. Dan was okay, or so he said. While the gift of cornbread had confused her, maybe it meant something? Like ordering the wounding and not the killing of Lorenzo? Perhaps, despite Foster's brutality, he at least cared enough to make sure those here could work. It made some twisted sense that he was interested in their wellbeing and survival.

"If you need to leave for any reason, please wait for Doctor Malum to take you or send for me directly. Once you're more familiar with the landscape and the procedures, I will increase your movements." His hand trembled, curling into a fist. "Please, it's for your own safety."

Foster turned to leave as Malum slipped in, hands clasped behind his back, dipping slightly—like a peasant bowing before his king.

She pursed her lips.

When his majesty was out of sight, Malum's hands emerged, one clutching a small, frayed sack covered in dirt.

Hannah exhaled, her pulse still hammering. She couldn't keep playing this game—lying to Foster, praying for a signal, watching Alisha fade. They were trapped, and time was running out.

In front of her, the grubby Malum smiled and held out an empty palm.

"Phone?" he said.

"Wait a minute." She paced to the entryway and looked out at the rain. Foster was at the bottom of the hill chatting with one of his weapon-clutching cronies. His mannerisms were bizarre, moody. Maybe that was just his way?

She returned inside to Malum.

"Phone?" he asked again.

Cautiously, she reached into the same box she'd dropped the carton into before Foster surprised her. Her hand circled its interior, and she bent further. But it wasn't there! She yanked the cardboard box from the plastic shelf. Oh my God!

But Malum pointed.

Behind the crate, resting sideways against the wall, sat their busted phone.

She'd accidentally tossed the device behind the crate. That's why Foster didn't see it.

She reached over and handed it to Malum.

His shaking hand cradled its face.

"See?" he said.

He pressed a button on its side.

The phone came to life.

"Yes!" she cried, reaching to grab it.

"No," Malum said.

Before her eyes, the amber screen blinked off. No welcoming reset messages had time to form on the LCD screen.

She thought about this.

"Of course!" she shouted. The damn thing's battery had drained— just like her old cell when it died. It must've scavenged a faint spark overnight, enough for Malum to coax it alive for a heartbeat. And all they needed was… was power to recharge it.

Fuck.

She closed her eyes and shook her head.

Malum held up his dirty bag and beamed.

36

Inside the sack, Malum unfurled a set of black wires.

Hannah guessed he'd kept the bag somewhere on the grounds and had retrieved it last night.

He mumbled with excitement at the square electrical plug attached to the wiring.

"For the phone?" she asked.

Malum nodded. He slid each wire into his mouth and tore the plastic insulation with his teeth, exposing their silver cords. He removed the phone's battery and attached an end of bare wire to each terminal, and then applied tape to hold the connections.

"Great," she said. "Now, where the hell do we plug it in?"

Malum walked to the entry, and she followed.

"There." He pointed across the mine to the silver camper on the opposite hillside.

The one with lights at night.

Foster's trailer.

"Are you out of your fucking mind?"

The words burst out, raw, before she caught herself. He'd been a lifeline—shaky, strange, but vital. She touched his shoulder, softer now.

"I'm sorry, I didn't mean that," she said.

But Malum's smile remained.

"How?" she asked. "How can either of us get inside that place?"

"Me, sneak," Malum smirked and pointed again. "Sneaky-sneak."

This required thought. Should they even try it? What if Foster caught them? She had no idea what his routine was, and he entered and exited the trailer at varying times. How were they supposed to plan around that? And could she trust Doctor Malum with this critical task?

Behind her, Alisha stirred on the examination table. Despite Foster's words, Dan's return was still in question. Hannah would only believe it once she saw him with her own eyes.

But what would become of that child if she didn't reach the outside world? A coldness struck her. No, even though he'd aided in the phone's rebuild. No, even though he could walk the grounds unrestrained. No, because this was far too important a task to leave to the erratic doctor with trembling hands.

Fixing that phone meant rescue for Alisha and Dan and their unborn child.

"Please give them to me," she held out a hand.

Malum looked at her strangely.

"Please," she repeated.

He shrugged, handing her the battery, wires, and plug.

She stuffed the objects into a pocket of her cargo pants.

"Okay," his grin was now gone. He raised an open hand, with his fingers and thumb spread apart.

"You want me to wait?" she asked.

Malum shook his head.

"Five," he said.

"Five what?"

Malum pointed to his wrist.

"Five minutes?"

"Yes, yes."

"Charge for five minutes?"

Malum nodded vigorously.

"Why?"

"Hot," he said, tapping his temple.

Did he know something? She froze, eyeing the devices in her hand. "This plug—it's not compatible?"

Malum tilted his head, lips gnashing softly.

"It could fry the battery," she muttered.

Malum's five fingers shot up again.

How did he know? What if he was wrong and the battery melted—or exploded, like those horror stories in the news? She had no choice but to trust him. Five minutes—enough for a call to emergency services? Enough for a signal to reach out of this hellhole? A chill hit her. She'd hold the battery while it charged, feel for heat. No mistakes.

"Alright, five minutes."

Malum's gaze drifted to the foil package in the crate, sniffing its aroma.

Hannah tensed. He'd been here forever—months, years?—and might know if Foster's "gift" was laced with something. Poison? Drugs to keep them docile? She reached for it, then paused. If Malum ate and convulsed, she'd have her answer—but at what cost? She'd sworn no harm, even to him. It was best she be honest, and tell him where it came from, and gather his reaction.

"Would you like a piece?" she said. "Foster made it."

Malum nodded anxiously.

"Good," he said. "Very good."

Had he eaten it before? She opened the package, broke off a sizeable chunk, and put it into his shaky hand.

Malum nibbled an edge before taking a large bite.

"Yum." He chewed.

She hadn't eaten in more than a day and was so hungry her stomach ached. Gingerly she broke off a section for herself. Her eyes closed. The flavor was spectacular, and her taste buds exploded with delight.

"Tasty?" Malum asked, crumbs on his lips.

Foster's treat was so delicious that she had to remind herself he was the same asshole keeping them captive. She wanted to gobble all of it. But Alisha required nourishment, and Dan if he ever returned.

"Water." Malum's eyes flicked to the crate.

"The jug in the other room?"

He shook his head, sharp. "Danger. Poison."

She swallowed hard, the food souring in her gut. What was he saying?

CHAPTER
37

They marched onward through the jungle back to the vehicles. Phinn relayed a story concerning his country's football team that included the term "geez a gobble," which Kendrick was thankful the others did not ask him to translate.

Rosales cut in, changing the subject.

"Sir, I've been thinking about that hidden path and those semi-trucks."

"Yeah—and who's using it," Nelson added.

"What route?" Phinn asked.

Nelson flicked a twig off his sleeve, turned to Phinn and filled him in on the details.

"Near the dead bastard?"

Nelson nodded.

"And you're all coming to the conclusion that someone involved with that route took our three assets?" Kendrick said.

"I also think so," Bennett said. "No other real roads out here. That 4Runner takes a detour to dump a body, someone witnesses the deed. Seems probable."

"I think that, also, sir."

Nelson and Phinn agreed.

For the next few minutes, they trampled through the foliage in silence, until Kendrick's earlier tale stirred a question from Rosales.

"Sir." She turned, her voice sharp with purpose. "You said the Silk Road was a great network of routes. Like this one we're chasing now?"

"Yeah, what happened to it?" Nelson said.

Kendrick carved a path through the tangled undergrowth, boots sinking into the muck.

"One of the greatest empires in history couldn't hold its massive self together."

"Aye. Give me a mite. I needs to piss," Phinn said, wandering into a nearby bush.

The others stopped as Kendrick continued his story.

"In terms of connected land mass, Mongolia was the largest empire in history. Its kingdom controlled a quarter of the world's territory. But the Mongols were known for their viciousness."

"Viciousness?" Nelson fished out his canteen for a swig. "How brutal were they?"

"Brutal enough the Ming Dynasty finished the Great Wall of China to keep them out." Kendrick raised his brows. "Mongols were nomadic and took no prisoners."

"Sounds like the cartel." Bennett cracked his knuckles. "Same fucking playbook."

"Quite." Kendrick nodded. "You want to know why trade stayed safe on those ancient arteries? It's because the Mongols wiped out enemies with no mercy—and every trader knew this. And as Mongol territories grew to include most of the Silk Road's passages, it was the Mongols who appointed themselves as police to stabilize the entire route. Raiders and entire kingdoms were under severe threat of Mongol punishment and war if they didn't let travelers pass safely."

"But wait, couldn't the Mongols just steal everything from the traders?" Bennett said.

"It might've worked once or twice." Kendrick shrugged. "But trade would've stopped. And the empire was so vast, it had to protect the supply chain to survive."

"Makes me wonder who our Mongol is here," Nelson said.

"Yeah, somebody is policing this road." Bennett eyed the area.

"Safe passage for some, bullets for others." Nelson took another swig.

Rosales eyed Kendrick. "What killed the Silk Road, sir?"

"After Genghis Khan's death, infighting started. Greed and mistrust fractured the empire." A mosquito circled, and Kendrick slapped it off his neck with a curse. "The route fell apart—paving the way for the Ottoman rise."

"Did the Ottoman go to war with the Mongols?"

"No war was needed." Kendrick shook his head. "Just one chokehold on the Europe-Asia bridge did the trick. A narrow strip of land the Ottomans controlled—heavily taxing anything that moved through it."

"Constantinople," Rosales said.

"Right. That single maneuver sped the end of the longest trading route in history."

"That's too bad, sir," she said.

"Protection is why governments exist in the first place. People, commerce." Kendrick flashed a frown. "And while closing the Silk Road was unfortunate, trade was evolving—moving from land to sea. And it forced Spain to search for an entirely new route to India to avoid the Ottoman, changing our world forever."

Nelson whipped his head around. "Wait a damn minute. That's what sparked the–?"

Bennett frowned, rubbing his temple. "I don't understand."

A glint came to Kendrick's eyes and he nodded to Nelson.

Nelson cleared his throat. "The Ottoman Empire halted free access to the Silk Road. That cut off trading to the entire European continent. And those countries needed to find an alternate route around Constantinople to continue trading with Asia." He bobbed his head, chuckling. "And that's why Christopher Columbus set sail for the new world."

"No shit?" Bennett frowned. "I always thought he was just out for gold."

"Oh, he was. But the Spanish Empire backed him to avoid trading through Ottoman territory." Kendrick tilted his head. "Do they teach anything of value at those schools in your country?"

"Rarely." Bennett chuckled. "But I hear the new math is awesome."

Kendrick also laughed, sharing a rare moment with the fickle Marine.

"Of course!" Rosales said suddenly. "Protection—that's it."

"What?" Nelson said.

"The shells by the trucks, sirs."

"What of them?" Kendrick said.

Rosales fished a brass shell from her pocket and tapped it against her thumb. "I got it wrong—those weapons weren't shooting at the truck."

"They weren't?" Nelson said.

"The truck's holes—clean, no shrapnel." She rolled the .44 casing between her fingers, squinting at its base. "Headstamp says "two"—U.S.-made, hollow-point, 90% sure."

Phinn zipped up as he stepped from the bush. "Aye, that ammo's bloody everywhere."

"Right," Rosales said. "But hollow-points mushroom on impact. These holes didn't. We didn't see any shroom-shapes in the truck's metal, did we?"

"They could've missed," Nelson said.

"From fifteen feet away, sir?"

Nelson's jaw shifted side to side.

The team resumed their hike to a peak, where they sighted the SUVs in the distance. Kendrick thumbed at his eyewear again, his third attempt to reach Adler. Static hissed—too long a silence for a man who never missed a check-in.

Eyeing one of the spent shells in her hand, Rosales halted the team. "We saw clean piercings in that ambushed truck and all about the same size. Yet we have shotgun and handgun shells here, sirs, and I don't recall seeing any scattershot marks in that vehicle."

"What's the significance?"

"Cartels tend to stick to AK and AR rifles." She pursed her lips. "That's who I believe was shooting at the vehicle."

"Okay, but –" Kendrick uttered.

"And if my theory is correct, whoever spent these shells was protecting the truck, while the cartel was ambushing it." She returned the brass to her pocket.

"Interesting." Kendrick scratched his chin.

Nelson turned. "Hold up—didn't you say FARC was likely helping the cartel?"

"Several of FARC's guerrilla groups are rural farmers and landowners, sirs. Regular people fighting to keep their land from being taken over by those drug lords. Though FARC also has its fanatics, it's full-timers, as all groups do. And at first, I doubted those types are involved because, you're right, they're more likely to work with the local cartels." Rosales paused. "But that's what's got me puzzled, sirs. I think whoever's controlling these routes is using these hard-core types to protect their cargo."

"So fanatical FARC versus the local drug cartels?" Nelson said.

"Based on weapons evidence, sir, I'd say it's likely."

"Christ, we've walked into a damn warzone." Bennett gripped his weapon.

Nelson's brow furrowed. "Still doesn't explain who was riding on top of those rigs."

A heavy silence settled over the group.

Kendrick stiffened. That was a question he hadn't dared ask until now. Who had the money and power to turn FARC—a formidable guerrilla force—against the well-funded drug cartels?

CHAPTER
38

Four injured. One patient had a dislocated shoulder, but the other three bore marks of punishment from Foster's men—thugs enforcing his grip on this muddy camp. No gunshot wounds, though, which was a relief.

The three battered patients never spoke. Their eyes were glazed over like Lorenzo's when they arrived in the filthy shack.

All of them smelled horrible. The young man with the shoulder injury also had five or six missing teeth, but she couldn't determine if the damage was from disease or a rifle butt to the face.

When she tried to question him, he laughed, like Bandana. In fact, each of her questions was met by non-committal body language and a strange stare. His bony hands also trembled.

She patched each man as best she could. Alisha helped bandage a fractured wrist on one as Marko stood guard, smoking by the doorway. But as soon as the grubby riflemen collected his repaired workers, he left the shack without a word.

Smoke crept through the air. She'd rationed the last of the cornbread for herself and Alisha for this evening. Dan still hadn't returned, but she put his portion aside. She hoped the remainder would be enough for them because going down into that awful muddy place for food while Foster's men hovered with their guns was something she intended to avoid for as long as possible.

She broke out two pieces of cornbread. Alisha, tears finally stilled, took hers, cradling it in her palm. A faint, strange giggle escaped her.

Hannah turned.

"Elmo," Alisha chuckled. "He wanted to name our baby Elmo if it was a boy."

"What?" Hannah cracked a slow smile. "But that's a child's toy?"

"Yes, but apparently it's also a family name. A great uncle."

"What if you have a girl?"

"Oh darling," she wiped her cheek. "So far, I've talked him out of Morna, Teeka, and Kimber."

"Where the hell is he getting these names?"

"I have no idea, but I love that he's trying," she gave a small smile. "You know he wants to open a family practice when we get back to London?"

"That'll be wonderful."

Alisha nodded.

"Of course, if you name the kid after a Muppet, you'll need a therapist on staff."

Both women laughed. They talked a bit longer, and she could tell the exchange made Alisha feel better. A brief time later her exhausted friend retreated to the flimsy plywood table and fell asleep.

Outside, quiet yammering from those resting around the pits echoed. Near Foster's trailer, a fire roared at the east hill, and several men stood and chatted around the flames.

Hannah grabbed the phone battery and its sketchy charger and tucked them inside a pocket. At the open entry, she scanned the perimeter. Darkness in every direction but Foster's silver caravan. She inched into the open air, keeping in the shadows. Instead of descending the trail down the hill, she rounded a path to the rear of the shack and crept through the heavily overgrown hillside, keeping watch on Foster's distant fire and the men gathered around it.

She passed the halfway point between the shack and the trailer on the opposite side and continued her quiet trek until a large divot caught her foot.

Something tickled her leg. Many somethings. She looked down. Ants from the mound she'd stumbled over marched with fury up her ankles. Several breached her loose pant cuffs and clamped their tiny pinchers onto her flesh.

She held back a scream and bounded into a giant bush for cover, not realizing the shrubbery was hiding a steep slope. She tumbled down the hillside, clawing at the rushing ground until her spinning finally ended. She'd rolled about thirty feet.

Most of the ants had held on for the ride. Hannah slapped them off in a frenzy, scraping the last stragglers from her clothes. The itching hit hard. She clawed at the ground, mixing damp clay with puddle water to smear over the bites, soothing the sting.

She shook off the last of the ants. Fucking jungles. She checked her pockets. Both the battery and charger were still inside. She bear-crawled back up the hill, careful not to stick her face into that ravenous mound of army ants.

At the top of the slope a faint glow broke through as she scanned the area for any more insects or animals, then cautiously resumed her crouched walk toward Foster's trailer. She could hear the generator's loud motor pumping power to the muddy site's king and his mobile Shangri La, almost a hundred feet away. She crept closer. On the other side of the camper, men sipped and smoked their tequila and marijuana.

Carefully, she rounded the camper's backside. Seeing was difficult. No moonlight. No glow from the trailer's fire. Only blackness, except for the generator's gleaming green light.

She readied with a deep breath.

Cautious of making any noise, she soft stepped along the aluminum siding toward the smidgen of green. Her own team's generator at their last village had two external receptacles on its panel, in addition to the outgoing service cords. She moved forward, fishing out the battery and its charging cable from her pocket.

Fifteen feet away, the ground softened. She shuffled her steps to avoid slipping, should the sloppy ground challenge her balance.

Eleven feet. A rank smell grew, but she pressed onward, focusing on the generator's little green light of hope.

Five minutes. She would keep the battery in her hand. If it got too hot, she'd immediately pull the charger from the generator's receptacle.

After she made the call, this place would swarm with rescue teams, United Nations soldiers, and health aid groups within 24 hours. This satellite phone would save them—save every one of them.

Nine feet and closing.

She'd keep them on the line for as long as possible. The authorities would locate her using GPS and come swooping in with their Blackhawk helicopters. These crooks would be cuffed and carted off to prison for life plus 1,000 years. The workers and her team would all be freed.

But something happened. Something she'd only seen on television as a child—a sitcom or an old movie, she couldn't recall which. Though she knew it didn't exist in the real world. But now, she was experiencing the sensation, and the one word her mind could conjure up was… quicksand. Or, more rightly, quick mud.

She toppled forward. Her right leg plunged into the muck. An adrenal kick juiced her spine. She was being sucked in, and her foot couldn't feel the bottom. She grabbed for anything to stop from sinking into this bowl of disgusting slop.

The pit consumed both legs. A hinge attached to the trailer's underside came into focus. Desperate, she reached as far as she could with both hands and seized it. With all her strength, she tugged. The dirty bandage around her fingers slipped off and fell into the guck. But she held firm and extracted herself.

That's when her ungrateful brain became aware of the horrible smell, with the thick rottenness making her gag instantly. She'd unknowingly wandered into the trailer's open septic dump. Mercifully, the generator's strong hum covered her retching, but if she started coughing, those on the trailer's other side would hear her.

Once free, she stood, breathing through her mouth. The round hole was ten feet in diameter, fed from the underside of the trailer. She'd have to find a way to navigate around it, in the pitch dark, to reach that green light and plugin.

But when Hannah sunk a hand into her pocket, her blood ran cold.

Oh God, no! The phone's battery and charging cord were gone—sunk into that nauseating cavity.

"Ola, señora," a voice huffed behind her.

A dark figure emerged, swaying unsteadily next to the trailer. It was Marko.

JACK J. WYATT

Deceleration meant death—Lorenzo knew they would find him. The moon's broken shine hunted him, slicing his path with blades of unwanted light.

He sprinted over rocks and dirt, plunging into the vicious jungle where woody arms clawed at his flesh and thorny greens stabbed without mercy. Upward he fought—stumbling here, crawling there—his breathless body refusing surrender. He crested the first mound and gravity now favored his descent. He skated down a slope of loose soil, weaving past timber, vaulting shrubs. A sharp branch lashed at his chin. Blood welled, a sharp awakening.

There was only this. Racing ahead in the darkness. A broken pickaxe in one hand, a hammer's steel claw in the other. He'd attack, slaughter, whatever tried to stop him. Rage and fear powered his limbs.

Over the second hill, his foot snagged a root, and he pitched forward, tumbling over a craggy bluff. He struck the ground hard, pain flaring through his side in a white-hot jolt. No timeouts. He surged upright and charged on, legs shaking yet defiant. Night creatures scurried from his path as he tore through their jungle.

He emerged through a clearing on a cliff overlooking a river half a kilometer wide. He dove headfirst from the bluff, breaking the river's surface in a silent splash. The briny water stung the cuts and scrapes on his skin. Undeterred, he stroked—carving relentless arcs—legs thrashing with a fury that defied exhaustion.

He swam north, northwest maybe?

Down in the pits, those weeks ago, the sun had reached its height. A distant standing tree aligned as east. Foster's trailer was opposite to the west. That orientation provided his best guess toward that glow in the forest, and Jesus willing, someone who could help him.

On his back, he slowed his arms, kicking instead, swimming further from the cliff. The tools wedged at his hips dragged at his strokes, but he needed them to survive. To hunt. To fish. To reach that light. Otherwise, he'd have let them sink to the river's bottom.

Above, stars charted his wake to the river's promising side. The water's chill bolstered his will. He clawed the sand and lurched into a fresh sprint.

He'd endured so much, as did they all, for so long. Men huddled in the mud who cried themselves to sleep. Painfully, steadily, converting to obedience, like a belted native to a new God. Resigned to their fate in those pits of horror as rifled demons hovered over them.

The fact that he'd survived the pits at all was a miracle—adapting to the grueling labor and the brutal punishments for disobedience. When he and the others were first brought in and realized they'd never leave, the group split: some obeyed, moving like sleepwalkers through back-breaking tasks. Others resisted—and often disappeared.

But over time, even the obedient ones lost hope. In that hellish place, survival drained every last drop of will and identity.

A man without promise in his future carries a lifeless glaze in his eyes. Tormented beyond reason, stripped of morality, he becomes something else—savage, feral, no longer tethered to who he once was. In those desperate holes, civility dissolved, replaced by fear, hunger, and madness. They fought for scraps, for air, for the idea of themselves, long after the world forgot they existed.

He had no idea how far the city was, any city. He may not even be in the same country. Yet any place was better than what he'd just left behind. The others like him, he'd work to free as soon as he was able.

Towering mountains swallowed the moonlight. He scanned for the lonesome glow he'd seen those nights ago, but he needed to scale higher again to see it. Without that, he was lost in this dense prison of tangled wilderness.

He stole a glance at the stars, whispering his wish into the night. Isabella, please be safe.

202

CHAPTER
40

Marko stood at the rear of the trailer, blocking Hannah's path back to the shack. Behind her, the awful pit of shit she'd escaped.

He stepped closer.

"Why here?" He picked at something in his teeth. "You want Marko, yes?"

He was drunk or stoned or both. Whatever his poison, it must have dulled his senses to the point that he made no remark about her smelliness, something she could barely tolerate.

Moonlight hit his thick frame, sweat streaking his cheeks. Though, he wasn't carrying his usual weapon.

He flashed a nasty smile.

Hannah's stomach dropped. What could she do? She'd lost the battery and the charger. There was no way she'd reenter that crater of crap for the devices. But even if she could fashion a rod and netting from items back in the shack, the sludge had likely fried the device. The phone's critical core and power supply were gone, along with any chance of the cavalry swarming into these pits with combat choppers.

Marko fumbled with the front of his pants, coming closer.

Would the strange cornbread king rescue a woman caught behind his living quarters without any questions? Should she knock on Foster's trailer? Or would she be trading one maniac for the other?

Marko ambled forward.

Then an idea. She'd lure Marko in, grab his arm, and, with all her might, swing him into the trough of liquefied filth behind her. He might yell or scream, but she'd sprint as fast as she could back to the medical shack. Lord willing, he'd drown before he could tell anyone she'd been sneaking around Foster's kingdom.

"You pretty, woman," Marko grumbled.

She planted her feet in the slop.

Marko slid a hand over his potbelly and up his filthy shirt. He rubbed the left side of his eager chest.

Against everything inside of her, she reached forward. Marko's clammy hand took hers. Firmly, she pulled him into her body to test his weight.

He barely moved, and this scared her. She should've been able to yank him forward, but she'd misjudged his mass severely. There was no conceivable way to pull him in the pit. This plan would never work. Even if she locked onto his heavy frame somehow and skewed him off balance, she'd likely fall into the sludge herself along with Marko. And there was a good chance they'd either both drown in that brown goo, or he'd force himself on top of her trying to get out. She'd be dead either way.

"Here stinks," Marko said.

She looked past Marko at the hillside, the path she'd trekked to this trailer. An idea captured her. Could she? Did she have it in her? Without the help of rescue, things would only get worse if Foster found out she was sneaking around. He'd collected and punished Dan for the same offense. Hers was now a fight for survival.

"Yes," she said coolly. "It does smell here." She let go of his hand and flirtatiously moseyed past the large man. "We should go someplace where we can be alone."

"Mmm," Marko moaned, following close behind.

The two remained out of view from the others cavorting around the fire near Foster's camper. Marko stayed on her heels. He tried reaching for her hand again, but, thankfully, in the darkness, she'd caught sight of it in her periphery and sped her step, remaining inches from his sweaty paw's reach.

She led him down a slight incline.

His heavy feet marched faster.

Hannah, too, increased her speed but tried to do so playfully. She steered them around the next set of high shrubs, leading Marko the way she'd come. A faraway light flickered, which meant she was close.

Hannah skipped, teasingly tugging the bottom of her shirt, while moonlight beamed on her body.

Groans and grumbles came from the stumbling beast.

She found the spot, coyly turned, and put up a hand.

The intoxicated man halted.

She yanked off her shirt, tossing it to the ground. Her fingers seductively traced the underside of her sports bra, snaking down her tummy to her pant line, and slithered over her thighs.

The monster licked his lips.

She closed her eyes, swaying slowly, and unfastened the top of her khakis.

Marko's bellied shadow shuffled closer. "I take you now," he slurred.

Her thumbs hooked her pants, moonlight baring her skin.

Feet away, Marko growled in desire.

Her stare met his wanting eyes.

She retreated, bounding over the humming mound.

His boot cracked the earth—and the hive beneath it.

The mighty South American invaders marched up his body, engulfing his legs, rapidly overtaking his mid-section. A chaotic dance ensued. Marko staggered, slapping himself wildly. But the insects wouldn't relent, infesting his neck and face. The panicked man quaked, lost his balance and collapsed. His heavy body cracked the colony's underground fortress, bulldozing the nest, infuriating the venom-pricking parasites.

A shudder swept through her, not from cold, but from some deep, animal part that knew she'd crossed a line. She hadn't expected it to work this fast—or this violently. The ants had become her weapon, but watching them dismantle a man was something else entirely.

Hannah couldn't look away. The ant attack was savage. Payback for Phinn's murder and their kidnapping.

At her feet, she seized a heavy boulder, hoisting it with all her strength. She came as near to the infested man as she dared, enduring numerous stings herself. Her hands trembled. Not from pain—but from what she was about to become.

Marko's screams invited more ants inside his gaping mouth.

She heaved the massive stone forward, aiming for the center of Marko's stomach. The sickening crush drove all the air from his gut. Bones crunched.

The sound turned her stomach, but she couldn't stop. She slapped the insects attacking her legs, withdrawing farther from the attack zone.

Astonishingly, bug-covered Marko came to a knee. But the venom was too much, and hemotoxins overwhelmed his circulatory system.

He convulsed and dropped to the dirt.

Hannah watched for any movement, but none came.

Her body pulsed with adrenaline. She'd just led a man to a death no animal deserved. Marko had tortured and killed, yes—but what she'd done wasn't clean. It wasn't justice. It was survival. And it had changed something inside her—something she didn't yet recognize but knew would never come back.

She tried to collect herself. She'd need to make more clay paste, cover the fresh bites on her legs. But first she had to get back to the shack before anyone found her here. She turned toward the hillside but stopped.

A laugh erupted from a nearby bush.

Beyond the ant-riddled corpse, Foster glared, Bandana at his side.

CHAPTER
41

"I'd thought my rules were understood by each of you?" Foster said.

Bandana grappled Hannah's mane. Her hands locked around his to control the yank on her hair.

"I suggest you don't lose your footing," Foster crooned. "As my partner will maintain his hold."

Marko's corpse, infested with insects, was unrecognizable.

They dragged her in the direction of the trailer, veering past the small fire. Foster led them down a hill she'd never seen before.

His tone came icy. "There are no steps here, so please, as I've said, maintain your balance." He side-stepped down the embankment. "I'm sure you're curious as to where we took your friend?"

Bandana giggled.

"All I asked of you and your colleagues was that you follow the rules. Rules I patiently explained."

They slid down the earthy incline. The cinch on her hair never loosened.

Below, faint voices moaned.

Bandana's clumsy feet trampled hers when she didn't move quick enough.

At the bottom, barren, unlit terrain. A wasteland where troublemakers rotted. In the distance were the three men she and

Alisha had patched up earlier that day. Each chained by the ankle to a stake in the ground. Eight men, staked like beasts.

Then a familiar face. Dan. He sat, shoulders slumped, staring at the ground, unaware. She wanted to run to him. But Bandana's hand clung to her hair.

"Now, for your breach, it has become necessary to reeducate you on those policies. You may wish to know how long I will keep you here but that I won't divulge. Besides, I must replace my trusted guard with another, which will take some time and training. I'll begin calculating your sentence once the camp is fully staffed again and not before. That is my priority."

Most of her torso was exposed, but the sports bra held snug. Her soiled pants had fallen below her hips.

"This way," Foster pointed.

They pulled her to a vacant space away from the others. A long steel rod stuck up from the soil with a rusty chain and open clamp.

"Please try to keep this clean," Foster said.

He ratcheted the clamp around her ankle, and Bandana finally let go of her hair.

"If the locking mechanism gets too much dirt inside, it does not operate when we return for release. Then we'll have to cut, and I'm not talking about the iron cuff."

Bandana delivered a cynical high laugh.

"This is your new home. You will sleep, eat, and everything else while fastened."

Her terrified eyes met his.

"We have two guards roaming this area. It would be wise to keep them on your side, for they are your only protection from anything which may come to feast on you out here."

She looked down at her feet. One shackled. A steel chain bound to a rod pounded in the ground.

"It is also wise to keep your voice down. Screams and such can rile up the others, and your protectors with the guns don't like it much. Disregard this warning, and we'll have to give you something to calm your nerves. A special cocktail of the opiate variety, supplied by our friends out here, served up in a syringe."

Motherfucker. That's how he did it. Injecting the "troublemakers" with narcotics, sending them into a stupor. And poor Lorenzo—they'd put a bullet into the unlucky kid to break up the brawl and jabbed him. That's why the awful medical shack had no analgesics. Foster could administer the perfect painkiller at any time.

"You might try asking your friend about its effects when he comes around again."

Dan sat thirty feet away, head slumped.

There had to be a way out of this. How deep was the stake? Could her lingering strength pry it loose?

"Unfortunately, you lost your top," Foster said. "The spraying of kerosene down here is sporadic, as we ration the chemicals to protect our productive workers on the other side from mosquitoes." He pointed up the hill.

Something flew into her hair and crawled up the side of her skull. She smacked her head. The creature buzzed off.

"Pity, that."

A smiling Bandana nodded.

"Otherwise, please enjoy the fresh air and think on what I've said."

She eyed the stake which held her chain.

Foster halted, and then spun around and met her eyes.

"Before I forget, if you're planning to brew some form of lubricant to slip that brace off, or, cut your chain using a blow torch hidden in your back pocket, or maybe work that steel rod from the ground? Please don't. I can assure you it's exceptionally durable, and the shaft it's welded to goes down for three meters. If my guards catch you monkeying with it, I'll have no choice but to prick your skin with my needle." He pointed up the hill. "Yet should you execute a miracle escape, I'll simply have your pregnant friend take your place. Deal?"

The iron apparatus around her ankle was clamped tight. Even at the chain's full length, she could tell it wouldn't allow one staked prisoner to reach another. Outside this desolate valley was total darkness, and the circle she could roam contained nothing but sand and small pebbles.

Hannah dropped her chin and gave a weak nod.

"Very good, have a pleasant night."

Bandana and Foster made their way up the hill, toward the glow over the mountain.

Once out of earshot, she signaled to Dan.

No response.

"Dan?"

Her friend, someone she'd spent the last ten months traveling with from village to village, who she'd come to admire and love as close as anyone in her life, sluggishly raised his head.

The night sky's faint light struck the side of his face, and drool leaked from his mouth.

She stared at her friend, or what was left of him. Her breath caught—not from fear, but sorrow. All her training, all her strength, and still she was chained here like an animal. Every part of her ached to scream.

But it wouldn't save them.

CHAPTER
42

Creatures shrieked from the tops of trees. Lorenzo bounded through the undergrowth, penetrated a clearing, and came upon a stream. A slice of cloudless sky exposed the shimmering ripples.

He held, catching his breath. A few minutes of rest but no more. Anything could strike in these wilds, especially the two-legged predators—if he stumbled into their drug territory.

An eager frog readied to catch a meal in the running stream. A tiny pill bug skated across the creek's surface, and he hopped into the water, lassoing it with his tongue. Polluted waters did not attract insects. The frog's meal was a good sign.

Lorenzo shifted, the busted hammer and pickaxe jabbing his waistband. He crouched, plunging cupped hands into the cold creek. Runoff from higher elevation, it was pure and unpolluted. He gulped a mouthful, then another—unsure when he might find more to quench his thirst.

High in the sky, a dim silvery light blinked and moved. An aircraft—heading toward the north star.

Lorenzo slurped. He'd traveled the same course since escaping the pits. He was, indeed, headed in the right direction.

Keeping his eyes skyward, he drank a final scoop from the stream, aligning the airliner's path to a patch of stars.

At his feet, the frog returned to its rocky perch, no doubt waiting for a second helping to float by.

Lorenzo rose from his squat.

"Estar bien, mi amigo," he said.

The frog croaked.

Lorenzo jogged away from the stream into the dark forest. Guided by a string of stars, he sensed something, but his mind, shattered by months in those muddy quarries, buzzed like a frayed wire at every shadow. Every rustle, every snap could be danger or nothing—his ravaged nerves couldn't tell.

Death had haunted him—bodies in the ravine, men wasting away beside him—twisting his gut and blurring pain into peril. His escape had been fueled by euphoria, but now terror surged again, the pits still clawing at his soul. Would it ever fade? Or would anxiety flood his mind forever? Would he ever know inner peace again?

An eerie quiet surrounded him. Something was wrong. Where were the birds? The macaws, the cries for mates?

Above, a faint rustle, too deliberate to be the wind.

The jaguar sprang from a tree, bounding to the ground.

Lorenzo broke into a sprint. Strong climbers, deadly claws and teeth—the jaguar could crush his skull with its massive jaws.

Dashing at full speed, the animal was gaining on him.

In the distance, a pair of large trees. If he ran straight for them he might have a chance. Flat out, with every ounce of strength inside of him, he sprinted.

One small stumble could kill him.

The pickaxe tumbled from his waistband, clattering into the undergrowth.

Four paws pounded, the force vibrating in his skinny chest, readying to strike.

He struggled for speed—one chance to save himself, and it had to be enough.

The creature closed in behind him. In a few more strides, it would pounce.

Lorenzo dove between the trees, latching an arm to one, swinging himself around. The pull tore at his shoulder, but he held.

The jaguar leaped, raking its claw down his spine as it soared by.

Lorenzo staggered, wrestled the busted hammer from his waistband, clutching its jagged edge.

The feline turned, roaring in his direction.

Lorenzo raised his arms with a wild shout, but the animal crept forward.

His heart pounded—blood oozed from his bicep, the gunshot wound split wide without its bandage, a hot sting flaring across his back, unnoticed in the chaos.

The jaguar's growl rumbled through the earth.

Fight or be eaten.

Gripping the metal, he timed the jaguar's pounce, breaths quickening.

The big cat sprang, jaws gaping.

Lorenzo swung down as hard as he could, striking the nose square with the hammer.

The jaguar stumbled.

Lorenzo pounced again, smacking the crown of its skull.

The big cat collapsed in a daze.

Lorenzo sped up the hillside, blood pulsing as the jaguar rose, eyelids fluttering. The bewildered cat staggered into the forest, its limp swallowed by the jungle's hum.

"Lo siento, mi amigo," Lorenzo whispered.

He was not the jaguar's enemy, but their paths had crossed. He continued up the hill, the north star blazing above, urging him onward. His breath slowed. The stench of blood clung to him. Alone on the slope, beneath a blanket of stars, he realized his hands were still trembling.

He wasn't sure if it was fear… or relief.

CHAPTER
43

They would die here.

Hannah had counted the chain's links for an hour—seventy-nine, roughly six feet—useless data that wouldn't free her. The welded rod didn't budge, not even when she kicked it.

"Dan!" she whispered firmly.

This time he turned to her.

"Dan?"

He wiped his chin.

"Can you hear me?"

Dan's head bobbed, and Hannah breathed a sigh.

"Are you okay?"

He nodded again, slow.

"What'd they do to you?"

His arm raised slowly, and with his other hand, he pointed to the muscle in his forearm.

Hannah could make out the tiny round punctures and bruises even in the moonlight. Foster's men had indeed drugged him. They hadn't used a vein—just sunk the needle into muscle for a slow opioid drip, not the lightning-fast kick most addicts craved. The injections kept him in the same stupor she'd seen in the others. Saucer eyes, dissociation, sluggish behavior.

"Dan, I'm sorry," she offered.

He dropped his arm, and his chest rose and fell. "Alisha?" he said weakly.

"She's okay, still in that shack, but okay. She misses you horribly." She bit back the rest. "We have to find a way out of here."

He shook his head.

"We have to. We'll die if we don't." But, as the words left her mouth, despair swept through her. The battery was gone, the satellite phone useless. She'd never hear from the outside world again. No one would ever know they'd been taken here, and there'd be no rescue.

Marko's screams, ants swarming him, flashed fresh in her mind. A vicious end she couldn't unsee. What had she become? Had this dreadful, demented place ruined her soul? How had she become someone who could do that—even to a monster like Marko? No, no, it couldn't be real. But the awful truth was this place had turned her into a killer.

She couldn't share any of this with Dan or anyone. There was no point. Admitting her failure with the phone or Marko's murder aloud would only further the hopelessness and guilt.

Stroking the iron clamp around her ankle, she sobbed silently.

Dan stirred next to her.

"Their food, no good."

"What?" she sniveled.

His breathing was slow, difficult.

"The baby," he managed.

"Alisha, your child?"

"The mining," he wheezed. "The barrels."

A strange gloom overtook Dan's face.

"Using mercury."

"Mercury?" Hannah sniffled.

"Rocks." Dan cleared his throat. "They're cleaning with it."

Hannah had forgotten about the reddish-yellow clump he'd handed to her before they'd taken him down here.

"But it's poison," she recoiled. Mercury—an invisible, insidious metal—had saturated this place. Its vapor clung to skin, burrowed into organs, and dismantled the nervous system one trembling nerve at a time. Speech warped, thoughts frayed. And then she remembered—Malum. The tremor in his hands, the disjointed way he spoke. His deterioration hadn't been just stress or trauma. It was mercury. He was poisoned.

It explained everything.

His cryptic warnings, his sudden bouts of confusion—he wasn't just unraveling emotionally. His body was losing its fight.

The toxin coursed through his bloodstream now, winding through his organs, tightening its grip on his mind.

And if it had gotten to him… how many others had breathed it in? Drank it? Absorbed it through their skin?

Dear God—Alisha was still up there. Alone. Exposed.

Hannah's body shook. Their meals and anything they drank were riddled with the stuff. Poor Dan had likely consumed the poison since they'd leashed him down here among the others. The toxins in his body were probably already at dangerous levels.

Hannah's fingers trembled. She reached again for the metal clamp bracing her ankle. Alisha was isolated, the phone was gone, and she and Dan were shackled like animals.

Fresh tears trickled down her cheeks.

Bats shrieked overhead, wings slicing the dark.

They would die here—all of them.

CHAPTER
44

Lorenzo clawed his way up the rainy hillside, every muscle in his battered body shrieking in protest. Dawn loomed on the horizon, threatening to snuff out the stars that had steered him through the night.

The jaguar—his flailing strikes had stunned the beast, its yellow eyes flashing in the dark—but the predator wouldn't stay down long.

Rain pounded around him. He prayed the water would wash away his scent before the big cat found him.

The slope rose endlessly, steep and treacherous, its mud sucking at his hands and knees. His chest burned with each ragged breath, the air thick with humidity and the bitterness of blood.

The gash on his bicep wept red, the warm trickle mixing with the rain as it slid down his arm. Infection was a silent killer here, as lethal as the jaguar's jaws, festering in the damp heat.

Thirty meters from the mesa's peak, hunger gnawed at his core. A sharp, hollow ache. Months in the pits starved, shriveling his muscles, stripping away the man he'd been. He knew if he stayed in those pits any longer he'd never have the strength for escape.

He paused, chest heaving, forehead pressed to the muck. Every instinct told him to stop—but stopping was death.

Their food. Heat killed bacteria—but the communal jugs of water in the hellish quarry repulsed him. He couldn't trust water touched by others, teeming with unseen filth. Instead, at night, he sought out a clean spring, sipping only what he knew was pure. That caution paid off. While the others in those pits drank from the tainted jugs and lost their minds to poison, his stayed sharp.

That sharpness was fading now.

With ten meters left to reach the hilltop, dizziness crashed over him. His legs wobbled, threatening to give out. He clawed the mud, hauling himself upward. The jungle wouldn't claim him. Not yet.

A sudden jolt ripped through his spine, electric and cruel. He dropped flat, like a felled tree, his face smashing into the ground. Mud clogged his mouth with a bitter grit. His limbs went numb, his racing heart felt like it might explode. He gasped for air.

He couldn't see. Couldn't think. Just the roar of blood and the slap of rain.

Rain pounded the earth. He could not die here—he could not leave her. The wind lashed his bare back, and he crawled forward on his belly, driven by his own agony.

The ground leveled. He crested the mesa.

Heaving, trembling, he forced himself upright.

A deafening rumble rolled through the clouds, and a flash cleaved the sky. Beyond the trees, a flicker—steady, warm—a light. One, maybe two kilometers away.

Civilization. Or something close enough.

The downpour softened. He caught his breath. His strength was gone—nothing left but sheer will now. He eyed the steep trail below, rocky, winding downward. It would take everything he had.

Behind him, thudding paws slammed the ground.

Panic surged, wild and sharp.

He bolted down the narrow path, feet pounding. Rain and sweat blinded him, ribs throbbing from the ascent. The trail steepened, slick with mud. He skidded, breaking into a frantic, uncontrollable sprint. The slope pitched sharper still.

Branches clawed at his skin. Gravity took over.

He lost his footing, tumbling into chaos.

He rolled, clawing at the mud. Twigs whipped his face, rocks stabbed his sides. Hurling downward, he pitched over a cliff, reeling sidewise, crashing hard to the ground.

Pain exploded, white-hot.

His scream caught in his throat—lungs crushed by pain and panic. He gasped, rain prattling around him.

A low hum shook the ground.

Lorenzo's eyes fluttered shut, the void of darkness swallowing him whole as the vibration drew closer.

CHAPTER
45

The team dedicated the afternoon to scouting the camp's outskirts, investigating the few trails that wound through the mountains and valleys. The majority of the trails were too narrow for the Rover and Yukon, so Nelson instructed them to patrol on foot, cautioning everyone to stay close together.

Regrettably, Kendrick found himself paired with Bennett once more.

"Don't see shit here," Bennett said. "What about you, British Intelligence? Any intel you want to share?"

As the sun dipped below the horizon, the promising cantina and its barbecue were already closed, forcing them to settle for a bland MRE from Rosales's backpack. Kendrick's mood soured.

"Do you and I have an issue?" he glared Bennett's way.

The Marine stopped, stretched his back, and gazed at the encroaching twilight.

"Known people like you. Dealt with them my entire career." He drank from his bottle. "Ask how many I trust."

"Earning trust is–" Kendrick began, then wished he hadn't.

"First," Bennett interrupted. "We came up differently. I didn't get to go to college. Paid my dues in mud and blood and worked my ass off to become a pilot. Nobody slapped bars on my shoulder because of some ass-down degree."

Kendrick's education was piecemeal, and despite spending most of his life as a field operative, he had climbed the ranks through grit and determination. Still, he allowed Bennett to vent.

"Yet my entire career, I took orders from clean-handed college idiots. And when I finally move up the ranks, it's the "intelligence" chumps calling the shots. And they're the worst of the bunch. Screwing with the regimes of countries in the name of democracy or freedom, or what-the-shit-ever. Doesn't matter if you come from the U.S. or the U.K., arrogant assholes in your branch are why soldiers are driven into battle in the first place." Bennett jeered. "Bullshit Iraq "weapons of mass destruction," convincing us to train those drugged-out buffoons in Afghanistan to fight the Taliban—when we should be arming the women. They've got the most to lose. But you over educated know-it-alls won't listen and put agency and politics before country. Pumping out blackhole intelligence with no goddamn accountability. Distorting facts to feed shadow agendas that put good soldiers in harm's way. And it's criminal."

"I can assure you my role has never–"

"Man, I need to know I can rely on you when shit lights up," Bennett shook his head. "You may know everything, you might even be a nice guy, but I question whether you're a real soldier. That's my issue."

The Marine's anger wasn't misplaced. Kendrick's agency had taken similar, questionable actions in the past as those of its American counterpart. But Kendrick had never once fed any administration unverified or agenda-driven intelligence. Quite the opposite. As an expediter, he had an extraordinary ability to uncover the truth no matter how deep it went or who the information implicated. It was his gift, but one that had put him at serious odds with his command in the past.

Perhaps he'd have a chance to explain this to Bennett at some point. But would further discussion do any good? The Marine's frustration ran deep.

They trekked quietly until Rosales, Phinn, and Nelson came into view over the adjacent ridge.

Bennett sealed his bottle and quickened his step.

Kendrick trailed behind, keeping some space.

The group made their way back to the vehicles. Lost in thought, Kendrick was jolted by a chime in his earpiece, pulling him away from his reflections on Bennett.

"Second Lieutenant Adler, sir,"

"Good to hear from you," he said. "I tried contact earlier."

"Sir, I'm not certain how to explain what's going on here. There's a lot of hush, and the Brigadier hasn't checked in today. He's unreachable, which is unusual. I did hear some chatter about mobilizing medical teams, but no mass casualty event was reported. It could be a drill, but security at the base is remarkably tight. It took hours for me to get through."

"Understood. My team remains committed as of last. But if you're calling to change–"

"No, no sir, nothing like that. I may have some data. Uh, but I'm not officially authorized to relay because of chain of command."

"I'd argue your observation of unusual activity may be enough to supersede such directives at the moment?"

Adler paused.

Kendrick then realized the dilemma.

"Second lieutenant, I order you to divulge whatever information is in your possession that may aid our operations."

"Thank you, sir. On your orders, then, I must relay."

"Good lad."

"Sir, I need to bring images up on your eyewear's screen. It may impact your visual field, which might affect your movement. I need you to stand still if possible?"

Kendrick halted the others. They were within sight of their vehicles, and Rosales looked at him quizzically. Bennett, Nelson, and Phinn were engaged in conversation about where the team should search next given that nighttime had rolled in.

"We're in fairly quiet territory. Go ahead with the intel."

"Yes, sir, good." Adler's clicking trickled into his ears.

Seconds later floating boxes materialized in his eyewear's visual field, a two-dimensional topographical rendering of the Colombian jungle on the right. On the left, a series of numbers, dates, and times.

"Sir, we're at plus four."

"Yes, I've seen this map, and–"

"Sir, there's been a development."

"A development?"

"Well, sir, I scanned for RF in the vicinity, but then I recalled how rogue actors in the area tend to blast static and other EI noise to jam communications and shroud their movements. But for some reason, the noise in the region flutters at about five gigahertz."

Kendrick rubbed the bridge of his nose.

"So, I set a wide array to pick up everything in both the upper and lower L-bands, all the way up to infrared. A broader net. And when any signal popped up, I sent the hits through the big box using this quick subroutine I cooked up–"

"Adler?"

"Yes, sir?"

"Cease the chinwag?"

"Sorry, right." He cleared his throat. "Now it was only visible for a few seconds, but I've triple, and quadruple checked and..."

"Adler?"

"Sir," he said. "They turned their satellite phone on."

Kendrick's arms shot into the air.

The conversation between the others stopped.

"Where? Tell me you have a location."

"Sir, while the signal is positive, there remains a problem."

"Problem?"

"Watch your map, sir."

At last, a solid clue. The signal meant either the hostages' location or the location of those who took them. He longed for the former.

"There you are, major," Adler said.

Kendrick's eyes tried to string together the yellow specks on his eyewear's map. But the location was unclear.

"Broaden the map for me, would you?"

"Sir, I need to explain. The jamming equipment they use down there does funny things to GPS, even at this high frequency. Where a clear line of sight can home into a square meter, this equipment's EI clogging saturates the signal to a five-kilometer radius. Makes a mess out of the waves, really. The Chinese do the same thing, and–"

"Adler?"

"Yes, sir."

"Please broaden the map's area?"

Each enlargement took several seconds to render. Once the Gulf of Mexico came into view, Kendrick said, "Stop there."

"Yes, sir."

"Fuck all," Kendrick muttered aloud.

The others fell in around him.

"Sir, I've done my level best to clean up the signal. Yet I'm only able to lock it down to this saturated spread, which is more of a perimeter, really. I've even tried–"

"Adler?"

"Sir?"

"How certain are you this was the signal from their phone?"

Adler cleared his throat. "One hundred percent, sir. I've cross-referenced the terrain to roadways and small villages but found none. Then I overlayed satellite photos from the past three years. I'm afraid we don't have many because it's a remote region of no real value. Yet, I did find large vehicles moving in and out from the zone on unmarked routes but could not follow them to any solid destination. It's mountainous, tree-covered terrain."

Everyplace out here was, and the position on the screen was an easy one hundred kilometers away from their current spot. Kendrick rechecked the topography on Adler's map one more time, closed his eyes, and inhaled deep.

"This changes things," he said.

Adler's inability to pinpoint the signal was one concern, but of most worry was the boundary line on the map. If Adler's calculations were correct, and he had no reason to doubt them, it meant one thing: in the lengthy list of unfriendlies, cartel crazies, lawless bandits, and utter parasites infecting this dangerous countryside, their three assets—the doctors—had been hauled deep into a country at literal war with itself.

"Sir, they've been taken into Venezuela."

Kendrick exhaled. "Yes, Adler. I can see that."

CHAPTER
46

Heavy clouds masked the half-moon overhead. Rosales switched on her vest's red light, and the team gathered between the Rover and Yukon.

They debated whether Phinn should take a vehicle and head to a hospital due east of their location for further treatment. Phinn, though, defended his health with several colorful sentences, concluding the argument by grabbing a rifle from the Range Rover, dropping out the magazine, checking the chamber, reloading it, and uttering, "Aen no gowk. Can handle me self!"

"I love that guy," Bennett chuckled.

"Good. The two of you and Nelson can ride together. Rosales and I will take the Rover."

Adler sent a series of images to each of their eyewears. The satellite's high-resolution digital pics allowed the flexibility to view the overhead countryside and expand the lower detail to find a route to their target.

Bennett shared his eyewear with Phinn. The Scot was shocked with the technology but not as surprised as the AI was with his accent. Phinn attempted the commands he'd overheard, but his thick Scottish accent left the AI bewildered. Angry, he shouted commands in his native tongue, telling the AI what he thought of its mother.

It took Rosales and the Marine a solid minute to clear the multiple screens Phinn had inadvertently activated.

"They only sent four pairs, sir," Rosales said.

"Probably a good thing," Bennett winked.

Kendrick stepped forward, calling their attention.

"Alright, we need to prep for the country we're about to enter," he gestured around the area. "In Colombia, we were dealing with farmers and at least one random cartel envoy."

"Crossed paths with the cartel?" Phinn asked.

"More of a welcome committee who dotted up the Rover," Bennett said.

"You's got fuckin shot at?"

Kendrick eyed the two men. "Now, we have a whole new set of dangers. Venezuela is a volatile nation. Its current leader is ruling the cities using his armed forces, which many of his citizens are staunchly against. Remember, Venezuelans went from what many considered a socialist utopia to a military dictatorship in a matter of months after their economy collapsed. In their hills, we won't encounter the military, but we may cross paths with more bandits, likely better-armed, and roaming hostiles. This includes cartel protecting their lands and their product."

The others listened intently.

"Our mission is to locate and extract our three physicians—and to do so with as little interaction with others as possible. That means do not shoot unless lives are in danger. In fact, we should remain out of sight and undetected if possible. Our armed presence in that country is a violation of Venezuelan sovereignty and will be considered a measure of aggression by our respective countries and an act of war."

He studied their faces before continuing.

"Hide all identification. No passports, licenses, credit cards, or photos. Nothing that ties us to our homeland."

Rosales tore something from her neck. Phinn removed his wallet and stuffed it deep inside a seat cushion in the Yukon. Nelson flung his cell phone into the truck, and Bennett simply nodded.

"If you're captured, Maduro's men will parade you as a trophy in the media. If you are not killed, you will be convicted at trial, period. There is no guarantee any government agency will ever come to retrieve us. We are here to rescue these three civilians, and nobody is backing us up. There are too many political dominos waiting to fall if any outside force attempts our retrieval. Keep your heads low and fingers off those triggers because any firing will expose us all."

Kendrick looked at Phinn.

"Unloading and loading is one thing."

"Aye. Had me a cousin across the splash. Spent me summers plugin targets. A'can work the bullets from this bastard." He gripped the rifle's butt-end with one hand and the barrel with the other. "But I'll keep'r tame less the others start eruptin."

Kendrick looked at Bennett, who bobbed his head.

"Alright, the first obstacle is the border," Kendrick said.

"Sir, all the main crossings are heavily guarded. Our best chance at entry is to follow unmarked routes through the mountainside, stay ourselves north of Cerro Pintado."

"Shit tough country," Phinn uttered.

"We'll punch through it," Nelson said. "We have to."

"We'll take as direct a route as we can but avoid all main thoroughfares. We've got over a hundred kilometers to travel before we get to the site of where their signal went off."

"Sir, how large is this grid?"

"We have a radial perimeter, it's not the best, but my command is certain it's where their signal pinged."

"How big's the area?" Bennett repeated Rosales's question.

"Five," Kendrick began.

"Five-hundred meters? It'll take some time but–"

"Five kilometers," Kendrick said.

Bennett's head shook.

"I know it seems impossible, but we track. Look for vehicle prints and other signs. Hunt the area."

"Three-mile circle, a hell of a challenge." Bennett flexed his cheek muscles.

Rosales and Nelson nodded.

"Protect and hide the vehicles. They're our only transport."

Bennett regarded Phinn for a moment.

"You know, even for experienced infantry, these obstacles are pretty hairy."

"Oy, Merican, eye me daft again, and I'll shoot ya," Phinn grumbled.

"Alrighty, then." Bennett smirked.

Phinn headed for the Yukon's wheeled side. "Let's get da fuck on with it."

Bennett chuckled. "Guess he's driving."

Nelson followed both men to the SUV.

A sudden downpour intensified.

Both engines revved up, and the Range Rover raced behind Phinn, Nelson, and Bennett in the Yukon.

CHAPTER
47

Despite fresh bedding, sleep escaped Foster. Recent unsettling events gnawed at him like vermin. He lay awake in the trailer, the night humidity suffocating.

His men reported a missing worker that day—another fool lost to the jungle. Soon, buzzards would circle, their lazy spirals marking another corpse in the wilds below. He sneered. The stupid savages in those pits never learned, he was the only thing keeping them alive out here.

But his new arrivals left him puzzled. How had a nothing-sized woman taken down one of his biggest men? Unplausible, or was he missing something?

He rose from the bunk, filled a cup from the tarnished urn, and dipped a teabag. A jolt stabbed his neck, buckling his knees. Scalding tea splashed his hand. He cursed, steadying his pour.

Years in these jungled shitholes had taken their toll—poor circulation—an ill reward for all he'd done. It took a special breed of man to squeeze riches from this wasteland, and if health was the price then so be it.

He shuffled to the trailer's filthy window. Eight of his twelve guards lounged by a fire. Their coarse laughter mixed with liquor and marijuana scents. He watched them, tools dulled by drugs and drink.

But these goods were sourced by Marko and his grubby Datsun-driving contact. What would happen when they ran out? Would the men turn on him? Did they have the courage?

He and Marko were not friends. The fat man fetched liquor, teas, and opiates to keep the workers docile. Marko's loyalty was bought, not earned. Now gone, replacing him would be a hassle.

Foster peered out at their fire. He didn't speak the guards' rough tongue—a language beneath him. But he'd need a replacement soon.

He sipped his tea. Bitter—the jungle's stench tainted even the finest blends.

His mind drifted to the unshirted woman chained down in the gully. Marko, three times her size, fell into her trap. Was Marko that easy a target? Or, was she trained in such techniques?

He swished his tongue. Yuri's hand was in this—had he sent her? A ploy, a bid to seize this place and cut him out?

Yuri had killed Diego, seizing the routes with precision. Was his next move sending these three physicians here as spies?

Foster winced, slamming his cup down on the counter. "That fucking Russian," he growled.

Yuri thought himself clever, but he'd outmaneuver him.

The woman who killed Marko was a professional—Yuri's pick, unsuspected because of her sex. Chaining her had been smart. He'd underestimated her once. Not again.

Catching the male physician roaming should've warned him—scouting the mine, tracking rounds, probing weaknesses. The man's excuses were too smooth.

The chained woman planned her capture, sparing Marko to escort her spies. It was a ruse to find his hidden mines. She played it well, but he saw through her now.

A darker idea hit: kill them now? End the threat fast?

He poured water into the urn, warmed it, and refilled his cup. No, he'd break them first. The round-bellied woman—pregnant, or a ruse? If real, it was leverage.

Inside his trailer, he checked the electronic panel. The device hummed, jamming signals. Yuri's trackers were useless. He smirked. Something was finally working.

"I'll be ready," Foster muttered, voice thick with disdain.

He drained his tea, vision sharpening. He'd need his wits to beat Yuri—and he would. These pits were his, and no Russian would take them.

JACK J. WYATT

CHAPTER
48

They avoided the truck routes. Whatever was being stripped from these lands had cartels warring with FARC, heavy weapons in play, numbers unknown. Stumbling into that crossfire would be a nightmare. Instead, their two vehicles rumbled east through a muddy track, cutting across the mountain into thicker rainforest.

The path twisted, narrowing one moment, widening the next. Enormous leaves and branches slapped the SUV's frame, then fell away, the moon breaking through before the jungle swallowed them again. Rosales kept the Yukon ahead at a safe distance, dodging stones its tires kicked up. After a heavier rain, mud smeared the windshield. She flipped on the wipers, their steady tick cutting through the hum of the engine. The trail dipped into a valley, leveling out as the forest pressed closer.

"Venezuela's really that bad, sir?" Rosales eyed the jungle path as they sped through it.

Kendrick scanned the shadows. "Wasn't always this way. When most think of oil, they think of the Middle East—Saudi Arabia, Kuwait."

"Sheiks with their skyscrapers," Rosales said. "Because they've got the most oil, right?"

"That's a misconception, you see. The country with the most oil on the planet is Venezuela."

"Really?"

Kendrick nodded. "More proven reserves than the next two countries combined. And that's just onshore. Offshore is a guess—foreign ships can't get close to Venezuelan shores."

Rosales swerved around a rut. "So what happened? Why is the country in such a mess? Couldn't they just pump more oil and stay rich?"

"You'd think," Kendrick said. "But it's not that easy. Chávez took over in '99. Oil prices shot up—$20 a barrel to over $150. Billions rolled in. He dumped cash into social programs—schools, food, housing, clinics. His people were happy."

Rosales nodded. "He kept the masses fed, and that kept him in charge."

"Right. But then things went pear-shaped. Chávez bet everything on oil. He didn't invest in farming or factories. They were rich, and he figured why grow bananas when you've got the money to import them?"

"But then the price of oil dropped, and everything went to shit?"

"Yes. To shit everything went. The recession hit in 2008. Oil crashed to a third of its peak. Chávez then quietly dipped into state savings to keep the party going, as it were. He believed he could bankroll things until oil prices rebounded."

"Did they?"

"Not fast enough. He then passed a referendum eliminating Presidential term limits, to keep himself in power."

"Wouldn't that make him a dictator?"

"Dictators hold power using force. Socialists hold power using handouts."

"But what happens when socialists run out of handouts?"

"Venezuela happens."

Rosales frowned. "But wait, sir, didn't Chávez die?"

"Yes, 2013. Nicolás Maduro stepped in when the economy was already in free-fall."

The trail tightened, branches scraping the Rover. Kendrick wiped a bead of sweat from his forehead, keeping his stare sharp.

"What'd Maduro do?"

"He only made things worse. There were shortages everywhere—food, jobs. Inflation went wild."

"What about OPEC? Don't they control prices?"

"With the ongoing recession, those devious bastards saw the opportunity to flood the market with product. They ramped up production, sinking prices further."

"But why?"

"To undercut the competition. The Saudis have rigs everywhere, linked by a seamless network of pipelines. No transportation costs." He turned to her. "The Saudi's can do with the turn of a valve that which takes the U.S. a rig, crew, road and rail transport. Nobody can compete with them."

"I had no idea the Saudi's infrastructure was so extensive."

"Efficiency is the most effective weapon in a price war."

"Venezuela's screwed then?"

"The country's a mess now. Riots, scavenging. Money is worthless, no food or medicine. Maduro is using the military to control his people, you see."

The Yukon ahead slowed, easing through a muddy patch.

"No more handouts. Now it's a dictatorship."

Kendrick nodded. "A devolving cycle. With the military tied up in the cities, the countryside's been left wide open. Drug trafficking, bandits raping the minerals. It's a free for all."

"Fucking hell, sir." Her knuckles tightened on the wheel.

"Quite," Kendrick said low. "And we're nearly there."

CHAPTER
49

Hannah went from volunteer to chained prisoner in a few days. It was carving into her body. A tightness gripped her chest, her limbs. It was as if her bones were clenching.

The rain stopped, clouds peeling back. But the strange stars above taunted. Pricks of light twinkling, mocking her chains in this cursed jungle.

Two or three weeks until Foster, their captor, replaced the guard she'd killed. Only then might he reconsider freeing her from this iron stake—its shackle rusted and biting into her ankle.

Dan wouldn't make it much longer. Mid-conversation, his head drooped, exhaustion shutting him down like a child fighting sleep. His chest stuttered with shallow breaths. A few more days, maybe. Injured, drugged, fed poison. Vomit stained his shirt. Dehydration was already starving him, his body soon to cannibalize itself—muscles first, then intestines, liver, kidneys. Finally, his heart. A slow rot from within, an agony she could only watch, chained mere feet away.

Alisha was already devastated. Her unborn child surely felt the weight of its mother's dread. A husband who might not return, a father to an unborn child he'd never meet.

Then there was her. So much in her own life, she'd never really dealt with. Her parents unhappy marriage had driven her to isolation when she was a child. Academia became her outlet—or really, overachievement.

Goals, attainments, more goals. She avoided emotional connections. People had only hurt her or let her down. And when that happened, she retreated into solitude. In this instance, all the way to South America. Men like Roland never had a chance.

She'd been a fool, dismissing the men in her life as too immature, too self-absorbed for real connection. But now, as those stars looked down on her, she realized she'd been at fault all along, keeping them at arm's length with judgments and biases and other defenses. She simply didn't dare to open herself up, to be vulnerable, to take any real chance. She'd been bound by her own fears for years—fear of connection, fear of loss.

Now she'd never know if she could change and conquer those failings. There was no way she, Alisha, and Dan would leave this hell alive. How had it all turned to this so fast?

A distant figure circled in the darkness. One of Foster's henchmen, guarding the king's prisoners. Pacing back and forth, watching her in this valley of death.

If she screamed, would he shoot her?

Would death be kinder?

CHAPTER
50

The vehicles motored through a maze of backtrails. They'd curiously discovered another path hidden by a tunnel of leafage, as if someone had carved the lane on purpose but wanted to keep it secret. This single-lane channel with few gaps ran for sixty kilometers through the valleys and mountains. They hadn't seen any other vehicles nor passed any town along its mysterious winding route deep into Venezuela.

Rosales suggested this strange jungle route might connect to the same path they'd seen the semi-trucks rumbling through on the Colombian side, and Kendrick agreed.

They'd crested a bend when Bennett's voice crackled through static.

"What the fuck? Bogey ahead."

The Yukon's brake lights went solid red, muddy tires sliding to a stop. The doors sprang open. Bennett and Nelson leaped out—but Phinn vaulted from the driver's side and outraced both men to the crumpled figure.

Rosales and Kendrick parked and hurried to join them.

"Where ya hurt, lad? Where ya hurt?" Phinn cried.

"Is he conscious?" Nelson asked, kneeling.

The injured man on the ground wore ratty dirty denim pants, but no shirt or shoes, and his upper body and face were covered in scratches.

Phinn cradled his neck and poked his chest.

The young man groaned.

"Hands and feet giving the proper wiggles," Phinn said.

"Agua," came a whisper.

Rosales passed her canteen to Phinn, who brought it to the injured man's lips.

"Watch him while I check his abdomen," Nelson said. "Make sure he doesn't drink too much. Few sips at most."

"Aye."

Rosales turned on her vest light.

The man's gaunt frame bore bruises and scratches across his torso and limbs. A large gash marred his arm.

Nelson probed his ribs and stomach, pausing at a flinch. He aimed his light into the man's face. "Pupils normal. Maybe a cracked rib or two."

"Cuál es tu nombre?" Rosales said.

"Can he stand?" Kendrick asked.

"Says his arm hurts, sirs. Said he might have blacked out." She glanced up at Kendrick. "Sir, I think he might've been running from something. An animal."

"Stay alert." Bennett tapped Phinn on the shoulder, and he rose. "Let's make sure nothing is out here that might want to take a bite out of us."

Phinn grabbed his rifle, and he and Bennett took point while Kendrick and Rosales aided the man on the ground.

"Sir, his name is Lorenzo."

"Do you think we can get him to his feet?"

"We can try, sir."

They braced Lorenzo's arms, hauling him upright as he swayed. Nelson stepped in, hands swift across his torso.

"I see an open wound," he said. "Jesus, he's been slashed."

Rosales and Kendrick also took in the injury. Three parallel gashes on his left side, under the shoulder. Layers of torn skin and muscle were covered by dried dark blood.

"Yeah, something big took a swipe at him."

Bennett, several meters away, shouted to Phinn to keep his eyes sharp, muttered something about "fucking tigers," then returned to patrolling the bushes.

"No tigers here, sir. Not in South America." Rosales traced the gashes on Lorenzo's side, her jaw tight. "Jaguars, though."

"Right," Nelson said. "We should sterilize, mend, and cover this with gauze. After that, why don't you take him, talk with him, find out who he is?"

"Good idea, sir."

Nelson had a steady maturity about him. Cool and pragmatic. No wonder his Navy wanted to reinstate him. Kendrick couldn't believe those American imbeciles had sacked this man.

Headlights stabbed into the jungle, shadows twitching beyond. Sitting still out here was an invitation—to what, Kendrick didn't want to guess. A twig snapped beyond the headlights' reach. Whatever had ambushed Lorenzo might still be circling, drawn by the scent of blood. The beast's escaped meal had now attracted five more. He drew his weapon, eyeing the darkness.

Rosales and Nelson finished patching Lorenzo's wounds as the others stood guard. A rustle in the brush snapped their rifles up, but the eyewear's screen showed nothing.

Kendrick scanned the area, moving toward the vehicles. "Let's load him into the Rover and get moving."

Rosales guided Lorenzo into the backseat and Kendrick jumped behind the wheel. Rosales and Lorenzo began chatting. The Yukon and Rover growled eastward, jungle thickening as they neared a hill's base. Kendrick checked the eyewear's map—eight kilometers to target, unchanged for ten minutes, as if the signal mocked them.

"What's your distance show, Nelson?" Kendrick said.

"My map—shows eleven klicks." Nelson's transmission crackled. The voice interference thickened the deeper they pushed into Venezuela.

Now it seemed like their GPS might be compromised. Was someone jamming their signal?

Kendrick slapped a switch. "Turn off the beams."

"Say—again?"

"Headlights. Turn off the lights."

"Copy—that," Nelson said.

In the rearview, Lorenzo's sunken eyes flared wide, terror fracturing his fragile calm as he whispered to Rosales. It was a look Kendrick had seen in the past, on fields of battle.

"What is it?" he said, guiding the Rover through the underbrush.

"Sir, I was asking about the wound on his bicep. He says he was shot."

"Shot, by whom?"

"He's vague, sir. He keeps mentioning a place in these hills—somewhere he escaped."

Lorenzo tugged her arm, uttering more Spanish.

"He thought we were taking him back there, until I explained who we are. Now he wants to help us find that spot he fled from."

"Tell him we'll do our best to help, but right now, we're on a mission. Once we're back in Colombia we can–"

"Hold on, sir."

Lorenzo lifted his head.

"What's he saying?"

"He's fighting the pain meds, sir. Spat out the fent-pop, and won't touch pills—says he needs to stay sharp."

"Tough kid." Kendrick frowned. He'd been numbing himself for decades with alcohol.

"But, sir, there's something else. He says a woman patched the gunshot on his arm."

"A woman?"

"Yes, sir. A doctor."

"Doctor?"

She and Lorenzo exchanged more words.

"Yes, sir. Doctor Hannah."

Kendrick's grip on the wheel locked, gut tightening.

They were close now.

JACK J. WYATT

CHAPTER
51

Kendrick gunned the Rover past the Yukon, tearing into the jungle's gauntlet of shadows and thorns. The 4x4s bounced over rocks and debris, burrowing a new path over a maze of shrubs. A jagged branch slammed the windshield, spiderwebbing the glass with a vicious crack. Kendrick's foot held firm on the gas pedal.

"Nelson?" he said. "Bennett?" No response came. Communications in the eyewear were no longer functioning out here.

"Sir," Rosales bellowed from the Rover's backseat, her voice cutting through the jungle's roar. "Lorenzo says we're two klicks out."

"Let me find a clearing," Kendrick hollered back.

He wrestled the Rover a few hundred meters farther, the ridge flattening into a rare stretch of open ground. The air reeked of damp earth and rot, nocturnal birds shrieking faintly through the trees as rain streaked the cracked windshield.

Rosales repositioned Lorenzo longways in the backseat and covered him with a mylar blanket.

"Gracias," he said.

Rosales smiled, closed the door, then made her way to the Yukon with Kendrick.

Kendrick explained to the others why they'd stopped here and that Lorenzo may have had contact with one of their assets.

"Doctor? What'd she look like?" Phinn asked anxiously.

"Didn't get a description, but he knew her name," Rosales said. "And we've got a direction, sirs," she pointed southeast. "Two kilometers, that way."

Bennett fumbled with his eyewear. "Damn things went dead."

Each confirmed the radio communication in their eyewear no longer functioned, and the GPS was frozen. Rosales stood to the side, trying to reset her pair but had no luck.

Without the tech, pulling off a rescue would be a brutal long shot. Even so, Kendrick held for a moment. One of Bennett's comments had stuck with him. A tactic he'd been accused of in the past, and Joyner had passively mentioned. He had to lean on his team's skills, relinquishing control—a bitter lesson carved from past failures.

"PFC Nelson," he said. "As a SEAL, you're the incursion specialist. Would you do us the honor?"

Nelson, without delay, stepped forward, looking each in the eyes.

"This piece of real estate is our base. If anyone is separated or lost, make your way back here and wait. I also suggest we leave Lorenzo a pistol in case he needs it."

"Sir, I gave him my SIG," Rosales said.

"Alright, we do this in two stages. Our first challenge is to get close enough for verification and assessment. We have no sat-images. We don't know how many unfriendlies we might encounter. Most features of the eyewear no longer function, including communications. So, we'll have to rely on voice and hand signals. We still have night vision and compass, but make sure you each take a flashlight in case we're separated."

Rosales, Bennett, Kendrick, and Phinn nodded.

"Rosales, you're on point since you have first-hand intel from Lorenzo."

"Yes, sir. He gave me the direction."

"Phinn, we're shorthanded, and I hear you have experience with firearms. Since you're able, I want you to tag along, be our backup."

"Aye," Phinn nodded.

"Darkness is our advantage, but when the sun comes up in 90 minutes, we lose it. Remember that. We're approximately two kilometers from our target location. Because we're scouting for three assets, we'll break off into two teams for reconnaissance once we reach a proper assessment barrier. Then, if we establish the possibility that our assets are there, we'll plan an incursion and exit."

Nelson moved to the Range Rover's rear.

"Once we leave this base, it's critical communication only. We remain together, in a straight line behind the Sergeant to hide our count. Does everyone understand?"

Each nodded a second time.

"Does anyone have any questions?"

Silence.

"Double check weapons." Nelson gave each a quick nod. "Take only as much as you're able to run with. Let's gear up, and don't forget we're in the Amazonian rainforest. We're food to a lot of creatures out here."

The young SEAL's instincts were razor-sharp, sparking Kendrick's pride. He nodded to Nelson with a wink.

Nelson flashed a tight grin, his eyes glinting.

The team gathered their weapons.

"Geared to go," Bennett said.

"Heading out, sirs," Rosales added.

She guided the men down the hill and instructed them not to use any lights unless it became critically necessary because doing so would interfere with the eyewear's night vision. They slogged through the woods past all manner of large leaf, until vines of Mandeville and grape ivy corded through their path. Rosales drew her serrated machete, slashing through the vines barring their path, the jungle yielding reluctantly. Every other branch, plant, weed, or thorny shrub was theirs to wriggle and twist through on their own.

Phinn attempted to relieve Rosales when they came upon an especially severe section of tangled wilds, but Kendrick grabbed his arm.

"Put chivalry aside," he whispered. "Rosales will tell us if she gets tired."

Phinn shrugged and settled back into formation.

Adler hadn't understated things. Whoever was out here used something powerful to saturate the airwaves. All communications in or out were met with static; video efforts yielded a series of screen errors on their eyewear. The night vision's internal software could track "things." Still, because the device's outbound link to any database couldn't be established, the glasses could no longer distinguish between an enemy hostile and a bunny rabbit. Animated boxes could still frame objects on the eyewear's internal screen, but the teeny shapes had lost their digital captions.

"Fuck," Bennett grumbled, tumbling before Nelson caught him by the elbow.

"You alright?" Nelson whispered.

"Twisted my damn ankle." Bennett massaged his foot.

"Let me look at it."

"No, chief. I'm good." He rose.

For the next hour, they followed the would-be Green Beret in a loose-stack formation with one behind the other, down the hill and through the jungle in silence.

Bennett's limp became a hobble, but he kept up with the others.

Rosales signaled a stop. She had them hold position while she vanished into the jungle. A minute passed, she returned and gave the signal to move again. Shortly, the team emerged from the woods into a small valley at the foot of a large hillside. The sandy ground was studded with knee-high bushes, a lower terrain that likely transformed into a river during the rainy season.

Rosales raised an arm and clenched a fist.

With her back turned, she rotated her arm and moved the signal up and down. Kendrick, Phinn, Nelson, and a limping Bennett huddled around her position in silence.

Plumes of smoke rose over the mountain into the night sky. To the west, a steady light pierced the dark—through the eyewear's grainy night vision, it burned a cold bluish-white.

Rosales put a palm to her ear.

A faint rat-a-tat-tat echoed over the hill.

"Motor?" Phinn whispered.

Rosales nodded, then turned to Nelson and said quietly, "This is our front line, sir," she pointed. "According to Lorenzo, they're over that hill."

Nelson circled the group into a tight huddle.

"Bennett, get some wrap around that foot. You and Phinn both hold position here," he whispered.

Bennett lowered his chin and Phinn bobbed his head.

"You two are the safety net. If one of us needs help, I'll signal with three flashlight bursts. Phinn will advance, but Bennett, you stay here. Understood?"

Both affirmed the order.

"Otherwise, if anyone comes over that hill that's not us, or we don't return by daybreak, you two haul-ass to the transport. Do not look back. Jump in one of the rides and get the fuck over that border. Take yourselves and Lorenzo to safety at all costs. That's the priority. Confirm?"

Bennett gripped his rifle and nodded to Nelson.

Phinn, though, looked past Nelson at the terrain behind him.

"Phinn, copy last?" Nelson said quietly.

Phinn's gaze didn't waver from the dark, hilly landscape in the distance, but he nodded.

"Okay, we three are going to split the ridge, 150 to 200-meters between, stay as parallel as possible. Rosales, you take Kendrick. Any questions?"

Phinn's attention suddenly returned to the team.

"Oy. It takes two teams to flank the hill in pitch dark," Phinn said to Nelson. "I'm going with you."

"But you're not–"

"You need me," Phinn said, stoned faced. "I'm going."

Nelson eyed him. "Alright, you're with me. But do exactly as I say, copy?"

"Aye," Phinn said.

"We need to scout as stealth as possible. If we spot assets, we'll regroup for a strategy," Nelson said firmly. "Our mission right now is recon only. No engagement, and absolutely no firing unless I fire first, got it?"

All nodded.

Nelson eyed the Marine. "Bennett, anything happens–"

"And I haul ass, chief. Confirmed."

Nelson turned to Rosales and both rechecked their weapons.

Nelson and Phinn trudged east toward the running generator's loud whirr.

They were marching toward a black void, fortified by an unknown enemy of unknown forces, using intel from an injured man they'd picked up on an unmarked dirt road. There were only four of them, with no outside support. If shit went sideways, at least Bennett and Lorenzo had a good chance at escape. But if Rosales, Nelson, Phinn, or himself became wounded or captured, no one was coming to help. The discovery of their very presence could spark an international incident, amounting to war crimes for each.

Kendrick gripped his rifle, trailing Rosales up the hill.

From the trees, a swarm of bats surged, wings slashing the air. A jolt of adrenaline spiked Kendrick's pulse as their screeches passed overhead.

CHAPTER
52

Nelson and Phinn crested the hilltop as Nelson's eyewear flared, swarming with jagged, shifting fragments. He raised his arm and Phinn halted.

A flood of green boxes danced like hornets across the eyewear's flickering display. Then the pixelated ground twisted, a tide of glitched targets inching their way toward the men.

Nelson whispered tersely, "Move, move!"

Both men bolted, cutting parallel on the hill.

"Wha' the fuck gotcha spooked?" Phinn huffed.

"Not sure," Nelson whispered. "Looked like a miniature... army." He slid a thumb and finger under his eyewear and rubbed the sweat from his eyes. Did the ground move? Was it static? No, it couldn't be. Static didn't shift, did it? More massaging of his pupils. Outside the wire for over a year, but he'd kept himself in solid shape. Was he imagining things?

On the bluff, he and Phinn hugged the shadows, invisible.

A dying fire pulsed faintly in the black valley below.

Phinn moved forward for a better view.

"Eerie," he whispered.

A blanket of smoke settled over the dark gorge. To the east, rain bled through towering floodlights, glinting off a weathered aluminum trailer.

The eyewear's software glitched again. But instead of tiny static, the eyewear clocked a field of green boxes in every direction. Maybe the damn glasses were drenched and malfunctioning? Or the humidity fried their circuitry?

The clash between the bright LED lights of the distant trailer and the eyewear's infrared sensors produced a snowy flash at certain angles.

Nelson ripped off the eyewear, jamming them into his pocket. He'd rely on naked vision.

A generator snarled nearby, its growl clawing the silence. It had to be powering those overhead beams and possibly that trailer. This place was deep in the mountains and in the middle of fucking nowhere. Was this the command center Lorenzo told them about? The one Lorenzo said was ruled by that straw-hatted bastard?

"Smellin of shit here," Phinn whispered.

He was right. The scent was rancid. They kept low, Nelson carving a path over the crest toward the silver trailer's gleam.

In the distance, a slumped figure, sprawled in a folding chair.

"Tango, ten o'clock," he breathed, aiming his rifle at the stranger. "Can't see a weapon. Might not be alone. Let's stick together and circle–"

Phinn tapped Nelson's shoulder.

"What?"

"Listen," Phinn said.

Nelson could only hear the generator's hum. "What is it?"

Phinn shifted, moving east.

"Phinn?"

The Scotsman melted into a snarl of thicket shadows.

"Fuck," Nelson growled. "I'm gonna shoot him."

Low, he tracked Phinn to jagged brush wall.

"Down, down," Phinn whispered.

"What is it?"

Phinn held up two fingers and pointed west. In the moonlight, fifty feet off, two men slumped asleep in a gully's cradle. Their rifles rested against a nearby log.

With no heads-up, Phinn moved swiftly down the slope.

Nelson shadowed him, renewing his vow to shoot the damn Scot at the next opportunity.

The darkness was challenging, but they'd made it down the hill into a dark valley. He squinted at lumpy forms dotting the ground, spaced like graves every twenty feet. Beside each, crooked poles stabbed up from the dirt. A loose cable was attached to each.

Nelson zeroed in on the twisted silhouettes, neck hairs bristling like wire. Heads, arms, legs. The contours were human.

These were prisoners.

Those two dozing bastards uphill had to be the watch. Nelson prepared himself to revisit their alcove.

A form in the gorge twitched, a faint whimper echoing in the dark.

"Ain't fucking real," Phinn growled, sprinting toward the sobbing.

CHAPTER

53

Rosales spotted the shack once they'd crested the hill. It was fifty meters south of their position.

"Sir, movement."

The shanty structure was made of mudbrick and hastily constructed. The tin roof fluttered under the wind and raindrops. The shack had a low, uneven entry and one windowed cavity but no glass or screen. Inside appeared a flickering light and a moving shadow.

"I'll go front, you go rear," Kendrick said, gripping his weapon. They split and slowly approached from opposing sides.

After several meters, a black crater gaped to Kendrick's right, its depths choked with swirling smoke. Its basin vanished beneath a dense shroud of haze, too thick for the smart eyewear to pierce. Green targeting boxes flickered erratically on the eyewear's screen before winking out. He raised an arm and waved sharply inward.

Rosales weaved through the puddles and crouched beside him behind a row of bushes.

"I see something," Kendrick whispered. "The glasses are picking up a flicker down there." He pointed.

Rosales gripped her weapon tight as they squatted in the high bushes overlooking the pit. Together, they scanned the dark, smoke-filled crater before she panned her vision left to right.

"Hold here, sir." She slung her weapon around her backside and crawled on all fours, careful to avoid splashing in the wet grounds. She descended the void's incline, ten or so meters down below the haze.

Kendrick held, quiet. Did she see something?

Moments later, Rosales reappeared, chest heaving and breathing ragged.

"What'd you find down there?"

"Sir," she rasped. "Need a time check—now."

"Time check?"

"What time's your eyewear show?"

"Zero five two-niner."

"Copy that." Rosales tilted her face to the rain, breaths sharp and unsteady. "Mine shows the same. How many green markers registered on your screen, roughly?"

"Not certain, ten or fifteen maybe."

She removed a Sharpie from her vest and wrote the time they'd confirmed on her forearm, along with the date.

"What the hell's that for?"

She pointed. "Sir, look southeast for me? And read the eyewear's digital compass. It uses ULF, not GPS, and should still give an accurate reading."

Kendrick didn't know where this was leading but did as she instructed.

"Sir, can you focus on that starred skyline? Do you see the bright orange one over the horizon and below the rain clouds?"

"Yes," Kendrick said quietly.

"Keep your eyes fixed on it. I'm betting that's the constellation Aquarius. Hold your vision steady near that point."

Kendrick stared at the stars beneath the clouds and over the vista. Rosales focused elsewhere on the skyline.

Then, Rosales said her name, Kendrick's, and the command, "Go snapshot."

A red dot flashed in the corner of Kendrick's eyewear.

"Sir, look at my arm and make sure you have a clear view of these numbers."

His eyes lowered to the figures.

"Go snapshot," she said.

Another red dot flashed in his eyewear.

"Let's hope that worked," she muttered.

"What is this for?" Kendrick said.

"Replication, sir." She capped the marker and returned it to her vest.

"What're you not telling me?" he whispered.

She spun her rifle around to ready. Wind and light rain rustled around them for long moment before Rosales spoke again.

"I have a daughter," she said softly. "Leena, she's six. My brown-eyed bundle of energy." Rosales sighed, her voice softening. "My mom loves taking care of her. Only wish I could spend more time."

Kendrick sensed she was steering him away from something but held his tongue.

"Got married at eighteen, before I really knew who I was." She shrugged. "Kind of had to with the pregnancy and all."

Kendrick nodded.

"But Dwayne liked partying with his friends more than he liked me and our daughter. We split short of a year. He went to prison months later." She shook her head. "Turned out his buddies were also his customers."

"I'm sorry," he whispered.

She peered over the rim, into the misty pit.

"Though without that shithead, I wouldn't have her," she said quietly. "And when people ask me why I do this, it's because I want to make the world a wonderful place for her." She turned. "Scrape off some evil because there's a lot of it."

Scrape off some evil. It was an uncomplicated philosophy and an honorable one, given Kendrick's experience. Especially for a young soldier.

"Do you have any children?' she asked.

He shook his head.

"Anyone special back home, sir?"

Kendrick sighed. "I'm afraid the last time I made a woman groan, I'd swiped her spot in the carpark."

Rosales chuckled. "Sir, once we're out of this mess, I'll debrief on what I saw down there. But for now, we should focus on the assets. I don't want to confuse the mission, sir."

Confuse the mission? What the hell did that mean? He glanced over the fog-filled cavity below, then turned back to Rosales. Something inside of him told him to trust her.

"Understood," he said. "I won't press."

"Sir," she motioned to the distant shack. "I'll take the window"

"Roger. Stay clear of the light."

Rosales slipped back to her perch on the opposite ridge, and they pressed on toward the adobe shack, its tin roof rattling oddly in the wind.

Rain pattered around them.

A silhouette appeared in the window, backlit by the flickering candle inside.

Kendrick signaled Rosales and mimed choking, hand to his throat. She raised a fist.

The individual moved out of sight. Rosales hustled to the makeshift window, put her back against the adobe wall, and readied her weapon. Kendrick paced quietly to the entry.

Beyond the doorway, warped plywood planks sagged on the dirt floor, tangled with filthy rags. He moved next to the entry and suddenly realized he had no way to signal Rosales for a breach because the radio communications in the headwear no longer worked.

Kendrick took a breath, clutched his M16, and entered slowly. Raindrops rolled down his face, but he didn't wipe them clear. Instead, he scanned the interior.

The space was dreary and empty, except for a stack of plastic crates shoved up against a wall and some plywood sheets resting in the dirt. There appeared another cavernous chamber to his left, candlelight quivering in the moving air. He snuck across the soil until his backside met a passageway wall, and he went low.

A low, steady weeping drifted from the next room.

Kendrick was in a precarious position. If the woman were being held prisoner and the aggressor was here, he needed to remain ready to fire. But he also didn't want to startle whoever was crying and set off a scream that could compromise a rescue.

Kendrick looked down and picked up a small pebble from the dirt. He tossed the rock underhanded toward the sound.

The weeping stopped.

"Who's there?" a high, shaky voice sniveled.

Kendrick raised an open hand, with the other carrying his rifle upward so as not to scare the woman. He entered slowly and gazed down at a blanketed figure in the corner clutching its knees.

"Miss, we're here to help," he said quietly.

A shadow grew over him, then another, a chilling click sounded from the doorway.

Outside, Rosales froze, hands raised high.

Next to her, a shorter man held a rifle to her temple.

On the ground, the blanket snapped open. A pale man jumped to his feet, his silver pistol trained at Kendrick's chest.

"I've been waiting for you," Foster said.

CHAPTER
54

Kendrick dropped the rifle. He lifted his hands, elbows low.

"Come through," Foster said, aiming at Rosales.

She scaled the barrier, joining Kendrick.

A wiry man in a red bandanna clutched an AK47, tracking them.

"I know why you're here." Foster waved his silver pistol. "And who has sent you." His accent bit the words.

Disarmed, guns on them, Kendrick eyed Rosales.

"My name is Foster, but I'm sure you already knew that." He swiped dirt off his clothes, adjusting his straw hat. "Spies, spies. What do we do with spies?"

The wiry man laughed, rifle steady.

Foster rubbed his eye.

They'd been baited into this place. Foster had sniffed them out, set a trap. Had Lorenzo, their rescue, sold them out? How? The kid was half-dead when they found him. Their radio was unusable. No way for the kid to signal.

"One of yours is in my camper, crying about her crew. Too pregnant to fight."

Pregnant?

"But you sent someone tougher, didn't you?" Foster craned his neck, wincing. "However, I'm afraid she exposed herself by murdering one of my men."

Was he talking about one of their assets?

Foster sidestepped, pistol on them.

Kendrick's elbows tightened.

"She's below, soaking in the rain, softening for questioning." He blinked hard, clearing his eyes.

Foster had them pinned. Had they stumbled into a drug field? This man wasn't cartel. His accent—familiar, sharp—eluded Kendrick.

"I'll escort you down soon for the same."

Or Kendrick could draw his pistols and end this conversation another way. But that would risk Rosales. He'd try words first.

"We're here for–" Kendrick started.

Foster jabbed his gun.

"Another word, and you fucking die!"

Kendrick shut up.

"No deals!" Foster blinked hard. "I know who you work for and the lies he sent you with."

Did he have advanced intel? How the hell did he know they were coming?

Foster's gaze fell to Kendrick's unbuttoned overshirt. "Fish both of those out when you have a moment, please."

Shit. Kendrick pulled a Browning from his shoulder holster and dropped it to the dirt. Then he dropped the second, butt-first, to his feet.

Foster blinked fast, tilting his head. He swapped the pistol to his left.

If that was his weak hand, Kendrick had a shot. But there was a hitch. He could tackle Foster, maybe disarm him. Rosales couldn't reach the little guy's rifle—a gun that could shred them in seconds.

"I've unearthed more gold than Raleigh and Cortés ever dreamed. Though that's not the real prize, and Yuri knows this."

Yuri?

"If he thinks he can take these fields from me without a fight, he's misguided." Foster aimed at them. "I rule these mountains!"

Kendrick figured the straw-hat man had been here ages. Did he think someone was coming to topple him, take this place? Was Yuri his enemy?

"My stones." Foster rubbed his eye, pulled a black lump from his pocket. "Heat resistant. Never corrodes. The perfect ingredient to stabilize those bits of energy."

A dark blue rock glinted in the candlelight.

Kendrick's eyes flared. Same mineral from the shot-up truck on the Silk Road. And days back, in Alexandra's container.

Foster turned and paced to a corner.

The short man aimed, rocking on his feet.

Rosales edged closer.

"Tantalum," she whispered.

"Right!" Foster spun. "And a remarkable purity of ore here." He stepped toward them. "Let me ask, with trillions at stake, do you believe any technology company or government cares where their gold or this mineral comes from? When the newest model phone is released, or smart bomb is born, is it possible that the slightest bit of conscience affects any of them?"

Minerals. Is that what this place was?

"Your Yuri thinks he's boxed me in? Moving in his people to squeeze me out. I won't let him!" he roared. "This is mine! And once you're dead, that freighter's mine!"

If Kendrick could convince him they weren't with Yuri, they might slip free. But one word, and Foster might fire. Why wouldn't he? What would this madman lose by pulling the trigger?

Something smacked the tin roof, rolled off.

Foster snapped to it. "Who's there? Show yourself!"

A projectile zipped past, hitting the mud wall.
Foster swung, blasting into the dark.
The short man froze, rifle on them, eyes on the door.
Kendrick readied to pounce.
But Rosales yanked his shirt, hurling him through the door.
Kendrick tripped into the rain.
Bullets ripped the air.
Rosales barreled into him, sending them down the mountainside.

CHAPTER
55

Bennett raced behind Rosales and Kendrick, limping but fast. Their two assets held pace, as Rosales broke from the group.

"Weapon!" she shouted.

Nelson tossed the sprinting Rosales his Desert Eagle.

The firefight erupted up the hill.

Nelson sprayed rifle bursts into the shack.

Rosales charged east toward the floodlights. As the slope steepened, her boots slid in the mud, but she pressed on. Floodlights around the camper flared her eyewear, blinding her briefly, but she held low and slipped to the silver caravan's rear. She dodged a grim pool of muck and grabbed two cables from the humming generator.

Voices shouted beyond the trailer.

She ripped the cables free, killing the spotlights.

The area went black.

She crawled under the camper's front. In the distance, a smoky fire crackled in the drizzle. Feet shuffled in the mud. Belly down and hidden, she waited. The tip of a firearm dipped into view.

She aimed the Desert Eagle and fired.

The .50 caliber round shattered a knee, dropping the man.

She fired again, silencing him.

More feet rushed to the body. She spotted a banana clip on a rifle from beneath the caravan.

Rosales blasted the rifleman's ankle, dropping him screaming to his side. His eyes locked on hers. She put two rounds in his skull.

Her chest heaved, adrenaline fading into a cold hollowness. Were these men the abusers—trapping and torturing these souls—or mere underlings? There was no time to reckon in the fog of duty. She had to keep moving.

The fire's crackle hissed as rain fell.

She lay under the caravan, watching for movement, then slid out. Rising to her feet, she drew a combat knife and edged along the caravan's siding. She circled to the front, hugging the doorframe, and yanked the knob.

A rifle poked from the doorway.

"Drop it!" she shouted.

"¡Vete a la mierda!" the voice spat.

Rosales held out of view, her back against the camper. She eyed the open doorway in her periphery, but couldn't see inside. Where was the pregnant woman? Even at speed, if she crossed the hatch and fired, the gunman inside could be using that woman as a shield.

Voices shouted nearby.

Rosales had to end the standoff before she was outgunned. Sheathing the knife, she took a ready breath. She tossed the handgun by the open door.

The hostile's rifle dipped to the discarded Desert Eagle.

Rosales sprang across the doorway, seizing the rifle barrel.

Bullets sprayed past her waist as she wrestled the weapon. The barrel burned her hand, but she held tight. She yanked and twisted, tumbling the gunman down the steps. She pounced on him. But the rifle stayed slung on his shoulder.

Rosales rolled them left, clawing for the knife in her vest.

More firing.

She sank the knife into his side and twisted.

He dropped the rifle.

She rolled off, grabbed the handgun, and shot him between the eyes.

A scream.

She swung the Desert Eagle to the doorway, finger on the trigger.

A lanky man in grimy clothes stood, hands trembling high. He was unarmed. A pregnant woman appeared behind him, wide-eyed.

Rosales leaped to her feet.

A shadow, meters off, closed in.

Rosales aimed.

Kendrick threw up his hands.

She dropped her aim.

Kendrick pried the AK47 from the corpse.

Rosales faced the trailer. "Doctors Bannister?"

The woman nodded. Her partner shook, fear-struck.

Rosales seized his arm. "On me!"

She and Kendrick hustled the two assets down the dark mountain. Bennett and Nelson shielded their six, firing blind bursts up the hill for cover.

They fell back to the sandy ravine where three figures emerged.

Phinn signaled them in. "Oy! Oy! Here."

The group paused to breathe.

The female near Phinn embraced the pregnant woman and the lanky man.

"Three down." Kendrick panted, hands on hips. He locked eyes with Rosales. "No hesitation."

She'd killed one other in combat. But a body drop through a scope was entirely different from a close kill. Doubt plagued even the best-trained troops in close quarters. Some couldn't rise. Uncertainty, fear, hesitancy—cripplers of even the toughest. Inaction endangered the squad. Special forces weeded them out, but that mental wall stopped many. Her squad leader dubbed it the deadly adrenal reflex. True fighters locked on, neutralized threats, and faced the red without flinching.

Being a woman fueled her superiors' doubts. They needed proof she could operate solo. That's why they'd sent her out here. This was her final test.

"You're a warrior." Kendrick caught his breath and put a firm hand on her shoulder. "The best of us, now."

Rosales flashed a grin. "Thank you, sir."

Dawn split the sky. Figures shifted on the summit as gunfire snapped.

Nelson's jaw tightened. "Here they come."

CHAPTER

56

The team tore through the jungle. Nelson hauled a limp Dan on his back, while Hannah braced Alisha's waist, matching their stride. Bennett pushed forward with a limp until he buckled, forcing Malum to drag him up and sling Bennett's arm over his lanky frame. Kendrick and Phinn brought up the rear, taking turns firing on the approaching posse trailing them.

They hit the vehicles fast.

"In, in, in!" Nelson rushed to the Yukon, easing Dan into the backseat. Alisha slid in next to her unconscious husband. Bennett limped to the Range Rover with Hannah and Kendrick, as Malum rounded the passenger side of the Yukon, sliding into the front seat opposite Nelson.

"We're plus one?" Nelson called out.

Hannah ripped open the Rover's back door. "Doctor Malum. He's coming with us."

Inside the Rover, Bennett cranked the engine.

"Oh my God!" Hannah shouted from the rear.

Bennett turned, hand quick to his sidearm.

"Lorenzo! You're here! How the hell did they find you?"

Bennett frowned. "You know this kid?"

She crushed him in a fierce hug. "Yes, yes I do!"

The injured man from the side of the road received a hearty squeeze.

"I thought I'd never see you again," Hannah cried.

From the other vehicle, Nelson hollered. "Count off!"

"Yukon, five loaded," Kendrick called.

"Five in the Rover, too, sir." Rosales jumped in the rear, yanking down the tailgate.

"All accounted!" Nelson bellowed. "Head out! Move, move, move!"

The Range Rover spun a half circle, bouncing down the mountain with the Yukon tight behind.

Quickly, the vehicles found the same hidden path they'd used for their arrival—a leafy tunnel through the jungle that would take them to the border.

Phinn tossed Hannah a big red shirt. "Missy, put this on."

Hannah slipped it over her head.

Kendrick tugged his seatbelt, words itching for the Marine. It was Bennett's bullet that had come zipping through the window, distracting the straw hat lunatic and allowing him and Rosales to escape.

"Thank you for–"

"Knew I'd have to save your ass," Bennett chuckled. "It's called soldiering."

So much for expressing his gratitude.

The Rover jolted over rough ground as Bennett flicked his eyes to the mirror.

"When we hit Colombia, should we head to the embassy?"

"Not sure," Kendrick said. "The mission, it seems…"

"Yeah." Bennett turned. "Tossing us misfits together, command bailing." He torqued the Rover's wheel onto a dirt trail. "Good thing your guy didn't, or we'd have been screwed. I'm not sure who sanctioned this, but I sense fuckery."

"Yes, fuckery. Might be best we keep everyone together until we get some answers."

The Rover picked up speed.

"North, then," Bennett nodded.

Ahead, a gap opened, sunlight stabbing through the canopy.

"Should be able to make it across without stopping," Bennett said. "Ma'am, how you two doing back there?"

Before Hannah answered, the Rover and Yukon roared into the clearing, a gray Datsun truck tearing in behind, guns blazing.

"Oh shit!" Bennett floored the accelerator.

The Yukon hugged close until a round from the Datsun tore its side, smoke spilling out.

Bullets slammed the Rover's shell.

Kendrick shoved the AK47 out the window, ripping bursts at the Datsun as the Yukon swung wide. Through the shattered tailgate window, Rosales returned fire from the rear.

A round punched the Datsun's grille, smoke curling as it slowed.

"Watch your ass. Here comes the jungle!" Bennett shouted.

Kendrick recoiled into the Rover before the arms of an enormous Babassu palm slapped the SUV's windshield.

The Datsun spat its final shots, gunfire fading as the SUVs surged free. At near full speed, the vehicle cut into a dense, narrow trail.

Hannah screamed.

Barreling toward them was a giant semi-truck, the same type they'd seen earlier, bullet-riddled and abandoned, on the jungle's treacherous Silk Road.

Bennett jerked the wheel left, smashing through brush, then carved back onto the path.

"They still behind us?"

Kendrick turned.

The Yukon swerved, Datsun rounds grazing its tail. The two SUVs sped away from the giant truck, though Kendrick kept his eyes on the Yukon. In another kilometer, that vehicle began to slow.

"They may have a problem," he said.

Bennett eased off the accelerator.

The Yukon lurched to a smoky halt, doors flying open.

"Backing up," Bennett said. He shifted into reverse, stopping alongside the Yukon. The doors flew open. Alisha, Dan, Malum, and Nelson piled into the Rover's rear.

"Secure," Rosales called from the windowless tailgate.

Bennett threw the Range Rover into drive and started off again as the others adjusted to their limited seating.

Kendrick checked the AK's magazine. Half a clip. If any other chase vehicles caught up to them, he could fend off one, maybe two, but no more.

Risky as hell, it was their best shot. The battered Rover, ten packed inside, roared west down the jungle's brutal Silk Road.

CHAPTER
57

"Eyewear's live, sirs," Rosales yelled. "Map reads two-seven-zero klicks to the airport."

Kendrick immediately tried to contact Adler but got no response, and there was no way to leave a message.

No chase vehicles showed in the next hour as the Rover churned through mud and slipped over the Colombian border. Strange—Kendrick had expected much more resistance and pursuit than a single flat-bed truck they'd been able to fend off with a few bursts. Sure, they'd lost the Yukon, but it was all too easy. Maybe the cartel was too busy consuming its products?

Dan was still unresponsive, but Lorenzo was alert and drinking water.

"Need a go at the fucker who shot me," Phinn mumbled aloud. "Batter the prick." He rubbed a dry spot of blood that had formed under his torn shirt at the shoulder.

"You got shot? Why didn't you say something?" Nelson said.

"Let me see that." Rosales wriggled over the Rover's cargo barrier and rolled up his shirt sleeve.

"Just a flesher," Phinn said. "Starting to sting, though."

Rosales checked the wound.

"He's right, sirs. The bullet carved a nice streak, but he wasn't hit directly. I'll glue and gauze. Very lucky."

"Lucky, hell! I'm Scottish!"

"Anybody else got any holes?" Nelson called.

There were murmurs but no one else reported injuries.

The Rover's tires bit asphalt, rejoining Colombia's highway grid. Seventy-Secondary connected with National 45 north and would take them toward the Caribbean Sea and Ricardo Domini International Airport, where the jet was waiting.

They had to stop twice to refuel during the mountainous, six-hour journey. Bennett, Nelson, and Kendrick also checked the SUVs gauges. Hauling ten souls across hilly roads had the engine running hot, and the sweltering temperatures weren't helping. Nelson grabbed two coolant bottles and added them to the Rover's overflow reservoir.

They were heading west with less than 50 kilometers to the airport when a heavy downpour started. Amazingly, the Rover's windshield wipers worked flawlessly.

"I think we'll make it." Bennett, hands clamped on the steering wheel, stared at the roadway ahead.

Thirty-seven klicks out, the Rover's engine coughed, thick white smoke billowing from the hood.

"I may need to revise my previous assessment." He pointed to the smoke and wiped sweat from his forehead.

A tone pulsed in Kendrick's headwear.

"Kendrick, answer com."

"Sir, Adler here."

"Tried to call earlier," Kendrick said. "We did it. All assets and team, plus two."

"Great work, sir," Adler said. "Head directly to the airport and get back to the states."

That was curious.

"Are we that wanted?" Kendrick said. "We made mostly a clean getaway and wouldn't the embassy–"

"Something's coming, sir. You'd all better leave as soon as you get to the plane. It's not good."

"Who's after us, Adler?"

"Sir, they're closing down the airports."

"The Colombians? Why would they do that?"

"This hasn't gone out over the wire yet, sir. But it will in a few hours. They'll stop all inbound and outbound flights," Adler said.

"What are you saying?"

Kendrick finished the call and turned to face the others.

Chatter inside the SUV fell silent.

"There's a developing situation. An infection, a pandemic, hitting the general population." He looked each in the eye. "Unknown lethality, but it's bad. Public alerts haven't gone out yet, but disease control centers are preparing to announce as we speak."

"Pandemic?" Nelson repeated. "What?"

"It's taken lives," Kendrick continued. "And my command says it's only a matter of days before this thing circles the globe. There's talk of quarantine."

"Quarantine? Where?" Phinn asked.

"A lockdown for every person, every place in the world."

"What the fuck?" Nelson said.

"That puts a clock on things." Bennett stepped on the gas.

"Do they know the origin?" Hannah asked.

A thought struck Kendrick. Rescuing three doctors. Was this virus what the retrieval was all about? With the exception of Rosales, using non-active personnel to keep things quiet? Doctor Hannah being the priority. What did she do precisely—Atlanta, that University research facility? Did the American government know this was coming? Did the Kingdom?

"Doctor Mitchum, what's your specialty?" Kendrick said.

Hannah stared at him, the scratches on her face and neck covered by dried blood.

"Virology."

"Did you have a specialty? I mean, within the field?" Whoever orchestrated this retrieval must've known not only about the oncoming outbreak but also had the power to initiate this rescue op.

"Did a lot of protein studies, zoonosis for my last year in the lab."

"Zoonosis? Does that mean what I think it means?"

"If you think it's studying the likelihood of an illness jumping the animal-human barrier, then yes."

"That must be it. This disease must have a component requiring that expertise. Your retrieval was the priority."

Hannah put up a hand and shook her head.

"Even if this infection is zoonotic, there's… I mean, that field of study is a specialty, sure, but it's in no way rare. It's not as if I have some secret knowledge or skill where–"

She stopped mid-sentence, and Kendrick watched her eyes.

"What is it?"

"It's got to be him."

"Him who?" Kendrick said.

Hannah closed her eyes and sighed.

"The Senator from the great state of Massachusetts."

"Senator?"

Hannah dropped her head, jaw tight.

"My father."

CHAPTER

58

The Rover lurched, its dying engine gasping for life.

Bennett gripped the wheel, pounding the dash with an angry fist. "C'mon, you boxy piece of shit!"

Tires shredding asphalt, the Rover sagged while the motor coughed and metal clanked, jolting everyone inside.

"Two klicks!" Rosales shouted over the roar.

Sweat beading on his brow, Kendrick clung to the handle as the SUV lurched forward. Beyond the cracked windshield, Ricardo Domini Airport shimmered ahead, taunting them with its nearness.

The quarantine Adler had warned them about loomed, its timing maddeningly uncertain. Kendrick eyed the others. They'd be stranded in Colombia's chaos if they didn't make it out soon.

But their escape gnawed at him—why so little resistance at the Venezuelan border? Had they been allowed to leave? Was it the lockdown—or something else?

And the mission felt off. Hannah Mitchum was the priority. The others, Kendrick figured, were just along for the ride—maybe thanks to her senator father. Perhaps he realized she'd never abandon them?

Bennett nailed it—political fuckery.

He needed Adler and answers, but first, they had to reach the jet. Once airborne, he could unravel this mess—and breathe.

Grayish-black smoke billowed from the hood as Bennett wrenched the wheel, cursing under his breath.

"Damn, power steering's dead!" he shouted.

The private terminal neared. They didn't expect to be searched—still, they'd handed the weapons to Rosales, who stashed them in the seats.

Kendrick kept his Colt tucked in his six-slot, staying cool until they were clear.

By some miracle, the battered Rover staggered to the gate.

A Colombian guard in faded fatigues barely glanced at Bennett's papers.

Smoke swirled, cracks spidered the windshield, and bullet holes peppered the Rover. Yet, the guard waved them through with a lazy flick.

The Rover rattled past small aircraft and into the hangar, its engine choking out one last, pitiful cough. Inside, the hangar swallowed sound, its cinderblock walls stretching wide under harsh fluorescent lights, rusted oil drums stacked against the edges.

The doors flew open and the team tumbled out, battered but breathing. Kendrick exhaled as cool air hit his face, though a thousand things could still go wrong. But soon, they'd be in the skies, and that thought steadied him.

Rosales, Nelson, and Phinn helped their rescued assets from the back. Dan stumbled out, eyes glassy.

Kendrick watched Dan wobble forward, Alisha's hands catching his shoulders. For a tick, the blur of this nightmare lifted. They were out. Shaken, bruised—but whole enough.

He lowered his head and drew a single, silent breath of thanks before reality came rushing back in. Rosales's strange snapshot. The mysterious things said by Adler. Too much still hung unfinished.

The air swirled with fuel and metal. Kendrick scanned the hangar, adrenaline buzzing in his veins. They had to leave, now.

Bennett circled the jet, checking the tires and the exterior. Rosales stashed a duffel of weapons under the wing and then ran back for another.

From the hangar's far side, a man in greasy coveralls approached briskly, clipboard in hand.

Kendrick eased a hand back, fingers brushing his Colt.

"Hold up, amigo." Bennett hustled by with a snort. "Don't cap the guy who filled the tanks, okay?"

Kendrick eased his grip as Bennett met the man near the tail to sign off. None of the team had slept in 24 hours, some of their assets even longer. They all needed rest.

Bennett returned, chatting with Nelson about flying duties. It caught Kendrick off guard—despite the report calling Nelson a hothead, he'd led them flawlessly through a hairy rescue. When they returned to the States, Kendrick vowed to fix that record.

Rosales approached, carrying another duffel.

Something else came to mind. The pictures she'd taken. The stars, the numbers she'd written on her arm. The story about her daughter. The strangeness of the moment. He had to know what it was all about.

"Rosales?" he said.

"Sir?" She shoved the final duffel into the compartment.

"Back in the field, before the shack, you clocked our spot when the GPS died and snapped those photos—"

"I'll debrief once we're airborne, sir."

"Okay."

She latched the hatch, head down. "What I found down in that trench is critical, sir. But I think it's better if we're both seated when I tell you."

A chill crawled up his neck. "In the air, then."

"Yes, sir," Rosales said before hustling away to aid the others.

Whatever she had to share was undoubtedly significant. But what else was there beyond their escape, the tending of their assets, and the oncoming pandemic?

The mysterious kid, Lorenzo, was speaking on a landline inside the hangar. He pleaded with someone on the other end in Spanish, then hung up in frustration.

The young man wasn't part of the deal. They could take him back to the States, but then what? He lived here and wanted to go home, too. They might never know his entire story, and that was okay. They'd saved him from the elements in that dangerous countryside. Now it was time for him to leave, to reconnect with his life elsewhere.

Lorenzo seized a water bottle, marched past the Rover, and vanished from Kendrick's view. He was a loose end in this tangled mess.

As for the rest, they'd fly out and offload the physicians at Hartsfield as instructed. Then Kendrick would rent a car and make the easy drive south—back to his island town. With good timing, he'd reach the Saloon during working hours to shake off this mission with a pint or three.

Nelson helped the shaken physicians up the jet's stairs.

Bennett finished his check and approached, a frown creasing his forehead. "Something worries me," he said. "It was a little easy getting in here. There were four, maybe five guards at the airport's gate when we left. But only one dude here now? Do you think they know about the virus deal?"

The private terminal was near-deserted. The man in coveralls clasped his clipboard on the hangar's far side. In fact, besides Kendrick and his team, that worker was the only person in this ordinarily bustling area.

Kendrick nodded. "I was wondering that, too," he said. "Feels off." It was good to know he wasn't the only one feeling jumpy.

The two men stood by the jet, scanning the main runway outside of the hangar.

"Commercial flights," Bennett pointed. "Normal cadence out there." He shrugged. "Maybe I just have the jitters. I know I'll feel a shitload better when we're wheels up."

"Yeah, we should get the assets back to the States. The sooner, the better," Kendrick said.

Bennett gestured at something.

"You think that guy's pissed about the Rover?"

"Pissed?" Kendrick said. "Who?"

A slim man in a weathered t-shirt and jeans sauntered into the hangar. Even from a distance, the scar on his upper lip was familiar. It was the same bloke who'd supplied the team with the beat-up Range Rover, then scampered off days ago.

"I'm sure one of our governments will make amends. Can't be but a few pounds to replace."

Bennett raised a brow. "Yeah, but someone still owes me a pair of sunglasses."

Kendrick laughed. This was the most easygoing conversation he'd had with the Marine. Maybe being in the shit together had changed him—perhaps he'd come around. Kendrick was about to make another comment when movement in the distance caught their attention.

Behind the scarred man, a dark Mercedes SUV sped toward them from the runway.

"Incoming," Bennett muttered.

Nelson and Phinn stood chatting at the jet's stairway. Rosales, though, was nowhere in sight.

The vehicle stopped. A tall man in a suit and crimson boots stepped from the passenger side. His long, ashy-black hair caught the light. Two other men in suits exited from the rear.

The booted man paced toward them, smiling.

He was likely the owner or part of the airport's security team. Nonetheless, Kendrick casually felt for his weapon.

As he did, the two men flanking the black-haired stranger drew guns.

"Oh shit," Bennett said.

"Let us see your hands," said the stranger.

Both he and Kendrick slowly raised their arms.

The man scanned the Gulfstream from tip to tail.

"Please," he said, raising a palm and wriggling his fingers.

Kendrick removed the pistol from the small of his back and set it at his feet.

"Better if your friend puts his away, too," he said. "We do not wish this to get messy."

Scowling, Bennett nodded to Nelson, who unhitched his weapon and lowered it to the concrete.

One of the suited strangers pointed a pistol at him until he rose. The goon motioned with his handgun for Nelson to stand beside Kendrick and Bennett.

The lip-scarred worker in jeans skipped over, snatched a thick envelope from one of the men, and zipped away without a word.

The booted man brushed his long hair aside. "I must thank you," he said, motioning to the Gulfstream with a crooked smile. "For returning my jet."

CHAPTER
59

"Awkward without introduction," he said. "I am Yuri." He smiled thinly, circling Bennett and Kendrick. "I am wondering how you came in possession of my jet. Care to share explanation?"

Kendrick's pulse hammered. The jungle chase, the lone guard's lazy wave at the gate—it all clicked. No one was trailing them because they knew exactly where they were headed. Straight to Yuri's Gulfstream, a fucking trap he never saw coming.

"I know of your grab in the gorge, across the border. Colleague was very shaken by the breach. But he will like this… roundup."

Yuri's man corralled them into a tight group with waves of his handgun.

Malum staggered off the jet's airstairs. Hannah stumbled behind, eyes darting, clutching Dan's sleeve. Dan swayed, face gray, as Alisha steadied him, her eyes still teary.

With three weapons aimed at them, Kendrick knew they had no chance of escape, even though his team outnumbered their captors three to four. He glanced toward the wing—Rosales had latched the hatch, but where was she?

Yuri regarded the group. "Who is pilot?"

None of them moved or said a word.

Yuri gestured to the hangar's archway. "There is issue with enclosure as this. Structure refracts sound, and shots leave terrible ringing in the ear." He raised his handgun. "Do not make me shoot one of you for an answer."

Bennett stepped forward, eyes steeled. "I'm the pilot."

Kendrick's gut twisted.

"Excellent. Have you been enjoying my aircraft?"

Bennett stood silent.

"Okay, here is proposition. You will take jet back across gulf to small strip in United States. Do you think you can do this?"

Bennett squared his shoulders, stare locked on Yuri's gun.

"Please, ringing in ear is unpleasant, we don't–"

Bennett dipped his chin, hands flexing at his sides. "Yes, I'll do it."

"Excellent. And to ensure you get there safely, I will take all women with me, and you passenger men. If anything happens to my man or my plane, then you never see them again. Deal?"

Bennett lowered his head.

"Words, please." Yuri's pistol twitched upward.

"Yes, deal," the Marine said, jaw tight.

"Very good." Yuri turned to the large man beside him. "Vadim, you will be their escort on plane. I will stay with ship, as our friends in Kiev are counting on goods. Also, please call cousin to expect plane on landing. I will take these ladies to port. Colleague should arrive shortly. And we will all meet up in two days."

Vadim dipped his head.

"Very good." Yuri faced Kendrick and Bennett, eyeing them curiously. "Those glasses you wear. Are they corrective?"

Before Kendrick could answer, Yuri stepped forward.

"Appear to be same brand." He cocked his head. "Very curious."

Kendrick and Bennett stood stoically.

Yuri extended his palm. "Remove them, now."

Each handed Yuri their eyewear. He examined both, then slipped a pair over his ears. Next, he exchanged one set for the other, looked around the hangar, and smiled strangely.

"Interesting prescriptions." He removed the eyewear, dropped both pairs to the concrete, and stomped them with his boot heel. The prototypes broke into tiny fragments.

A ping struck Kendrick's gut. Without the eyewear, they'd lost their connection to the outside world—and, most concerning, to Rosales.

"Put all that in car," Yuri instructed. The man to his left gathered the handguns and the rifles they'd stacked near the jet's port engine.

Yuri flicked a wrist. Vadim stomped forward, shoving men toward the jet's stairs with a meaty hand, barking at the women to stay put.

"No," Alisha screamed, clinging to Dan.

Vadim looked to Yuri.

Yuri nodded, slow.

Vadim yanked back the slide on his handgun. Click.

"Wait, wait!" Kendrick shouted. "It's not their fault, let me." He lunged forward, steadying Alisha by the shoulders, her sobs shaking his hold. "It'll be okay, it'll be okay. I promise."

The two broke their embrace, Alisha sobbing as Vadim ushered her alongside Hannah.

"Okay, we have our assignments," Yuri said.

"Hold up." Bennett pointed to Nelson. "This man is my copilot."

Yuri gave a crooked nod. "Then both of you, please be good to my jet. It is costly machine." The corners of his mouth turned down. "I would hate to have to toss women friends into ocean if cousin reports damage."

Phinn's knuckles whitened, Nelson's jaw clenched, and Hannah's breath hitched—fingers twisting her sleeve as Yuri loomed closer.

Wherever Rosales was, she'd been smart enough to stay hidden during all this. If she had her rifle, she could drop all three of these men in as many shots and even fewer seconds.

Kendrick climbed the airstairs, Malum trembling ahead, his gasps sharp. He and the others were going to take off in a jet guarded by a gigantic, armed man named Vadim, whose loyalty probably couldn't be reasoned with or bribed. Two of their assets were being taken somewhere by a man he'd never seen before. They had no weapons, and his Green Beret had gone MIA.

Yuri herded his hostages to the Mercedes, tires screeching as it roared across the tarmac, vanishing into haze.

Kendrick dropped into a seat, sweat stinging his eyes. Through the window, a container ship hulked north at the port, its silhouette swallowing the horizon. Was that where Yuri was taking them?

Rosales burst from cover, sprinting across the tarmac to the Rover. Its engine coughed, smoke trailing as it peeled after Yuri's Mercedes.

No one else had seen her leave with the vehicle.

As the airstairs retracted with a hydraulic whine, Bennett gripped the lever, then squared his shoulder to ram the door—but Vadim's pistol jabbed his ribs, shoving him toward the cockpit.

CHAPTER
60

"Ident 1443, intentions unknown. Acknowledge?"

Bennett had taken off without clearance from runway 10R, with the barrel of a Lebedev PL-15 pressed against his neck. Nelson sat to his right, and Vadim hovered like a gorilla behind both, finger foolishly on the trigger.

"Gulfstream 650, ident 1443, what is your intended heading?" the anxious air traffic controller called.

Max thrust kicked in as he banked left, the Gulfstream skimming the Atlantic like a stone. They were level at 400 feet, nose pointed zero-five-zero. The aircraft rocketed above the ocean for three miles to clear any inbound traffic. Beneath, a fishing boat rocked as the Gulfstream cut the air wake just above their vessel, engines screaming.

They couldn't pressurize. Once clear of the holding stack, Bennett climbed to six thousand feet and held—as anything above ten risked hypoxia and death.

"Avianca 2400 expedite climb to twelve thousand for separation and maintain VFR."

Yes, get them the fuck out of my way! Playing chicken with a 230-passenger Airbus 321 would shred the Gulfstream into turbofan confetti, their remains chumming the waters for those fishermen below. Bennett gnashed his teeth. Karma loved her some irony.

"Unknown 1443." The incident had attracted a senior ATC operator with a gritty voice. "We will not provide IFR clearance while airborne. Instruct you return to the runway immediately. Acknowledge 1443."

The low altitude had to be scaring the hell out of his passengers, but with thick clouds and no help from the tower, Bennett had no choice.

The fucking idiot with the gun wouldn't let him communicate with air traffic control. And this was no game. Flying through Bravo airspace in low-vis was like sprinting across the Daytona 500—blindfolded.

"SKSM traffic control considers Gulfstream 1443 actions unknown and possibly hostile. No info. Aircraft is level at six thousand. Escort for 1443 inbound."

Bennett gripped the stick. That was the one he was waiting for. The good old Colombian Air Force would scramble their Kfir fighters, missiles hot, and spook this Vadim asshole into landing. Then Bennett would dump the fuel, turn back, and boot this bastard down the jetway before the authorities put him in chains.

"Heading three-three-nine," Vadim growled. "Deviate and you're dead." The pistol jabbed at his neck. The huge man was taking orders from someone on his phone—probably the jet's old pilot. That communication would die once they were out of range and the Gulf of Mexico swallowed his signal.

Bennett adjusted the heading.

Vadim leaned forward, flashed a photo on his phone, and conferred with his listener on the screen's settings.

"Kill transponder," he barked.

Bennett deliberately reached for the wrong knob.

Vadim raised the pistol to his temple.

Bennett switched off the correct one.

Vadim and the mystery pilot chatted, a meaty finger pointing over his shoulder. "Now the other."

The color drained from Bennett's face. "If I do that, we lose TCAS, and collision–"

The gun's cold barrel stabbed his neck.

Bennett switched the secondary transponder knob off.

"ATC SKSM. Gulfstream 1443 off scope," gritty said.

"Maintain," Vadim growled, knocking the weapon against Bennett's shoulder.

Ripping through rain and clouds, the Gulfstream shook as turbulence clawed at its frame. Next to him, Nelson sat silent but kept a white-knuckled grip on his side panel.

Minutes ticked by. No word from air traffic, no sign of Colombian jets. Their radar should've picked up the Gulfstream by now, right?

"Hello? Hello?" Vadim fussed with his phone until he finally grunted and slipped the cell back into his pocket.

Bennett held them at six thousand feet. Where the fuck are those fighter jets?

He could deploy flaps, yank the stick for a hard pull-up, and let G-forces teach this unbelted idiot a lesson. Best case, Vadim slams into the overhead, cracks his skull, and blacks out. Worst case, the giant bounces around, gets pissed, and smashes Bennett's skull through the windscreen.

Bennett shot a glance at Nelson, then thought of the others strapped in the cabin. Yeah, bad idea.

The storm they were flying through worsened, and clouds filled the screen's radar. Vadim shifted behind the seats, eyes locked on Bennett.

Could he lunge for the gun? Turn it on Vadim and end this? But Vadim might shoot first—or bash his face in. Either way, Nelson would be stuck flying, and the kid only knew the basics. Shit, that wouldn't work.

He rechecked the radar. No inbound traffic. They were clear for now—then it hit him. He could set the G650 on autopilot, slip out, find a weapon, grab Kendrick, and storm the cockpit. Three against one— they could take this bastard down. First, he'd demand to use the head.

Bennett clicked on the autopilot. "I need to take a leak," he said calmly.

Vadim pressed the gun to his shoulder blade. "Piss in pants."

Bennett clicked off the autopilot.

Forty minutes out, the clouds broke. Vadim hovered behind them scanning the screens.

Ninety minutes out, Bennett accepted that the Colombian military wasn't coming. They were deep into international airspace, no longer a threat. Fuel's too precious to waste on a rogue jet. Now, they were someone else's headache. Air traffic might provide a courtesy call to the Cubans or the Americans, but without the transponder signaling the Gulfstream's position, it was like trying to find a contact lens in a fucking swimming pool.

Bennett did his best to avoid Cuba's western airspace, but now they were crossing the Yucatan traffic lanes on their north heading. With no way to be seen and the asshead behind him making sure he didn't contact ATC, he was flying on raw eyesight.

But piloting airspace isn't like racing a car, a boat, or anything else. When two opposing jet craft converged at altitude, they arrived at nearly twice supersonic speed—faster than a bullet.

Nelson screamed.

The Boeing 777's tail number flashed past in a blur. Bennett yanked the stick, banking full. The jet rolled sharply, slinging Vadim into the bulkhead with a crack. He hit the floor hard.

The gunshot was inevitable—Vadim had no trigger discipline. But the sharp pain in Bennett's chest? That was a problem.

CHAPTER
61

Sitting copilot during takeoff scared him more than combat. The Gulfstream ripped through the sky at 541 knots, which, according to Nelson's frantic calculation, was 625 mph.

Tearing through chunky clouds was surreal—grayness and roaring rain, brief silence, then pounding drops, and finally a clearing.

Terrified, for some reason, he thought of Eden—the pretty young woman watching Noodle. She'd texted five or six times since his departure, sometimes just to ask how he was doing. She ran an online store, selling quirky vintage jewelry. Noodle's tail had suspiciously appeared in her most recent postings.

The stench of gun oil filled his nostrils. Would he ever meet the girl down the road in person? Would he see his furry pal again?

Bennett boosted their altitude above the cloud cover. The beefy, foul-smelling gunman moved behind him and was now literally breathing down his neck.

Nelson gripped the side panel, staring at the video screens on the dash—something he thought a copilot would do. He scanned the digital gauges, nodding as if confirming the pilot's actions. Though, beyond banking right and left, he knew next to shit about controlling this jet.

They'd flown for a couple of hours and were passing over eastern Cuba when Bennett arched forward, wide-eyed, staring outward.

A shimmer flashed in the distance. A fleck at first, then lost in a sea of dark clouds. Next, an enormous white heap filled their field of vision.

The Gulfstream banked hard.

Someone screamed.

His insides whipped left.

A massive jumbo jet roared by, missing the Gulfstream by yards.

Behind, a crash—then a crack of gunfire. His ears rang.

Vadim fought to regain his footing, his handgun lost.

Phinn and Kendrick busted through the cockpit door.

The Scot pounced on Vadim.

Stuck in the tight aisle, Kendrick could do nothing to help.

From the ground, Vadim struck Phinn with a heavy blow.

Phinn tumbled backward.

A strange, high-pitched whistle pierced the cabin.

Vadim leaped to his feet and charged the two men.

The melee shifted to the main cabin, where the bone-crushing blows continued.

Nelson scanned the floor but couldn't find Vadim's weapon. He reached for the latch on his seatbelt. Three on one, they could take this son of a bitch.

Fingers clamped his forearm.

It was Bennett.

"Stay… strapped in," he wheezed. The pilot's other hand clutched a spot on his chest, blood inking his shirt.

Nelson froze. "You're hit!"

"Full metal round. Got me good, chief." He motioned to a small hole above his sidestick. "And breached… the craft's shell."

The whistle. "There's a hole in the plane?"

Bennett shook his head. "She'll hold, but…"

Nelson unbuckled. He couldn't see the others, but grunts and shouting erupted from the galley. He shifted up from his chair.

"No, chief. Stay."

"But I need to put pressure on the wound!"

"Get back… in your seat." Blood seeped from his chest and he coughed.

This wasn't looking good. But Nelson held, strapped in, heart racing.

Bennett winced. "We never… talked about it."

He stared at the bleeding Marine. "Talked about?"

Bennett swallowed. "They did you… dirty, chief. On the Salvo, that was… bullshit."

Despite the hijacking, the near-collision, the brawl raging behind them, and Bennett bleeding beside him—a flood of memories filled Nelson.

Late summer. His vessel, the Salvo—a San Antonio-class transport ship, churned the eastern Pacific. They were on a logistics mission. The USS Kelvin, battered by Typhoon Jebi, was running on single auxiliary, limping its way back to the mainland.

Its 1,500-person crew was suffocating, trapped in a steel box adrift in the ocean. No air conditioning, suffering dry rations after the food spoiled, and hadn't seen an ice cube in 26 days.

The Salvo would be their lifeline, bringing critical parts to restore their second boiler, their mains, and bring her up to full power again. It was a feel-good mission, but it would be Nelson's last.

Finishing rounds at 3 a.m., a sound stopped him cold—high shrieks cutting through the stillness. He followed the noise into the mess, where no crew were permitted after chow time. Near the kitchen came whimpers.

A small sailor—head freshly shaved and stripped bare—thrashed against a large crewman pinning him down. The kid's face purple, eyes wide and wild. He clawed at the arm clamping his throat, gurgle bubbling from his lips.

The aggressor, a hulking man, squeezed.

"Hey!" Nelson shouted. "Let him go!"

The bigger man whipped around, fury in his gaze.

"Teaching this newbie some manners," he growled.

The naked kid yelped for air.

Nelson reached for his sidearm. "Let him go, now!"

The attacker hurled the kid at Nelson, their bodies crashing together. The big man lunged, fists a blur of fury.

Nelson pushed the kid clear.

A punch hit his gut, and Nelson countered with a jab to the nose. The two men bowled over a table, where Nelson wrenched an arm, snapping it at the elbow.

The man screamed.

Nelson bounced to his feet and reached for his radio.

"What the fuck's going on?" a voice boomed.

Nelson looked up.

The XO stood in the doorway.

"Sir, there was a disturbance, and I–"

The man on the ground shrieked and squealed.

"Restraints, now!"

Two men rushed in, grabbed Nelson, and put him in handcuffs. No chance to protest or plead, they dragged him to the brig.

The charges came fast—assault, disorderly conduct, a laundry list of bullshit. He tried to explain, the kid choking, the hazing. But no one cared. The naked sailor he'd saved? Gone, melted back into the ship's ranks, silent.

His lawyer, a pudgy lieutenant who smelled of sweat and cigarettes, pushed for a single judge over a full panel. "Quicker this way," he'd grunted.

He was right. The trial lasted 11 minutes.

Nelson was named the aggressor. The gavel dropped, "conduct unbecoming." Eight years of service—a career he'd bled for—gone in less time than it took to brew a pot of coffee.

Later he'd learned the man's arm he busted was Chief Petty Officer Ratkin, the Captain's nephew. The fix had been in from the fucking start. Cheated out of a career he loved.

The Gulfstream jolted. Beside him, Bennett's shallow breaths rasped. From the cabin, Vadim's growls mixed with the smack of fists.

"You're a damn good… soldier, chief," Bennett huffed.

A lump grew in Nelson's throat. He hadn't thought about any of that since leaving Alexandra days ago. Here, with this team. He'd felt every bit the soldier he once was. People who trusted him, who fought alongside him without question, being part of something bigger than himself. Back on the Salvo, he'd been betrayed by those he thought were his brothers. Here, he had a family again.

But there was no time to dwell. His friend was dying, and the jet was in danger. He had to help him. He unbuckled.

"No," Bennett wheezed. "Keep her on course,"

"But I have to help you!"

"More lives than me… need you." He pointed a finger. "You gotta… land us."

Nelson's face went flush.

Bennett gestured to the flat panel—a strip of land labeled 4R9. "There, four klicks out… ease down to 500 feet."

Nelson nodded anxiously.

"Hit landing gear, deploy flaps." He pointed to a switch. "Throttle back… 130 knots." He nodded to the horizontal stabilizer. "Keep nose up… and speed. Don't stall her."

Nelson searched for something to write with, but found nothing.

"Steer center, runway."

"But–"

"When tires make contact… pull back, full." Bennett tapped the thrusters. "Runway's short. Watch sheer… wings level."

Nelson glared at the controls. "I don't know if I can do this."

Bennett coughed. "You gotta, chief."

Nelson trembled. This was not possible. He'd only ever flown in clear airspace, once, for a few hundred miles, feathering a damn joystick. Now he had to land the jet? His head spun. He had to concentrate, recall everything. Four klicks, 500 feet, gear, flaps, slow to—shit!

"Slow to 150 knots?" Nelson pointed to the air speed.

Bennett did not respond.

Nelson turned.

The Marine's head slumped forward.

Nelson hit the autopilot, buying time but even he knew it couldn't land them. He bounced from his seat. Bennett was still breathing—shallow, but his chest was moving.

The fight in the fuselage raged, but he couldn't intervene. He had to focus. Desperate, he grabbed the jet's guidebook, ripped out a page, and found a black marker in the seat pocket.

Lightning split the sky.

A wall of red grew in the radar's display.

The three men in the galley continued their brawling—thuds, yells, and grunts.

His chest tightened. He scribbled what he could recall of Bennett's instructions, oblivious to the anvil-shaped thunder cloud engulfing their approaching jet.

CHAPTER

62

Phinn battled on, even as the bigger man overpowered him. The damn Scot could take a fucking punch, there was no doubt.

Vadim's pistol had disappeared near the cockpit. But since Kendrick couldn't get past the two, the challenge now was to keep Vadim from finding it before he did.

Behind, Malum and Dan were belted in the plane's rear. The trembling doctor looked Kendrick's way, terrified, as the drowsy Dan fought to remain conscious.

Heavy booms erupted outside the aircraft, rattling the frame. The Gulfstream plummeted.

Phinn, Vadim, and Kendrick were flung in the air—then all three men slammed to the deck.

For a heartbeat, there was silence. Kendrick's cheek pressed to the cold floor, the taste of metal and smoke thick in his mouth.

Then came the groan of fuselage and the pound of feet.

Phinn and Vadim lunged at each other again.

Beyond the men, the cockpit's door swung, and Bennett's limp arm dangled over his seat. In the other seat, Nelson fumbled with the controls. Was he flying the jet?

Phinn rocked the Russian with an uppercut, but caught a fiercer blow in return.

The jet lurched. A rattle jerked Kendrick's attention to the door—an ominous clanging followed. Maybe the high speed and low altitude caused it? Outside, blackness and lightning flashed.

A second thunderous bang shook the jet. The cabin flared white, then a clang seized his focus. The fuselage door shook violently, its latch unsecured.

Kendrick retreated as the men grappled near the trembling door. Lightning struck again, the tremors intensifying.

The only plan he could devise was drastic—it required speed and force. Kendrick planted his feet, braced his arms, and charged at Phinn's back.

The impact sent them sprawling, all three men hitting the deck. He ripped Phinn from Vadim, shoving him into a seat. Kendrick threw himself atop Phinn, clutched the armrest, and looped a seatbelt around his forearm to anchor them.

The Scotsman struggled, but Kendrick held him.

"The fuck ya doing?" Phinn cried.

Wind roared from the jet's entry.

"The door!" Kendrick shouted.

A bloody-faced Vadim got to his feet, careened toward the pair, and hooked Kendrick by the neck.

A thunderclap blasted through the fuselage, ripping the door from its frame. Winds howled from the gaping passage.

A second bang rocked the jet.

The Gulfstream shuddered, plunging into a steep dive.

Vadim's fierce yank ripped Kendrick from Phinn, the seatbelt slipping free. The Russian grabbed his wrist and jerked him forward. At the same time, Phinn clawed Kendrick's belt, and an absurd tug-of-war ensued.

Heavy rain and freezing winds blasted through the open hull. The aircraft yawed wildly.

Vadim's grip tightened while Phinn's loosened, and Kendrick slipped toward the gaping hole.

There was one move left—a primal last resort. Otherwise, he'd be hurled into the storm, plunging to his death.

He drew his leg back and, with every ounce of strength, unleashed a kick. His steel-toed boot pulverized Vadim's groin, wrenching a shriek from the giant. The stocky man's knees buckled, and his grip broke from Kendrick's arm.

But before Kendrick could mount an attack, Phinn shoved past him. He landed a bone-splitting punch to Vadim's hand, crushing it against the wall.

Vadim let go of the frame, his body instantly sucked out of the flying craft.

Kendrick had seen a lot of death, but this was nasty, gruesome. He stared out the opening until Phinn pulled him into a chair.

The jet kept plummeting.

Both men scrambled to belt in. Outside, faint moonlight glinted off churning waves.

"We ditchin?" Phinn's shout was barely audible above the roar of the wind.

Kendrick didn't know. The plane was hurtling toward the sea, fast. Flames licked the wing, flickering in and out. They'd probably lost an engine.

Phinn cinched his belt as winds whipped his clothes. He closed his eyes, gripped the armrests, and braced himself.

Kendrick clamped his eyes shut. He pictured a soft breeze, his hand caressing her shoulder, the scent of her hair.

Tremors rippled beneath his feet.

Outside, rolling waves appeared. A palm tree flashed past. Then another, and another.

Had they made it to shore? Were they landing?

The jet's nose pitched up, then down, up again, until the tail struck the ground. A tire exploded. The aircraft lurched forward, veering sharply left. Blinking runway markers streaked past the oval windows.

Sparks spurted from the aircraft's belly as the body scraped against the pavement beneath. They were decelerating, but the pilot struggled to keep the plane on the runway.

The grinding ceased, but the jet continued its slide, plowing through wet sand. It slid from beach to surf—a blast of seawater flooding its breached hull.

CHAPTER

63

Rosales tasted grit and ash on her tongue. She wedged into a narrow gap between containers near the freighter's midsection.

The freighter dwarfed any structure she'd seen in motion. Spanning the width of a football field and over three times its length, the freighter was crammed with cargo containers. What stunned her most was the vessel's staggering depth. The ship was a vast metal chasm, stacked with thousands of tractor-trailer-sized containers rising twelve to fifteen levels across its deck. Those same containers plunged five stories deep into the ship's hold, hidden below the surface.

The sky was still dark but wouldn't be for long. She had to find cover and reach Kendrick—or anyone. No one answered through her eyewear. Electronic interference likely jammed the signals. The eyewear's local functions still worked. Night vision, zoom, and tinting held steady. At least she'd look cool when they spotted her in the daylight and shot her. A grim chuckle escaped—she'd have to save that quip for Bennett.

She crept along the deck, slipping between container stacks to stay unseen. Near the ship's stern, a white tower of windowed chambers rose above the container stacks. The tower held multiple spaces, its peak— two hundred feet above deck—bristling with antennas and radar gear. Her eyewear caught crew members moving behind rectangular panes,

307

marking the tower's top chambers as navigation. Lower windows revealed a mess hall, then crew quarters, one holding a familiar face.

Doctor Hannah Mitchum gazed from a window several stories high.

Rosales darted between containers to stay hidden. She needed a way into that towering block to scour its rooms. The pregnant woman must be close.

She'd spotted two men with pistols, their faces pale in the dim light. They didn't move like crew. They likely guarded that Yuri man. Another figure, glimpsed briefly, sported a grimy red bandanna and clutched a rifle.

She'd dropped to the ship's lowest deck. Dim amber lights lined narrow pathways along the ship's inner rim, giving way to stairwells and ladders like the one she'd taken. The air felt cleaner below, but cloying. Containers rose in groaning stacks, shifting with the ship's sway. Metal grated on metal, the sound ricocheting when the vast ship struck rough seas. A faint thud echoed from within one. Shifting cargo?

Two men approached from stern. One clutched a clipboard. Rosales hunkered between containers, her breath easing out. She needed a spot to hide and assess. A watertight door labeled "Electrical" stood twenty-five feet off. She edged through a tight gap between containers toward it.

No rain fell, and she stood at the lowest deck near midship. Yet liquid dripped onto her neck from above. A faint, acrid whiff hit her first. Had a wave breached the deck? She advanced, scanning the passageway. All clear.

The dog lever resisted, then turned counterclockwise with a grudging clank. A thick click, and the door swung open. She felt along the metal wall for a switch, finding none. Her eyewear flicked to night vision, revealing a tight area. It could fit two workers tending the panels inside. She yanked the door shut. No dog lever graced the inside—just a fixed handle she tugged tight.

A toolbox at her feet held wrenches, screwdrivers, pliers, switches, and six bungee cords with hooked ends. She lashed two cords to the handle, securing their hooks to a conduit pipe along the wall. The cords held, sealing the door.

"Electrical" fit the cramped nook perfectly. A ceiling brushed her head, joined by six breaker panels, the toolbox, and a dented soda can on the floor. She could sit, legs folded tight to her chest. It felt like a car's trunk. Tiny LEDs on the panels blinked erratically.

The liquid that had dropped from the container stacks onto her neck trickled into a cut near her collarbone, burning fiercely. She touched the wound, then inspected her fingers through night vision.

Her pulse quickened. The fluid reeked of sharp ammonia. Those containers above—she wasn't alone.

CHAPTER
64

Seawater surged through the jet's breached hatch, flooding the cockpit and dragging the Gulfstream's nose downward. Smoke swirled, stinging Kendrick's eyes.

Phinn hauled Dan from his seat, seized Malum, and the trio plunged into the churning sea.

Kendrick waded through the flooded cabin to the flight deck, boots slipping on the wet floor. Red and amber lights flashed across the consoles, alarms shrieking as chest-high water climbed fast.

Nelson wrestled to free himself from his waterlogged seat.

"My wrist," he cried. "It's busted."

Kendrick heaved the SEAL over the center console, steadying him before turning his focus to Bennett's limp form in the water.

Nelson clutched his injured wrist. "He's been shot."

Blood spread across the pilot's chest, staining his soaked shirt.

"Can you get out by yourself?"

Pulsing lights caught Nelson's grim nod.

"Then get out—I got this."

Nelson staggered from the cockpit.

Kendrick turned to Bennett, pressing two fingers on his carotid, searching for a pulse. It ticked faintly, and the Marine's breaths were shallow.

As the jet's nose plunged, seawater engulfed the cockpit. Dash monitors fizzled, sparks snuffing the last of the instrument lights.

Kendrick covered Bennett's mouth and nose to shield his airways from the flood.

The cockpit vanished beneath the surface, fully submerged.

Clutching Bennett's limp form, Kendrick kicked through the inky flood, surging toward the jagged breach in the jet's hull. The current shimmered with fiery reflections as he thrust them upward.

With Bethany, there had only been love—and a future brimming with plans. Her auburn hair, long and glowing, cascaded to her mid-back. Her infectious smile, shy laugh, and robin-blue eyes, endlessly deep. Tiny freckles dusted her nose, vivid up close when their lips brushed.

She was charmingly clumsy, and a terrible liar.

"Carnations are fine," she'd said, brushing a lock of hair behind an ear. She adored costly calla lilies, and despite his strained budget, he'd always deliver.

At twenty-three, his assignments kept him close to home. They'd crossed paths by chance in the market, between bananas and blueberries. Her runaway cart slammed into his toes. She squeezed his bicep, her warm apology disarming. The pain in his foot vanished.

She craved ice cream weekly, an unshakable ritual. Vanilla scoops dotted with chocolate sprinkles—her "yummy crumbs." Her hand clasped his, humming softly as she nibbled the cone. Only ice cream coaxed out her soothing, joyful purr.

"Will they play our song?"

He'd make sure they did.

She adored his stories, spun with playful theatrical flair. Some true, some embellished, they kept her soft hand in his.

"We'll seat favorites at the main table!"

There would be fifty guests, though his relatives were few and distant. His favorite would already be beside him.

She dreamed of children, and he eagerly agreed. A girl, then a boy, in that order. He promised to do his best.

Strolls along the shore, savoring the rushing tide and distant boats. They made a home in his apartment overlooking the Taff, windows open to the cool sea breeze as they nestled close.

It began one Sunday. Tearing bread, they tossed crumbs to eager seagulls by the river. Hands entwined, they chatted, savoring ice cream. A ship sailed across the scarlet horizon when Bethany's hand spasmed. He caught her swiftly before she collapsed.

"My legs!" Her terrified eyes pierced him with dread.

A flurry of tests followed, and days later, numbness crept into her hands. Scans uncovered a cancerous mass gnawing at her brain. Inoperable, the doctors declared. She faced the news with grace he couldn't muster.

Each day grew more precious.

They talked endlessly, smiling through tears until her medicines lulled her to sleep. Weeks later, brutal chills racked her. He raced home, returning with thicker blankets from their apartment. He wrapped her snugly, kissing her forehead with care.

"Thank you." Her lips were dry. Her shivers eased but persisted. His grip steadied her trembling palm. Bethany's eyes fluttered, fighting to stay open. "I love you," she whispered.

Fifty unsent invitations lay untouched in their nook.

The fucking treatments weren't working.

Within weeks, her soft hand stilled forever.

The tender memory faded, replaced by the briny taste of seawater and the weight of Bennett's limp body. Kendrick locked his arms around Bennett's chest, guiding them through the fiery current.

Phinn hooked Bennett's shoulders, dragging the unconscious Marine to the runway's muddy edge.

Thomas Ryan Kendrick collapsed in the dark, marshy soil, heaving and coughing. The jet's blazing flames churned on the tide beneath the glinting stars.

Her voice echoed in his mind.

"Do you think we'll get lots of gifts?"

The softness of her neck beneath his lips.

What a life they almost had.

CHAPTER

65

Two uniformed officers from Dauphin's Police Department shuffled around the treatment ward, questioning Malum and Nelson. Dr. Bannister had been x-rayed to check for internal injuries, hooked to an IV, and currently slept in the critical care ward under monitor for possible respiratory depression. There'd been no word on Bennett since the crash.

The crash landing was catching up with his body, and soreness spread through Kendrick's neck and shoulders. His limbs were also tight, and he paced the room, trying to work out the stiffness. He'd tried to phone Adler, but there was no answer despite three attempts. Had the authorities shut down Adler's command?

Phinn sat in the waiting room, holding a cold pack to his cheekbone. They'd both refused care, though an adorable nurse with a gentle smile insisted on cleaning the Scot's facial cuts, applying fresh gauze to his wounded arm, and explaining a proper icing cycle. Phinn was annoyed by the attention.

Kendrick torqued his neck to the side.

There was no doubt Rosales had made it onto the freighter with the two assets, headed to parts unknown. But without Adler's help, there'd be no way he could track them. Even if he found their position, he had no transportation or weapons. He was hesitant to reach out to domestic authorities. Doing so could wrap him up in days or weeks of debriefings, effectively ending any hunt for the women on that ship. Also, once Yuri found out the plane hadn't landed with his man at the correct airport, which would occur within the next twelve hours, he might follow through with his promise, and they'd never see Dr. Mitchum or Bannister again.

He made his way down a long corridor to a bank of vending machines. What he really wanted was a frothy pint, but as he stared at the two-meter high, fancy brewing mechanism in front of him, he'd settle for a single button labeled "black coffee."

Kendrick dropped his head. All weapons had been seized by Yuri. He had no information regarding the women's whereabouts. No transportation, even if he did know where they were. The brave, impulsive Marine who'd saved his life might not make it. Nelson, who'd incredibly landed the jet when Bennett became incapacitated, had broken his arm, and there was no way he could continue the mission.

Beyond all that, even if he could decipher the bizarre terminology on the giant contraption in front of him, he couldn't have a coffee because the bloody thing only took credit cards.

He balled his fists and took a deep breath. Maybe he was a relic? A man with useless knowledge, ineffectual, and obsolete? His former charge thought so. Perhaps they were right?

A vibration came from his soaked trouser pocket.

An exasperated Kendrick fished out the phone.

"Tommy?" a voice said.

"Yes?" Kendrick replied.

"Hey, it's Jed. I have some news."

Something inside him relaxed. His fisherman friend from Alexandra, the shrimper he'd befriended who'd asked those odd history questions. It was, as they say, nice to hear a familiar voice.

"Good to hear from you." He tried to sound upbeat.

Jed excitedly shared news of a recent adventure. He wanted to tell him the entire tale in person and hoped they could celebrate soon at the pub. He was buying.

Kendrick sighed.

"You alright, Tommy? You don't sound like your usual self."

He wasn't sure what weighed heaviest—exhaustion, soreness, his dire situation, or that damn coffee machine. Maybe all of it. Still, he headed down the corridor to a set of auto doors. He stepped outside into a small courtyard, took in the night air, and, without filter, began telling Jed everything.

Jed was stunned when Kendrick admitted he was former U.K. intelligence.

"Wait, you're not a professor?"

He shared other details of the mission, Colombia, Venezuela, told him how their jet had slid off the runway into the water.

"A jet crash? Are you okay, Tommy?"

He wasn't, but there were larger concerns. "Rosales followed the two hostages onto a freighter and I've got no way to track them."

Jed pressed him for the ship's name and relayed it to a woman on his end. They spoke, though Kendrick couldn't quite make out their conversation.

"You need to tell the authorities."

"I am the authorities, Jed. That freighter is Colombian flagged, and those onboard are heavily armed. Even if your Coast Guard could board them, they'd be walking into a fortified trap. And the people holding the two hostages have no principles. The bastards will heave those girls overboard the moment their freighter is threatened with boarding. I don't know if there's anything I can do."

He closed his eyes. He was sharing too much, something he'd avoided most of his life. He'd always kept banter concerning his missions and his person secret and vague. It was best not to involve others.

But, as he spoke, an unfamiliar feeling grew. Truthfully, he'd held people from his private life, away from his troubles, for so long, he'd forgotten the benefits of being open and truthful.

Kendrick rubbed his eyes. Bethany had taught him that—but the payback for his vulnerability then was her sudden and tragic passing. It left holes in his soul that had never mended.

However, as he shared more detail of his life with his friend, his breathing eased, and the soreness in his neck disappeared.

Still, he found it difficult to let his guard down.

"Sorry, Jed, I don't mean to burden you with this. It's been a long several days." He caught a double breath, and his eyes welled. He cleared both with a quick cough and a wipe, then glanced around the empty courtyard to ensure nobody witnessed his break.

"Where are you now, exactly?"

"Dauphin, emergency room." Kendrick cleared his throat again. "We're waiting on word."

Jed told him how sorry he was for his friend Bennett.

"Listen, we're docked in West Palm right now, taking the ship for a test run with its new engines. We're coming your way. It'll take a few days. But there's someone I need you to go and see, right away."

"Right away?" Kendrick repeated. The man's support touched him, but what could any mate of Jed's possibly do for him?

"If anyone can help, Tommy, it's him," Jed said. "I'll call ahead."

"Jed, please, it's late and—"

"Tommy, trust in this," Jed said calmly. "He's one of you."

Kendrick wasn't precisely sure what that meant, but he had no other resources at his disposal, couldn't reach Adler, and time, in many ways, was running out.

He agreed, and Jed provided directions before the call ended.

The hospital's auto doors opened, and Phinn sauntered outside into the courtyard.

"Put a damn tube in em." Phinn's head turned side to side. "Bullet poked his lung but passed right through, lucky bastard. Said that Malum bloke saved his life, jammed fingers into his chest and kept him breathing." Phinn stomped in half a circle. "Bennett's stable, but this daft, scrub-wearing prick wouldn't let me see him."

Kendrick rubbed his chin.

"Can't believe that Nelson kid landed the plane," Phinn said. "We hit the drink, but it could have been a shit ton worse."

Kendrick couldn't believe it either. They all owed that SEAL their lives.

"Aye," Phinn said. "Nelson wanted you to have these."

He handed Kendrick the SEAL's eyewear.

At last, a break! Kendrick immediately put the lenses on. He tried contacting Rosales. No answer. He tried Adler. No Answer. Shit. The device appeared to be working, but his eyewear was useless if nobody received his damn signal.

He exhaled, slipped the pair into his pocket, and his gaze returned to the night sky.

"Wha?" Phinn said after a long moment.

"I need to go and see someone."

"Who?"

"Someone who might be able to help, and–"

"I's going with! They was my charge!" Phinn barked.

He tried to convince the Scot otherwise. He didn't know if Jed's proposal would pay off at all, and he wanted Phinn to stay here and mind the others. But reasoning with the Scottish man was like trying to pet a porcupine.

Kendrick relented. "Alright, then," he said. "We'll need a car."

CHAPTER
66

Rosales tried to sleep, but the stifling heat and oppressive darkness of the cramped electrical compartment made rest impossible. Her body was slick with sweat, salty streaks etched paths down her skin. She shimmied up, unhooked the bungee cord holding the door, and carefully cracked it open. A rush of cool air filled her lungs, relief from the compartment's suffocating heat.

The passageway hummed with the ship's groans and vibrations, but it was absent of footsteps or voices. She eased the heavy door wider and slipped into the shadowy corridor. She needed to find the source of those mysterious drops on her neck. She retraced her steps.

A sharp whiff of ammonia stung her nostrils. She scanned the towering stack of containers for the source of the leak. Midway down the row, she spotted a puddle on the floor. Tracking it upward, she pinpointed the dripping to the fifth container from the bottom.

The leaking container was secured with a padlock. She'd need to bypass it, but first, she faced a daunting climb. The stack loomed 50 feet above her. Once at the top, she'd have to disable the mechanism, open the steel box, and see if its contents confirmed her horrible suspicions.

She snatched tinsnips from the toolbox, sliced an aluminum can into T-shaped shims, and pocketed them with the pliers—all while listening for trouble. She peered into the passageway to ensure it was clear, then sealed the door and secured its lever.

Grasping the container's central locking bars, she began her ascent. The climb was grueling at first, but she found her rhythm, reaching the fourth level with steady determination. Pausing to catch her breath, she noticed the dripping from above had stopped—at least for now.

An echo of footsteps approached. A beam of light pierced the darkness, dancing along the passageway walls. Rosales pressed herself flat against the container, thirty feet above the deck, and held her breath. The corridor's blackness cloaked her. The figure with the flashlight passed below, oblivious to her presence.

The ship lurched violently to port.

She dropped ten feet, flailing, until her left hand snagged a locking bar. Her right middle finger smashed into the metal with a crack. Her boot snagged the door lever, halting her fall. A jolt of pain shot through her injured hand.

Below, the footsteps stopped, as if the searcher sensed something amiss. With the light now sweeping from the port side, she scrambled down the stack as quietly as she could. She darted out of the row just as the flashlight beam grazed past, narrowly escaping detection.

She'd survived worse than this. Heart pounding, she sprinted into the starboard passageway. Returning to the electrical compartment wasn't an option—not without crossing the searcher's path.

Her right middle finger throbbed, clearly dislocated. If confronted, she'd need both hands to fight or flee. Gritting her teeth, she grasped the injured digit with her left hand, took a steadying breath, and yanked it back into place. Pain seared through her hand, but she clenched her jaw, refusing to let it slow her. The finger clicked into its socket, aching but usable.

The beam crept closer. Her pulse raced—one wrong move, and she'd be exposed. From a sheath on her thigh, she drew a seven-inch combat knife, its blade catching the dim light. If it came to a fight, she'd strike fast and silent, then hide the evidence in the electrical room. After that, she'd need a new refuge until she could signal for help.

The footsteps grew louder, and flashes of light flickered from the left, casting erratic shadows along the corridor walls.

"¿Qué estás haciendo?" a voice shouted.

"Escuché algo," a closer voice replied.

"Tengo hambre. Vamos."

The voices drifted off, their casual banter easing her nerves—they hadn't sensed her yet. The beam probing near her feet swung away, and the footsteps faded into the distance. With a quiet exhale, she slid the knife back into its sheath.

After confirming the coast was clear, she steeled herself and resumed the climb, determined to reach the fifth level. At last, she arrived at the padlocked container. Its u-shaped shackle gleamed defiantly. She retrieved the aluminum shims from her pocket, ready to execute her plan.

She wrapped the first shim around the lock's shackle, forming a tight collar. Using the needle-nosed pliers, she maneuvered the aluminum into the lock's mechanism, pressing it against the internal pin. A careful twist and push released one side of the shackle. She repeated the process with a second shim, and with a satisfying click, the lock sprang open.

A faint smile tugged at her lips. Her makeshift tools had worked. She lifted the lever with a gentle push, wincing at its faint squeak. The massive metal door swung open slowly, and she pulled herself up into the container's dark interior.

In the shadows, something stared back at her.

Rosales's heart drummed. Ancient trade arteries, protection at all costs, dark commerce. These shipping lanes were the new Silk Roads.

JACK J. WYATT

CHAPTER

67

Despite the late hour and closed rental agencies, Phinn arrived in a sleek black BMW 5 series. Kendrick bit back his questions. If there was one thing he'd learned, it was that the man driving next to him bulldozed through problems without much concern for consequence. And, truth be told, that was what they needed right now.

Phinn guided the car east along I-10. Kendrick gulped his second coffee as his phone vibrated.

"We have info on that vessel you saw in Colombia," Jed said.

Kendrick switched on the speaker for Phinn to hear.

"The Malusnavi is a Neopanamax, and Tommy, she's massive—like a 110-story skyscraper stretched across the water."

He rattled off the ship's staggering tonnage, dwarfing even Nimitz-class carriers. The seasoned shrimper admitted he'd only seen these giants in photos, each hauling 15,000 containers. They demanded at least five stories of water beneath them, tying them to the world's deepest ports.

"Anything shallower and one of these super-heavy cargo freighters might hit bottom and crack the planet," Jed said with a chuckle. "But that works to our advantage because there are only a few places it can dock."

"Where'r ya thinkin?" Phinn asked.

325

"Based on its last known pings, it passed the Panama Canal marker and headed north into the Gulf. Then its GPS vanished, which isn't normal."

"So, we can't be sure where it's headed?" Kendrick said.

"I have something!" A new voice broke in, brimming with excitement.

Quick introductions followed.

"It's very nice to meet you, Aldous," Maya replied.

The dash glow caught Phinn's wide smile.

"I tried to find the ship with GPS but couldn't. I think they're hiding their position to throw off trackers," she said.

"They can do that? A ship that big?" Kendrick asked.

"Easily, smugglers do it all the time. There are even apps to mock another location. It's not difficult. And the only way to spot a spoofed vessel in the open water without GPS is basic marine radar. But a ship has to be pretty close to show up on it."

"How close?" Phinn asked.

"Even with my equipment, the best range is twenty nautical miles," Jed said.

Kendrick's frown deepened. The freighter could be anywhere in the Gulf's endless stretch.

"Fortunately," Maya began, "our shrimping boat, the Gypsea Moon, predates GPS. It relied on a different navigation trick."

"Wait," Jed said. "You mean LORAN?"

"Right," Maya said. "Long-range navigation. A land-based system using signal towers. Captain Bill left a pile of gear below deck, which I found while rummaging."

"Snooping?" Jed said.

"When we left harbor, you wouldn't let me steer the boat," she chuckled. "So, I got bored and looked around in the hull."

"But those signal towers were turned off a dozen years ago. Even in the U.K.," Kendrick said.

"Yes. But among the gear below, I found an old military radio that scans global frequencies."

"And that helps us?" Kendrick said.

"Navigation systems varied—British, Russian, Chinese—using different frequencies from 2 to 100 megahertz. This gear lets me scan the entire spectrum," she said.

Kendrick's brow arched. She was good—Adler good.

"Because those LORAN towers are now turned off, all I could do was get a range fix between the ship's distance and ours. But once I found the frequency, I waited for the receiver to provide an approximate distance."

"But how did you find the frequency?"

"Monitoring chatter of ships in the sea lanes. Seaspeak's in English, but I heard a captain relay his ship's position with a stuttered accent."

"Russian accent?" Kendrick said.

"Yes," Maya said. "A passing freighter called out this ship's flag, and I fixed on the vessel's outgoing radio signal as best I could," she paused, "And this is the only Colombian-flagged, Russian speaking vessel in the entire Gulf. Have a listen."

Static buzzed, then a voice cut through the noise.

"That's them!" Phinn cried.

"The location isn't exact, but I'm sure that freighter passed the Yucatan channel about three hours ago, and she's going northwest," Maya said.

"Got to be headed to NOLA," Jed said. "They've dredged the Mississippi to over fifty feet for inland ports. NOLA's the nearest and biggest international container port in the Gulf. They must've completed a deep lane."

"You've got about eight hours till they reach it," Maya warned.

"The port is huge, a lot of areas to cover. You've got to find them before they dock," Jed said.

"Why?" Phinn cut in.

"Because they might move our hostages to another boat," Kendrick said. "And then we'd lose them."

"Truer than you know. The Mississippi runs for 2,300 miles north all the way into Minnesota. A third of domestic goods travel through those lanes on feeder boats. If your assets are moved off the ship, there are thousands of places they could take them, and hundreds of rivers east and west connect to the Mississippi. And if they're relocated to a car or truck, the odds of finding them get worse."

Typing clattered through the phone.

"Royal Cargo West," Maya said. "Dredge started in 2018. Got to be the area."

"Yeah, looks like they have a landing for Foreign-Trade, too," Jed added.

Kendrick mulled over the plan, staring out the window. The BMW hummed toward their contact, dawn creeping over the horizon.

The freighter was headed for New Orleans. Their mission was to infiltrate the port, locate the ship before it unloaded, extract their people, and disappear. One misstep could spark a firefight—or worse, they could lose their assets forever.

The BMW cut through the pre-dawn gloom, racing toward their contact as light bled over the horizon. They rolled up to a low brown house, white-trimmed. An oak sprawled across the yard. A lean man in his mid-sixties, skin weathered by decades of sun and salt, greeted them in the driveway.

"Ted Salvador," he said, seizing Kendrick's hand like a vise.

CHAPTER
68

Locked in. Onboard the freighter, Hannah and Alisha were taken to the accommodation block—a hulking rectangular tower rising from the ship's last third. It held crew sleeping quarters, nothing more. Their room offered a single bed, a desk fixed to the wall without a chair, and a cramped bathroom with a trickling shower. Their door was locked from the outside.

While Alisha burrowed under the covers, Hannah stepped into the bathroom. Water ran cold, no soap, barely cutting through the sour mud smell clinging to her from their last prison.

They were on the sixth or seventh level, window blocked by a rusted stack of containers. No radio, no phone. Just two outlets and a toggle switch at chest height.

Hannah could turn the lights on or off, or electrocute herself if she got bored. Still, it was a small miracle she was in control of anything.

Back in the mud-soaked hell of those ungodly pits, when those strangers descended that hill in the dark, she thought it was her imagination. A wild vision born from helplessness in that cursed valley, shaking beside a fading Dan and the dim shapes around her.

But that squad—soldiers or mercenaries—proved real, rushing to pull them out. Then Yuri, that bastard, rolled in with his crew. He shoved the men onto a jet, Dan and Doctor Malum too. She prayed they were okay.

She paced the cabin, craning toward the window's edge again. Rain streaked the glass, revealing only dark waves churning below. She'd rummaged through the desk drawers—nothing to smash the pane. Even if she broke through, sixty feet stretched straight down to the deck, slick containers impossible to grip. Even if they escaped this room, they were still in the middle of the Goddamn ocean.

Bolted in, they were Yuri's prisoners—trapped, with no one to save them. Captain, crew, all of them had to be evaded. It was hopeless.

A knock at the door jolted her. She darted to the mattress beside a sleeping Alisha. They'd been told to stay put when someone knocked, or food vanished. Any attempt to flee or fight would be met with severe punishment.

The door swung wide. A guard shoved a cart inside, his boots scuffing the floor, then slammed and bolted the door

Water, bread, beans. Plastic bottles, no cups, no forks—just two cloth napkins. Hannah sneered. How thoughtful.

She snatched a bread slice, scooped up beans. Hunger raked her empty stomach. Sauce dripped onto the red t-shirt from Phinn, smeared away with a swipe. Her mind flashed to Phinn's blood-soaked shirt in the tent—how had he survived that blade? It was astonishing. She'd barely had time to thank him before they were taken, again.

She shook her head. If these kidnapping assholes wanted money, they hadn't mentioned it. She had only a few hundred dollars in savings and a mountain of student debt. She could give them nothing.

She turned to Alisha. A new mother caught in the middle of all this chaos. Without her husband, Hannah had to protect her.

She set the bread back onto the cart, then vowed silently. If it came down to it, she'd trade herself to get Alisha back to Dan. She'd learned young—the world bit hard. But her friends had carved out something precious, a new life on the way. That deserved guarding. It was the one good thing she might be able to do in all this madness. A broken smile grew on her face.

Another rap struck the door.

She slid back to the bed beside Alisha.

The bolt clicked, the knob turning.

"Comfortable?" a haunting voice asked.

It was Foster.

A chill stabbed Hannah. What the hell was he doing here? The son-of-a-bitch must've trailed them from his mud-choked pits to the port. Yuri and he must be partners. Her shoulders stiffened, rage surging through her.

He staggered into the cabin, unsteady on the swaying floor. He'd swapped filth for a clean ivory suit, loose, topped with a straw hat. He looked like an old-time Southern plantation owner.

Hannah averted her eyes.

"Fine," she managed.

Foster eyed the cart, jabbing the bread.

"I'll send more nutrition in the morning—juice, fruit, cereal with fiber. We need you strong."

His voice prickled her skin. She stared, steady, as his gaze roamed.

"You're very attractive for a physician." His stare slid downward. "Married?"

Hannah folded her arms tight.

He fingered the brim of his hat. "Things would go much better for you if you cooperated."

Was this straw-hatted prick coming on to her?

"Go fuck yourself," she said.

Foster laughed low, brushing at his face.

"You must understand where you are and who you're talking to. You are not free, and you're alive only because you're still useful."

"What the fuck does that mean?"

He edged closer.

"Never mind now. But I will say this. The room you're in, this food you eat, this air you breathe can all be taken away at my say-so. I

recommend you change your attitude and soften that tongue of yours."
He pointed to Alisha. "Or I'll remove you from your friend."

Hannah clenched her fists, nails digging into her palms.

Foster's smile was cold, predatory. "Cooperate, and you and your friend stay together, treated well. Defy me, and I'll have you removed." He tilted toward Alisha, still asleep on the bed, her chest rising faintly beneath the thin blanket. "She'll stay here, under my… personal care." He frowned a tsk. "Fragile thing like her—alone, so far from home. It'd be a pity if she found herself in hands less gentle than my own."

Hannah's breath hitched, a cold knot tightening in her gut. Alisha—defenseless—left with this monster. She pictured Alisha's baby, alone without her, and the thought was unbearable.

"You wouldn't dare."

Foster's cruel grin widened. "Oh, I would."

She wanted to lunge from the bed, attack this animal, rip out his eyes. She tightened her jaw, readying for battle.

He flicked the rim of his hat. "Try me."

But there was no way she could overpower this man, not as weak as she felt. She needed food, strength, and a better plan than grappling and clawing him. She had to find a way off this ship to safety, for both her and Alisha.

Hannah's knees went weak, and she sank beside Alisha. Fear knotted her chest, her fists shaking with rage.

Foster lingered, his grin unwavering, then turned sharply. The door slammed shut behind him. The bolt squeaked, pinching to a stop.

Hannah went stiff. That sound—she had to get them out.

CHAPTER
69

Tina Salvador, a small energetic woman in large sunglasses, attacked Kendrick and Phinn with bear hugs. Phinn was utterly grateful for the squeeze.

They were treated to a spread of juice, eggs, and toast. Discussion during the meal centered around Tina's gardening, Ted's frustration with Florida's college football teams, and the weather. Tina lit up when she talked about their son, Jed.

"He bought us a beautiful powerboat! Now Ted can go fishing, and I won't worry that he is stuck out there fighting those dang winds."

Ted nodded between chews.

Phinn and Kendrick finished their meals.

"Too kind. This was delicious, thank you," Kendrick said.

Tina rose from the table.

"Allow me, lass." Phinn grabbed several plates. He arched his eyebrows at Ted, and the two strolled into the kitchen for a quick conversation.

A smiling Tina moseyed into the living room.

Phinn returned moments later.

"What'd you two—?"

"Beamer wasn't exactly a rental. That scrub twat'll be missing it soon." Phinn shrugged. "Ted said he'd take care of it."

Kendrick groaned quietly, shaking his head with a faint smile.

Ted entered the room, nodding toward the side door. "C'mon, let's talk outside."

As Tina trailed Phinn back into the kitchen, Ted led Kendrick into the backyard, the screen door creaking softly behind them.

"Heard you're in a spot?"

"Gracious for your aid, sir."

"Please, no sirs." His voice was smooth and commanding. "Friends of my boy are family."

The faint scent of freshly cut grass filled the air, as Ted led Kendrick across the lawn—its perimeter blooming with red fire spike and sprouting purpellias.

"Loves her gardening." Ted gestured to the shrubbery as the two men crossed. "I had to fix the gutters last season, damn rains eroding the soil. Patched the roof, too."

Kendrick supplied what he thought were the proper grunts of admiration as Ted led them to a detached outbuilding in the rear of the yard.

"Heard three females?" he said.

"Yes," Kendrick said. "Fortunately, one's Green Beret. She can hold her own, but adversaries are… too many."

"Green Beret?" Ted's brows shot up. "Then before the freighter makes berth, she'll scout the ship but not attempt action until she formulates a solid exit. Green Berets are trained pragmatic, solid tacticians—used to working in isolation. But even the best can get pinned down if the odds are bad enough. You'll need to move fast."

Ted opened the outbuilding's lock and slid open a steel carriage door. He switched on a bay of interior LED lights, their harsh glow cutting through the dimness, illuminating the cement floor. The air smelled of fresh sawdust and old varnish, and the hum of a distant fan barely stirred the stillness. Scattered across the space were heavy woodworking machines—band saws, planers, jointers.

An unfinished rocking chair sat on a workbench, its spindles expertly carved. The man was good with his hands.

"What was your branch of service, if you don't mind me asking?" Kendrick said.

"Went Army. Did a solid ten. Moved ready reserve when Jed was born. A couple of skirmishes. Then Kuwait."

It was impolite to press for particulars unless Ted offered those details himself. Besides, the best soldiers were modest and rarely discussed time in-country openly. Yet, there was something about the way this man carried himself that was poised and familiar. His time in theatre wasn't spent peeling potatoes.

Ted marched past a worktable and its bandsaw to a six-foot standing metal cabinet at the shop's rear. He pressed a sequence of numbers on the front panel, and a green light flashed.

"Wait, you'll need these." He fished a set of keys from his pocket. "Speedboat, tri-motor, fast as anything. Spot 61A in the marina. You'll want to take the Gulf Intercoastal from Lake Borgne to the Mississippi and lock-through the Industrial Canal. Should be open. Then head down river and wait for your freighter."

"Are you sure?" Kendrick hesitated.

"Take the speedboat," Ted grunted. "It's a beauty, but I love sailing. Hoisting the main, keeping stiff, fighting the splash, earning my turns." He nodded to himself. "Makes me feel like I've done something with my day."

For some reason, Kendrick understood that perfectly.

"Dozen years ago, I'd be going with you," Ted said.

"What was your specialty?"

Ted Salvador flashed a grin, turning the lever.

"Flank force," he said, sharply.

The locker opened.

Kendrick's eyes widened.

A pair of SIG516 semi-automatic rifles, a scoped jet-black x-bolt Winchester Magnum with muzzle, two close quarter Heckler & Koch MP7 semi-automatics with suppressors, and numerous handguns were mounted within the cabinet's insides. Stacks of olive drab metal cartridge-boxes, holding hundreds of rounds of ammunition, filled the locker's bottom third.

Kendrick gazed at the firearms, chuckling. "Snipers and their hardware."

Ted bounced a nod. "Take anything you need."

CHAPTER
70

Hannah was nine when her world shrank to a sagging trailer park on the edge of town, where she and her mom landed after the divorce. Her nurse mother often worked double shifts at the hospital, coming home with in stained scrubs, eyes heavy with exhaustion. Hannah had to fend for herself most nights.

Usually, Hannah locked just the trailer's door handle, a quick twist to seal herself in. But when her mom was home, bone-tired, Hannah made sure to slide the barrel bolt too, its sharp snap echoing in the quiet. It was a small ritual to world out, a fleeting sense of safety as they slept. A click that promised protection.

She'd heard no snap.

Foster had left the bolt loose, a mistake she could use.

A flare, a radio—anything to call for help. She'd tear the ship apart to find it. She stood, ran her fingers along the door's cold frame. When they'd forced them into this room, she'd seen the door's bolt swaying upright. If she was right, shaking the door might make it drop.

She pressed against the door and waited, but there was only silence. She twisted the handle—it was locked. She yanked the door in and out, and the bottom shifted. She shook it harder. A click sounded, and the door swung open.

Her heart slammed in her chest.

She shoved the door shut, stepped back. If any guard heard the breach and came, she'd act confused—blame the door, the ship's movement.

She stared at the knob, waiting for it to move. It didn't. The ship creaked, but the hall stayed quiet.

She edged to the door, turned the handle. It opened. She peeked out—the hall empty, shadows swaying with the waves. Alisha slept on, unaware.

She slipped into the dark corridor.

The ship groaned, rocking with the waves. Doors lined the narrow hall, most for the crew. She closed the door quietly, reached up and slid the bolt shut, locking it tight. Alisha would stay locked inside—it was the safest place for her right now.

Hannah swallowed, picturing Alisha's crooked smile, the way she'd snort when she laughed too hard. She couldn't lose her.

Hannah crossed to the outer platform, metal grates slick underfoot. Warm, wet wind hit her face, carrying the tang of salt and rust. A "7" on the ceiling marked her spot—seventh floor of the freighter's tower. Good thing she hadn't smashed the window, tried climbing down those containers. One slip, and she'd be dead.

The wind whipped harder now, mist stinging her skin. Waves smashed the hull far below, spraying the rail with saltwater. Containers stacked ten, twelve high, stretching up the tower and out to the bow. Green lights traced the ship's edge, flashing off the waves.

The terrace led to tight stairs, a ladder bolted beside them, running the height of all twelve floors.

Voices bounced down the corridor. A door creaked open nearby, then slammed shut. Hannah froze, holding her breath, waiting for footsteps. If they caught her outside, Foster would do it—take Alisha, for good.

She had to climb down, hide under the grates. It was dark enough they wouldn't spot her. She reached over the rail and grabbed a rung.

The ladder was slick with water. It groaned under her weight, metal cold against her burning palms. Seventy feet up, she swung from the terrace and started down. The ship rocked hard, slamming her into the tower. Her feet slipped from the rungs.

She hung in the air, legs kicking, heart pounding. Alisha's face flashed in her mind—pale, sleeping. She had to make it back. Reaching for a rung—she missed and almost fell. The ship steadied, and she swung back in.

Wind bit her eyes, making them water. She clung to the ladder, breathing hard. Another shake like that, and she'd hit the deck, dead. The ladder was too high, too slick in this storm—even just to hide.

She pulled herself over the rail, onto the terrace, shaking. She slumped against the rail, chest heaving, the storm's roar swallowing her ragged breaths. Her palms burned from the ladder's slick rungs.

A distant shout cut through the crashing waves.

She couldn't stay here—she was too exposed. She gripped the wet rail, and took the outer stairs toward the deck.

Below, a shadow moved.

Hannah gripped the railing and crept down the stairway to the deck. A sharp, metallic clang echoed from below. Then—a low voice, too faint to make out, came closer.

JACK J. WYATT

CHAPTER
71

The sun sank below the horizon, casting long, jagged shadows over the restless water as Phinn sped past Grand Island on Lake Borgne, entering the narrow channel at Tower Dupre. A bitter tang—oil, maybe, or something chemical—lingered in the thick sea air, stinging Kendrick's nostrils.

Phinn's steady hand navigated the water lanes like he'd done it a dozen times, scanning the buoy markers and the speedboat's glowing dash. Kendrick had a bundle of questions for the Scot when they were finished with all this.

Ted's boat was a beauty, sleek and gleaming even in the fading light. It seated eight on deck and slept four or five in the bow's cabin. The boat boasted top-tier satellite navigation, an entertainment system, and a high-tech dashboard. The craft oozed wealth, sleek and lavish. Kendrick was itching to hear more about the find Jed and his mates had come across.

They motored west along the coastline for nearly two hours, the engine a steady hum beneath the night sky. Distant lights flickered along the shore as Phinn steered under the rusted span of Seeber Bridge, through the Industrial Canal Lock, and between the weathered edges of Musicians' Village and The Lower Ninth Ward.

Smaller ships and barges drifted lazily between the Mississippi and eastern inlets, flanked by towering concrete flood walls—rebuilt after

Katrina's fury scarred the land. The river pulsed with engine growls and water slapping hulls, shattering the stillness.

Phinn throttled down as the canal widened into the vast Mississippi River. At no-wake speed, they idled through the shipping lane. Glowing channel markers bobbed in the 500-meter-wide waterway, a sprawling highway of steel giants. The ships' scale defied belief—massive freighters stretched into the dark, their decks alive with lights.

"Woah, these are monsters," Phinn muttered.

Kendrick nodded. "And ours is bigger."

He wasn't wrong. Each three-hundred-meter cargo vessel glowed like a floating city, some hauling over five thousand containers through the channel. Dozens of massive vessels clogged the river—oil tankers, merchant ships, and freighters stacked with cargo, each a floating giant. Their target, the Malusnavi freighter, loomed larger still—triple the capacity, a colossus waiting downriver.

The passage from the Gulf twisted over 100 miles through inlets near Pass A Loutre, past the murky waters of Black and Barataria Bays, up to the Port of New Orleans. Low tidal marshes stretched along the Mississippi's outlet, their bayous thick with Spartina grass and teeming with the hum of wildlife—crickets, frogs, the occasional splash of a fish breaking the surface.

Kendrick chewed on Jed's intel. NOLA's massive container port and its Foreign-Trade Zone sparked a hunch he couldn't shake.

"Let's head north to Royal Cargo West."

"Oy, but they're upriver?" Phinn's brow creased.

"Right, but I want to scope their destination," Kendrick said, voice firm.

Phinn nodded, swung the speedboat starboard, and sliced past anchored ships in the wide river, the wake rippling behind them. Fifteen minutes later, after weaving through the sluggish current, he pointed ahead. A row of towering yellow gantry cranes loomed like skeletal giants, their arms frozen mid-reach over the deserted docks.

The port stretched silent under the dim glow of sodium lights, its shoreline littered with shadows.

"There it is."

Phinn eased the boat to a nearby pier, its single store shuttered tight, windows black as pitch. A lone seagull screeched overhead, its cry swallowed by the oppressive night. They tied off, stashed the rifles—borrowed from Jed's father—beneath a tarp in the boat. They tucked the handguns into their waistbands, Kendrick's Glock fitted with a laser sight from Ted's custom work.

Kendrick's pulse quickened. He pictured Rosales and the hostages, trapped on that beast of a ship—counting on him, their time bleeding away. If he and Phinn failed, the three could be lost forever.

On foot, they crept through knee-high grass and scattered gear—rusted chains, a busted crate—to the port's perimeter fence. Beyond, a labyrinth of 20- and 40-foot containers stood in neat rows, their metal sides cool and slick as he brushed past.

He paused, weighing their next move. The mission was the rescue, but a detour nagged at him. Would Phinn be okay with breaking into the port to check a container or two? Maybe Phinn could stand guard while Kendrick slipped inside for some recon—after all, it was dark and this was their only chance.

"I was thinking—"

"How the fuck do we get in?" Phinn squinted at the wire fence.

Kendrick grinned. Bennett was right—he liked this guy, too.

"Oy, cameras." Phinn pointed.

Three cameras perched on poles inside the fence, the closest trained on the yard. Phinn's sharp eyes missed nothing, and Kendrick felt a flicker of relief having him along.

"Stay here," he said. He stripped off his overshirt, flung it over the barbed wire, and hauled himself up.

The fence rattled under his weight as he dropped to the other side, sprinting to the camera's pole. Kendrick tore the cable free with a sharp snap. He froze, breath held, waiting for an alarm that never sounded.

"C'mon!" He waved Phinn over.

Phinn scaled the fence, snagging Kendrick's shirt from the barbs. The fabric tore with a sharp rip, but Kendrick pulled it back on, ignoring the gash. They slipped into the container maze, footsteps muffled by the night. A distant clang echoed through the yard—metal on metal. Kendrick tensed. Was that the wind, or a guard? They pressed on, hugging the shadows.

"Move fast before patrol shows up. We need the Freeport," Kendrick said.

Phinn frowned. "Freeport?"

"Foreign trade zone."

Phinn's look lingered, so Kendrick elaborated.

"Freeports are Customs-free zones—private security, no oversight. Cargo sits untouched until it's shipped out. It's perfect for smuggling— fake machine parts, knockoff handbags, you name it. This is where that all comes from."

"Who runs 'em?"

"If they dock there, they can shuffle cargo to any foreign ship, no questions asked. It's a smuggler's dream—load up, swap ships, and vanish before anyone's the wiser. Stay in the zone, and no one can touch them without a warrant."

Phinn nodded. "Aye, shady as hell."

They slipped between containers.

Phinn's gaze flicked west, past the fence. "Why're them cameras facing the other way?"

Kendrick followed his gaze, then scaled a container for a better vantage. Beyond, a high concrete wall encircled a separate zone, its interior crammed with containers stacked like a blocks, edges glinting under harsh floodlights. A stack of pallets nearby could boost them over, but sleek dome cameras lined the boundary every 50 feet—far sharper than the cheap bullet cams in this yard. No cables to cut, no blind spots to slip through. Kendrick drew his Glock, the laser sight piercing the dark.

345

CHAPTER
72

Hannah ducked into an alcove stuffed with emergency craft and flotation gear. The space stank of mildew and rubber. Overhead, a bulky orange vessel—25 feet of battered fiberglass—swung from rusted pulleys above the railing. Its small propeller jutted out at the rear, and tiny, scratched windows lined its sides.

She held beneath its shadow. An escape craft. Would it be fast enough to carry her and Alisha from this nightmare? Shit, Alisha—she was still in that tower. How in the hell could she get her down here without being caught?

Hannah rubbed her sore hands. Salt and humidity layered her lungs. The ship chugged through a narrow channel, its engines shuddering the deck. Dark, she was blind to almost everything around. Across the moonlit water, flat, barren land ghosted into view—shadowed bushes and stunted trees clawing at the shoreline.

A red buoy blinked in the sea, pulsing like a heartbeat. She timed the flash, one about every five seconds. Was this a river delta? A coastal strait? Wind watered her eyes. The bobbing channel marker had a "92" painted on its side. But there were no other landmarks, no bearings— just endless black water and a gnawing unknown.

She scanned the deck. If she could locate the pulley's control switch, she could lower the boat. Then she might slink back to the seventh floor, grab Alisha, and drop that orange lifeboat into the waves before anyone spotted them. The plan was simple, brutal in its clarity. Even if they pulled it off, where were they? Miles from shore? Drifting into open sea? The boat could stall, its fuel tank dry, or the rainstorm could flip it like a toy.

Hannah crouched beneath the rescue boat, pressing deeper into the shadows, and closed her eyes. Yes, there were risks, but sitting still wasn't an option. If Foster caught them trying to escape—or caught her on deck—the consequences were dire, he'd made that painfully clear. She had to get Alisha and herself off of this ship at all costs.

In the distance, a crewman grappled with a coiled rope at the stern. His shoulders hunched against the wind, hands rough and deliberate as he fought the tangle. The rope slid across the deck.

Was he prepping to dock? Maybe they were nearing port? If she held out until land, she could bolt, find a phone, scream for help. On solid ground, Foster's crew would be slower, trapped by roads and walls. But waiting meant betting on a schedule she didn't know, dodging guards she couldn't see. Too much guesswork. Too much time.

With the deckhand's back turned, she darted between containers, wedging herself into a tight gap. Water streamed down, soaking her shoes, pooling around her ankles.

She had a better view of the water now. Still dark, it felt like they were moving north, maybe toward the southern U.S. coast. It was a hunch—the marshy flatlands, the numbered buoy marking their path, and the humidity. But if she was wrong, and they did launch the boat, she and Alisha could be caught adrift, lost to the currents.

Her attention returned to the ship's deck. A few yards off, a round container gleamed faintly, bolted to the railing. There were symbols etched its surface, a cross for medical supplies, and a tiny outline. A gun—a flare gun.

Her pulse kicked up. If she could grab it, she'd have a chance at signaling shore. Maybe she could even use it as a weapon and scorch the Foster bastard's face if it came to that.

Rain stung her eyes, blurring the world into smears of gray and orange. She edged closer, crouching low, the slippery deck treacherous.

Dan and Malum—wherever they were, trapped or still in the clutches of Yuri's men—she didn't know. But if she and Alisha broke free, she'd claw her way to the authorities, spill every name, every detail. Yuri or Foster—one of them held the key, and she'd choke it out of them herself if she had to.

A flicker of movement. A man in a rain slicker and hard hat prowled the deck, flashlight slicing through the downpour.

She flattened against the container, breath locked tight. He grumbled past, voice lost to the storm, then his boots sloshed toward the accommodation block.

She lunged for the container, yanking it free from its brackets. It was heavy, awkward. She bolted back to the hanging rescue boat and pried it open.

Gauze, bandages, tape, a scalpel—sharp enough to matter—but no flare gun. Shit! Their only hope, and someone had gutted the box and left her with scraps. She pocketed the scalpel and a few bandages.

A shout ripped through the storm.

She peeked from the gap.

Four men advanced from the bow. One jabbed a finger in her direction.

Her heart pounded. She dropped the container and ran, skidding through the downpour. She dove between the container stacks, zigzagging a path through the metallic maze.

Heavy footsteps echoed, closing in behind her.

"And where are you going?" said a voice.

JACK J. WYATT

CHAPTER

73

Phinn went first, leaping onto the freeport's concrete wall and lowering himself over. Kendrick held the Glock's laser sight on the security camera's lens until Phinn trained his Walther P99's beam on the same. Then, the Welshman made the leap.

Inside the freeport, they dropped low between the container stacks, slipping out of sight. A small dimly lit building housed the area's security patrol. Kendrick observed the structure. No movement, no voices, no flashlights.

"What're we looking for?" Phinn whispered.

Kendrick honestly didn't know. The cargo here had slipped past customs. Based on what he'd found on Alexandra, Kendrick suspected some containers held more than nuggets of gold and rocks of coltan.

"Oy, this one's unlocked," Phinn said. He pulled the lever and eased open the creaking door.

A broken pallet, abandoned shoe, a filthy shirt, and several empty plastic water bottles scattered everywhere. Otherwise, the shipping container had been cleaned out.

Kendrick picked up a bottle, examining it. It bore the same NGO logo he'd seen on Alexandra—two hands clasping over a globe. Strange.

But then something Nelson said days ago, a reminder really, struck Kendrick. Four pints, minimum, of water per day. Kendrick scanned the bottles. There were hundreds of empty containers at his feet. Was someone living in here?

Phinn shuffled by. "Smells rotted, like dead critter."

He was right. Quite possibly a creature had wandered inside, died and decayed. But the rot came with something sharper—the strong smell of ammonia.

Kendrick found something curious on the door. The container's PELG designation—the same code he'd seen on that container in Alexandra.

They found another PELG tagged container a few steps later. This one, however, secured with a disc padlock.

"Damn," Kendrick said. If he could pick the key mechanism, he might align the tumblers, but he didn't have the tools.

Phinn stepped over.

"Pancake lock," he grumbled. "We'll see about that."

He strode out of sight, but quickly returned gripping a rusty pipe wrench. Seizing the lock, he worked the wrench's jaws over it and torqued the tool's handle, snapping the lock in two.

Kendrick shook his head. "How?"

Phinn yanked the lever and opened the doors.

Inside were cardboard boxes, packed floor to ceiling, with Chinese writing and emblems. Phinn pulled one from a stack.

"Got fancy shirts in here," he whispered.

Kendrick examined another. His box held clothing too—American designer labels, probably counterfeit.

"What the hell?" Phinn said. "She's heavy."

He held a foil-wrapped package, dense and weighty, about the size of a brick. He split the foil with a nail, revealing a vacuum-sealed, mylar pouch.

Kendrick's spine went rigid.

"Don't!" he shouted.

He lunged toward Phinn, seizing the brick.

Thank God—Phinn hadn't punctured the seal.

He checked the seam. Still intact.

Phinn recoiled. "What the fuck is that?"

Kendrick shut his eyes.

Conflict minerals from Venezuelan mines moved unchecked—police and military either blind or bribed. Gold, coltan, and other resources flowed out, unregulated, dug by the same slave labor that once fed Sierra Leone's diamond trade and the Congo's crystal markets.

Back on Alexandra, the container with the PELG mark held a splintered crate—and the 5.56mm magazine Rudy's crew had dropped. That vessel had carried gold and coltan too, likely ripped from those same mines. Weapons and minerals, bundled together, traced to the same bloody source.

But this brick hadn't come from South America's mountains. It had bled out of Asia, moved halfway around the world, and landed in this harbor.

This freeport—and others like it—weren't just loopholes. No inspections. No oversight. Someone powerful was laundering shipments through here.

This was all far bigger than Kendrick imagined. The rescue mission had collided them into a significant smuggling artery—a Silk Road connecting the east and west. But the semi-trucks and freighters moving goods north were only one path. And now, this container from the east—proof the web spanned continents. They were smuggling far, far more than mere minerals.

Kendrick's pulse drummed. Inside the pouch, pale powder clung to the plastic, glinting faintly under the light—enough to kill cities. He gazed at all the unopened boxes still stacked inside this container, and the many other containers across the freeport yard.

Guns, forced labor, conflict minerals, and now this.

He turned to Phinn and exhaled. "This brick is pure fentanyl."

JACK J. WYATT

CHAPTER
74

"There you are." Foster swayed under the rain, sporting a smile and aiming his pistol.

Hannah had nowhere to go. The way up was a climb she could never make—and if she slipped or lost her grip, the fall would kill her.

She raised her hands in surrender.

"Quite the search we launched," Foster said. "My associate is still sweeping the lower decks for you. Though I don't know if I'll ever see him again on this monstrous ship." He chuckled to himself. "But I must say, I'll never understand how you were able to escape your room."

He waggled his gun, and Hannah stepped from the gangway onto the main deck.

"I won't let you get away again, though," Foster said—a slight slur to his words.

He grabbed her by the wrist.

She didn't struggle.

Small puddles splashed under their feet as they slogged back toward the accommodation tower.

She might leap over the side and escape—or drown before she ever reached shore. However, even if she were successful, that would leave Alisha in the hands of this deadly sociopath, and Hannah could never abandon her friend, even if their fate was now to die together.

"You're a feral one," Foster jeered. "Feisty, feral."

"Fuck you," Hannah grumbled.

"Fuck me? Nasty tongue. But we'll get those wild urges of yours under control soon enough." He searched for something in his pocket. "Yet before we do, I want to make certain you've got some appreciation for what I do in those fields."

Listening to his ramble, something struck Hannah. His cadence had a peculiar pattern.

"Soon this will be my ship. And it will carry my gold, tantalum, and nickel. In fact, many of those minerals used in your modern electronic appendages come from my mines."

Modern appendages? What was this crazy man talking about?

"This world depends on men like me." Foster smiled strangely as rain poured around them. "Sure, we've taken advantage of instability down there. Looting the ore, like plucking marshmallow bits from a child's breakfast cereal." He blinked. "But aren't you curious as to where all the minerals are going?"

If she had the strength, she'd force them both over the side right now and drown the prick.

"Fuck you," she repeated.

"I admire your resolve, but nobody will take this away from me."

He stared coldly into Hannah's eyes.

She met his dead gaze, refusing to flinch.

A slight twitch torqued one side of his face.

"I will take back control of those routes. I will run this ship!" Foster blinked unusually. His head jerked left, his face twisting in pain.

Hannah did a double take.

Water streamed off the brim of his hat, and the fingers of his left hand trembled.

"My minerals, my ship," he slurred.

Symptoms, patterns—holy shit!

During her residency, she'd seen it all—back pain masking kidney infections, depression hiding undiagnosed Celiac Disease. Diagnosis wasn't about the obvious symptoms. It was about piecing together the unseen ones.

She stared at Foster.

He was extremely sick and didn't realize it.

And he was the one steering their fate.

But it wasn't mercury poisoning.

On this freighter, under stress and away from those muddy pits he controlled, his symptoms were flaring. She thought back to the first time they'd met several days ago and didn't recall seeing anything severe—though she'd been terrified then and would've easily missed it.

A shout erupted on deck.

"Get fuck over here, now!"

Hannah turned.

Far in the distance Yuri stood in the rain, alongside another figure. The freighter's overhead beams did not light the deck well, especially with the falling water.

"Now!" Yuri screamed.

Foster squeezed her arm tight—he was using her to balance himself. They followed the rail along the high container stacks.

As Hannah got closer, her stomach dropped.

Yuri stood in his dark suit and boots—holding Alisha tightly by the wrist.

CHAPTER
75

They snuck out of the Freeport, through the customs yard in the same direction they'd arrived. Each hopped the wired fence and scurried from the grounds undetected. They were making their way back dockside to the speedboat when Phinn spotted a lone eatery whose neon sign boasted a dozen chicken wings and drink for $5.99.

"Oy, I could eat me a horse and jockey." Phinn wandered over and read a menu taped to its window.

While his palate wasn't quite that adventurous, Kendrick was starving, too. He checked his breast pocket for cash but came across a strange lump instead.

The eyewear! He'd forgotten about the smart glasses Nelson had given him! If Rosales was within RF distance and her pair were activated, they might be able to communicate.

Kendrick yanked them from his pocket, slipping them on.

"Rosales, Rosales? Can you hear me?"

Several seconds passed.

"Rosales, are you there?" Silence. Kendrick shook his head. This may have been too good to hope for.

"Sir?" a static-filled voice came. "Can you hear me?"

Kendrick nearly jumped in the air.

"Yes! Are you okay? Where are you?" he said excitedly.

Rosales was breathing heavily but her tone was quiet.

"Doctors are being kept in the ship's tower, sir."

"Are you safe?" Kendrick said.

"Sir, yes. I counted six hostiles onboard. Each armed. But the rest are crew."

Kendrick reconfirmed the figures.

"Sir, there's a lot of interference down here–"

"Down where?"

"I've been using the ship's lower section to stay hidden, sir. Once I heard your voice break in, I made my way stern and the signal got better. But I can't stay here long."

"Understood."

Phinn rushed over to join Kendrick.

"Is that the lass?"

Kendrick nodded.

"We know the ship's headed to Port NOLA, and I'm here with Phinn in the channel waiting for it to pass."

"Thank you, sir." She paused. "I've been staying out of sight inside a junction closet below. The switches inside enabled me to bypass the electrical lock of a watertight door in the freighter's ass-end. Port side. You should be able to open it without setting off any alarms."

Smart, tactical, and she'd figured out a way to let them board. Provided Phinn and he could sneak up behind the freighter without alerting any crew or the ship's armed cronies, this could work.

"Sir, I need to–"

But Rosales cut out.

"Rosales? You still there?"

"Sorry, sir," she whispered. "Had a close call there."

Kendrick breathed a sigh.

"Thank God you're okay. We–"

"Sir," she interrupted. "Do you remember the pictures we took at the mines with the eyewear? When I climbed from that smoky pit?"

"Yes."

"Said I'd debrief later, sir, because I didn't want to confuse the mission?" she said quietly.

"Yes."

"You said you saw ten to fifteen of those green boxes with the eyewear's tracking software?"

"Right, but the smoke." Kendrick paused. "Rosales, what are you trying to say?"

"Sir, those were persons down there," she whispered. "Alive in that valley. It's where Lorenzo escaped from."

The thought instantly sickened him. They could've retrieved the lot and taken them from that hell. And if Rosales knew, why hadn't she told him?

"Sir, I was able to upload those photos to my command's server and yours. We can use them to geolocate, get a satellite fix on that site since our GPS was being jammed in that area."

Though it would've been tight, they could've freed those souls with the others when they had the chance. Rosales had to know this. And if she did, what plausible reason could she have for not allowing them to save those poor workers?

"Why are you telling me this now?" He didn't want to press, but anger built anyway. Why would she abandon those men?

"Sir, your count at the hill's top was obscured by the smoke and interference. When I scaled down, I got a much better view. Sir, my tally was 191."

"I don't… 191?" Kendrick said, confused.

"Sir, there were 191 persons down in those pits."

Kendrick's mouth fell open, and his gut wrenched. One person forced to work that slurry was too many, but almost 200? That was atrocious, ruthless, unthinkably cruel, and warranted so many ungodly descriptors he didn't have the mental wherewithal to assemble them now. How the fuck had that single criminal mining operation been allowed to happen?

"That's why, sir, I didn't tell you."

She was right. It would have been impossible for him to walk away, had he known. She'd had the smarts to use the equipment to pinpoint their position for a later rescue. Kendrick on the other hand might've tried to devise an escape plan, which would've put the assets in grave danger. Besides, even if the team could've escaped with all two hundred, they'd only brought two vehicles, and wouldn't have gotten far. Ultimately, Rosales saved him from making that tough call.

"Sir, there's something else."

But he couldn't shake off the shocking news—two hundred souls trapped in that illegal mine. It made him sick and furious.

"Sir, down b—"

She cut out.

"Rosales?"

Kendrick repeated her name for two or three minutes, then tried Adler, but could not connect with his U.K. contact either.

The eatery's neon sign flickered off, and its keeper vanished from the area. River traffic thinned to nothing. Incoming clouds diminished the moon's glow, and thunder rumbled in the distance.

The two men made their way to the river. Frog and cicada sounds echoed around them, and lapping swells softly bounced the speedboat against the dock.

Phinn was making the climb from the planks to the vessel when he stopped unexpectedly, swallowed hard, and pointed downriver at a growing mountain of shifting lights.

"Oy, that's a jumbo fucker."

CHAPTER
76

Far below deck, the eyewear's RF signal cut out again.

"Kendrick? Kendrick?" Rosales called.

Static met her ears.

The enormous freighter had traveled up the Mississippi channel for several hours and was nearing the docks. Attempting to reestablish contact would take time she didn't have.

She sprinted through the corridor opposite the electrical room and peered down the long passageway. Rain streamed from above in waterfalls that pounded the ship's bottom. The sound was deafening.

No workers or armed patrols—she was clear.

But it wouldn't last.

She had to hurry.

Across the aisle from the bulkhead, she snatched a spool of heavy rope, slung it over her shoulder, then rushed from the outer perimeter back to the passage between containers. She seized the intermodal's locking bars and climbed its front side, pushing and grappling up the corrugated metal as quick as her burning muscles allowed.

Her chest pounded, and both hands burned with pain. She gasped for air. A few more feet, she was almost there.

She struggled upward, finally reaching the fifth container. She secured the line and removed the spool from her shoulder, letting it fall.

The rope's free end dropped straight down. Mercifully, the line hit the vessel's bottom—only barely—though it was enough.

The most excruciating part of this entire mission was leaving those suffering souls in the pits. Hundreds of bodies squirming in the mud, desperate for food, sleep, rescue. Lorenzo had told her how horrid it was, though until she'd seen and smelled it herself, its ghastly evil hadn't registered. Hundreds of them, starving, hopeless, waiting for death. It was something she still couldn't fully comprehend. Desperation beyond tears. Her small team wasn't prepared for anything on such a large scale, even if they could shepherd them from the mine unscathed. And that excruciating decision to abandon those dying men had eaten at her every second since.

But this was different.

Dangling from the rope, Rosales worked the container's latch. The heavy eight-foot door swung outward.

Urine inside the dark prison seeped from its ledge.

Sobs echoed and many frightened eyes stared her way.

A hand reached for hers.

But she couldn't grab ahold.

Sharp snaps tore at her ears and a sting bit her neck.

Her legs deadened.

And she fell.

When her father got home, they always played a game she'd invented called "kick and score." She and her dad would stand at opposite ends of the backyard, him still in his uniform. The object was to boot the soccer ball past the challenger on the opposing side. A ball over the fence didn't count—the offender had to take the shame walk to the neighbor's yard. However, each time the ball hit the fence, the metal chain links rattled, and a score was registered. They enjoyed many evenings kicking the ball back and forth across the yard. Somehow, the fence links on her father's side always rattled a little more often than hers.

Give more than you take, respect others.

He conveyed advice as the soccer ball traveled between them. He told her how important schooling was, and she studied tirelessly. She treasured the smile on her father's face. They chatted about her classes, but especially science, which was her favorite subject.

One afternoon, she asked her father why he wore the uniform. His answer was simple and would forever change her outlook on life. "When others need our help, the able and strong should rise to the challenge. All we have is each other, Catalina." Although she was young, that philosophy stuck with her.

But then came the rainy day.

Seven soldiers fired their rifles into the air three times. Another uniformed man placed a collapsed flag into her mother's arms. Hugs from strangers, some of whom followed them back home. Food on platters and hot trays. The dining room, where she was never allowed to play, filled with adults who shuffled over the carpet holding their paper plates and cups. Her sobbing mother remained seated. Well-wishers approached one by one, clasping her hand, speaking in hushed tones.

At some point, she escaped to her bedroom, crawled under the covers, and looked out the window. A wet soccer ball sat quietly in the backyard, and the chain link fence was silent.

They soon moved off base and into a smaller house. Her mother remarried. A bearded man who went to work in a shirt embroidered with his name and returned late, tired, and smelling of grease and gasoline, a man who had no time to kick a soccer ball.

She hyper focused on school and, later, work. Staying busy didn't leave much time for friends or play, but it didn't leave time for sadness either.

After her failed marriage, her mother took custody of Leena, and a friend provided Rosales a ride to a recruiting station. She left town on a bus to Fort Benning two days later.

During Basic, she endured the cackling from the male recruits. Those stopped, however, once she'd mastered the hand-to-hand techniques and sent the biggest bigot away with a whimper and a sore arm.

After that, her drill sergeant called her "SmackDown," and so did everyone else. She liked that. Her father would've liked that.

Water splashed from the container stack above.

More desperate souls she'd failed to help.

She'd landed on her back, and a scorching deadness rode up her spine. Blood streamed from her neck. Her lower half wouldn't move as her brain commanded, and her limbs were fiery, heavy.

A giggling man approached, clutching a smoking rifle.

She was cold and her vision blurred.

The laughing man neared, his weapon trained.

"Ken… drick," she coughed. Despite the four-story fall, the eyewear had stayed on, but each breath now became a struggle. An immense pressure was building in her chest, rising to her throat.

Static bled in and out.

"Ken… drick," she huffed again, her lungs forcing each syllable as the bitter taste of iron filled her mouth.

"Ro-sales!" a broken voice called. "Whe—are--you?"

She felt for the gushing wound in her neck. She found the hole. Despite the pain, she put pressure on the wound. Pins and needles crept about her entire body.

The laughing figure approached with something tied around his head.

"Rosales! Where are you?"

Tiredness swam through her.

The cackling man and his rifle stood above. A red bandana came into focus.

"Sssir," she gasped into the eyewear.

"Rosales!" Kendrick called.

Bandana smiled oddly.

Her pressure on the wound gave out.

And sleep beckoned as never before.

CHAPTER
77

"What goes on here?" Yuri barked. "My men check on women and find only this one in room."

She and Foster lumbered to the wet platform at the tower's base.

Alisha's head hung down, and her long hair was soaked.

Across from Yuri, two henchmen waited in silence. Like him, they were taut, stocky white men sporting shoulder holsters.

Foster released Hannah's arm and tottered forward.

"Yes. Seems we had an escapee."

"Escapee!" Yuri shouted.

"Somehow, she got out of her room," he slurred. "Feisty, she is. Feisty and feral."

"She and the other must not jeopardize cargo!"

One side of Foster's face twitched, and he spoke slowly.

"Not to worry, I've just the remedy." He pulled the softbox from his pocket with a shaky hand, unzipped it, and removed a syringe. "This will calm her."

Yuri stepped forward.

"What in the fuck is that?"

Foster held the needle under the ship's overhead light.

"Sedative, opiate," he said proudly. "Keeps the animals tame."

Yuri pointed. "Where in fuck did you get it?"

Foster pulled out a syringe. "Outside the fields, neighbors, a small operation nearby that Marko–"

"You fucking idiot!" Yuri's jaw clenched. "You are consorting with Venezuelan cartel! Goddammit! They are the ones attacking my trucks!"

Foster staggered backward.

Yuri drew a weapon beneath his black jacket.

"You stupid mudak! The Soles cartel have no loyalty—not like Colombians! They have found trail and are stealing minerals! What in fuck have you done? Those goddamn podonok have infested route!"

Yuri raised his gun.

Foster shoved Hannah aside, lurching to draw his weapon.

Yuri fired.

Foster staggered off-balance—and Yuri's shot tore through empty air. Foster returned fire twice, striking the six-foot Russian square in the chest.

Yuri collapsed.

Foster took immediate aim on Yuri's two men before either had opportunity to unholster.

Yuri squirmed on the rain-soaked deck, coughing and wheezing.

"Do we have a problem with this?" Foster said.

Both men shook their heads.

Foster turned his attention back to the dying Russian.

Yuri gasped like a drowning man. Blood spread across his chest, mixing with the rain, pooling onto the deck.

Foster stared down at him. "You should've made me a real partner," he said.

Yuri coughed violently, a wet, rattling sound. His hand twitched toward his jacket—a second weapon, maybe—but Foster was faster. He kicked Yuri's wrist, the hand flopping uselessly aside.

From across the deck, one of the henchmen shifted his weight. Foster snapped his pistol upward, warning sharp in his eyes. Neither man moved again.

Foster steadied himself against a cargo strut. "When we get ashore, I want the women with me. Secure them, please."

The two men hesitated.

Foster wiped rain from his face. "Now!"

Boots splashed toward Hannah and Alisha as thunder rumbled overhead.

CHAPTER
78

Kendrick and Phinn jumped from the speedboat and snuck aboard using the freighter's port door, precisely as Rosales had guided them to do.

Kendrick withdrew the Glock 19 and his arms extended in aim as they rounded another high stack of shipping containers.

"Rosales?" he called into the eyewear.

At the freighter's lowest level, there was near complete darkness. Containers creaked and groaned while water cascaded from the stacks above through the floor's steel grated walkway. Phinn held behind, wide-eyed, grasping the SIG516 with both hands.

"Sssir," her weak voice panted through the eyewear.

He and Phinn moved forward. Her signal painfully clear. But where was she? Was she trapped? Had someone or a team of someone's cornered her? Where?

"Rosales?"

A narrow, pitch-black path afforded just enough space for a single person to pass through. Guided by the eyewear's night vision, they hustled up the alley past soaring rows of intermodals. Some rose higher than two hundred feet.

Kendrick sped to a quick jog and Phinn raced behind. Kendrick held his aim parallel to the stacks. They had to find her, fast. Wherever she was, the signal was getting stronger, and they were close.

The eyewear's internal screen shuddered with two green boxes at the next gap.

Phinn sprinted past him at full speed. His weapon's barrel struck the corrugated siding of a container, and the SIG516 tore from his grip.

Undeterred, the Scot rocketed through the passage and pounced. He clawed the smaller man's rifle away and sent it skidding toward Kendrick.

Phinn launched a heavy fist into the man's ribcage.

The ferocious impact sounded like the snap of branches.

"You's fuckin stabbed me!" Phinn roared.

Phinn grabbed the man by his headscarf and pounded him mercilessly. It looked like a game of human paddleball.

Kendrick was astounded at the Scot's power until a dangling rope caught his attention. A shape lay beneath its end, and the sight took his breath away.

He darted over and fell to a knee. Blood pooled around the body.

One of Rosales's legs was twisted at a sickening angle.

Her eyelids flickered.

"Rosales!" he cried, reaching to apply pressure on a dripping wound in her neck.

Her lips parted, but no sound came.

Kendrick used both hands and pushed as hard as possible on the gash but could not stop the leak.

Thick blood seeped through his fingers.

The bullet had ruptured her jugular.

A familiar sadness washed over him.

"Sssir," she uttered.

She was dying, and he couldn't help her. She was an incredible soldier. Determined, clever, kind. The way she'd surrendered her candy to those happy children in the village. Always, always addressing him as "sir." And making that impossible decision to leave those captive workers in the pits—knowing abandoning them was the right decision but one that would've crushed Kendrick.

Her hand lifted... then slipped away.

He caught her hand and held on tight.

"Be still. We have to–"

"Please," she wheezed.

"I know," he said softly. "Leena. I know."

Her mouth opened but couldn't speak. Then her eyes fluttered to a close.

"Stay with me!" he begged.

But a cough rattled the chest of Sergeant Catalina Rosales, and she fell still.

Kendrick held her hand until the warmth drained. A silence pressed down—deafening in the space where her spirit had been. He'd seen so many go. But this one left a hollow in him he couldn't yet name. He closed her eyes with trembling fingers.

"We'll scrape off that evil for you," he whispered.

Foster loomed over the gasping man sprawled across the rain-slick deck. "I always knew it would come to this, comrade. It's time for a change. This is my freighter. My cargo. My routes. My operation." He lifted his pistol.

Gunfire cracked through the storm.

Yuri twitched once, twice—then sagged into a heap, blood spreading beneath him.

Foster swung his weapon toward Hannah and Alisha.

"Now, you two! I have concluded your presence on my ship is far more work than benefit."

He slurred the words, his left eyelid spasming. Hannah's gut twisted. If she was right, he'd lost vision in that eye—one more signal of his accelerating breakdown. Stress had torched whatever failing grip he had on his central nervous system. The damage was gaining ground fast.

"But I do believe you still hold some value," Foster garbled. He blinked, gathering himself. "Return with these men to your cabin and behave. But if I sense the slightest issue—one of you steps out of line—I'll kill you both."

A shadow moved fast across a container, leaping the gaps with feral speed.

Hannah caught the motion from the corner of her eye—and recognized him. Rain hammered the deck, plastering her hair against her face. She shifted a few steps to her right, edging into Foster's blind side.

"Where are you going?" Foster slurred.

Another step. Careful. Quiet.

"Stay put!" he barked, but the pistol trembled in his hand.

The shadow vaulted up the tower's third level, then sprang off the balcony.

Foster flinched—too slow.

The attacker slammed into his chest. The pistol flew from Foster's grip, spinning across the slick platform.

Foster staggered back, shoes slipping, arms windmilling.

The high container stacks groaned under the weight of rain and wind.

Foster slid belly-first across the flooded deck toward the gap—a dark throat yawning between the ship's towering cargo holds. He teetered at the platform's edge, legs kicking over the void.

"Help me!" he shrieked.

The attacker stepped into the light. Shirtless. Barefoot. Rain streaking his face.

Lorenzo.

"¡Dónde está Isabella!" he shouted.

Foster flailed. "Help me!"

"¡Dónde está ella!"

Foster clawed desperately for Lorenzo's ankle. "Pull me up, you savage!"

Instead, Lorenzo gazed up into the pounding rain, as if asking the sky itself for permission.

Then his eyes dropped—dark, furious—and he drove his bare heel into Foster's forehead.

The straw hat spun into the dark.

Foster's fingers slipped. His white linen suit flashed once in the ship's floodlights—then he dropped like a rag doll into the abyss.

Lorenzo stood over the empty space, breathing hard, rain streaking his skin.

He turned toward Hannah, his expression unreadable.

Yuri's men opened fire.

Lorenzo twisted, sprang for the rail, and vaulted overboard in a clean, arcing leap. A splash rose from the ship's side.

Yuri's men shouted in Russian.

Hannah grabbed Alisha's hand and yanked her behind a cargo strut.

"Stop!" one of them barked.

The other turned from the rail. "Get them!"

The gunmen closed in, weapons raised.

One flicked a glance to Yuri's body. "Does not look good for us."

"We call Alexi," the other said. "He will help dump bodies."

Rain sheeted across the steel deck as thunder shook the ship's spine.

Hannah tightened her grip on Alisha's trembling hand.

They'd escaped the muddy pits, survived captivity, dodged druggings and worse. Somehow, they'd come this far.

And still—it wasn't enough.

She closed her eyes, clutching Alisha.

We were almost free. I'm so sorry, Dan.

The sharp crack of gunfire tore the night.

She braced for pain—but it didn't come. No jolt. No tearing heat. Had they shot her in the head? Was this death? Was this the last feeling she'd ever know? The grip of Alisha's hand in hers?

Behind her, a voice—steady, familiar.

"You ladies all right?"

Hannah opened her eyes.

Yuri's men lay sprawled across the platform, bleeding onto the deck.

She turned, heart pounding.

Kendrick stood beneath the ship's floodlights, a pistol in each hand, smoke curling from the barrels.

80

The backyard party was missing a few guests, but Ted Salvador worked the grill, flipping thick, delicious burgers.

"They do em' better at The Jetty, but what can you do in this damn pandemic?" he said.

Tina passed out napkins, hovering by her son Jed while her husband manned the grill.

Hannah was grateful for the food.

Alisha and Dan caught a late flight to London just before the skies locked down, texting her the moment they arrived. Hannah had held her breath since waving them off at the airport. But now, the lovebirds were home safe. Alisha and Dan, together forever, once again.

Doctor Anthony Malum was recuperating in the hospital, and she went to check on him each day. The medicine and therapy were working. His shaking had stopped, and he could speak normally. She found out he'd been in those pits nearly three years, abducted as they had been while doing volunteer work in northern Brazil. His wife was trying to fly in from New Zealand, but the lockdowns made that near impossible. Hannah, though, promised him she'd visit every day.

Michael Bennett was also in the same treatment ward. They'd removed the tubes, and he was breathing on his own. When she learned what he'd done for them, she wanted to hug the scruffy man but had to settle for a handshake. She did sneak a peek at his chart, however, and in a few more weeks, she could give him that squeeze.

Lorenzo, though, was most curious. After everything that happened on the freighter, he'd disappeared into the water. She had no idea if he was even alive. The Coast Guard search turned up nothing. And, when authorities ultimately gained access to the giant freighter, its captain and crew had scattered. Lorenzo was simply gone. But she had a feeling the man with the soft brown eyes was still alive, somewhere.

She'd seen too many die to confuse hope with denial. But something about Lorenzo's will—the way he fought the jungle and the pits and the dark inside himself—stuck with her. Some spirits didn't break. They just disappeared for a while.

Maybe, one day, he'd find his way back.

Tonight, she made new friends. Ernie Nelson, a good-looking young man with a broken wrist, had been with Phinn when they'd shot the locks off their ankles, freeing her and Dan. The seven others chained with them in that ghastly valley were also freed, but all disappeared into the jungle. She prayed for their safety.

Ernie shared a photo of his cat Noodle and told her of his place on Alexandra Island. Beautiful and peaceful, he said—everything her life hadn't been for weeks. During their conversation, his phone chimed—a wide grin growing on his face.

"Girlfriend?" Hannah teased.

"Working on it." He winked, ducking away.

Maya was stunning. They were about the same age, but Maya had perfect olive skin and a glowing smile. She excitedly told of how they'd helped find the cargo ship using forgotten technology through radio frequencies and calculations which Hannah did not understand at all. But just listening to Maya made Hannah feel normal.

Shortly after, Phinn slid into the seat next to her and handed her a fresh beer.

"Thank you," Hannah smiled. They chatted for almost an hour. This incredible man had suffered a stabbing, a terrifying jungle trek, a plane crash—and still, he'd come for them. He was everything her father would never be. A genuine hero. Now, if only he were twenty years younger.

When Hannah was told of Sergeant Catalina Rosales, though, her heart sank because without Rosales, none of them would be here tonight. A young, promising soldier who'd given her life helping to rescue them. Rosales had snuck aboard when they left the South American port, working in secret with the others to track them. Her sacrifice was something Hannah couldn't fathom. Ernie and Phinn spoke of her extraordinary soldiering and how much she meant to them.

Thomas Kendrick, the fine-looking Welshman with the salt and pepper hair, socialized with the others but appeared preoccupied. He paced the yard, deep in thought. She'd given Tommy a hug for saving them from Yuri's henchmen, and that seemed enough for him. Before the evening's end, he asked to borrow something from Ted's toolshed and left with Phinn shortly after.

After his text session, Ernie launched into a puzzling story about a stone he'd surfaced during a dive, which enthralled Maya and Jed for some reason.

But the best surprise came when a large strapping man with brown curls introduced himself.

"Bobby Tucker," he smiled.

A commercial fisherman, part of Jed's crew. First mate. Strong, handsome. They talked and laughed until the dark settled in, and Bobby's arm found her waist, steady and sure.

CHAPTER
81

Seventy-one degrees and overcast, but the District of Columbia's Constitution Park was far less crowded than it should have been at three in the afternoon. Senator Spencer Mitchum readjusted his face mask and found the specified bench in a secluded enclave facing the Garden's Pond. He brushed off the surface debris and sat.

The pandemic was the perfect opportunity, they'd told him. Wodehouse and Steadman were busily collecting private funds behind closed doors, while Jordan and Hicks flooded the internet with memes in his favor. There'd been no official announcement—that would come after the 2022 midterms.

He'd been a horrible father to Hannah, and those mistakes had haunted him the older he got. Twenty years ago, he'd been caught up in the trappings of a profession that fed his ego a steady diet of spotlight, praise, and money. And now, his political career was like a train he couldn't stop.

Once this meeting in the park was over, the driver would take him to Gregg's Smokery. He'd enter using the alley because the establishment's doors were currently closed to the public. Vice-Chair Brown would meet him, order a pitcher of Coors Light, then drink it all himself as he commanded Spencer on his upcoming run. Others would undoubtedly join them, a blur of faces he'd pretend to listen to, nodding along with their ideas.

But after that, it was finally home to Mandy and Owen, his five-year-old son. The boy was his proudest achievement. Despite his grueling schedule, he tried to do things differently this time around. He showed up to his son's tee-ball games when he could and checked his homework on the weekends. Days ago, Owen lost his first tooth and Mandy happily informed their son of the tooth fairy. But under his pillow that night, along with the missing fang, was a carefully folded crayon drawing of a puppy. His son didn't want money from the tooth fairy; he wanted a dog. He and Mandy had already agreed to take the weekend and find him one.

These were things he should have done with Hannah.

She and Lydia seemed like a lifetime ago.

Back then, partner positions at the firm required tireless work, the proper social connections, and a spouse of a particular pedigree. After his first big case they'd thrown him a party. Though, during the celebration, he'd overheard a senior attorney refer to Lydia as "Pennsylvania mountain trash." He let those words rattle around inside his head. And, instead of defending his wife, he became a coward to his career.

He'd convinced himself that he'd outgrown Lydia, that divorce was inevitable. He went from associate to partner in three years. Next came district attorney, and then mayor. He had a knack for politics. At the end of his mayoral term, they pushed him into his first Senate run. He learned of Lydia's death during the campaign—but was so wrapped up in himself he never made the time to call his daughter.

Now leadership "handlers" demanded he run for the highest office in the land. However, as with all dealings in D.C., the inner workings of the arrangement were far more complicated.

His public image had, indeed, become a runaway train. But he was too spineless to say no. If he did, they'd take away his Senatorship, obliterate his reputation, and he might even meet with a tragic accident.

There were the lenient plea deals he made with defense attorneys. One kept a 23-year-old habitual offender, and the son of a wealthy executive, out of prison after killing his girlfriend in a drunken car wreck. There were his unscrupulous connections with Bryson, Huntsman, the shady contracts awarded to Pellgrin, and many, many other things.

They'd expose them all if he didn't run. Blackmail with a handshake—a sickle over his head.

When the kidnapping happened in Colombia, they saw it as an opportunity to bolster his image even further. Concerned Father Stops at Nothing to Bring Daughter Back Alive! A rare headline of victory in these trying times. Name recognition would shoot through the stratosphere.

Spencer sighed.

Though, he really did want to make up with Hannah. But they were handling that, too. Phone calls were made to the right people, and they'd secured Hannah a lead position at the CDC's research center. Spencer knew it wouldn't earn her forgiveness, but he hoped the new job might mend a fence or two—even if borne of unsought cronyism.

In the park, parents with strollers, joggers, and those simply sick of being locked indoors meandered about. Each wore protective face coverings. Two agents they'd assigned to him also strolled the area, examining faces.

A blonde woman in a long, gypsy skirt and sleeved blouse, accessorized with a teal shoulder bag and matching personal protection mask, approached the bench. She wore tinted glasses and a large white summer hat, presumably to protect her skin from further wrinkles.

Spencer thought of waving her off. But any scene, particularly in today's politically charged pandemic climate, brought out those fucking cell cameras. Video of a 58-year-old Senator shooing a female away would go viral in seconds, followed by the headline: Senator Mitchum of Massachusetts Doesn't Believe Women have the Right to Sit.

When the man who called did arrive, Spencer would seat them elsewhere, away from the woman and her teal bag. That change in position would also alert the two agents across the waterway of their mark.

For now, the unwelcome woman sat at the bench's far end, keeping a proper amount of social distance. She hunched at the waist and picked at something on the side of her two-inch heel.

Spencer continued scanning faces and reflecting on his life.

Still fiddling with a heel, the figure in the dress spoke.

"Don't look at me."

The accented voice was deep, masculine.

Spencer froze.

"I know you've employed surveillance, so here's how it'll work. I'll ask a series of questions. You'll respond to each, keeping your eyes straight ahead."

Spencer turned. "I believe we–"

The stranger rose from the bench.

"Wait, wait, wait," Spencer said quietly, returning his head forward.

The stranger brushed something from the skirt and sat back down.

"I'm sorry, force of habit. Just tell me—"

"The physicians are safe, back on American soil."

"Where is my daughter?"

"Don't look at me again, or I'll leave, and you'll never see her."

Spencer gazed ahead toward the pond. The two agents wandered far in the distance, inspecting masked faces, but neither glanced his way.

"The private army. This was your doing?"

Spencer nodded slowly.

"Arranged through Senator Garner Wodehouse of the Armed Services "Threats and Capabilities" committee?"

Spencer gave a small nod.

"Which means you knew about the Russian and his gunrunning?"

Seconds passed.

"Look down."

Spencer did. A crimson dot danced over the fabric of his pants, lasering directly on his crotch. His heart quickened.

"Unless you want a painful limp, I expect answers."

Spencer inhaled heavily through his nostrils. "Yes, but it doesn't have anything to do with–"

"You're funding a revolution? Where?"

The Senator turned.

"Look my way again, and you'll have a second hole to piss through."

The two clueless agents strolled around the Garden's large pond farther from view.

"Not a revolution."

"Then where are those weapons going?"

The Senator crossed his legs.

The red dot floated over his heart.

The Senator uncrossed his legs and grimaced.

"Ukraine."

The stranger's head shook.

"A Russian smuggling weapons into Ukraine? Your government's trying to ignite something, aren't they?"

The Senator was silent. He honestly didn't understand it himself.

"That pasty South African—the one mining down there. Where are those minerals going?"

Spencer frowned. "Minerals?"

"The illegal mines. You're using an NGO to transport minerals. I've seen the packaging and manifests."

"I don't—"

"Lie to me and my man will put a bullet in you."

"Okay, okay." A tightness gripped his chest. "There's no money. Guns. They use guns—that's the currency."

"Who is "they" exactly? These are M4s, Senator, which means–"

"I know, I know. But this is all I could piece together. It's some kind of trade."

"Weapons for minerals? Where's the ore going?"

"I don't know. It's not the U.S. We have our own sources."

"Yet, your country is supplying these guns." He paused. "Wodehouse, what's he getting in the exchange?"

Spencer shook his head. "No idea. He doesn't tell me these things."

The dot rose to his neck.

Spencer recoiled. "It's something else. Shipments headed to U.S. ports. I overheard them talking about it once. I don't know where and I don't know what."

"You know more."

The dot danced to Spencer's forehead.

"God damn it, alright. The NGO. They handle logistics." The Senator gritted his teeth. "Water, something about bottled water. They needed it. Pallets. That's all I know."

"Fucking hell." The stranger hunched forward, clenching his jaw. "They're smuggling people."

"Woah, woah. I don't know anything about that." And he really didn't. That was awful, but given the types he'd dealt with recently, he wasn't surprised. Still, he wanted no part of it.

The stranger sat in silence.

"Look," Spencer said. "I can help you. I will help you. I know people, we can –"

The man in the dress turned to him, unblinking. "We lost a soldier in that mess, Senator. A damn good one."

Spencer nodded, carefully. "I'm sorry."

The man in the spring hat turned toward the gardens. Moments passed. Then he spoke again, and it sent shivers through Spencer.

"There will be no negotiations with this, and I'm only saying it once. You'll give $3 million to the daughter of Sergeant Catalina Rosales. The girl can use what she needs for college, but the bulk should remain in a binding trust until her 21st birthday. And her shitbag father better not see a dime of it."

"Three million?" Spencer whined. "Where am I supposed to get that?"

"Adler?" Then a pause. "2016-2585-1987-04."

Fuck. Spencer knew the account number by heart. It was every dollar, legitimate and otherwise, he'd managed to save. At present, a little over six million. A secret nest egg. It wasn't enough to escape his handlers yet, but it was something he could leave his wife and son in case he pissed off the wrong people.

He slouched.

"Next, you'll expunge the record of Ernie Nelson completely, and provide a formal apology for his dismissal. You'll also see that he gets a nice bonus for this mission, and personally spearhead the effort to reinstate and promote him to Senior Chief."

Spencer no longer saw the two agents in the park.

"Third, you'll pay the same bonus to Colonel Michael Bennett, and Aldous Patrick Phinn."

"Who's Phinn?"

"A civilian. Loyal, honest. Virtues foreign to your sort. Also, you'll offer him a fast track to citizenship if he wants it. He's a good man who deserves a fresh start."

"Okay."

"And you'll sign the rest of that bank account over to your daughter. Repayment for ditching her and her mother so you could become the egotistical political swine you are today."

The red dot held steady on his trousers, and Spencer felt like weeping.

"Anything else?" he managed.

"Yes. Consider our meeting here a formal lobby to the Senate Security Council. They'll set up a commission to fight illegal mining and human abuses in South America, specifically Venezuela. You and your buddy Wodehouse will pull your strings and rescue every person from those mines."

Spencer exhaled. "When do I get to see my daughter?"

A double-hull commuter bus approached a stop on Constitution Avenue.

"When your money is in those two accounts, I'll let you know how you can contact Hannah." The stranger in the skirt rose from the bench. "I'm not certain she wants to speak with you, though."

A sheet of folded construction paper came from the teal purse.

"This list includes the coordinates of that blood mountain. I want those men freed within a week. Adler and I will be watching."

Spencer shook his head.

"What if I encounter red tape? I may not be able to control everything."

The bus's pneumatic brakes hissed to a halt.

The folded paper fell next to the Senator on the bench.

"Fill those accounts."

Spencer opened the paper sheet. Its texture was vaguely familiar, and on its surface were handwritten account numbers, along with a list of longitudes and latitudes.

Then a bold thought came. He had allowed this man too much control. Spencer cleared his throat and sat up straight.

"This is extortion. I'm a U.S. Senator, you understand? I can signal my men and send you to jail for life."

The stranger's spring hat received a twist.

"He's a grand artist."

Spencer blinked. "Who? What?"

But Thomas Ryan Kendrick straightened his skirt and strolled toward the bus without another word.

Spencer scanned the figures again, then flipped the thick paper. On its backside, etched in orange crayon, was a floppy-eared puppy—and in the corner, a crooked signature that twisted his insides.

Owen.

A Special Request

Your review really, really matters. Whether you bought this book in a magical mom and pop bookstore, online, or swiped it from a friend. Please visit one of these sites and tell me what you think!

I personally read each review, grateful, laughing, looking for character names.

Amazon.com

Goodreads.com

(Amazon review link)

ACKNOWLEDGEMENTS

To my patient, wonderful wife, who suffers through my typing and mumbling until dawn. You're my Princess.

In memory of my friend Jamie. We lost you too soon, buddy.

To Shelly and Bobby. Your enthusiasm keeps me motivated, and I treasure your honesty.

Thanks to David K., Michael Peck, Big Jon, Tyler Z., and Navy Dave for your stories and insights. You are the best of us.

Doctor H., Jesse R., Doctor Genny, and Barbara B. for your help on medical matters.

Pilot and author Ivan Luciani for allowing me to pick his brain and pick apart his aircraft.

Lockmaster Richard M. for guiding me into the Mississippi.

Thanks to Holly Tavel for making my words sparkle.

The owner prefix on a container code is actually three digits, but the story uses four to keep me out of trouble.

Purpellia would be an excellent name for a plant.

For my furry pal Charlie.